THE GO

THE GODLESS

Children

Book One

BEN PEEK

TOR

First published 2014 by Tor
an imprint of Pan Macmillan, a division of Macmillan Publishers Limited
Pan Macmillan, 20 New Wharf Road, London N1 9RR
Basingstoke and Oxford
Associated companies throughout the world
www.panmacmillan.com

ISBN 978-1-4472-5124-8 HB
ISBN 978-1-4472-5126-2 TPB

1 3 5 7 9 8 6 4 2

A CIP catalogue record for this book is available from the British Library.

Map artwork © David Atkinson 2014: handmademaps.com

Typeset by Palimpsest Book Production Limited, Falkirk, Stirlingshire
Printed and bound by CPI Group (UK) Ltd, Croydon, CR0 4YY

For my Grandparents,
Clifford and Muriel Mamwell

Acknowledgements

A novel is not just a collection of words. It is a collection of people, as well. My partner, Nikilyn Nevins, read this book in parts, in sections, in wholes. She listened to my worry and complaint. I would have left me, but she stuck it out and bought me beer. Tessa Kum (the Book Whisperer) and Kyla Ward (the Occult Expert) were the first readers, and both I cannot thank enough. My agent, John Jarrold, was surely as surprised as I was by the reception – a piece of string is at least this long, I believe – but truly, none of it would have happened without him.

Lastly, a thank you to my editor, Julie Crisp, and the American bad cop to her British good cop – it might have been the other way around on different days of the week – Pete Wolverton, without whom the book would have been a lesser creature. It would not, I feel the need to add, have had a decapitated head without either.

Let us start at the beginning, shall we?
With the start that was the end.

—Qian, *The Godless*

Prologue

The Spine of Ger had been made from stone, by hand. It ran across the Mountains of Mireea, along its peaks and valleys, an uninterrupted length that followed the vertebrae of the dead god, Ger, who lay beneath the mountains. The being who had been known once as the Warden of the Elements had been a giant whose head cleared the clouds, a figure that had been stationary until the final decades of his long life. His dark, scarred hands had held long, spiked chains with collars that, upon his fall, tore apart the land and created the crevasse that his long body would lie in. For hundreds of years after, his voice was heard in the rustle of leaves around him, in the storms above, in the floods of rivers and the crackle of fire that began by lightning. It continued long after Ger had finished building the mountain range around himself, a tomb wormed with mineral-rich excesses to hide his ravaged body, but died long before the last brick of the Spine had been laid. In the eleven thousand years since that final stone had been placed, only the roots of ancient trees had caused the Spine to alter its shape – large roots lifting stone, or hollowing earth beneath – though none had broken its flow and it stood now, old and

1

weathered, its construction as subject to fiction as the god beneath it, the stone patterned green by mould and moss when covered and bleached by the sun's exposure where the old, thick canopy fell away.

Bleached by Sei's cracked palace, the young soldier, Ciron, corrected himself as he looked up through the branches, at the second of the three suns that rose as the first set. *The midday's sun rises, the morning's sun sets, but it is just the remains of the Sei's home orbiting the bones of the God of Light himself.* His horse walked beneath a thick, low branch, and he shifted around it. Sei had been the first god to kill another, though it had not been Ger, but rather Linae, the Goddess of Fertility. That act had begun the War of the Gods, though no one knew why he had done so, not even after so many generations. In class, the teacher – a young man who wore narrow, thick glasses that Ciron himself had envied – had argued that it had been a lovers' fight. Why should the gods be so different to them, he said, and the class had agreed, much to Ciron's distress. Even at the age of five and ten, he had known that such a simplistic answer was inherently flawed, based as it was in the desire of the individual to see him- or herself in the divine. He had spent a lot of time reading about the gods, spending hours in Yeflam's public libraries and he knew that the gods had not been like them, knew that they had not been human, and that the reasons for their war were so difficult to understand because their very experience of life was so alien to that of any dreamed by humanity.

'Boy, you're daydreaming again.'

'I'm sorry.'

His voice sounded young, nasal and strained, and he heard a grunt from the older man ahead of him. 'Don't apologize, just pay attention,' Ira said. 'The trail is leading to the flooded shafts.'

'Then it's leading nowhere?'

'Don't be smart, boy.' The other spat a stream of tobacco to his left. 'What do you think will happen at the end of this trail if the raiders are standing there?'

Nothing.

No one would be standing there. Ciron knew that, so did Ira, but the young soldier was being paid to pretend otherwise. The thought made him angry, but he had not been in the Mireean Guard long enough to say that, especially to someone as senior as Ira. Besides, since Ciron had arrived, he had felt like he had been carrying a black mark because of how he had come to Mireea, the large city state that had formed itself behind one part of the Spine of Ger. Unlike the other new recruits who were drawn from the city, he had arrived from the Floating Cities of Yeflam, a letter in his hand a week after his sixteenth birthday, a week after his father had told him that he had purchased a rank in the Mireean Guard for his eldest son. On the day that he had said it, Ciron had thought that his father had meant it as a joke. Surely, his father was not going to send him to a city where all talk of the gods was based on fear, and would instead send him to the Universities in Yeflam, to study theology beneath the Keepers from the Enclave, to become the scholar that he dreamed of. But no, in a humbling moment, Ciron realized that his father had no desire to send him there, did not have the political will to admit to his peers that his son was a scholar, not a soldier, and so had done what others had done, and purchased him a rank in Mireea.

'Remember,' his barely literate father had said, the day after his birthday, 'that you are our ambassador to Mireea, our hope and our future. Everything you do reflects upon us.'

For the first time in his life, he had almost agreed with his father and told him exactly how it did reflect on him, but his mother had stood beside the short man and one pleading look from her had seen him swallow his bitter words.

Yet, his father's decisions had proved worse than Ciron had originally thought. The raids by Leera against Mireea and its outlying villages had begun to escalate into a war by the time he rode up to the Spine of Ger, and whatever safe, easy position he had hoped to find had been stolen from him in the first week. The sword he had been given was too heavy in his hands, the armour he wore had bruised his shoulders, and the rank his father had purchased was one step up from a squire. Before the first week was out he saw his first fight, felt sick during it, was sick after it, and managed to stay alive only because of those in his unit. To further insult him, on the trail back to Mireea, his unit had met the mercenary group Steel, a replacement for an earlier group, Mirin, which had left under a controversy he had never had explained to him. Yet, in Steel's ranks were fighters as young as he, boys and girls already veterans, each one a rising star of a cheap fiction where he would be placed, in contrast, as a boy in need of rescue.

Rocks skittered before him as Ira's horse slipped, but the soldier was a decent rider, and his stocky body kept it under control. Ciron, only slightly more inept a rider than he was a swordsman, let his horse navigate the short drop, stroking her neck and murmuring his thanks when they emerged without stumble. She was an older horse, brown and white, a sturdy child's horse. He had sighed when the sergeant had led her out for him, but the tall man — who had seen and anticipated the response — had said, 'She knows the mountains as well as any of the men and women you're with. If you get lost, she will return here. When you're a little firmer on the land up here and a little better with the horses, I'll find you a new mount, but until then, she will keep you alive.' Since then, Ciron had been thankful with the choice. He had gotten lost twice already, only to have the horse lead him back to the unit. After the second time, Corporal Jennis had threatened to tie him to Ira's saddle if it happened again, and he had flushed beneath her anger, impotent to respond.

'Boy?' Ira said. 'You still with me?'

'Yes.'

'You didn't answer my question.'

Ciron caught a bug on his neck, wiped the bloody smear away. He did not remember hearing a question, though to do so would mean admitting that he had been daydreaming, again . . . 'Sorry, I did not hear.' He began to say something else, but stopped and shrugged. 'Sorry.'

'Don't apologize so much.' Ira spat to his right this time. 'I was asking if you'd been to Leera.'

'No.'

'Travel is hard there during the wet season, but that'll be over, soon.' Above the pair, the green tinted canopy began to lighten. 'We've been seeing their raiders coming up here more and more as the season draws to a close. Things are going to get worse than what we just left.'

Ciron could hardly imagine anything worse. With half the week gone and the other half to come, his unit had found the burnt-out village midway through their patrol, the morning's sun a solitary dot high in the sky. Following trails of smoke, they had found the remains of twenty-seven men and women laid out around a huge cooking pit, one woman on a spit above it. Ciron had been sick at the sight and smell, and though he had seen it before, he felt no shame – for even now, he could see the looks of revulsion on the faces of the others around him, and knew they were close to vomiting as well. It had also got him sent out of the village: the corporal had sent him out with Ira to follow a trail two hours old, a trail that all knew would end in nothing.

The sound of a waterfall emerged and Ira slowed his horse at the edge of the canopy. When Ciron drew next to him, he saw the clearing the other man was examining. There, the green light gave way to the bright heat of the midday's sun, leaving it looking briefly washed out and sun faded. In the centre of the opening waited a decaying wooden cover over an old tunnel, but the tracks went around it to the edge where the drop there led to the river and the waterfall that began it. After what felt like an hour, Ira slipped from his horse and, with one hand on his sword, entered the clearing.

Ciron followed, stopping at the cover. 'You don't think they went into the tunnels, do you?' he asked.

'It's flooded, boy.'

'But—'

'Look if you want.'

Carefully, he reached for the cover. The wood cracked beneath his fingers, but it shifted, and the sun's light caught on the murky water.

The tunnels were mineshafts, sunk deep for gold, the gold

that had given rise to Mireea and its first fortune. They were empty, now, but when they had given out gold, the mines had killed as many as they had made rich; now they just killed when people – children mostly – fell into the abandoned and flooded holes. People still believed that there was gold in the mountain, and there was, Ciron knew, if you knew where to look. In the second week of his time in the Mireean Guard he had heard that the Captain of the Spine was going to send divers into the flooded tunnels, and he had tried to get assigned to that duty to look for his gold, but the sergeant had shaken his head. He said that most ended in dirt and cave-ins, and that there was only the possibility of raiders, not gold, but he had misunderstood why Ciron had wanted to go. Some of the mines broke into the old cities beneath Mireea, the cave cities that men and women had built to honour Ger in the years after his fall. They were dark, haunted relics, boxed in by intentional cave-ins from the last days of those people, but it was rumoured that if you went deep enough, you could find the remains of Ger himself.

Leaving the broken openings, Ira walked to the edge of the clearing. 'No, they went to the edge and then their tracks stop. It looks like they leapt over.'

Ciron approached, timid in his approach to look out and over at the waterfall, at the massive drop. 'They didn't, though,' he said. 'There's a few scuffs here, where they went to the left.'

'Yeah.' The other man sounded pleased. 'Tell how many there are?'

'Two?'

'Three, at most. Not the fifteen we've been following.'

'That's no different than before.'

'No, it's not,' Ira said. 'Come on, the corporal will want us back before the afternoon's sun is up.'

The fact that he had been right did not give Ciron pleasure. At school, proving himself had been important – necessary, even. He had needed excellent marks to prove to his father that he was dedicated to an academic pursuit, needed them to break down his resistance to the Enclave and the teaching that took place there. He saw the men and women who made up the ruling body of Yeflam as abominations. 'Cursed,' he said, once, when Ciron had been younger. 'That's the name we ought to give them officially. They're not Keepers of the Divine. They're cursed. They are the shattered sun and the black ocean of people, the burden that ordinary people have to carry.'

An older Ciron had examples to counter him, had arguments to make, but his younger self had sat at the dinner table and stared at his plate. 'I know you think I'm stupid,' his father had said, the silence of his family an awfully familiar one in the face of his rages. 'But when you're older and you step out of the Floating Cities, you will talk to witches and warlocks and you'll hear a different story about the gods. You'll hear that they aren't dead like you and me, but that they're both dead and alive, that they have been dying for over fifteen thousand years, with their blood spilling into the ground, into the water, and into the air, spilling so that we breathe it and drink it and wade through it daily. That's how the cursed get their powers – that's why they're such a danger to us. Outside Yeflam, people aren't confused about that.'

The silence between Ciron and Ira stretched out for the ride back to the village, the former thankful that the latter had not asked him any questions. Yet, soon, the younger soldier noticed that the silence between the two of them had extended, that it had now come to take the air, drowning out the susurration of insects and animals, the sound of mountain's breath. The leaves on the trees did not shake, did not drop, and the green tinted light showed the thick, damp patches on Ciron's jerkin, the sweat of fear.

It was only when the horses began to hesitate in their steps that Ira finally stopped.

Cast in a shadowed green, the soldier ran his thick fingers through his hair and flicked out the moisture. Slowly, he slid from the saddle. 'Tie the horses here.'

'Are you—' Ciron stumbled, cleared his throat. 'Are you sure?'

The man's hand hooked the bridle of his horse. 'This is no time to be weak, boy. What lives on this mountain is telling us our friends are in trouble.'

They weren't his *friends*. He didn't have friends. Yet Ciron shifted and lifted his leg, his new boots touching the ground with caution. Ahead, Ira was strapping his short sword around his waist and Ciron followed suit, fumbling with the long sword that the sergeant had given him on his first day. He then pulled out his bow. He was awful with both, he knew, and he felt that failing as he had in the first fight he had been in, the memory of it sharpening as Ira slipped through the trees ahead, his boots avoiding twigs and mulch, leaving no sound. Desperate to do the same, Ciron followed in an awkward, hesitant mirror of Ira's steps that alleviated his noise only slightly.

The bush turned thick ahead, but even as he pushed back

branches and began to make his way up the rocky incline, the silence of the trail only grew. Each bent branch echoed loudly. Each step a clear signal to anyone on guard. Yet nothing responded. Passing one thick root striking darkly from the soil, Ciron saw a brown snake, thick and mean, as if it had been pulled from the ground itself. It was still, its tongue not even flickering as he passed. It watched him as it lay unmoving, a creature known to strike swiftly and deadly that was seemingly – impossibly – trying to draw as little attention to itself as it could.

At the top of the rise, the village appeared, and further behind it, the green mottled stone of Ger's Spine. The village was a collection of buildings and tents, a half-built village unofficially named Jand's, after one of the dead they had found, Ciron had been told. Its small population was the reason for the attack, the corporal had said after they had taken the woman's body off the fire, and it was bad luck that the squad was there now, rather than a week earlier. The Captain of the Spine had planned to draw in all the villages around Mireea as the raids grew, but a storm had kicked up and left them in Mireea for a week longer than planned.

Gazing upon the village for the second time that day, Ciron did not at first notice any difference. The smell of smoke was in the air, the odour of cooked flesh and vomit mixed with it, the men, women and children lying across the ground . . .

Only, there were more.

Beside him, Ira stepped from the bush and into the village, the pressure of his boots on sticks and mud resounding loudly. His sword was drawn and he held it tightly in his hand. Caught off guard, Ciron scrambled after him, desperate not to be left alone, his imagination alive with horrors, his stomach starting to rebel against what he had seen and what he had not, images piecing themselves together in a slowly dawning horror. Side by side, he and Ira closed in on the bodies, the still form of the corporal becoming clearer and clearer. Blood pooled around her chest, but the flow had stilled long before.

An arrow hit the ground between them.

The two dived to opposite sides. Dirt flew into Ciron's eyes and the hilt of his sword jammed in to his waist. He dropped his bow in a desperate attempt to clean his eyes. He heard Ira cry out and, through his blurred gaze, saw the other man hobble, a metal bolt sticking from his left calf. Horrified, Ciron watched Ira drop his sword, grab the bolt and, as he went to yank it out, topple to the side, a pair of bolts hitting his back and shoulder.

Fumbling with his sword, Ciron began to run to his aid, but tripped. Stumbling, he glanced at his leg, but saw no bolt. But he could not see where the injury had come from, could not . . . and then, from the trees – the very trees he had stepped out of – emerged men and women, thin and pale beneath their leather armour, as if their muscle was being burned away. *Raiders.* Scrambling to his feet, ignoring the sharp pain, Ciron turned to run, to run as fast and as far as he could, only to feel a hard object punch into his stomach, piercing him as if he were fruit. His heavy sword hit the ground and, in shock, Ciron followed the line of its trajectory. There, a dark-haired man finished cranking his crossbow, and lifted it.

His last thought was of how much he hated his father.

Beneath the Skin

We do not know how the world was created. We do not know *why* it was created.

Yet, there have always been stories, myths, ideals. Each one of these was a symbol in which meaning was encoded, an attempt to answer the question of how and why.

As a child, a witch told me, just as she told all the children, that one by one, the gods had torn a piece of flesh from their body to form the world. When the gods took back what they gave, she said, the world would end.

—Qian, *The Godless*

1.

'Your eyes,' Illaan said to her, before the sun rose. 'Your eyes are made from fire.'

At the edge of sleep, tangled in their sheets and shaken by his rough hands, a deep fear was awoken again in Ayae. It took her back to the age of five, a month after her arrival in Mireea, when the matron of the orphanage said that rooms were warmer when she was in them. The large, red-faced woman had died days later when the oil lamp in her room overturned and, with a child's logic, Ayae had blamed herself for her death. For years she feared she would awake surrounded by flames or suffocating in smoke, the cause igniting from her own skin. Such an offhand comment had resulted in years of paranoia. She had never forgiven the unfortunate matron her ill-timed words. Life was hard enough without thinking you were a freak: she was small, brown-skinned and black-haired, born in Sooia and in a minority among the tall, mountain whites who lived and traded in Mireea. Her dark brown eyes were a map of hardships that only a child from a continent torn apart by war could carry.

A child, now an adult, who was seeing war again.

Mireea was being raided. Villages were gutted by flame and sword, an event unforeseen by anyone. To a degree, it was unfathomable. Strewn across the mountain range that was referred to as the Spine of Ger, Mireea was the city that had begun as a trading post before turning into the capital of a borderless trade empire. In the North, where the Kingdoms of Faaisha sprawled, Mireea was the gate by which half their wealth emerged; in the East, the Tribes of the Plateau had for generations been pacifists and rarely travelled over the Spine of Ger, stopping there instead to buy and sell; everything they wanted they purchased in the stalls and fairs that ran in all but the wettest days; while in the South, the Floating Cities of Yeflam and the home of the Keepers Enclave claimed a quarter of their wealth came from trade with the Spine; and in the West, in Leera, the wooden kingdom of vine-covered fortresses and hot, steaming marsh, Mireea had funded the birth of the nation after war-torn refugees from icy mountain ridges had been forced across the world, to a new climate, and a new life.

But it was from Leera that the raiders came.

At first, Ayae believed that the attacks were minor, nothing more than robberies on the roads. There had always been bandits, she knew. Others had thought the same and there was reassurance in each other's denial of the truth. But then trade stopped, letters between cities went unanswered, and the stories of priests, of churches, began to circulate.

The ageing Lord of the Spine, Elan Wagan, moved to stop the raids – by treaty first, and then force; but his ride into the sweating swamps had left Mireea's small army decimated by the enemy and he had returned haunted and blind. His wife,

Muriel, petitioned for aid from the Enclave, from the body of men and women who were thousands of years old, who claimed to be in ascendancy to immortality and godhood, but who in the meantime were the most powerful of Mireea's allies. In response, they sent two Keepers of the Divine, Fo and Bau, one old and one new. If any but the Lady Wagan had seen the pair since their arrival Ayae had not heard of it, but as Lady Wagan had began to build huge gates around the city while also hiring mercenary armies to supplement her own, Ayae suspected that the Lady had been told to expect the worst from her visitors.

Composing herself in the warm quiet of the night, Ayae whispered to Illaan that he had only dreamed, that the horrors he had seen the day before had dug into his subconscious.

It was one of the last raids that had seen Illaan return to her, the shadow in his already dark gaze haunted with memories. He was a soldier who — though Ayae would never tell him — was best suited to the mundane: organizing those under him and training new recruits, and then coming home to children and dinner. He was not a man who led soldiers to pick their way through charred buildings and the bodies of men and women he knew, one of whom was no more than a child. On his first night back, he sat in the stuffed cushions on the floor of her tiny house, silent, his long fingers flicking periodically at nothing. Now he'd woken her with a harsh whisper about her burning eyes.

'It was just a dream,' she told him, stroking his shoulders as he shuddered. 'Nothing but a dream.'

When he slept, he was cold to her touch.

In the morning she awoke to an empty bed, the sight of the

rumpled sheets bothering her. It felt as if Illaan was barely in her life lately, a crease in sheets that could be straightened. Rising, she found him with his long body bent over the fire that stifled the room, turning iron tongs as he cooked the last of her bread. It didn't need to be cooked, but Ayae bit back her words and dropped her hand to his still cool shoulder. He smiled, but it was narrow and did not touch the rest of his pale face.

'There are mercenaries arriving in the city. They meet where the markets were held,' he said. 'They sell swords instead of cloth, blood instead of corn.'

'Are they not employed, then?'

'They will be. We are expecting a new group called Dark. Lady Wagan has hired them, though she won't tell us if they number a dozen, or a hundred.' Brown cloth wrapped around his long fingers, Illaan turned the tongs. His voice, when he spoke, was heavy. 'Do you know what kind of people sell their swords from one war to another for money?'

'They're just the kind of—'

'People we don't want,' he finished. 'They're not their stories.'

She squeezed his arm, said nothing for fear that the spark of anger in her would work its way out. What he had seen had been terrible, but she also knew that once the memory of it started to fade, his cynicism would follow. Ayae would not be the first person to welcome another company of men and women who arrived road weary, with glints of metal in boiled leather. But she was not the last person to acknowledge their importance, either: without them, the raids from Leera would have escalated into a full-fledged attack, and the city would have already been under siege.

Illaan pulled out the toast, smoke trailing from the burnt edges. With a rueful smile, he said, 'I was going to surprise you, to apologize for last night.'

She ruffled his hair, made her way to the tiny kitchen. Beneath the floorboards was a small chute of hard ice, where she kept juice, milk, butter and occasionally meat. They froze on the edges when the rainy season came, but mostly they were kept only chill.

'Maybe we should go out for dinner tonight?'

He dropped the burnt toast on the board before her. 'Tonight?'

'No?'

'Just . . .' He poked at the burnt edge. 'I was thinking I might go home tonight.'

'You're not still thinking of this morning?'

'Yeah.' Illaan shrugged, rubbed at his narrow face. 'I'm sorry. I'm trying, but it was just so vivid. Your eyes. I swear the iris was alive. I could see each line in it, burning.'

An angry reply was on her lips, but she pursed them together.

'I'm sure you're right, though,' he continued. 'It wasn't – the bodies. I mean, I knew – one of them was only sixteen. They cooked him after they killed him. After they killed all of his squad. I just need some time to get it out of my head. That's all.'

'You've been gone two weeks,' Ayae said, softly. 'I missed you.'

'I just need some time to myself.' He did not meet her gaze. 'That's all. Just a night. A night so I can wash out what I saw from my head, get away from burnt bodies and Keeper talk.'

'Keepers?'

'They hide in rooms all day for fear that we will see them and have hope.' Illaan picked a burnt edge from the toast, held it between his fingers. 'In Yeflam they're no different. They sit inside that giant white monstrosity they call the Enclave and rule by their so-called power, by their curse that makes the rest of us nothing but animals. They are not here to rescue the animals.'

'Was one there with you?'

'No.'

She smiled to take the sting out of her words. 'Then you shouldn't let talk bother you.'

Illaan shrugged, crushing the burnt remains between his fingers. 'Sometimes,' he said quietly, 'talk is true.'

2.

After the door closed, a low, frustrated breath escaped Ayae. She had not wanted to argue with him after he had just come back, but it was difficult.

Leaving the half-eaten burnt toast in the kitchen and walking to her wardrobe, Ayae considered that maybe it was for the best he wouldn't be returning tonight. She knew that she was quick to attack verbally when frustrated, and Faise – a plump, brown-skinned girl who had grown up in the orphanage with her, her best friend now living in Yeflam – once told her that no one cut as hard and sharp as Ayae when she was angry.

She dressed in brown leather trousers, a light black-buttoned shirt, and boots made from thin, hard snakeskin – her standard outfit when huddling over a large table, working on a new map for Orlan. She was very rarely seen in the front of his workshop and the elderly white man had no strict dress code, so Ayae dressed for comfort rather than style. It was also perfect for the morning's martial training. When the lessons had begun over a month ago, Ayae had been initially reluctant: she could remember all too well the sway of the old ships on the black waves as they left Sooia, the country of her birth.

The scrappy, flame-ridden, walled compound she had spent her first years in had slowly receded, the marks of battle scars she could see miles out, and for a moment she felt as if that ship were returning to it. As if she would wake and find the Spine of Ger similarly pitted and ruined. Yet, after a few days of the training, she found that the morning exercise focused her mind and alleviated the anxiety she felt about the raids. Exposure to the soldiers also made her realize that the Lady of the Spine's plan to train her populace as a last-minute army was as much about empowering the people as it was ensuring that the Lady could protect her home, a notion that Ayae had begun to appreciate more and more as the training continued.

She opened the door and stepped into the warm morning's sun. Lady Wagan's decision to train the Mireeans had come weeks before the first refugee camps on the north of the Spine of Ger had been established. On the day the ground was broken for the camp, the first company of mercenaries, Mirin, had arrived. By that night, however, the story of one Mirin soldier attempting to rape a young teacher was made known. His victim, one of those trained alongside Ayae each morning, had fought back and managed to stab him. Despite Lady Wagan's swift retaliation against the culprit, Ayae felt as if the previous security she had found in the city, as a dispossessed child, was suddenly lost. That night, she had dreamed again of the refugee camps in Sooia, something she hadn't done since she was a child. She dreamed of fire catching on the fabric of the tents, of the faceless figure of the Innocent, the immortal general Aela Ren, who had decimated her country and whose fear and reputation had spread where his armies did not. In the morning, she awoke to the news that Lady Wagan had dismissed the entire company outright and, on the following day, Ayae had stood at the window of Orlan's shop as the mercenary troop were escorted out of the city, the body of their rapist left swinging on a gibbet over the main entrance.

Along with the training, there had been further announcements that she was less enthusiastic about. Her house was in a modest neighbourhood, one built around narrow, cobbled paths that looped around blocks of four or five, and were hidden beneath a thick canopy of the trees lining the streets. It meant her house and the road had shade in the hottest parts of the day. Or used to have. As Ayae follow the cobbled path, she could see the empty sky and the morning's sun – the first sun – above the single-storey, red and brown brick houses, a new, harsh sight after the dense canopy had been brutally cut back. The lumber from the trees had been taken into the main streets and used to build a series of walls and gates, blockades designed to cut off a section of Mireea a piece at a time if it was breached. It left the newly exposed skyline of the city jagged, as if an ancient fortress made from roughly hewn wood had raised its shadow amid the bricks and mortar and struggled to assert dominance over its modern descendant. Ayae guessed that it was supposed to be reassuring, a promise that the city's populace would be defended, cemented by the straight figures of the Mireean Guard patrolling the wooden barriers in chain and leather, pikes and crossbows in hand.

That saddened Ayae. With an adopted child's logic, she had loved Mireea from the day the refugee wagon had entered the city, led in by representatives of an aid group that owned the orphanage and had brought the children across continents. It was so different from Sooia. There, the land was ravaged, the ground so hard that the bodies of her parents, like so many other parents, had lain above it in cairns of stone, a site still in her earliest memories: a pilgrimage made in a child's act of disobedience that she could no longer remember the reason for. The hardship of the camps had made it an easy trip to begin with, a difficult one to endure, and by the end, her four-year-old self had learned no more of the people who sent her to safety as the Innocent's conquering forces emerged on the plains. In contrast, Mireea, untouched by war, had been a place of security and peace after the death and bloodshed she'd been born into. She'd even found comfort in the stories her rescuers had entertained the children with, about the dead god Ger and his bones which lay buried deep in the mountain beneath them. It had been a camp fire story, part horrifying, part amusing, part comforting, and she had taken solace in it. If a god lay beneath them, surely nothing could harm her. Even now, looking upon the Spine of Ger, the huge monolith that ran along the entire mountain range, gave her a sense of calm, a barrier to the rising tensions surrounding her. It was said that the Spine followed the broken back of the god, that the stone sank into his vertebrae and that its path altered only as Ger's bones sank further into the ground. After Ayae had walked up the two hundred and thirty-three steps to the top of the wall, the sight of the mountains around her and the empty blue sky left her with the feeling that she *was* standing on the back of a god.

Today, however, what awaited her on the top of the wall were rows ten people deep made up from men and women, young and old. Ayae's spot was behind a thirteen-year-old bakery apprentice, Jaerc, and next to two women, Desmonia, who worked in the bar *Red's Grin*, and Keallis, one of the city's planners.

Shielding her eyes from the sun's glare, Ayae saw Captain Heast, a lean, grey-haired man with his left leg made from steel, make his way slowly to the platform in front of everyone. It still surprised her that the old soldier joined them every day and led them in the stretching and light exercise. Once, she had seen him walk past her with a ring of blood seeping through the leg of his trousers.

Behind him, two men took up positions by large drums, beginning a slow beat, accompanied by Captain Heast's voice directing exercises. After thirty minutes of synchronized movements, the drums stopped and soldiers emerged in front of each column, wooden swords at their feet. She did not like sword practice: it reminded her too much of the camps, of the empty-eyed men who walked the walls, but she had come to accept it. In part, it had been made easier by the fact that she was paired with Jaerc, who was slim and quick and made a game out of it that did not begin to approach the reality of what real weapons could do. They had even begun to joke that it was a duel of apprentices, and that their masters gambled on who performed better; but she had seven years on him and a little more speed, and the contest invariably ended in her favour.

With a grin, Jaerc broke the line and rushed forward to grab a pair of swords and a rope. The pair were seldom bothered in sword practice. Both were quick, did not fear a bruise and required no guidance from the soldiers who walked along the lines, helping others with basic instructions: how to hold a sword, how to thrust, how to block. Despite her reticence with the acts of war, Ayae had never had any trouble learning the first steps.

After the rope line had been made, the young baker's apprentice came in first, thrusting low. She met it easily. There was warmth in her limbs, an energy that she felt more keenly now that she moved around Jaerc, blocking and parrying, and then snapping high at him. Every time their swords hit she felt her grip tighten, her breath catch, and the energy in her press her forward. It almost got her caught twice, but a third and fourth time her attacks caught Jaerc – once on the thigh, then on his shoulder; the fifth time she moved too eagerly, and he slapped his blade against the side of her chest. Pushing that aside she readied to leap forward again, only to stop as she felt a presence behind her.

Turning, she found herself staring at a large, bald black man. The only hair on his face was white stubble on his chin, hair that looked to have been dyed to match the spiralling white tattoos that twisted across his bare arms, disappearing beneath his clothing, a dark shirt and dark leather leggings, laced together with white straps. On his hips he wore a pair of curved hand axes, the hilts wrapped with worn, sweat-stained leather grips.

'You got good speed, girl,' he said, his voice deep and heavy with an accent that betrayed his Ooilan nativity. 'A natural eye.'

The men and women around her stopped, while others accompanying him – three men and two women, road-stained, wearing similar black leather – watched.

Turning to Jaerc, he said, ''Scuse me, son, mind if I borrow your sword?' It was dwarfed in his grasp as he spun it around, his attention back on Ayae. 'Now, the problem is, your eye and your speed are not entirely in sync. You constantly leave yourself open, which against anyone with experience is going to have you hurt. You got a name, miss?'

She told him.

'My name is Bueralan. This a problem for you?'

She felt the gaze of the crowd on her. 'No,' she said. 'I'm here to learn.'

His grin was wide, revealing white teeth. 'That natural speed you got, that's more than what I have. I got some height and muscle on you, though.'

'I would never have guessed.'

Around her, the crowd laughed.

'Go,' he said.

Ayae's sword snapped up, quicker than she had thought she could move. He blocked, but only just, and she pressed her attack, adrenalin coursing through her. This was not Jaerc, but a mercenary, a seasoned soldier. A danger. This was the kind of man who had been drawn to the camp in Sooia, deserters, scavengers and thieves, men with no hope and no honour. That he probably wasn't any of that was, momentarily, lost to Ayae. His name meant nothing to her. He meant nothing. The fury of her past, the worries of her present gave her a strength and speed so that she pressed the mercenary backwards, forcing the crowd to part, and felt a thrill at doing so.

It was short-lived: Bueralan's sword slapped her own aside, the force of it putting her off balance, and quicker than she thought possible, the wooden edge of his borrowed practice blade tapped her neck.

'Balancing speed and eye,' he said, 'that's a virtue that goes missed by many fighters. A lot will try to hack their way through you with the first, think nothing of the second.'

'You backed up though.'

'That I did.' His nod was short, approving. 'You caught me a little flat on my feet and it took a few steps to find my balance. If your swings had been a little more controlled, you might have had me.'

Her eyebrow rose. 'Might?'

'Well.' Half a smile lifted his right cheek. 'In a real fight, I probably would have cheated.'

Despite herself, Ayae laughed.

'Learn to juggle.' The big man handed the sword back to Jaerc. 'Anything that helps with your hand–eye coordination won't hurt.'

Before she could ask him if he was serious, he nodded and walked through the crowd ringed around him. The men and women in leather followed him, except for one. He did not have the look of a mercenary about him: he wore a simple, loose-fitting shirt, his trousers tucked into riding boots. His plain, pale face and brown hair had nothing to recommend it and Ayae was not sure why he had caught her eye.

'Do you know who that is?' Jaerc asked.

'Him?' She turned, and saw he was looking at the big black man heading towards the podium. 'No.'

'That was the exiled baron, Bueralan Le, Captain of Dark.'

Shrugging, not having the background knowledge about mercenary groups to be able to share Jaerc's awe, Ayae turned back towards the other man who had been staring at her, but he was gone.

3.

According to the friends of the disgraced Baron of Kein, Bueralan's greatest character flaw was that after seventeen years in exile, he showed no remorse. One day, his enemies said, it would be the death of him.

Beneath the steely gaze of Captain Heast, that assessment – inaccurate, the subject of it had said more than once – returned to Bueralan. His lack of so-called remorse arose from the fact that he did not often think himself wrong, but he knew he had overstepped his boundaries with the girl he was walking away from. Heast, loyal, pragmatic, professional and capable of shocking coldness, did not appreciate others breaking his discipline, and would remember that: the captain had long ago earned the reputation as a man who had a library of memories, each of them meticulously annotated and referenced.

'I see the wilds and my cousin have taught you nothing,' the Captain of the Spine said evenly as the podium's stairs creaked beneath Bueralan's weight. 'I was hoping for humility, at the very least.'

'Only in death.'

Their handshake was strong, firm.

'She shows promise,' Bueralan said. 'A lot of promise.'

'The apprentices of cartographers are not here for careers in warfare.' Heast's gaze swept over the men and women behind the exiled baron. 'Your people can retire to the North Keep's barracks.'

Dark waited down the stairs, five in number, a mix of nationalities and ages clothed in aged, stained leather and bearing close-quarter weapons. Zean, who was all the family that Bueralan had left, stood at their head, tall and lean, an ugly knife on each hip and more hidden. Behind him stood the oldest, Kae, a pale-skinned swordsman who stood taller than Zean and whose left hand was missing the two smallest fingers. The sisters, Aerala and Liaya, dark-haired and olive-skinned, stood next to him, the first holding a longbow in her hands, while the second, younger and slightly smaller, carried a worn satchel over her sword. And lastly, at the end, stood Ruk, a white man with mud-coloured hair whose most blessed attribute was not the sword he carried but rather that he had nothing of note to distinguish him from another man on the street, not even when he spoke.

As a whole, they were formidable, dangerous, but to Bueralan they looked mostly tired. It was not the journey that left them so, but the last job. Paid by a small lord in the equally small kingdom of Ille, the mercenary group had been hired for work that had been mean and dispiriting, a month spent cutting out the heart of a peasant rebellion in the poverty-stricken countryside. At the end of it, they had had enough money to pay a widow poor compensation for her loss and, as he looked over them, he saw the scars of that experience, the weariness that was not so much about flesh, as it was about soul. With a nod to them they left to follow Heast's directions; when he turned the captain's fingers were pressed against his leg. A faint ring of blood showed at the hip.

'You ought to see a healer about that,' Bueralan said.

'I have.'

'A real healer. Not the ones here that cover you in herbs and stitch wounds.'

'You mean warlocks?' said Heast coldly. 'Witches? Heal with blood and pay with gold.'

Behind them, one of the drummers hit his skin softly, testing it. 'It would make it easier to climb stairs, at least,' Bueralan said.

'Ease is not something I concern myself with.' Approaching the drummer who was tapping out a soft beat, he said, 'I'll take this man to see the Lady, Oric. Ten more minutes and you can begin cleaning up.'

The limping captain led Bueralan off his podium, the latter slowing his pace for the former as he made his way awkwardly down the stairs.

Ahead sat the Keep of the Spine. Set against the solid stone of the mountain, it used the natural formation as a wall and a foundation for its four tall towers, the dark stones giving it the appearance of having been carved from the mountain, rather than built into it. The illusion had been recently broken by a huge wooden wall that ran from the edge of the Keep down into the Spine of Ger itself, the hard, warm light of the sun following each angle of the construction.

As the Spine's Keep drew closer, Bueralan saw that the walls in front had been reinforced, and the grounds there reduced to flat dirt. There had been gardens, once, and though they were not renowned, Lady Wagan's reputation as a proud gardener, the mercenary recalled, was because of the diversity that she had managed to grow in the tropical heat. As he followed the path up to the Keep's entrance, he remembered that previously the grounds had been an array of clashing colours, a living, visual equivalent of the diversity that swept through the cobbled streets of Mireea, and the trade found in its markets.

It had been different last time he'd been here, Bueralan thought. Then as he'd walked through the famed markets of Mireea, and followed each turn of the cobbled road, he'd been accompanied by the clamour of merchants yelling, the aroma of food, of spice and tobacco. The best and most expensive merchants had been here, within easy reach of the Keep, but even in the working-class sections around yards and small houses, there had been stalls selling everyday necessities. But now, from the gate, through the wide roads that led to the poorer parts, Bueralan saw only a city that was defined by its silence. The archways in the Spine that had once been so full of people, bartering, a good-natured bickering, were now bricked-up lanes with mercenaries gathered, singly and in groups, waiting to see if they would be offered work by either the larger mercenary groups already hired, or by Heast himself. Beyond them, the woods that had pressed against the Spine were gone, making way for a wide, loosely packed killing ground of dirt.

'Did he die well?' Heast asked abruptly.

'Does anyone?' They were talking about Elar, Heast's cousin, the man Bueralan had lost in Ille. 'He died hard,' he admitted.

'Don't we all?'

'We were forced to cremate him before we sent him home.'

Heast grunted, unsurprised. 'Was the business finished?'

'Yes.' A silence fell between the two, awkward for a moment. 'Do you not run the markets any more?' Bueralan asked.

'They stopped six months ago,' Heast said.

'And the city's economy?'

'You'll get paid, Baron.' The captain's tone was dry. 'You'll not have to fear for your purse.'

Bueralan chuckled. Both men knew the ritual, the mercenary's concern and complaint about money, and how they used it. Both had fought for more than one lord and lady and found, once the dying began, that there was no money in the coffers to pay for their services. Some mercenary troops, especially the larger ones like Steel, worked for money that would be paid in ransoms, rewards and debts to be settled after the battles, but Dark did not take prisoners or petition for the safety of others. They were a small group, a private group who tried to stay out of the public's gaze – unlike many other mercenary groups, they did not authorize cheap novels or plays about their exploits. Bueralan did not need to march into a city with flowers being thrown at his feet, accompanied by trumpet fanfares and mobbed by enthusiastic children. He did not need to look outside the window of his barracks and see youngsters re-enacting scenes from the fictions that were created from his exploits – in short he did not feel the need to be a hero or legend to anyone but the members of Dark.

Seeing how other mercenary groups had been short-changed or unpaid, Bueralan had changed the way they operated and ensured they were paid two-fifths in advance, the rest on completion, and their rates were reasonable. Until, that is, special requests were made.

It did not make him popular, but he wasn't out to win any contests in that area.

He liked the money, liked that no one would take on a job just to meet him in combat in an attempt to make a name for themselves, and liked especially that no one asked why an exiled baron needed to lead an army. He had, for a while, tried to keep his exile a secret, but the very nature of it made that difficult and, surprisingly, it had given him a reputation of trustworthiness, for it was clear that he was only interested in the money rather than feats of glory, that he and his company would get the job done, keep quiet and honest and then leave. Despite his attempts at anonymity, such was the nature of the fascination with mercenary groups that he was known in some quarters by enthusiasts with more passion for fiction than reality. The boy who sparred with the girl had known him, he was sure. Half a dozen others might have, as well. Ever since the fictions had become popular, it had become harder for people like him to keep a low profile, and the more he worked at ensuring that he and Dark weren't in books, weren't in songs, the more, it seemed, a select few spent their time try-ing to aggrandize their exploits into something glorious and thrilling rather than the blood, dirt and shortened life he knew were associated with his line of work.

The two men passed through the gates, leaving the empty streets behind and walking at a steady, albeit one-sided limping pace, to the Keep's heavy doors. These were made from the timber of ancient trees that had grown along Ger's Spine. Inside, the scent of spice drifted through the air. It reminded

Bueralan of the Plateau, where the vegan diets of pacifist tribes were similarly spiced — and where he had been, but once, officially — but the direction from where the spices came was not where Heast led him. They made their way down the hall, walking over warm tiles to a second grand door, where two guards revealed a spacious, well-lit room.

Inside, the floor was decorated with a sprawling, circular pattern, and at its centre was a silver throne. High on the roof, an intricate array of lights shone and, with almost theatre-like drama, a white light was centred on the throne whenever the Lord or Lady of the Spine held court. The immense throne was a relic of an older age, recovered from the cities that had been built in the caves throughout the mountains, by a cult who had been outlawed during the Five Kingdoms, but who had been destroyed by the men and women who came to dig for a new life in the ground, for gold, the men and women who would later build Mireea. Heast led Bueralan past it without comment. Through a door on the other side of the room, a narrow corridor turned into a spiralling staircase where, at the end of several levels, a single guard stood. He nodded as Heast emerged and opened the door to reveal another large room.

Inside sat the Lady of the Spine, Muriel Wagan.

Despite her reputation for being strict with an iron will, she looked like a softer woman, verging gently into fat, her dyed red hair that hung like a younger woman's ponytail over a gown of bright yellow and orange reflecting a mind that was anything but sharp and precise.

'Your ladyship, I present to you Captain Bueralan Le,' Heast said, his hands folding before him.

'My Lady.' Bueralan bowed his head. 'A pleasure.'

Her smile revealed discoloured teeth. 'My Lord. Captain, how are you feeling?'

'Fine.'

'I'll take that to mean in considerable pain, as always.' Her smile was affectionate, taking no offence at his grunted reply. 'Take yourself downstairs. Have that leg looked at.'

The captain glanced at Bueralan.

'Aned,' the Lady of the Spine said, 'don't make me dismiss you.'

With a faint inclination of his head, the briefest frown of displeasure slipping across his face, the soldier left the room. When the door shut, the affection left Lady Wagan's face and she turned her gaze on Bueralan. 'Dark,' she said, her pale green eyes holding his. 'Saboteurs.'

'Yes.'

'For *your* price, I could hire a small army.'

'You already have small armies,' he replied. 'What you don't have are soldiers who slip into the ranks of your enemy, who poison rivers and dams, who blow up bridges and collapse tunnels.'

'And assassinate generals.'

He shook his head. 'Not often. Once – twice, it has happened, but both were opportunities taken advantage of, rather than planned. First time, the army was so small that it did fall apart without the leader. Second time, another man took the spot and the army kept moving. My advice has always been that you are better to cripple the body than to strike the head of an army.'

'Aned speaks very highly of you, Captain,' she said.

'I'll try not to disappoint him.' He nodded to the chair. 'Do you mind?'

'No. I must confess, I don't know much about you. Where did you meet my captain?'

Easing into the cushions, Bueralan replied, 'On the western coast of the Wilate in a port called Wisal. Merchants had hired a small army to conquer it after it declared its independence from the Southern League. The Wisal Governor put Heast in charge of fighting what was turning into an ugly little war over trade routes. I think they expected him to hire an army, but instead he took on a group of saboteurs. It was the first squad I worked for, and the job took two weeks and two deaths before the war failed to start properly.' He met the Lady's gaze. 'He's a fine soldier. In another part of the world, there are books written about him. Important books.'

'I have read them.' Behind her, a large window displayed the cut-back canopy of the forest. The morning's sun had risen to its high point and threatened to flood the room. 'He told me that Dark numbered eight, not six.'

Stretching his legs out in front of him, he nodded. 'Lost two in Ille. The first was Elar — he had been with us for six years. You can't replace a man like that easily.'

'And the other?'

'He was new. This wasn't the kind of work for him.'

'Did he make the right choice?'

The question had never been asked of him and, as the light filtered into the upper half of the room, the saboteur paused. 'Any mercenary will tell you, people come and go in this work,' he said, finally. 'Sometimes, they have debts to pay. Other times, they're just going from one place to another. Mostly, mercenaries are just soldiers who only know this work and there's either no place at home for them or home has changed.

Occasionally, a man or a group gets famous, but most don't last that long. It's different when you're a saboteur. It is not a thing you can pick up and put down. If you know your job, you know too much. You keep professional, because you work for people you like, and people you don't. Sometimes, it is just numbers and maths and theories, and sometimes, you get paid to kill men and women, to poison wells, to kill crops and to steal cattle. At times, it is a hard thing to do to look in the eye of someone. Other times, you get paid to slip into a war you don't want to be part of, to spend time with people you don't want to spend time with. You've got to close off the enemy like a good soldier does: it is steel on steel, but it's harder when you share drinks with them for a month. You realize no one is born evil, just as no one is born pure, but the job is a lot easier if you keep the morals straight with the people you work with. The boy's first job was one I regret, a choice we made that we ought not to have made, and the price we paid was high. At the end, he thought we were a little too much like assassins and wasn't ready for a life of sleeping on the cold ground, eating last, dying first, and watching warm bits of silver and gold spend quicker than you could kill for.'

'A surprisingly philosophical response,' Lady Wagan replied. 'Why then do you continue with it?'

'My poetry sells poorly.'

Lady Wagan laughed. 'Would you like a drink, Captain?'

'I rarely say no.'

From beneath her table, the Lady of the Spine produced two glasses and a long, straight bottle of laq, a clear liquor from Faaisha. She poured a generous two fingers into each, and pushed one forward to the edge of the table.

'This war that I am engaged in is a terrible waste,' she said, leaning back into the light. 'Mireea is a neutral trade city. A city that runs off mathematics, I have heard it said. Whether you believe that or not, it is a city where only coin is worshipped. Your race, creed and colour do not matter — so long as you understand that the market can reward and punish you for both at the same time. This war has damaged my *coin*. No doubt you have seen my empty streets. My closed stores. Before the first force is sighted, it has cost me what is most important and ruined my belief in my neighbours.'

Bueralan's thick fingers closed around the glass. 'Your treaties?'

'Have ensured that all legal trade has been cut off from Leera. Anything else will require me to renegotiate at the cost of my financial independence.'

The candid response surprised him. 'You've not heard anything from Rakun, then?'

'The King of Leera has made no demands and sent no diplomats. No one has heard from him in close to a year.'

'A long time.'

'A long time for a lot of rumours, but let's assume he is dead.' Lady Wagan lifted her drink in salute, finished it in one motion. 'The last envoy I had from Leera claimed to work for a general by the name of Waalstan. Rumours — whispers, really — suggest that he is a warlock. I have no information as to whether that is true or not; what he wanted was to begin digging into the Mountain of Ger. He offered a token amount for the rights, but the land he wanted to take was so large that he cannot have thought I would be anything but offended. He didn't even offer a reason for wanting the land. I pointed out that the gold was mostly tapped, and the envoy told me that there were other precious things in the ground. You can use your imagination. Anyhow, after I told this envoy no, I heard nothing. It had been three seasons since we saw crops from Leera and five since there was any trade in fish or meat, and I figured that they would have to return soon enough, but then the attacks began, and the cannibalism followed.'

'They're starving?'

'Your guess is as good as mine. No one I have sent has come back with information. Not spies, diplomats or mercenaries.'

'Dead?'

'Yes.'

'How did you hear that?'

'I didn't, but the border of Leera tells many tales. The only rumour we have heard relates to two years of stories about priests.'

'Priests?'

'Yes.'

Bueralan placed his empty glass on the table. 'Any particular god they worship?'

'They want to dig up the mountain, Captain,' she said, the sun dipping further into the room. 'There has been nothing officially said, and this close to Yeflam, I can understand why. But the rumour is that they have put priests in positions of power, though they are probably nothing more than witches and warlocks. There have been a few signs of rituals in camp-sites, and my husband's torture was not the work of a simple man. I assume that the general is nothing more than the man with the largest bag of blood by his side for use in their blood magic, but regardless the information suggests I am caught in a holy war — or the appearance of one. I need to know for sure, however, and that is why I have hired you and your soldiers. I need to know who is running Leera's war. I also need to know what kind of feeling is in the country, whether food and water is low, how big an army it is, and how deep the chains of command run. I need to know if they can be stopped before a siege is laid, or if it will be a longer, more drawn-out path to victory.'

'But you would win?'

Her smile was easy, confident. 'Mireea is a small nation, but not a poor one. I will use my resources wisely.'

'Indeed you will, ma'am. Dark could do with a few days' rest before you send us out, if that's possible.'

'The wet season ended a week ago in Leera. Take a day or two, but don't wait too long. The roads will start to fill up soon.'

He nodded, pushed himself up, ready to leave.

'Captain?' The Lady's gaze was intent, unwavering. 'Speed and accuracy is important. There are already spies in my city.'

4.

The inside of *Orlan's Cartography* smelt faintly of incense. A decidedly religious odour for a man who, Ayae knew, viewed himself as anything but that.

She let the door close, the chimes sounding as it did, and did not bother with the lock. Ayae crossed the warm wooden floor, the maps on the walls around her a recollection of past and current events. Each was a finely detailed study of roads, borders and names, both current and obsolete, all of which fetched tidy sums. Ayae had still not gotten used to the money involved, especially for the older maps, and she doubted that she ever would. It was the oddities in these prices that struck her: how the slanting script of an Orlan two hundred years ago was worth far more than the initialled maps six hundred years old. She had been told – lectured, she remembered with a smile – that the younger Orlan's maps had been mostly lost in a fire a century and a half ago and their scarcity therefore increased their value.

Samuel Orlan was an important symbol. To say that there had always been one was not quite right, for the original Orlan had lived and died before the War of the Gods. He had been famous, but had become more so after the war, when the world had been so different. But a second Samuel Orlan did not emerge until early in the Five Kingdoms, where in the huge libraries of Samar, a slim man had stumbled across the original maps and taken it upon himself to make new ones. Since then, there had always been a Samuel Orlan – male and female, with the cartographer's final apprentice taking over the name, the legacy and the work of ensuring that the world remained mapped. Ayae was still constantly amazed at the stream of men and women, wealthy and famous, who came from afar to the shop to look for a particular map, or to contract the current Samuel Orlan for a specific job for fees of such amounts that she could scarcely judge them real.

The first time such a customer had come and left, Samuel had laughed at her expression. 'You can make a fortune with the name, if you take it on after me. If not, well, you'll still likely make a fortune, just without the necessity to grow a beard. It is tradition, you understand.'

A part of her felt guilty when he said that, for both of them knew that she would not be the next Samuel Orlan, but the guilt was not long lived. She did not have the dedication that Orlan had, did not have the sheer skill he displayed. But she loved the work, deeply appreciated the time that Orlan took to teach her his skills, the growing skill her own hand had, and the joy that came in seeing a piece of land or a continent come together on the parchment she worked upon. Both she and he knew that he had given her a skill that would enable her to live comfortably for the rest of her life, to fund her while she followed the other paths of her art, to the portraits and illustrations that were her first love.

Behind her, the door chimes sounded.

Ayae turned from the parchment she was examining, her hand resting on the large table that dominated the room. A man of medium height stood in the doorway. For a moment she did not recognize him, until the sheer ordinariness of him, the plainness of his white skin, close-cut brown hair and loose white shirt and trousers, sparked a recognition:

This morning. The Spine.

'We're not open yet,' she said, her voice so soft that she was forced to repeat herself. 'You'll have to wait half an hour.'

'The door wasn't locked.' The man's voice was polite, easy-going. 'I'm sorry, I didn't mean to just walk in.'

Yet, her hand gripped the table tight. 'The sign was on the door.'

He smiled, a faint, half curve of his lips. 'That's quite the work you're standing next to. The masterpiece of an artist.'

The map across the table she gripped was easily three times her width and a foot taller. Kept under glass, it showed the world as it was commonly known, with Orlan's confident, strong lines and use of colour as much a signature as the one in the corner. What set this map apart was that the corpses of the gods had been worked into the landscape: the Spine did not follow the spine of Ger, but *was* the spine, with Mireea the connective vertebrae to the neck and shoulders.

'I asked you to leave,' Ayae said, a flicker of annoyance alighting in her stomach. 'Don't make me ask again.'

'You're not going to ask again.'

Anger sparked. 'Leave now. There are strict penalties for thieves. You don't want to be on the wrong side of Lady—'

'Lady Wagan does not interest me.' Stepping up to the table, the man gazed down at the map. 'What is beautiful about this map – other than the craft that is, and we must always admire craftsmanship, child – what is beautiful is the gods. So many maps, so many lives are empty of them now. But not here, not on this mountain, not where Samuel Orlan lives. No, he understands that we sail upon the blood of the Leviathan, as sailors say.'

'You need to leave,' Ayae said, releasing the table, her anger strengthening her resolve as she walked to the door. 'I don't appreciate being followed. I don't appreciate you thinking you have a right to come in here uninvited.'

Unconcerned, he ran his hands across the glass.

'I said—'

'I heard you.' He turned to her. 'Don't you feel uncomfortable here?'

The table began to smoke, as if deep in its frame there was a flame, a single spark that was struggling to get out. With his hard, grey eyes holding her gaze, the oh-so-ordinary-looking man who was clearly not so ordinary left the table.

Ayae whispered, 'Who are you?'

'I have no name,' he said softly, his pale hand closing around her arm—

Her free hand slammed heel first into his chest.

It was a desperate blow, but it caught him off guard and caused him to stagger back. Yet he did not release her. Quickly, Ayae drove her foot down onto his. The man made no sound and fear threaded through her unlike any she had felt before. Behind her, the wood in the table ignited, and flames began to rush along the edges, spreading like burning pitch across broken tiles.

The flames jumped, leaping from the table to the wall, and Ayae panicked at the sight. She broke free and turned for the door, grabbing the handle; a hand grasped her hair and wrenched her back. Twisting, she slammed the heel of her hand into the nameless man's arm, hitting the forearm hard. Behind them, the flames found parchment, ink, paint, chemicals, and glass and black smoke ripped out. The man flinched, caught in the blast. Horrified, she tensed to strike out again, but the man turned and threw her against the wall – threw her *into* the flames.

Ayae screamed and slapped at her clothes, at her body – unable to feel pain, but sure, more sure than anything that her flesh was peeling, turning dark, that the fire was devouring the air around her, thrusting its smoke into her throat, and aiming to choke her. The fire leapt and twisted around her and the nameless man, his hands black, reached for her. Through watering eyes, her body twisting to get out of his way, out of the fire's way, she could do nothing – nothing but scream as, behind him, the fire took form, and a hand reached out and grabbed the head of her attacker, wrenching it back as a smouldering blade ran across his throat.

There was no scream.

No blood.

Nothing.

Flames roared, but Ayae had gone still. She had to move, she had to *get out*, but she could not. Flames cascaded across the ceiling, a mix of orange and black. She heard glass pop. A part of her screamed. A young part, a child's voice.

Then hands were on her roughly, were dragging her like a heavy weight to the door. Smoke hid the sky, and she felt a cloak drop over her, felt it smother her, wrap around her tightly as she sank to the ground, the trembling setting into her deeply before unconsciousness took her.

5.

When Ayae awoke, she was in flames.

They flickered without heat, hitting glass as if she were trapped inside a bubble, and they were searching, probing, trying to enter her. Fingers curling she grabbed sheets, exposed toes following, her panic subsiding as her consciousness registered the lamp directly above. Rising, Ayae pushed a hand through her hair and gazed around her. She was in a long, wide room, with dozens of empty single beds. The emergency ward of Mireea. There were guards at the door and windows at the top of the wall that showed the night and the moon — *the remains of a dead god*, the thought came unbidden.

She was in no pain. Pushing back the blanket, she saw her bare legs and arms beneath the simple shift she had been dressed in. Outside of the taste of smoke in her mouth, there was no indication that she had been in a fire.

The same could not be said about the room's other inhabitant. Wearing clothes stained by smoke and burnt by flames, he was a man of medium height, pale-skinned with long auburn hair. On the floor beside him sat a pair of ash-stained boots and a canvas duffle bag, a long, leather cloak resting over it. The strangest thing about him were the thin chains wrapped around his wrists, the bands a mix of silver and copper threaded with tiny charms made from gold, copper, silver, glass and leather. The charms were not isolated to his wrists, for she could see thin chains tied through his hair and one pierced in his right ear.

'So you wake.' His voice had a strange accent, one she could not place. 'I think they were going to bring a prince, eventually.'

'Have I been here long?' Her voice sounded smoky and harsh. She coughed to clear it.

'Since this morning.'

'You – you pulled me out of the fire?'

'Yes.'

'Thank you.'

His right hand touched a chain on his wrist. 'It was luck. I heard screaming and went in. I found you in need.'

Footsteps emerged outside the door. Ayae hesitated, then said, 'Did you – did you kill the man in there?'

'No.' He had dark-green eyes, darker than any she had seen before, and they met hers evenly. 'You want to avoid him,' the man littered with charms said. 'If you can.'

The door opened and Reila, the small, grey-haired, white healer, entered. 'There will be guards coming for you soon, Zaifyr,' she said, though her gaze was not on him. 'Pull on your boots.'

'They have holes in them.'

Ignoring him, the healer's small hands pushed aside Ayae's hair, and pressed against her forehead. 'How do you feel?'

'Fine.'

'You're warm,' she said softly. 'Still warm. Like you're smouldering beneath your skin.'

'Don't say that,' Ayae whispered.

The healer's words were too close to suggesting something that, beneath her skin, in her blood and bones, was a touch of a god, that she was cursed. It was the name that men and women in Mireea used for people with a god's power in them, the name repeated up to Faaisha aloud, but the name that was whispered in the streets of Yeflam behind the Keepers' backs. It was the name that implied countless horrors, stories told of men and women who, since birth, looked normal, acted normal, until one day they split down the chest as arms grew from their body, or their skin began to melt.

To be cursed meant that, inside you, was part of a dead god. Their very beings broke down around you, their blood seeping into the land, into the water, their last breaths polluting the air, each act freeing their divinity, leaving it to remake the world without restraint, leaving tragedy in its wake, creating madmen such as the Innocent and terrible empires such as the Five Kingdoms. The remains of the dead were nothing but pain and suffering that ordinary people had to endure.

Before Ayae could say more, the door opened and Illaan entered, flanked by two guards. At the sight of him, she dared a smile; but if he saw her, he gave no indication. His gaze was focused on Zaifyr as he pulled on his boots.

'Is he able to be questioned now?' Illaan asked.

'The only thing hurt is his clothes,' Reila replied. 'Both of them are extremely lucky.'

With a nod, Illaan indicated to the two guards. Standing, Zaifyr stamped both feet, a cloud of ash rising as he did. In the corner of her eye, Ayae was aware of him trying to catch her gaze, but she kept her eyes on Illaan. He had turned to her now, his lips parted in what might have been the start of a smile, or even, she thought for a second time, a frown.

'She needs rest,' Reila told him. 'She's going to be here for the night, Sergeant, no matter what she says to you.'

Illaan nodded, just once.

At the door, the healer turned to Ayae, a hint of sympathy in her lined face. Before it had any time to grow, she stepped out of the room, following the guards and the charm-laced man, leaving the two alone. Leaving Ayae to turn to Illaan and smile faintly. 'We should be happier,' she said. 'I avoided death today.'

'I know. You were in a fire.' In the awkward silence that followed his words, Illaan moved to the bed next to her. 'The shop looked awful,' he said, finally. 'It was gutted on the inside. All those maps just lit up.'

'The other shops?'

'A little damage.' He rubbed the top of his thigh gently. 'Orlan's shop is a total loss, though. We couldn't save that.'

'Do you know why it was started?'

'It's strange,' he continued, ignoring her. 'The fire was all around you in there. You were thrown into it. Your clothes – Reila was afraid to cut away the clothes, thinking they had melted so badly into your skin, but when she did, it was as if you had just been born.'

She shook her head.

'It's true.'

'It's good, yes? Lucky.' She reached out for him, but he drew back. 'Please, Illaan, I do not know why any of this happened.

51

The man who came into the shop making threats — he made the fire, not me.' There was a hint of hysteria in her voice and she quelled it. 'What do you want me to say?'

'What if I had not woken you up last night?'

Ayae's eyes closed.

'I thought it was a dream,' he said quietly, the words twisting inside her. 'But it was not a dream. Your eyes did burn and you stood in a room full of flames and emerged without a scar on you. You're *cursed*, Ayae.'

No, she wanted to yell. *No.* She wanted to deny the word, deny everything that came with it, but the words stuck in her throat. She reached for Illaan. Her fingers found air and, opening her eyes, she saw him standing away from her, his face cold. 'There will be a Keeper here soon,' he said quietly. 'That's why the room is empty. He wanted to speak to you, privately.'

'Could you—' She swallowed. 'Could you stay?'

But he was already walking towards the door.

6.

The shallow spit of oil in the dimly burning lamp of Captain Heast's office had been the only sound to greet Bueralan upon his arrival. Heast was there, sitting behind his wide, clean table, but he had few words to say and so the saboteur took the middle of the three empty chairs. Within minutes two other mercenary captains were led in, taking the remaining pair. The first, Queila Meina, was a tall, dark-haired, fair-skinned woman not yet thirty but who had taken command of the six-hundred-strong Steel after her father's death. Bueralan had met her twice briefly, and had been impressed by the discipline of her army. The result, no doubt, of a child raised among mercenaries and where loyalty to anyone outside Steel was bought in coin and trusted as far as it spent. The second captain, Kal Essa, was a squat, bald man, heavily scarred around the left side of his face, reportedly by a mace. He commanded the Brotherhood, an army four hundred strong that had arisen out of the remains of Qaaina after it had been conquered by his homeland of Ooila, three months across Leviathan's Blood. Bueralan had never met him, but he had heard that his men were fierce in battle, an army of refugee soldiers who had been driven from their homes and had no desire to find a new one.

The saboteur liked the choices that Lady Wagan had made: loyal, disciplined, capable, her gold well spent. His only criticism was that neither Steel nor the Brotherhood had much experience in laying siege to another kingdom and were too small for such a task. They were big enough to defend Mireea and hold the city range that the Spine ran across, but neither were conquerors. By hiring them, the Lady was making a statement of her intent – defence rather than attack.

When he had returned from his first meeting with Lady Wagan to the barracks earlier, Zean had been awake. It was clear that he had not slept – he still wore the same clothes he had when he entered Mireea. 'What,' the other man asked as the door opened, 'are we being paid for first?'

'A ride,' Bueralan replied. 'See the countryside, find a pet crocodile.'

Whetstone running across his dagger, the other man grinned and said, 'We can skip the war then?'

'I've almost forgotten how.'

The tall man glanced up the stairs. Up the narrow steps was a warm dark and there, stretched across the doorway, was a thin tripwire.

Bueralan chuckled drily. 'This one will be civilized.'

'Then I'll prepare my pie trays for the faire, sir.'

He had found an empty bunk near the door and, with the sound of Zean's whetstone working along the edge of his knife, drifted off to sleep. His dreams had been fragmented, images of houses with straw roofs, of cattle little more than bones wrapped in hide, of farmers whose children succumbed to disease and famine, of the weapons the peasants made by melting down hoes and shovels and picks, and of Elar.

Of late, it was always Elar.

He dreamed of the man lying flat beneath a sheet, stains seeping through, and Heast's voice: 'Did he die well?'

It had been a relief when Zean had shaken him and, crouching next to his ear, whispered that Captain Heast requested his presence.

'There was a fire today,' the same man said, his voice breaking the silence of his office, ten minutes later. 'In Samuel Orlan's shop.'

Kal Essa's thick arms shifted across his chest. 'You woke us to discuss a fire?'

'The fire was enough to raise the interest of the Keepers.'

'They show up and put it out?' Bueralan asked.

No smile cracked Heast's straight lips. 'They let the guard do that, but they did clear a wing in the hospital for Orlan's apprentice and the man that pulled her out of the fire.'

'What have the Keepers said?' Queila Meina asked.

'Very little.'

That didn't surprise Bueralan.

'Reading between the lines, though, I think we can all agree that something interesting has happened.' The captain's pale blue eyes met them all steadily. 'Part of it is explained by the girl, who appears to be cursed.'

The saboteur leaned forward. 'The Sooianese girl I met earlier?'

'Yes. She emerged from the fire completely unscathed.'

'I saw a dog do that, once,' muttered Essa beside him.

'Perhaps the Keepers will find *it* next,' Bueralan replied.

'She is not important,' Heast said, cutting in before the squat mercenary commander could reply. 'What is, however, is that someone burnt down Samuel Orlan's shop, destroying generations of maps, and that that man has disappeared.'

'Spies are not uncommon.' Bueralan glanced at Queila as she spoke. 'And there are plenty of maps of Leera.'

'There's a lot special in what Orlan does.' Heast leaned back, the faint light of his lamp casting him in shadows. 'The Orlan Maps, for generations, have been known as the most accurate of any kingdom. They go beyond street names and dominion lords. They follow sewers, trade routes, dams, crop growths, weather patterns, bolt-holes, escape routes, back doors and more.'

The captain's lips parted in a faint smile. 'My point still stands. It's not as if there was one map. Orlan's apprentices have drawn and redrawn his maps throughout the world.'

'She does have a point,' Bueralan said, looking at Heast.

'She does,' he conceded.

'Then what did this person want, if not the girl?'

'Orlan?' Queila asked.

'He hasn't been seen for about a week, but that's not unusual. His work often takes him out of Mireea.'

'Is he as neutral as they say?'

'Every Orlan has been,' Heast said. 'I think that's why so many of them have lived here. No need to worry about being pressured to change the lines in estates or conscripted into a war to advise on routes and supplying needs. Here, he offers no allegiance to anyone and his services bring all to him.'

'Strange to burn such a man's work,' Essa mused. 'Are you sure that this attacker was not after the girl?'

'No.'

Bueralan turned, hearing the door to Heast's office open. Four figures stood there, three of them guards under Heast. Solid men, though the sergeant had a nervous look about him, a twitch in his brown eyes that the saboteur found himself cold towards. It appeared that he was not the only one possessed of such a reaction for the fourth man, who did not wear a guard's dark-green cloak, regarded the sergeant flatly. The soldier looked capable with the longsword at his side, but the saboteur had the distinct impression that, for all the charms the other wore, he was not a man to take lightly.

'Thank you, Illaan,' Heast said, standing as the others did. 'Did you speak with Ayae?'

The sergeant hesitated, then said, 'Yes, sir.'

'Is she—'

'Fine, sir.'

The start of a frown tugged at Heast's lips. 'If you would rather return to the hospital, I understand.'

'I will stay here, sir.'

With the briefest of nods the Captain of the Spine dropped the subject and motioned for the man adorned in charms to be brought forward. The shadows of the room clung to him as he did, the burns and stains in his clothes lending him the impression of a figure not yet fully formed, of a man being created before Bueralan's eyes.

'This is Zaifyr,' Heast said. 'A man in my employ from Kakar.'

'Kakar,' Queila Meina said. 'That's little more than ruins now.'

'People still live there,' he said, accent sharpening his use of the letter p. 'Some of the older men and women still call it

Asila, but it has been a long time since I lived there. I spend a year here, a year there. My home becomes more distant every day.'

Stepping from behind his desk, Heast's steel leg hit the ground solidly. 'You saved someone today.'

Zaifyr's right hand drifted to the chain around his left. 'Luck, really.'

'I was told you slashed open the throat of the man who started the fire, but there was no body to be found.'

'Slashing that throat did very little,' he said.

'Tell me exactly what happened.'

'I heard Ayae scream.' At the use of her name, Illaan frowned. 'I could see fire coming out of the door of Orlan's store, so I ran in, mostly on instinct. I thought it was simply someone trapped, or panicking – I certainly didn't think I would enter just in time to see a man throw a girl across the room as if she were a doll. She was unhurt, but the man's skin was blackened, especially around the hands. When he took a step through the flames to reach her, I came up behind him, grabbed his hair and slashed his throat. It didn't stop him, though. It didn't even make him bleed.'

'Wrong angle?'

He shook his head and Bueralan glanced at the two mercenary commanders beside him. Kal Essa's arms were folded across his chest, the look of doubt clear, and Queila, though not as obvious, still seemed dubious.

'I dragged him outside,' Zaifyr continued. 'It was hard to see or breathe in there, but I had enough of him to drag him onto the road. There was a crowd starting to show, but as the man hit the ground, they scattered. It wasn't until he turned around that I could see why they did that: he looked awful, a mix of burnt flesh and aged bone. He stared at me, and ran with a growl. I was left with a choice of following him or rescuing Ayae – I chose the latter.'

'You don't sound particularly bothered by that,' Essa muttered.

The Captain of the Spine shook his head. 'It was the right thing. The smart thing. A man like that fights with no pain.'

'What do you mean?' Bueralan asked.

'Our friend here can explain.'

Beneath the gaze of everyone in the room, Zaifyr smiled faintly, and shrugged. 'It was a Quor'lo,' he said easily; 'a dead man possessed.'

7.

Ayae considered running. The windows in the hospital were not big, but she was small enough to slip through and, even in the gown she wore, she believed that she could make her way down the warm cobbled road to her house and be gone before the first of the sun began to soak through the canopies of the mountains' forest.

But she had nowhere to go. If she went back to her house, once she'd pulled on old trousers and new shirt, found her boots and filled her pack, hiding what gold she had at the bottom, she would step to the doorway and simply stop. The dark shadow of the tree before her would offer no hint of direction, other than to point back into her house with its cut branches. It would urge her to stay. To stay in the place that was the only security she knew. A small spark of anger ignited in her stomach with the thought. She had not been born in Mireea, but it was her home.

Her home.

The door to the ward opened, revealing the two guards who stood straight and still as a large, hairless man stepped between them. Dressed in expensive red leather trousers and grey silk shirt, and wearing boots made from soft, supple leather, it was his hands that drew her attention. They were littered with scars. The succession of tiny white marks looked as if they had been made by a plague thousands of years old. His eyes, when they turned to her, were similarly afflicted, faint, white specks drifting over the pale grey iris, as if once a milky blindness had threatened him.

'My name is Fo,' he said, approaching her, his scarred hand held out to her. 'I'm a Keeper from the Enclave in Yeflam.'

Fo, the Disease. He looked neither sick nor afraid. Ayae shook his clammy hand and introduced herself hesitantly.

She was aware that she was in the presence of a man who did not age, a man whose life was meshed in myth and rumour, but whose his grip was firm. He was a Keeper of the Divine, a man who had been cursed – or blessed, depending on who spoke – with immortality. Fo also had the power to infect a living creature with illness, design and create new diseases, but offer no cure. He was one part of the Enclave, the organization that ruled Yeflam, drawing men and women into their city on the promise of utopia on the day they ascended.

Still holding her hand, he sat opposite. 'I hope you're feeling better. The healer here tells me that you're fine, but - well, let us just say, I like to see things myself.'

'I'm fine.' Ayae attempted to pull her hand back, but could not. 'Reila knows what she is talking about.'

'Reila is a fanatic: a "healer" who would rather work with herbs and alchemy than magic, but who draws from her own blood when she must.' His voice was cool. 'A year ago, a young healer came to Mireea to set up shop. He had a touch of the gods in him. A tiny curse, you could say, enough that he could mend a wound and intuitively pick up an illness. He was a rarity – a young man who wanted to help, and sought neither riches nor fame doing so. The Lord Wagan sent him back to Yeflam in chains two months after his arrival, as your same healer had him arrested and roundly denounced him in front of the Lord and Lady.'

'He killed two people.'

Fo gazed at her, his grey eyes unblinking.

Unwilling to be put off, Ayae continued, 'One had a broken leg, the other a cancer in the stomach. Reila said he treated neither.'

'And you believed her?'

She had. With a quick tug, she pulled back her hand and rubbed the sweat from it. 'I'd never heard of anyone dying from a broken leg before that.'

The Keeper's eyes blinked, slowly, then he shook his head. 'I see I will have a lot of work to do with you.'

'You'll have *nothing* to do with me.'

His hairless eyebrows rose at her tone. 'You emerged from a burning building without a mark on you, child. You survived an attack from a Quor'lo—'

'A what?'

The large man rose, a frown added to his list of expressions. 'A Quor'lo. Moves, acts, smells just like it would alive, but its body is given life by a living person elsewhere.'

'Does the captain know? If this has—'

'He knows.' At the front of her bed, he met her eyes. 'Bau already informed Heast what it was, though I imagine that the captain's meticulous mind would have found it quickly enough. You needn't worry about the Quor'lo. Right now I am sure they are discussing it, wondering where it is hiding, and if they can capture it. I can only imagine that the man who pulled you out of the fire is helping them greatly.'

'Zaifyr?'

'That's his name, is it?' The Keeper's tone suggested familiarity, though not friendly in nature.

'Who is he?' Ayae asked.

'At this moment, I am sure he is nothing more than a man employed by Captain Heast.' Fo's scarred fingers laced together. 'However, you have changed the subject. I am here to talk about you. You emerged from a fire without a burn today, but should I hold your hand again I would feel it smoulder.'

Her hands slipped under the blankets, falling warmly against her legs. 'I was just lucky.'

'There's no such thing.' She met his strange gaze, but said nothing. 'I imagine, since you live on this mountain, you think anybody with a touch of power in them is cursed by the gods.'

'I don't want any of that,' she said, quietly. 'I just want to be able to tell my partner that I am just who I am. I just – I don't want this.'

'You think you can give up what is inside you?' Fo's scarred hands dropped to the metal end of the bed. 'What remains of the gods finds us. In wombs, in childhood, in the summers and winters of our lives. Once it has found us, only death can drive it out. If that two-bit copper healer told you she could do that, she has done nothing but lie to you.' His long fingers curled, one at a time, over the bed frame. 'But you have nothing to fear, child. Not from this. Trust me. Trust us. My brothers and sisters and I study the remains of the gods. They lay around us as they lived: on our land, in our oceans, and in our skies, the power that made us originally still there, wishing to create.'

'Wishing to create?' Ayae met Fo's disease-scarred eyes. 'What is it that you're implying? That I have been infected by a god?'

'Possession is not infection.' His smile was faint. 'I can tell you that on a number of levels, child.'

'Then what?'

'We are being re-created, reborn. The power in the gods does not wish to die with its host. It is searching for escape, for a new home, and it has found you, just as it found me. With it, you and I are in evolution to take back what was once ours.'

A laugh escaped her mouth at the ridiculousness of the statement, but a second did not follow. The bar beneath Fo's hands had bent and she waited for him to lash out. What did he expect? She had grown up hearing stories of men and women who were cursed, stories of wives taking children away from fathers who melted, of lovers devoured by their partner with teeth made from stone, and of blindness and deformity that resulted in abuse. In the orphanage, children had teased others with the term, used it to suggest that the newest among them might harbour such a power, that it might be the reason they had no family, no home, and could not be trusted.

'You'll see in time,' was Fo's soft reply. 'Tomorrow, I expect you at the Spine's Keep. You have a lot to learn, Ayae. It may be that you are no more than a copper healer, but I doubt that. A Quor'lo does not brave Samuel Orlan's shop for the cheapest of coin.'

Turning, he stalked away, and for a moment, Ayae wanted to call out to him, to demand an explanation of his last words, but her attention was drawn to the bar that Fo's hands had curled around. There, dented with a strength she did not have – did not know anyone to have – was the perfect impression of his fingers.

The City Beneath

As I grew older, none of the symbols I was taught as a child retained meaning. After death, the talismans of a god neither contained truth or moral lesson, neither comforted or protected. Instead, they became objects, relics that counted the existence of seventy-eight beings of divinity. Seventy-eight corpses.

—Qian, *The Godless*

1.

In the morning sun's light, Mireea smouldered. From the edges of the Spine, from the closed yards of carpenters and smiths, from the empty mills, from the wide cobbled roads of industry that flourished so much before the markets had closed and left them silent and boarded up, mist rose. It was as if, buried deep within his tomb, Ger's corpse had caught alight, and the flames were rising. It was a morbid thought and the exiled Baron of Kein tried to shake it off as he followed Sergeant Illaan Alahn and his squad of Mireean Guards along the street. The thought had too much potency this morning – especially with the charm-laced man, Zaifyr, beside him.

They were headed towards the graveyard outside the city on Heast's orders. As light began to flare in the morning, the Captain of the Spine, his hand held over his thigh where metal and flesh were welded painfully together, said, 'With its throat cut and half its face burnt away, it'll be hard for whoever is controlling it to keep it upright. Whoever is possessing it has to draw from his or herself and lend it a little life so that it can function, and the worse condition that it is in, the more that is required to keep it alive.'

'Why won't whoever's in control just have dumped it?' Queila Meina asked.

'It takes time. You have to withdraw every little bit of yourself, or you'll risk losing a part.'

'Part?'

'Your voice, your ability to move your left hand,' Zaifyr explained quietly. 'Think of all the things you do. You have to pull each conscious awareness out, one by one.'

'You know a lot,' Essa muttered, thick hand scratching his stubble. 'Ain't no one curious how a man learns this kind of thing?'

Bueralan was, but he waited and watched as the other man shrugged. 'Same way your captain does, I'd imagine,' he said.

'Fifteen years ago,' Heast answered, 'I watched a witch in Faaisha possess a child that had died during the night. The body had been sold to her in the morning, a trade she was well known for among the poor. The noble who I was employed by at the time wanted to know what his rival was doing, and so he employed her. She had me walk half a mile with that thing in my grasp, listening to it – to her – whisper to me the entire time as I knocked, pretending to look for its parents. Finally, I begged the lady of the rival house to look after the child while I went to work for the day. The next morning, I collected the child and the information. That witch was buried deep in the corpse for another day, getting herself out.' He looked intently at the man in half-burnt clothing. 'I remember that right?'

'You were there?' Queila asked, incredulous. 'Were you the child he carried?'

'No, but you've missed the point,' Zaifyr said. 'We saw it done, like bread baked.'

70

'How did she do it, then?'

'With blood and death,' the Captain of the Spine replied. 'We have a limited time to find the Quor'lo if we wish to know before Bau or Fo arrive. They're showing some interest because, like us, they think it has been sent from Leera, and if it has, then we want to catch it before they do.'

Bueralan did not think the last likely to happen and, given the speed with which Heast commanded his waiting sergeant and soldiers, the captain did not either. Of the four mercenaries only Bueralan and Zaifyr were instructed to assist in the search, the two mercenary commanders being dismissed. The evening had been an education for them, a glimpse into the kind of enemy that they would be fighting. Even should the Quor'lo prove not to have been sent by the Leerans – an unlikely prospect, given what Bueralan had already been told – the point had been made that they would not just be fighting with swords and muscle.

There would be blood.

The graveyard was a gamble, Bueralan thought as they made their way down the road, a roughly built wooden gate looming above them. A gamble, but an educated one. The safest place for a Quor'lo whose throat had been cut, whose hands were blackened and face burnt, was a yard full of men and women who would look no different.

Outside the city, thin trails of mist swept into a wide road leading down a gentle decline. On either side stood silent trees, their canopies woven thickly together to throw a queer light, a mix of green and orange, upon the path they walked. Further along it widened, turning into a large opening with old, cut-back canopies that the dawn shone through.

There stood intricate funeral pyres made from iron. Numbering eight lines of ten, the pyres were twice Bueralan's height and bolted to the ground, each with a god designed into the frame. The first he saw was Ger: the tall god looked introspective with his head bowed and hands over the hilt of his great axe; the Wanderer, who had walked the roads of mortal men and women, stood beside him, his hood lowered and his arms folded; next to him was the Goddess Maita, once goddess of his homeland, whose wings dissolved every morning as the sun rose. It continued, each pyre holding an intricate design, from the obscure gods like Hienka to those like the Leviathan, whose memory lingered in the ocean, until each of the seventy-eight gods were replicated.

'The last two,' Zaifyr murmured beside him, 'are empty of any design. Whoever is executed by the rule of the land lies there.'

Grunting, the saboteur said, 'Why would someone build this?'

'Because the gods did exist.' Sergeant Illaan turned to the two men. 'Is it so surprising that we pay homage to what they once were? The Third Lord of the Spine believed that we should. He had these pyres built by the blacksmith Juen Methal. It took him thirty years to build them all.'

'If I die, bury me in the dirt,' Bueralan said. 'I don't need the ceremony.'

'Our ceremony is an important part of our culture. A remembrance.'

The saboteur shook his head. 'Where I was born, people believe that you could capture a soul and hold it in a bottle. The bottle is very dark and made from a specially blown glass.

Once your soul is caught, a couple will make an offer to your family, the amount depending on what kind of life the dead has lived. Once an agreement is reached, the woman drinks from the bottle shortly after she conceives.'

'You believe that?'

'Plenty of children are conceived without a bottle being drunk.'

Illaan looked as if he were about to speak again, but pressed his lips tightly together and his gaze focused behind Bueralan. Turning, the saboteur saw a man of medium height, white-skinned and wearing a simple white robe, with soft leather boots. As he drew closer, his gaze ran across the sergeant, his squad, and lingered on Bueralan but for a moment before settling on Zaifyr.

The charm-laced man said quietly, 'The Healer, Bau.'

2.

Ayae could not sleep. She tried, pushing herself down on the hard mattress, willing herself to let go, to just drift . . . but each time she opened her eyes there was no light, and she opened her eyes so often that she lost count well before the morning sun's dawn soaked through the tiny windows of the hospital. By then she'd had enough. She had stayed too long, wanted no more and, running a hand through her hair, she rose and pulled on her smoke-stained clothing.

At the door, the two guards created a human wall of worn chain mail and professionalism. She met the gaze of both. 'I just want to sleep in my own bed.'

The left part of the wall shrugged. 'We have orders.'

'I'm not going to be kept here.'

'I—'

'Gentlemen, let her pass.' A small hand parted the chain mail and revealed Reila, who took Ayae's arm and drew her past the two-man blockage. 'Have we lost so much kindness already, just because of a Keeper?'

'Our orders—' the right part of the wall began.

She raised a hand. 'Think before you speak, Voren.'

74

The soldier's lips pursed, but he nodded, once, and retreated as Ayae was led down the pale, morning-lit corridor. As she stepped into the morning light, Reila told Ayae that she should rest for a few days, drink plenty of water and find her immediately if she began to feel hot. 'We will take care of you, child,' the healer said, the wet cobbles beneath their feet like drying tears. 'All is not lost.'

By the time Ayae had returned to her home, she felt that all was indeed lost. Her hope that no one would have heard what happened in Orlan's shop was gone and she felt a hollow pit form in her stomach. She saw the damage from afar, as if whoever had damaged the building had damaged her. As if the broken and trampled garden was her, beaten, as if the scrawled obscenities on the door were dug into her skin, as if the broken windows were wounds upon her and not her house.

Her house.

She had paid for the house entirely a year ago, after she had been awarded an apprenticeship with Samuel Orlan.

The day had been one that she could still remember with shock. Samuel Orlan took on one apprentice every five years, and men and women came from around the world to apply for it, with the competition becoming more and more fierce the older the cartographer became. To be the last apprentice of Samuel Orlan was to be the inheritor of not just wealth, but a fame that took you to any court in any part of the world. On the day that the apprenticeship had been announced, Ayae had not even gone to the ceremony to hear, believing that a choice had already been made, that the event of the day was, like many of its kind, a planned spontaneity. But at the time of the announcement she had heard a knock on the apartment door that she and Faise had shared, and her friend had gotten up to answer it, only to return in silence, the small old man following her, looking entirely too pleased to be missing his own ceremony.

After a month, the old man had advanced her the money for the house, telling her that neither she nor Faise could remain in that awful apartment they shared. The act had lodged such affection and loyalty within her that the sight of her house reminded her what would happen when Samuel heard about her. The thought was a cold one, dousing the anger that nestled in her stomach.

At the door, a hand fell once, twice, and finally, a third time.

If it was Illaan, he had a key and could let himself in; but even as the thought occurred to her, she knew it was not him. His betrayal, his rejection of her in the hospital, struck deeply and she would not forgive him for it. He would know that, as well. When the knocking sounded again, she swallowed a sudden lump of tears and opened the door.

Backlit against the morning's sunlight, the small, portly figure of Samuel Orlan stood, waiting for her. Dressed in fine but simple clothes of blue and grey, the elderly man's white beard and hair looked as if they were touched by fire. If his blue eyes had not been filled with obvious concern and had he not immediately embraced her, Ayae would have thought that such lighting was a sign of anger.

'I'm sorry,' she whispered into his shoulder.

'Don't you say another word,' he replied. 'That shop was old. Outdated. I was going to burn it down for insurance money next week, anyway.'

A short laugh escaped the mouth she pressed against him.

'Besides, I need a new project. I keep dating older women who want me for my money,' the small man continued. 'Do you know the look on their faces when I tell them that I have no personal wealth? That the money is part of the Orlan Estate, and not mine? Oh, but it reminds me of when I was a teenager and my first love rejected me. But you are Samuel Orlan, they say. I am forced to admit that, while that is true, I am also a fat old man born to equally fat parents who had no money. I find myself saying the exact words that dear old love said to me when I presented her with a flower. No, it has to stop. I need a new hobby. Also, I fear that word will soon be out on the street, and these women will no longer make me home-cooked meals and take – well, let us be delicate about that, yes?'

'Of course. They have reputations.'

'Awful ones, awful.' Slipping his arm around her waist, he stepped through the door and closed it gently behind him. 'Now, let's get you something cold to drink, and you can tell me who has ruined your garden and I can tell you about our new shop.'

Wiping wet eyes, Ayae said, 'You still want me to come back?'

'Why wouldn't I?'

Struggling – his flippant tone suggested that he didn't know about Fo's visit, though she did not believe such knowledge would remain secret for long – Ayae told him about the fire, her own reaction and the Keeper's visit. It was when she brought up the latter that, with the blind half opened to let in the morning's light, the old cartographer paused and said, 'And where was Illaan through all this?'

'Gone.'

He grunted. 'Useless man.'

'What the Keeper said doesn't bother you?'

'No.' He made a dismissive wave. 'In this part of the world the Enclave offers a rare moment of sanity in the debate about cursed men and women.'

A frown creased Ayae's lips.

Open now, the blind revealed motes of dust in the light. 'The Enclave is, relatively speaking, a new organization,' Orlan explained. 'A thousand years ago, the maps say that Yeflam was nothing more than a small crop of islands on the edge of Kuinia, the first of the Five Kingdoms. The area was mostly known for the cult that lived in the Spine of Ger, who built their cities in the mountains to be closer to the remains of the god himself. The gold rushes that brought men and women of a less virtuous mind to their peaks after the fall of the Five Kingdoms eventually saw the cult – which had become inbred and largely isolated – killed, and left the area open for anyone with a strong sword. In that vacuum, six men and women took control of the islands and began to build the Floating Cities of Yeflam, that huge artificial stone empire that covers the black ocean like a tomb. The people responsible for it are all long lived – immortal, if you take their word for it – but only Aelyn Meah, their leader, has any real power. You'll find it rarely spoken of in Yeflam, but she was one of the five who ruled before. Her kingdom was Maewe, the third kingdom, after Asila, but before Mahga and Salar. She is one of the oldest beings on the planet. Those with her in the Enclave are much, much younger than her and could not compete with her in terms of power or violence, not in the way one such as the Innocent, Aela Ren, does, but they do attempt to stop the needless fear of the cursed.'

'You talk about the years as if they mean nothing,' she said. 'The Five Kingdoms fell apart a thousand years ago and the Innocent began killing nearly seven hundred years ago.'

'I am the eighty-second Samuel Orlan.' The short man grinned. 'My perspective may be slightly askew.'

Shaking her head, Ayae lowered herself onto a chair. 'The Keeper said I was to go to him tomorrow.'

Dawn lit the edges of the cartographer again. 'Demanding sort, but perhaps for the best. The Keepers do understand their curses well. And—'

'And?'

'I am afraid,' he said, the light enveloping him, 'the only way to understand something is to ask the people who have experienced it.'

3.

Flies burst from the closest pyre as a Mireean Guard examined the body that lay there. It had taken him, Bueralan thought, ten minutes to mount the wooden ramp and check beneath the white linen. He could understand their reluctance, but he cursed them for it since it left him standing next to the Keeper, Bau. So far he had been nothing but polite company, but since he had said to Illaan that he was 'nothing but an adviser, a helper if you need one', a tension had crept into the air, growing further when the Healer said, 'Do you know how long it has been since anyone saw a Quor'lo in our world?'

Zaifyr replied, 'No more than twenty-one hours, I imagine.'

Ahead, the first line of pyres had been cleared and soldiers were working through the second. Bueralan wondered what the two men beside him would do if the Quor'lo was not found, if it had gone to ground elsewhere or the body had already been abandoned – to his mind, the most likely – when movement on the fifth pyre caught his eye. A moment later, a soldier cried out and the three men ran towards the sound.

On the pyre, a dead man held a young, blond-haired soldier

in his grasp. 'Another step,' it hissed at Bau. 'That's all it takes for this man to die.'

'You've nowhere to go,' Illaan said, stepping forward. 'Release him. Release him and I'll—'

The soldier's throat burst.

It happened quickly: a thin, bloodless smile spread across the ruined face of the Quor'lo, its burnt fingers tightened, a strangled cry caught in the soldier as his throat was torn out . . . and, as the soldiers around Bueralan moved forward, the body was flung off the ledge into them and the Quor'lo leapt from its perch.

Bueralan was a step behind Zaifyr. He burst through the soldiers who had run not at the creature, but to the body of their comrade. He heard Illaan call for Bau and glanced back to see the Keeper staring intently after them. For a moment it looked as if he would ignore the call for help, but then, with a snarl, the neat man turned. Doing likewise, Bueralan focused on weaving through the pyres, the dirt crunching beneath his boots as he chased the Quor'lo into the tree line.

The saboteur did not stop. At full speed, he left flat ground and began running downwards, his feet slipping as he skirted thick roots and potholes, not slowing himself even as he was forced to navigate the sloping terrain of the mountain. In front of him, Zaifyr cleared a ditch and the saboteur zigged, crossing the shallow end of the same indent, before clearing a dead branch and gaining on the Quor'lo, who had stopped to stamp its foot heavily.

Bueralan pulled one of his axes from his waist and launched it, head over handle, through the air. It cut deeply into a tree directly beside the creature.

Raising its burnt head, it snarled at him and reached for the buried axe just as Zaifyr crashed into it.

Bueralan followed, yanking the axe from the tree as he did. Drawing the second, he fell into a defensive position as the Quor'lo tossed its attacker to the side and rose to its full height. It looked awful: decay had set in around the wounds on its head, the body looked tired, bones showing through skin as if it were being eaten away. The Quor'lo's eyes focused on Bueralan. Holding the other's gaze, he watched Zaifyr rise slowly. With a sudden shift the saboteur darted forward, his axes coming in from the right side.

The Quor'lo spun, dodging Bueralan's attack and using the momentum to evade Zaifyr as he lunged. Scoring a brief moment of respite, it stamped its foot again and again, furious as Zaifyr rose with a knife in his hands to thrust—

The Quor'lo disappeared.

4.

Ayae sat quietly beneath the open window, the morning's sun filtering over her. She had spent her time since Orlan left searching herself, trying to find the seed of warmth Reila had mentioned, the burning ember that she could quench. So far she could find nothing. No, that was not true: as the minutes passed she became angrier at Illaan's behaviour, furious at the defacing of her house and bitter at the loneliness she felt. But that, she admitted to herself as the sun lazily made its way down her light brown arms, was not her 'curse'. That was just her, as Faise had said.

Faise.

How would she react to the news? Her friend, with such a quick and ferocious intelligence, had left Mireea eight months ago. She had married Zineer, who owned a small accounting business in one of the cities of Yeflam, and who did work for the Traders Union. She wrote weekly, telling Ayae everything, asking for the same in return, but how could Ayae write that she could still taste smoke in her mouth such that even drinking three glasses of orange juice did not rid her of the taste? How could she explain that if she relaxed her internal search, the memory of the burning shop returned and panic set in? How could she explain how she stared at her arms looking for scars she did not have?

Nothing would come of this, Ayae knew. It was a self-designed trap of smoke and flames, a hunt for a cause that she could not identify in the ruin of her life. She could not sit here and stop her life. Orlan had already shown her that not everyone in Mireea was like the people who had damaged her house.

Slowly, pushing herself up from the floor, she opened her neat and orderly closet and chose clothes that did not smell of smoke.

Outside, the sky showed empty through the cut branches and the defacing of her house was clearer. Under the morning's sun it appeared both more violent and more pathetic: the words on her walls were misspelt, her garden only half destroyed and salvageable. It would take a day, but she would be able to clean up both — but her footsteps along the narrow cobbled path did not take her to a shop, but to the Spine of Ger. It was not habit that saw her make her way to the morning's training, but rather a desire to do something, to be active; a self-conscious doubt began to seed in her, but that only strengthened her resolve. She would not let the words of a Keeper, or the rejection of her partner, stop her from taking part in an exercise that she enjoyed.

The thought strengthened her as she climbed the last step of the Spine and saw the heads of men and women turn to her. She knew they were not her friends but they were normally civil to her, as she was to them: they nodded and smiled and said hello. It would be no different, she persuaded herself, walking through them as the Captain of the Spine began his torturous climb up the stairs. By the time Heast reached the podium, Ayae had made it to her position, behind Jaerc, ignoring how the baker's apprentice shifted forward slightly.

Next to her, Keallis, the tall city planner, whispered harshly, 'Are you witless?'

Ayae whispered, 'Nothing has chan—'

'You're *scaring* him,' she said.

She stared at Jaerc's hunched shoulders.

'You're cursed!' the woman whispered. 'We all know that!'

She could not reply.

'Do you want to burn us alive?' the woman hissed again. Around her, others began the first of their stretches. 'We have all heard how your skin splits beneath fire! You destroyed the shop of Samuel Orlan!'

'I did not!' Her voice was raw, struggling for composure. 'There was another man there. He set it on fire . . .'

'Don't you understand?' Around her, men and women turned, their attention drawn by Keallis's raising voice. On the podium, Ayae saw the captain staring at her. In his usually stern face, she thought she saw sympathy there. 'We are meant to die,' she continued, not bothering to whisper now. 'That's what the gods taught us.'

Through the disordered people, a Mireean Guard was making his way towards Ayae, the order given from a slight nod by Heast. Closing her eyes, squeezing them tight, she said softly, 'I wouldn't hurt anyone.'

'*Leave!*'

And without another word she fled, aware that their eyes followed her every step.

5.

Beneath the shattered wooden covering was only darkness. There was water, though Bueralan could see but the faintest reflection of the morning's light off it. The rankness of the hole was not so shy, and with his hands on the rotten wooden edge that led to a frail, broken ladder he stared into the inky black, trying to gauge its depth between breaths.

He did not want to go into the flooded mineshaft, which he considered a reasonable state of mind to be in. The two men Illaan had sent to bring sealed bladders and pitch globes, brothers who rescued trapped miners in flash floods, had agreed with him. They arrived in an old, crumbling wagon pulled by an older, grey-haired horse. After one look at the shaft, they had laughed. Both men were white, diminutive and scrawny with dark hair and deep-set, squinting eyes.

Without turning to the sergeant, the First said, 'You don't have enough booze in this city to convince us to go down there. It's two decades—'

'Four,' interrupted the Second. 'Maybe five.'

'Six to seven decades old, rotten in its core, and flooded,' continued the First. 'In addition, there is a man down there who has not come up for air in a good hour.'

'We're not doing it,' concluded the Second.

Around them, the Mireean Guard searched for the openings of other mineshafts. When one was found, a soldier would pull back the covering, releasing a foul odour that he or she would then stand guard over. So far they had found five, unsurprising in a mountain riddled with wounds left from centuries of digging.

'You're not expected to go down there,' Illaan said evenly. 'I just want you to help these two men get ready.'

'You should have that Keeper down here,' muttered the First.

Bueralan did not disagree. Bau had not left the funeral pyres. Lost in concentration, the saboteur had been told that he was knitting the soldier's throat back together.

Rising, he met Zaifyr's gaze from across the hole and the charm-laced man grimaced, liking the decision no more. Yet both would swim down the shaft until they hit the bottom. There, the silt would be disturbed, and in water turning darker and murkier, they would swim down a tunnel with nothing but trapped air in their grasp. In theory, the tunnel would end in a low pit that had been designed to avoid flooding by being cut in higher than the tunnel to it.

'You're both just real unlucky,' the First said, he and his brother returning with shapeless, inflated animal bladders and two thick, glass orbs. 'This whole area has been scheduled for filling for the last year, if I remember.'

'Last two,' the Second corrected.

'Three then, probably.'

'Why wasn't it?' Bueralan asked.

'Why do a lot of civil projects not get done?' The First placed the glass orb he had been holding on the ground, the pitch inside it rolling sluggishly.

'Paperwork,' the Second answered.

'And a war,' Sergeant Illaan Alahn said, approaching the group. 'Let us not forget that, either.'

The First shrugged. The Second, his back to the soldier, rolled his deep-set eyes. Holding up the large globe, he said, 'These burn for half a candle in the water. Down there, these are your life. They'll tell you which way is up, which is down. They'll also stop you from being in the cold for too long – you go numb after a while, which is warning enough, really. You can move it if you need and you should. There's only a little bit of pitch in these, and we do that 'cause we like to move them. Once the first one is done on its time, we'll drop a second to guide you home in two hours. After that, one every hour until tonight. We'll assume you're not coming up, if you're not back by then.'

'You're filling me with confidence,' Bueralan said.

'At least it's not doubt and fear. That's a killer.' The small man grinned through his discoloured, crooked teeth. 'Once you're ready, I'll drop it down.'

With a nod the saboteur unstrapped his axes, pulled off his boots and his shirt. A long series of scars, a lash's touch, ran across his back. They were old, but deep, and the ends of his tattoos entwined in them, his old life, his new. If any of those around him had any thought about it, the splash of the dropping orb was the only statement made. Following its descent, Bueralan watched the burning glow get swallowed quickly.

'You sure we can't send the midgets down?' he muttered drily.

Zaifyr moved to the edge. 'Just pray that whoever has possessed the Quor'lo hasn't had time to pull themselves out yet.'

'Pray?'

The man dropped into the water.

'Time like this,' he said, rising from the black and cold water for but a moment, 'even a dead god is important.'

Then he plunged downwards.

6.

At first, Bueralan's trouble with the descent had been the cold. It seeped well into his bones before the light was gone and he thought about returning to the stench outside, to the smell that made his eyes water. It only got worse once the sunlight was left behind and the cold stillness of the water pressed in close. Coupled with the inky darkness, it became a psychological weight that combined with the tug of the bladder in his grasp and the saboteur felt a panic set in. Pushing it from his mind and using the physical act of swimming downwards as a focus, he moved quickly, the light of the orb guiding him. Soon, Zaifyr appeared next to it, his narrow face gazing upward. Seeing Bueralan, he picked up the orb and moved to his left, swimming into a narrow cut shaft.

A few metres into the shaft, claustrophobia set in. There was nothing but stone and water, the two elements mixing together. Bueralan was soon crawling more than swimming, and the sense of a crushing weight above sent a chill deep into his bones. Again, he pushed the thought from his mind, focused instead on taking a second breath from the bladder in his grasp. The valve had been easy to learn outside but his waterlogged fingers fumbled, a second of air bubbling out in a joyful escape. He closed it quickly, moved to catch up to the rolling orb and the shadow of Zaifyr, pushing ahead of him.

Suddenly the man stopped and released the orb, pushing upwards, his feet kicking out in an explosion of dirty water. Biting back a panicked curse Bueralan followed, pushing into a new shaft with a rotten ladder on the side. The light lasted but moments, and it went black. With panic threatening Bueralan almost turned around, but a pale green light bloomed around him as he burst from the water. Taking a deep breath and gagging on the stench as he did, he grabbed the edge of the hole and pulled himself out to stand in a small, dug-out room reinforced with rotting beams.

A bolt-hole: a miner would sleep, eat, live here for weeks, before the need for fresh air drove him or her up top.

The green light was cast by a seam of stone in the wall, a jagged line that highlighted a tunnel, and without speaking, Zaifyr crawled through it. The saboteur followed and found himself after no more than a dozen movements in a yawning cavern, the roof webbed with lines of crystal that emitted a pale glow. Beneath it were houses built into the walls, built from stone that had long lost its original colour to dripping water and were now cast sickly green beneath the light.

'A City of Ger,' Bueralan whispered, pushing himself up.

'Not nearly as empty as it should be,' the other man said, pointing up.

Recent beams had been put into place on the ceiling, the wood large enough that it would have had to be brought in by half a dozen men, and high enough that ladders would have been required. At the top of the beams were small, drilled tunnels pushing deep into the rock, back the way that they had come.

'Two midgets lied.' Bueralan's voice was still quiet, hushed. 'Someone has been down here in the last seventy years.'

'The last seven days, even,' Zaifyr said. 'Where do you think the holes go?'

'Beneath the roads.' He shrugged. 'To the killing ground outside the Spine. They probably dug it out to collapse under weight, making it difficult to move through but easier to kill on.'

The other man nodded. Then, turning, he pointed down through the city. 'The Quor'lo went this way.'

A single pair of footsteps were marked between worn stones, the edges of a street long gone. Following them, Bueralan wondered how they would be able to bring the Quor'lo back. The swim would not be viable, but if there was a second entrance, such as the one used by those who had set up the trap above them . . .

The rough dwellings gave way to extravagant houses, rising into two-storey buildings with blunted, crumbling balconies that peered over the street they walked upon. Broken lamp posts rose no higher than Bueralan's chest, the remains now part of the ground, lying next to the broken blades and hacked skeletons, a grisly reminder of the purging that had taken place once the gold diggers had settled on their state.

The saboteur heard the sound of moving water, the noise emerging from the slow drip of moisture in the cavern. Soon enough a chill began to seep into Bueralan, and the smell of fresh water reached him, pushing back the noxious odour that had followed him out of the stagnant mining tunnel. He paused there, turning his gaze to the pale lit river to where the light turned red.

'The people in this city must have read omens into this,' Zaifyr said, standing beside him. 'All manner of murder and betrayal.'

'You sure know how to reassure a man you just met.'

'They believed that Ger would rise again,' he said. 'They wanted a god, and any god would do, I suspect, but Ger was one of the first to react against the killing of Linae, and the reprisals that followed. He spoke out against both sides, and when neither listened, he began to stride across the continents, placing himself into the battles, stopping them with his sheer size and strength. At least that is what the cultists here believed. To them, he was a figure of responsibility, a guardian who would keep them safe.'

'And the light was for what the gods did?'

'For themselves, too. After all, they were killed while as close to Ger as they could be. Surely a betrayal for them.'

'Surely,' Bueralan echoed drily.

Half a smile slipped across Zaifyr's face and he began to follow the river. It was not strong, but soon the red light enveloped them both, lighting the tracks of the creature and its slow, injured walk. With each step along the path Bueralan's muscles tensed, his back straightened as he waited for the burnt, half-dead figure of the Quor'lo to burst out of a narrow cut in the wall.

Nothing.

Nothing except the edge of the river disappearing into a collapsed wall.

Zaifyr followed the water through the jagged rocks, so focused on the task that Bueralan believed himself forgotten. The saboteur began to believe that a personal desire had taken over the other man, had taken over any task of finding the Quor'lo for Heast – a notion that was only reinforced when he finally stepped through the collapsed wall and stared down off an almost sheer edge into a lake.

There, in a still, red-lit lake sat a huge building. Spread out in the water as if it were a long leech that had latched onto the dirt and drew nutrients until it had grown monstrous, it was one of the longest buildings that Bueralan had ever seen. In terms of height, it appeared to have been made with a re-verse in mind, as if its intention had been to dig through the rock of the mountain and push itself as deep as its design would allow. At the bottom of the wall Bueralan joined with Zaifyr, and they walked across the uneven rock towards the building and the slight shadow that knelt at the water's edge.

'Leave me,' the Quor'lo whispered harshly, not turning at their approach. 'Your presence is only angering here.'

Unmoved, Zaifyr said, 'Who are you?'

An ugly, bitter smile twisted the burnt remains of its face. 'I'm one of the faithful, not one of the faithless.'

'I asked for a name.'

'It is not important.' The dead man sighed, a ragged breath escaping the damaged chest. 'I am dying. I am stuck in this body and I am dying. Who I am will be gone soon enough. I might as well take a name that is meaningless, a jumble of letters, and present it to you as truth.'

'Dying men traditionally have no wit,' Zaifyr said, moving to stand next to it.

A dry laugh escaped it. 'I die before truth.'

'You die before an old building.'

The Quor'lo shook its head and turned, as much as it could, to Bueralan. Beneath the roof's red light it was a ghastly figure: skin torn, lips split, one eye closed and broken bone exposed and fractured. Yet there was no fear, as there had been when it had run from them at the pyres, no look of desperation on its face as had been when it stamped on the wooden cover of a mineshaft. There was a serenity that, given the nature of the creature before him and the pain the man or woman controlling it was feeling, was not easily identifiable.

'I can only imagine how I must look to you,' it said, its voice struggling to be heard over the crash of water. 'I cannot see this body. I only know there is blood, I can feel it – not here, but where I truly am. My skin is stained with it. Yet here I know only what is before me.'

It turned back to the submerged building, leaving the saboteur to follow its gaze. After the gods had died there had been temples, buildings erected to house the remains, relics and beliefs that were no longer in practice. Bueralan had never before seen one – they were, mostly, ruins now – and he felt a chill, as if a gaze had settled upon him. It enveloped him so fully that he did not know if he could step outside it.

'Do you feel him?' The Quor'lo's voice was barely audible.

'Yes,' Zaifyr replied.

Bueralan said nothing.

'We cannot find the remains of his wards,' it whispered, not concerned with his response. 'They are the air, the dirt, the fire, the ocean: Ger shattered their chains to him with what strength he had left. We are told that their remains are the anger in our weather, the floods, the droughts, the cyclones, the fires. They are lost to us.'

'They are not lost. They are here. They live without him, just fine.'

'No!'

The cry was sudden, angry, a denial that snapped Bueralan's attention away from the submerged building and forced him to take a step back, reaching for the cold dagger strapped to his leg. What started as a surge of the Quor'lo to its feet ended with a shudder. It fell to its knees. 'You and your kind,' it whispered. 'I will not listen to you and your kind.'

And there, its voice stumbling in an inaudible whisper of defiance, it fell still.

7.

Away from the Spine of Ger, Ayae dug her nails into the palms of her hands and fought for control. Part of her urged returning to the stairs to confront them all, to strike out, scream at the injustice of it just once; while another part urged her to keep walking, ignore the warmth at the tips of her fingers and the heat that soaked into the palms of her hands as her anger threatened to overwhelm her.

As the Spine fell behind her, Ayae found herself walking towards the Keep. Her first glance at the emerging structure saw her step falter, but as she drew closer and the gates that led to the empty gardens appeared, her step strengthened. Fo had not explained the curse enough to her – he had hidden everything behind his fanaticism, behind his dislike for Reila, and she had been in no condition to push him. Orlan was not entirely right that they were the only people to turn to about curses in Mireea, but they would certainly know the most, and she would press them for more information.

She was led from the gate by an elderly guard, his beard slivered with silver and his eyes the colour of wet stone. The warm, spice smells filled the Keep as the corridors twisted left and right, leading up flights of turning stairs cut into solid stone. With each step a series of doubts cracked beneath her, each one ending in the desire to turn around, to leave. To pave over what was broken. But the silence that she was treated to from the guard, and the way his back remained straight as if the muscles had frozen in place at her arrival, served to remind her of why she was making the trip. She knew that she could not walk away.

There were four towers in the Spine's Keep, each designed to mirror the towers that sat along the Spine, though without the practicality that those battlements actually had. The Keep's towers were named after the directions that they faced and were symbolic before anything else. The West Tower offered no strategic advantage, unless an army managed to climb the sheer drop it faced – and it was to the door of that tower Ayae was led by the guard, who left without a nod.

Alone, she stood before the door, her hands balled tight at her side. What would she say once she entered? Fo was a powerful man. He was a member of the Enclave, a Keeper who was, she had heard, over a thousand years old, and had a world view unlike her own. Ayae did not hate anyone with a curse – in truth, before today, she had never met anyone cursed – and she would not have raised her voice like Keallis, nor given into fear so easily, or at least she hoped; but she was not someone who enjoyed confrontation, or who saw it as a way to resolve her problems. How long she stood there lost in thought about how best to proceed, Ayae was not sure. It was entirely possible that she would have continued standing if a person had not emerged from the twisting halls of the Keep behind her and stopped at her side, his white robe stained in blood, his hands even more so.

He was a handsome man. When he smiled, faintly and with a hint of mockery, she felt herself respond. 'I believe you are the cartographer's assistant, yes?'

She said her name.

'Ayae,' he repeated. 'You are obviously not from Mireea, with that name.'

'Sooia.' She felt awkward. 'Some people struggle with pronouncing it. Few get it right the first time, unlike you.'

'But then I am not from here, just like you.' His bloodstained hands spread out before him and he paused. 'I'm Bau.'

'The Healer.'

'Most of the time,' he agreed. 'Some days, a life is beyond mine to save.'

'Today?'

'No, not today. Despite my distaste for this city, not today. Come, let us find you a chair and me a change of clothes and some water to wash myself.'

Bau pushed the door to the tower open with a touch of weariness, the smell of dried flowers and chemicals washing over them. The first thing that Ayae noticed was that beneath the windows were rows of cages, most no larger than what could be held in two hands – though three, sitting on the ground, would have required two people to lift them. Although the sunlight washed over the old wooden tables placed there, each cage had a cloth draped over it, plunging the inside into darkness and keeping its contents from her sight. Around the cages were glass tubes, burners, pipes and beakers, each connected in an elaborate skeleton that, at the end, in a small pot, was the cause of the chemical smell that was so strong in the room. It was there that the hairless figure of Fo stood with a steel rod in his hand, gently stirring what he had created.

'You're late,' he said, absently.

'And you have a guest.' Bau turned to Ayae. 'A moment, please. I need to clean myself up.'

She nodded and was left alone with Fo, who regarded her intently with his scarred eyes, his right hand absently stirring. Finally, with a faint smile creasing his lips, he said, 'It's good to see you today. I thought that we may have to chase you, come the evening.'

'I came here to talk.'

'Good.' Lifting the metal rod out of the beaker, he tapped it on the side. 'The God Ir knew every organ in every living creature. It was said that he had never had an original form, that he had shifted and changed to mirror whatever creature he came upon. He did this, or so his followers said, so that he could learn how better to kill the things he saw. It was this that made him so appealing to those who killed for a living, be they hunters of animals, or of men and women. It was said that they respected his knowledge and paid homage to it in their own work.'

Gently, the Keeper lifted one of the black cloths off the cage next to him. In it, twisted upon itself in a coil of dark, earth brown, was a brown snake. Still — impossibly so, Ayae thought — the thick creature watched the hairless man as he pulled a small mouse out from beneath a table. He dropped it into his beaker, then lifted the soaking, squirming creature out and placed it through the bars of the snake's cage.

A moment later, it was gone.

'Knowledge,' Fo said, as the snake settled back into stillness. 'Awful things are done in its name.'

Unsure what to say, Ayae was saved by the return of Bau, who smiled slightly at her. 'We might have a problem,' he said, changing the subject.

'Did they find it?' Fo asked.

'In a way.' In a fresh white robe, the handsome man lowered himself into a chair. '*He* was there.'

Fo turned slowly from his snake, regarding the other man intently. 'You didn't try and fight him, did you?'

'Do I look like a fool?'

'You look like a man who moments ago was covered in blood.'

'I know the laws as well as you do.'

'And you know just as I do that he has no time for the laws.'

Bau's expression was sour. 'A soldier was attacked by the Quor'lo. That was his blood you saw.'

'And the Madman?'

'Last I heard, he was chasing a Quor'lo down a hole.'

Behind Fo, the snake began to move in discomfort. 'What do you think he's doing here, then?'

'*He* sent him, obviously.'

'What if he came of his own accord? It is difficult to tell with him these days.'

'Aelyn would know,' Bau said, troubled. 'She watches him, closely.'

'And if she already knew?'

Ayae – tearing her eyes from the shifting form of the snake, the mouse still visible in it – said, 'Who are you talking about?'

'Your saviour,' Fo replied.

Bau's eyebrows rose. 'Really?'

She should leave. The thought was clear. She was out of her

depth. She would gain nothing by being here, would learn nothing that they did not already think she should know. There were other ways, other people. Ayae took a step backwards. As she took that first step Fo shook his head, his scarred eyes holding her. 'If you have questions, ask, child. You need not fear the asking.'

'You are scaring her, Fo,' the other man said, rising from his seat. Shaking his head, he closed his warm hand around her arm gently. 'Ignore his tone. Fo has a history with the man who saved you, though he is probably not even aware of it.'

'Zaifyr,' she whispered.

'Is that the name he's using?'

'Who is he?'

Bau guided her to a seat that was touched by the last of the morning's sunlight. She could see the snake's skin bulging, but worse, could see the outline of the soaked mouse. 'A man, like you and me. But a man thousands of years old, older than either myself or Fo. A man who talks to the dead, as if they were his own.'

'Which he once said they were,' Fo added, his tone heavy with dislike.

'How do you know this?'

Behind the hairless man, the sound of scratching began, the mouse's frantic movements tearing through the snake's skin. 'Because,' he said, 'a long time ago, my parents worshipped him as a god.'

The Boy Who was Destined to Die

The first god to die in my lifetime was Sei, the God of Light.

Considered by many to be the Murderer, the first god to kill another, his death was not one seen, but one experienced. My family knew of it only when the sun fractured and plunged the world into darkness. For a week, no prayer or offering could abate it. When the sun did return, it did as you see it now, in three broken shards, a trio of emancipated prisoners pulling the corpse of their friend on a litter made from his or her bones. The moon, never seen before, was a new object, cold and dark and dead.

It was a terrible sight, and many believed that we would have been better if darkness had never ended. If for nothing, we would have been blind to the famine that killed thousands, if not millions, in the decade that followed.

—Qian, *The Godless*

1.

Meihir, the Witch of Kakar, pushed her long fingers across the palm of the boy Zaifyr. Her rough nail ran through dirt, following the lines on his skin. Pushing hard at the base of his palm, she said that he would die at the age of twenty-nine.

He was not yet five.

Meihir, in contrast, was an ancient woman, the tiny bones braided into her hair yellow with age, the remains of a family long gone. For her age and her fragility in size, the witch wore the thick hide of a white bear as if it weighed nothing and spoke clearly and strongly, even when announcing the death of a child. On that day, as she foresaw the deaths of nineteen children in tragedies, her voice did not stumble once.

In Mireea, Zaifyr watched the afternoon's sun set before him, a brown bottle of beer slick with moisture in his hand. In the mountains of his childhood, the newly broken sun had resulted in cold, sleeting storms year round while stone bears – crafted by Hienka, the Feral God – roamed the valleys and roads. Hienka had made them before his hibernation, told Zaifyr's ancestors that the bears would care for them. It was only because of them that the years after Sei's death had taken less of a toll on them, and the villages thanked their god daily for his kindness until ten years after Meihir told the young they would die.

'I'm going to report to Heast. You coming?'

Bueralan. Earlier, after they had crawled out of the foul shaft.

'No.' Zaifyr flicked dirty water off his hands, drawn out of his hair. 'I'm not planning to go anywhere.'

The saboteur eased to the ground next to him, dropping axes and leather jerkin as he did. The hole they had crawled out of lay behind the pair, the soldiers spread out wide around them, as if they were afraid to step closer. 'You think we smell?'

'I don't smell a thing.'

'Me neither.'

With half a grin, Zaifyr pulled a copper chain from a pile of charms beside him and wound it around his left wrist. After Meihir's prophecy his family had wrapped charms around him, each one painstakingly made and blessed with all of the small magic they had. His mother assembled the chain he tied around his wrist, his grandfather melted and beat the pieces through his hair, his father made the studs for his ears and his grandmother engraved tiny blessings on each, some no more than a letter, others a word. In this, he was no different than the other children of Kakar who had been promised an early death. Nineteen was the most any witch had proclaimed and soon the charmed children were friends, isolated by the other children who did not play with them, and by the men and women who refused to teach them skills that the village survived on. There was only one blacksmith in Kakar, and Zaifyr, though he had shown an interest in the trade early on, could not be that. His father's pale green eyes had not blinked when he told him that. *You can hunt and track and marry one of five girls, girls you know by charms threaded through their hair and on their body. But no, son, you cannot follow my footsteps.*

You are a fighter, his father said when, with tears in his eyes, he had asked what he could be. *Keep your sword straight and make sure it doesn't drop. Fight until you cannot fight no more.*

As the afternoon's sun sank, liquid orange and melting over the Spine of Ger, Zaifyr saw all three of the new suns rising over Kakar eclipse, hidden behind a huge and terrifying darkness. Over ten thousand years ago, but he could still remember it. The town of his birth had organized the charmed children to walk to Hienka's cave hours after the midday darkness, fearing that the decade of famine that had etched across the world would return to them, only this time without the protection of a slumbering god. A god that they had never seen awake, that had never strode among them, but which had left its guardians to ensure that it was worshipped.

The thin figure of Meihir led them up a narrow trail, her bent figure a frail question none behind her could ask.

There were more questions when they found the stone bears, thirty-seven in number, sitting in rows before the cave.

Zaifyr and the other children had moved cautiously through their ranks after she entered the dark, empty mouth of the cave. He knew the bears, just as everyone did, for they padded paths from village to village, impossibly alive and unpredictable; but now their violent mouths were closed and they were still, returned to their original stone. Tentatively, he reached out, not the first to do so, but not the last, a skinny youth that neither set the lead nor followed. When he touched the side of one he jumped back immediately, thinking that it would turn its solid bulk towards him, but nothing happened. Zaifyr's thin hands reached out again, and again the stone bear did not move.

Inside the cave Hienka, his slumbering god, was gone.

2.

Axes strapped to his waist and leather jerkin chafing from damp, Bueralan knocked and pushed open the door to Heast's office. He found the grey-haired Captain of the Spine inside, seated before Sergeant Illaan Alahn, the weak light of the afternoon a shroud around each. 'I was told you would be here later.' Heast sniffed. 'Promised actually.'

'I didn't want to deprive you.' Humour exhausted, Bueralan was silent while he pulled a seat into place, easing himself down next to Illaan. 'My men and I will leave in the morning. The only question is: do we head down to Yeflam or to Leera?'

Heast's pale gaze did not waver, but it was Illaan who spoke. 'I was just explaining the city you found. We didn't think you could access it from there.'

'You already had,' Bueralan said.

'Yes,' Heast replied before his sergeant. 'However, we don't want too many people to know about it. I'm sure you can understand why.'

'What else don't you want to know?'

Heast's smile was thin. 'You mean, what else don't I want you to know?'

'An army with a warlock general, a Quor'lo, Keepers. Next there will be a god standing in this city.'

'It would be in keeping with the way my cards have been dealt,' the captain said drily. 'Am I keeping much from you? Probably. But anything relevant to your work? No. I really don't know anything about the army approaching us outside what you have already been told. Now, how did the Keeper react to the Quor'lo?'

'Showed a lot of interest.'

Heast grunted, unimpressed.

'He did heal your soldier,' Bueralan said.

'First decent thing he's done since he got here.' The captain's fingers steepled in front of him. 'For the most part he and Fo spend their time locked in a tower, having animals delivered to them. They have the staff in the Keep buy them from the market. The same staff collect the corpses a few days later.'

'What are they doing?'

'Playing, would be my guess.' Heast's hands parted, his left hand touching a collection of organized reports on his desk. 'In Yeflam, they were known for certain incidents relating to diseases. The latest was a small outbreak of a skin disease in one of the cities, Xeq, I believe. From what I understand, Fo released the initial carrier in the body of a rat, trying to see just how toxic a mix that the rodent could carry that would affect the human population. After the disease had spread enough to cause a panic, a quarantine was placed while Bau worked to heal those within. They were not subtle about the situation reportedly, and there was a lot of backlash. Times are changing in Yeflam. People aren't looking for gods any more. No one wants an infallible, almost godlike figure to rule them. The Traders Union has recognized that, and they are using Fo and Bau's exploits against the other Keepers. When Lady Wagan's request for help with the situation here arrived, it was, sadly, at the wrong time. None of us expected a Keeper to be sent, but politics have graced us.'

'They know Zaifyr,' the saboteur said, ignoring the sharp movement from Illaan beside him. 'That surprise you?'

'No.'

'Who is he?'

'Who he says he is.' Behind Heast, shafts of light faded from the window. 'But when I first met him, he was as he is right now.'

'A Keeper?' Illaan asked.

The captain's gaze pinned his sergeant to the chair, a silent reprimand for his outburst. 'No,' he said finally. 'But the Keepers are not the first or the last group of men and women with a touch of power in them to walk this world of ours. We may have no interest in the gods, but we would be naive to believe in a world where the sun is shattered, the sea dark, and our mountain a giant cairn, that the outcome of their deaths is not far and widely felt. But you should both know that I only hired Zaifyr *after* he arrived in the city, after I heard he was in hospital.'

'After he found the girl,' Bueralan added.

'I doubt it's a coincidence.'

'We should remove him.' Illaan rose from his seat. '*He* has no place in this city. *None* of their kind—'

'Sergeant.'

The young soldier's words faltered, stopped. 'I—'

'*Sergeant.*' Heast's voice did not raise itself, but its tone, its cold authority, allowed for no opposition. 'Sergeant, you will put aside such opinions. You have not distinguished yourself with your behaviour recently and outbreaks like this are entirely unacceptable. You will leave this room now and reflect on that. Dismissed.'

Illaan's hands bunched tightly together, the tension so strong that it could snap his bones. His teeth chewed his bottom lip into his mouth and for a moment it appeared that he was going to argue, though he must have known – as Bueralan did – the futility of such an action. With an abrupt salute he turned, pulled the door open and left with the sound of his boots ringing loudly down the hall.

As they faded, Heast pushed himself out of his seat. Moving slowly, he limped to the open door of his office and closed it. 'We are out of time, aren't we?' he said softly, without turning.

'Can't be sure.'

'But?'

'That Quor'lo was looking for something and I don't think it chose the cursed girl by some mistake.'

Heast turned and for the first time that Bueralan could remember, looked old, his age etched into the lines around his mouth and beneath his pale eyes. 'But why attack her, of all the powerful figures here? And what will Fo and Bau do when this general arrives? That is the question. Not what will happen when Leera lays siege to us. I know what will happen: we will cease to exist as an independent city if we stay and fight. The question remains to be asked, though: are we being used to send a statement to the rest of the world?'

'What about Zaifyr?' Bueralan got to his feet. 'You mentioned the others, but not him. Can we expect something of him?'

'We can expect nothing.'

The mercenary frowned.

'I know him,' Heast continued. 'He is a competent fighter, but he is not here because of money. He accepted a quarter of what I should have offered him — and did not even try for more. No, there is an interest that brings him here, and while I do not believe it is for Leera, it is not for us either. When the dying starts he will leave, as I suspect will Fo and Bau. They will leave us to fight with muscle and steel and to suffer the losses that we will.'

'You paint a bleak picture,' Bueralan said.

'Elar is dead and my city will soon be under siege. There is no other picture to paint.' Around them, the last of the afternoon's light died. In the deepening darkness, Bueralan heard the captain strike a match. The single flame lifted to one of the lamps, lighting it. 'Fortunately for you, that's when I am at my best.'

3.

Zaifyr's memory was fragmented, broken by a life so long that he could not recall it perfectly. Years, decades, centuries were lost to him. But he remembered hearing Meihir tell the village that Hienka's hibernation had been undertaken to avoid the War of the Gods. Thinking of survival only, the Feral God had plunged its land and its people into a brittle winter, forcing them to endure a cold harshness that hid it from its kin. 'We made a mistake,' she whispered, a week after the return from the cave. 'We thought we followed a god that honoured community, loyalty and strength, but we do not. It is primitive and feral and knows not of these things. It created winter not to protect us, but to protect itself. To hide, to kill all around it. We have worshipped an image that is false and now that it is awake, we find ourselves slaves to it.'

Thousands of years later, Zaifyr lifted the slick bottle to his lips, the dampness seeping through his fingers. As snow melted in the mountains, Meihir's new, intimate knowledge of Hienka brought a deepening despair to her eyes. It was she who first stopped calling upon the god for help, she who stopped calling the Feral God a him, and referred to the god as an it. 'We have taken from the sleeping,' she said, 'but it was not a gift offered to us. We have not understood the conditions of our worship. Our ignorance has blinded us to the bonds that we have created, the sacrifice that can be made without our consent.' Yet, she alone stopped calling on the god and life in the village, Zaifyr remembered, continued much as it had before Hienka had awoken, with only the weather changing. It did not take long for the people of Kakar to forget her words, to believe them a sign of her failings, of the god's rejection of her.

And then, months later, he awoke in silence.

'Mother?'

It was an eerie silence that stretched out from the bare room he slept in.

'Father?'

Pushing back his furs, and with the lower half of the chain around his wrist in the palm of his hand, he rose and drew aside the cloth door. Nothing stirred. The dirt was cold beneath his feet, the air still. Even the dogs were quiet. He repeated his call, though the sense of wrong that had compelled him to raise his voice saw him only call for his mother. Moving through the house, he pulled aside the door to their own room. There, he found them lying together in their furs, both still. No breath arose from them, no shift or twitch shifted the coverings and, as he bent over each and his fingers touched their skin, he found it cold.

In the hearth room he found the dogs, large black-and-grey beasts, lying still around the cold, black pit. Out the back, his steps directing him without thought, he stepped onto fresh snow and saw the animals in the pens. They too were dead. It was there, while staring at the bodies of ducks and rabbits, animals they planned to kill themselves for food, that the enormity of the situation hit him and he stumbled.

They were dead.

They were all dead.

His eyes blinked rapidly as the tears seeped down his cheeks, the silence broken by the sound of his bare feet walking across fresh snow.

Leaving the house of his parents, he continued into the centre of Kakar. He found the nineteen men and women he knew intimately. Each was wrapped in the charms of their family, the charms that would protect them at the age of twenty-nine, not at the age of nineteen; yet they had done that, the charms saving each of them. Half-dressed like him, and with looks of shock and loss upon their faces, they were silent. Their voices had been stolen by the growing realization that everyone but them was dead. He did not know how long he stood there with them, surrounded by their dead in houses of silence, but it was until a soft voice spoke:

'Hienka is dead.'

Meihir.

She made her way towards Zaifyr, thin, bent, her skin so frail that the light appeared to shine through it.

'How?' he whispered.

'The Wanderer and Leviathan.' The witch stood in the large firepit of the village, her feet black. 'Hienka took back what we borrowed to fight them both – to fight the God of Death and the Goddess of the Ocean. It killed the first. The Wanderer was weak from previous battles and Hienka struck so swiftly, a hunter to its prey, using our blood and our life to empower itself.'

'Why did he not take us?'

'The charms. They tied you to a different fate, hid you from it. It could not take you then, for it had agreed to take you elsewhere.'

'Why not you?' he asked, a hint of anger in his voice. 'Why not you?'

Yet, even as he spoke, he realized that the fragility of Meihir's skin was not due to her age, and that the light really did pierce her form.

4.

He was the only one that could see her, though the importance of that was not yet clear to him. In the cold morning he and the others agreed that it was a sign of Meihir's power, though the haunt of the elderly witch did not agree. As the nineteen charmed men and women talked, Zaifyr watched her frown, shift and look at herself, the harsh cold light of the morning breaking her body apart.

'This is not what I wanted,' she said, though only he could hear her. 'Who would ask not to be able to touch, to eat, to drink . . . and only to feel weariness, hunger and thirst?'

She followed Zaifyr into the house of his parents, where he lifted the fur-wrapped body of his mother first. She was a deadweight and he bore her body outside, his still-bare feet turning numb beneath the cold as he placed her in the pit. They had agreed to put all the dead there, to create a pyre so high that it would reach up through the mountains, a measure of their grief. Yet, as he eased his mother's body into the pit, placing it next to Soeran, he was aware of Meihir telling him that she had not planned her survival, that she had not wished for what she was, now.

'Maybe Hienka cursed you?'

The witch flinched, as if struck.

'I'm sorry, I didn't—'

'No,' she interrupted. 'No, do not apologize. You are right. I turned away from Hienka and it knew when it called to me. It saw what I believed and it denied paradise in death. It punished me for my rebellion, cursed me.'

It would be years before he heard the word applied to himself, centuries even. The cool bottle pressed against his skin in a wet, welcome kiss of cold that Kakar never had. Cursed. *Cursed.* That was a new term, arising out of changes that had emerged as generations were born without the kind or indifferent stare of a god over them. Attitudes changed, words changed, that was the nature of the world. When he had learned of his 'curse' he had been told he was special, different, that he was Chosen. The first Immortal, Jae'le, the Animal Lord, had told him to remember the morning in the village he had found his parents, to remember the smoke and the tart smell of burning flesh.

'How high did the fire burn?' Jae'le asked, the tall, brown-skinned man adorned in leather and a cloak of green feathers. 'High enough to make the mountains weep?'

'Yes,' Zaifyr replied softly.

'And your anger?'

He shook his head.

'You should have been angry.' The man's filed teeth showed in defiance. 'It was the failure of the gods, a lesson to us, their children.'

'I don't understand.'

'We have been shown their failure, my brother, and we must learn from it if we are to replace them.'

5.

'I don't understand,' Ayae said, hating the sound of the words for the weakness they implied.

'It's human nature, really.' Bau sat across from her in a plush chair, his legs pushed out into the fading afternoon's sunlight before him. They were in a small den divided by an empty table and dominated by an open window on the left. The strongest light in the room came from a single lamp burning over the stairwell, beneath which stood Fo, consumed by the now-still snake and his work. Unconcerned by the sounds of knives being moved, liquid bubbling and the hairless man's undecipherable words, Bau continued: 'After the gods killed each other, there were two reactions. The first was to create temples around the fallen bodies, believing that the gods had not died. There were seventy-eight gods and it was believed they would be back. The second was to look for new gods. Children, as it were. A century later, five had begun to estab-lish themselves. Those we named the Immortals. Back then, Zaifyr was known as Qian, the name I assume he was born with.'

'That's why I don't understand.' She focused on the man

before her, ignoring the sounds from beneath her feet. 'Zaifyr must be over ten thousand years old.'

'Eleven, actually,' Bau said. 'Jae'le, the First of the Immortals, claims that he was born a hundred and five years before the current calendar. Qian is said to be about the same age. The other three Immortals were born after the calendar began. That includes my lady, Aelyn Meah, who sits at the head of the Enclave.'

'Why don't people know about the others? Most of us know about Aelyn Meah, after all.'

In response to her frustration, the Healer shrugged, his movement barely visible in the weak light. 'Because they do not wish to be known. The first of us — those five — are the most pure, the closest to being gods at the outset. You and I, born and possessed by whatever way the remnants of the gods moves now, are shadows to them in terms of power. We have much further to go and our roads are much longer to walk than those.

'Those first men and women made the Five Kingdoms. It emerged two thousand years after the War of the Gods, a society of progression, restriction and, at times, genocide. The five who ruled did not believe they would one day be gods, but believed they were in fact gods. Any who rose with similar powers — like you or me — were given an ultimatum: to join or to die. Many were killed, but over the years, a number did join, and were sent out into the kingdoms, lords and ladies beneath the kings and queens of the pantheon. At its peak, the Five Kingdoms was the most powerful empire in the world, controlling just under half of it. It was poised to take the rest, and would have, had not that five turned on their creations. There are a number of theories about what brought about its end, but Aelyn claims that her brother's madness put them in such a position that they could no longer claim to be divine, that they could not rule as gods when they had been exposed to be anything but . . . Still, such was their power that they burned continents of literature, turned cities to rubble and then disappeared. Only Aelyn dared to begin anew in Yeflam.'

Beneath the wooden floor there was the sound of a sharp scrape, a stool pulled back harshly. 'Fo believes he is a god,' Ayae said, finally.

'Fo believes he is on the evolutionary path to becoming a god,' Bau corrected. 'All Keepers do. Aelyn is the closest to it, and when you meet her—'

'But you just said they were false gods!'

'I said the Immortals *claimed* to be false gods. In their youth, they claimed titles they were not ready to own. That affected us all and it is not until recently that we have sought to change that. We – the Keepers, that is – are here to do that. We are all that they were and more. We are the first evolutionary step towards omnipotence.'

'Is that what Fo is doing down there?' Ayae found it difficult to believe that both these men were gods, that they possessed any of the qualities that would be required to occupy such a state in the world. 'Is he trying to prove his godhood?'

He leaned forward. 'Fo is very dedicated to learning exactly what his power can do.'

'And you?'

'I'm dedicated.'

'Just like Aelyn Meah? Both of you are so dedicated that all you're trying to do is take the place of men and women who once ruled this part of the world.'

'You do not know her.'

'No, I've just met you.'

'You met Qian before me.' He leaned back, shadows closing over his face like tiny hands. 'Why did Qian pull you from a fire? Could it be he is looking to reclaim a part of this world, too? Is he jealous of the Enclave? That would explain why he thought the girl who smoulders beneath her skin need saving.'

'I don't—'

'You do.' Even interrupting her, he did not raise his voice. 'I feel it right now; Fo felt it when he saw you first. Qian – *he* would have felt it too.'

Ayae bit back her words. Her fingers curled into the palm of her hand and pressed deep. She found Bau to be a cold figure, his words clinical and his manner precise. It was as if he viewed the world about him as a series of connections, of veins and bones so that with the right incision or the right break, he could heal or hurt anyone before him.

'He can't be trusted, you should know that,' Bau said. 'No one trusts him any more, not even the Animal Lord, who is a brother to him. Until sixty years ago the man you know as Zaifyr, the man I know as Qian, was in a madhouse. Not just *a* madhouse, but *the* madhouse. One specially designed for him and built deep in the Broken Mountains. It was there that the other four Immortals used all their considerable power to lock him away. He had destroyed Asila, the kingdom he had created and ruled – no, more than that, he decimated an entire land. By the time the other four arrived to stop him, there was only destruction, and only further devastation followed when the others confronted him. It was of such a horror that in the aftermath, the Enclave made a law forbidding people like you and me from killing each other. All of us have agreed to it, bar Qian.'

'I have seen what the Innocent can do,' she said. 'Do you expect me to believe it was worse than that?'

'You should ask him, not me.'

'Then what,' she said slowly, each word sounded clearly, 'is the point of telling me?'

Bau chuckled, his smile a hint in the shadows. 'You have quite the temper.'

'I've heard that before.'

Below her, a squeal burst out.

'Fo bought mice the other day.' Rising, Bau approached the open window, the sound beneath fading.

'It's terrible.'

'Sacrifices must be made for knowledge.'

'I doubt—' Ayae's voice cut off in a startled sound as a lamp flew towards her. It was unlit, and appeared suddenly. Twisting her body out of its way, she made no attempt to catch it and instead stared hard at Bau, who said, 'Light it.'

'With what?'

'Your will.'

'I did not come here to be like you,' she said. 'I came here to find out how I can live an ordinary life.'

'You cannot.' He spread his hands. 'Why would you want to give this up?'

Ayae shook her head and nudged the lamp with her foot. 'You have no help for me, do you?'

'I will help you learn control,' he said. 'That is actually important.'

A second series of squeals erupted below her.

124

'Yes, such restraint must be,' she said, heading to the stairwell.

Behind her, she heard Bau call out that he would see her tomorrow.

No, he wouldn't. A day with him and she regretted her decision not to leave Mireea, even as she realized how deeply she did not want to leave. But as more and more people learned that she was cursed, Ayae knew that she would be either pushed out of the city or into the companionship of the two men, and that either way her home would be gone.

Leaving the stairwell, she saw Fo hunched over his worktable, a cage holding three brown mice next to him. Inside, the animals were scurrying around frantically, while his voice murmured 'Be still,' and 'Don't fight,' like a chant onto the table before him. As she drew closer, Ayae saw that his hands were stained in blood. He had pinned a white mouse to the table, a syringe lying next to it. As she reached the door, he said, 'It looks awful, does it not, child?'

Before her, the empty, warm night beckoned. 'It is,' she said.

'A decade ago, Bau and I cured a plague in a fishing village on Leviathan's Throat,' he said, his attention never leaving the mouse. 'We were the only people who answered the call of the magistrate there, the only people who were interested in descriptions of blood that seeped through eye ducts, nails and any opening the human body has. A quarantine had been put in place, no one allowed in or out. Any who tried to leave were shot by archers hundreds of yards away. By the time we had arrived, fifteen of the villagers had lost their lives to arrows, while another twenty had died from the disease. The village population was just over a hundred – those outside were planning to burn it to the ground when the last inhabitant died.'

'Why are you telling me this?'

'Do you think,' he said, his disease-scarred eyes meeting her own, 'that we found a cure by prayer?'

'I'm sure you used all the books you own.'

They were quick, cutting words that Faise would have known, punctuated at the end by the door slamming shut behind her.

6.

It would be another thirteen years before Zaifyr met Jae'le. Until then he lived in Kakar, the frozen mountains towering over the village and the sad form of Meihir haunting him.

Yet, in the latter, he was curiously unaffected. He agreed with Meihir that she was cursed, that Hienka had punished her for abandoning her belief at the end. There was no other explanation for her withered spirit and its aimless wandering around the village and, after he failed to interest her in the rebuilding of Kakar, he let her fate fall from his mind. She would not leave the area where her bones lay, and it would be years before he understood that she was no different in this way than the dead who followed her. She was waiting, just as they all were.

Other issues claimed his attention. After the funeral pyre of their kin had smouldered low, the nineteen charmed men and women of Kakar found themselves in desperate need of skills that they did not have. Uneducated because of their curse, they did not know how to safely cut open ice and sink lines to catch fish, nor did they know how to hunt the deer and bear that they had lived on since their birth. Their first attempts to do so relied upon their ability to fight, but the bears, who had been white for centuries, were lost in the snow and moved much more quietly and quickly than any thought they would. The deer, likewise, could hear them miles away and their swift darting away was done more to taunt than in fear. As the winter deepened, the nineteen tried desperately to teach themselves skills from the memories they had of watching others work.

In the end, however, they fell upon the skills they had been taught. In the cold, clear air, they left their quiet village and its dead and descended down the trails, to the foot of the mountains and the highways that cut a path through the snow. They hijacked and robbed before returning to the mountains, only to leave a week later, their stomachs sated, but a new hunger driving them. They cut down trees to block the road, then hid in the snow beneath white furs before emerging to speak to people who could not understand their native language. Zaifyr discovered a drawn sword was a language that was universal, and merchants and their mercenaries knew the language of robbery as well, if not better, than he and the remainder of his people did. Indeed, he suspected that the ease with which their first robberies took place had more to do with the familiarity that the guards had, than his own. They knew too that when they returned, months later, they would be better armed.

But by then, Zaifyr had killed his first man.

On that day he lay in the snow by the side of the road, his white bearskin cloak pulled around him, his gaze on where the horizon met the muddy road. In a week, the path would close due to the winter storms that had raged since Hienka's death, storms that turned bitter and deadly in the coldest part of the year. Truthfully, Zaifyr did not know if he would see anyone now, but it did not matter. Kakar had enough to last the winter – and the year, should the winter prove to be long and terrible. There was no need for him to be out with another six, waiting, but he was bored, as were the others. On a whim, no more, they had walked down the mountain and set up beside the road, in the hope that they might find a little excitement.

Ahead, a dead tree had been dragged over the road, just before the track began its winding climb that skirted the edge of the mountain range. Its position made it difficult for any driver to force his or her oxen into a sudden, hard run when they spotted Zaifyr and his friends. It was a good spot to sit and wait, but Zaifyr was careful not to use it all the time. If drivers knew where a robbery was to take place, they would simply alter their path and take detours through snowy fields and dead trees, adding a day or so to their journey, before returning to the road. Because of that, the robberies of the Children of Kakar looked without pattern.

He was on the verge of giving up for the day when the wagon appeared. It was the first in a train of three, the flat backs covered in tarpaulin and snow, the drivers hunched at the front with guards that held crossbows beside them. There were half a dozen other guards on horses riding around the wagons, but they were spread out, a thin defensive line that he did not expect any real trouble from. Zaifyr made out the subtle shifts of his companions, each moving into position as the wagons drew closer.

At the dead tree, three of the guards dismounted. It would

take more to move it, Zaifyr knew. They themselves had not moved it far from where it fell, the weight of the heavy trunk causing the tree to topple out of the thin ground it had been living in. As the guards gathered, one man, taller than the rest, placed his booted foot against the bark.

A crossbow bolt punched into the wood beside him.

Rising from the snow, Zaifyr pushed back his cloak. Beneath it he wore white dyed leather armour and a short sword strapped to his waist. He cut a strange mark on the horizon, he knew, the colour of his armour and skin allowing him to blend at a distance but for the shock of colour in his hair. As he approached, a second and third bolt hit the wagons beneath the feet of the drivers.

The lead driver, a thick, bald man, spat into the snow at his side as he dismounted. He spoke, but the words were foreign to Zaifyr.

Smiling, Zaifyr spread his hands and said, 'One last collection for the year.'

Behind the wagon driver, the tall mercenary pulled out the bolt next to him. He was staring out into the snow, but the charm-laced man knew that his dark eyes would see nothing but white and winter-stripped trees of brown grey.

The merchant turned to the tall man, who did not reply. With a shrug, he turned to the other drivers and barked a command, which saw the tarpaulins pulled back. As that happened the mercenary turned to the smaller man, his words making it clear that he held the man in contempt, and that he did not think they should pay. A few of the words made sense to Zaifyr as he spoke, the first relating to the crossbows, the second to the payment.

Then, suddenly, the merchant cried out, 'No!' The words emerged as the mercenary slammed a hand into his chest, sending him into Zaifyr. The charmed man deftly sidestepped and let the man fall into the snow as the mercenary's sword thrust forward. Turning, he spun out of the way, feeling the blade catching the edge of his armour, his own sword coming to his hand. Using his heel to rotate, Zaifyr's short sword parried a second strike and, in one quick thrust, hit the man's leather chest causing him to step back, allowing Zaifyr to step forward and slash up and diagonally across his throat. Gasping, he sank to the ground, blood splashed across the snow.

At his feet, the merchant cried out, rising to his knees, staring at the bolts that stuck out of the remaining guards and drivers.

Zaifyr, his body cold, hammered his sword into the man's neck from behind.

And as he did, the cold that was in him grew colder, grew into a stillness, not yet terror but close. As the merchant fell to the ground, his pale haunt emerged, broken through by sunlight.

7.

Zaifyr did not remember how he returned to Kakar. Later, much later, as the pale moonlight filtered through his window, he believed that the others had laid him in the back of the wagon next to the dead merchant and his guards – they would not leave them by the road this time – and led all three and their oxen up the narrow track to the village. If they had spoken to him, he did not know. They must have. He doubted that they would have been silent. They would have probed, touched, followed his gaze and then talked quietly among themselves. Gilan, a thick-necked, hulking, brown-haired man, his charms tied to his hair and beard, would have taken control. He would have told the others in his quiet voice to place the bodies on the wagons next to his, would have made sure they were buried away from the highway. But for Zaifyr, there was no memory of that. There was only the merchant following him up to the camp, his drivers and guards strung out behind in pale, shadowed forms broken by sunlight.

Gilan and the others believed that he was in shock and left him alone once he returned to the village. Freed from the cart, he found himself drifting along the hard, rocky ground until he reached the pelt-covered hut of his parents. It was his now, but in two years he had not made any changes. He slept in the same room as always, letting dust collect in others. As he drew closer to the cloth door, the haunt of Meihir paused and regarded not just him, but those that trailed behind him in a dull murmur of language neither could understand.

'Zaifyr,' she said.

His hand touched the heavy cloth.

'What have you done?' she asked, approaching him.

'I don't know.' His voice was barely a whisper. 'They are the spirits of men we killed down the mountain. I don't know why they are here.'

The murmur of the merchant and guards grew, the words unidentifiable.

'The God of Death is no more.' Meihir's attention wavered, the constant cold and hunger in her demanding. For the first time, Zaifyr watched her fight it. 'The Wanderer is gone,' she said again.

He had no response.

'What else can you see?'

Their words, he suspected, were complaints against hunger, cold and him. Zaifyr said, 'Nothing.'

'No birds, no animals?'

Around him, others in the village were gathering. 'There's nothing but you and them,' he said. 'Nothing but the dead.'

'Look for them!'

'There's nothing!'

She spoke again, but he shook his head, pulled back the cloth door and stepped inside, letting the heavy fabric fall behind him, though it did not muffle their voices.

Meihir's question lingered. Aided by the sight of the new dead patrolling between the village and the ravine where their bodies lay, the question was not allowed to slip his mind. He grew withdrawn from the others, spending more and more time in Meihir's small, dirty hut, reading what he could find. It was not much. She owned a handful of books, kept no diary. There were many times where he sat and listened to her telling him how unfair her punishment was, how she did not deserve this curse. But he did learn. He learned about the Wanderer, about how he had stumbled onto the rocky shore of Kakar with the Leviathan's help, an injured figure reliant on the giant god's friendship, left crippled from an early battle that saw the destruction of his pantheon, with the gods Maika, Maita and Maina, the gods of ascension, rebirth and finality, being destroyed. Meihir did not know why anyone would want to attack the Wanderer's pantheon, did not know why in the years after the first god fell he became a target, but she feared much, even if she could not explain it. Yet, what she did know in detail was the moments of the Wanderer as he was struck down by Heinka, as the Feral God had drawn on the lives of his believers to kill the other, in a seemingly suicidal attack before the might of the Leviathan. He learned about the gods, about the flow of magic and power that the witch had believed in, about how each power had been tethered by a god and how it would run wild through the world without them.

Finally, on a cold morning, he took one of the metal traps from the village and entered the snow fields to the north, with his white bearskin cloak around him. The stripped-bare trees watched him bury the trap at the edge of the Hoewa River, where the water did not entirely freeze no matter how cold. He settled back into the snow and waited.

It was a long wait. The empty, cold sky lit with the orange of the afternoon's sun and the cold set into his bones and he told himself he was a fool. Yet he stayed. Snow blanketed him. The ice in the river broke, the sound harsh and primitive. More than once he told himself to stand, to walk back to Kakar, but he never moved.

And then, finally, a stag stepped into the trap.

The metal crunched through bone, the animal cried out. It was young, its antlers not yet fully grown, and it thrashed against the trap, drawing on the chain spike that held it to the ground. Raising his crossbow, Zaifyr sank a bolt into its neck and saw it stagger and sag. Rising, his cloak dislodging thick snow as he did, the charm-laced man approached the dying animal and watched. He longed to shoot the stag again, to end his misery, but he had laid the trap for a reason and he would not weaken now.

The stag's breathing rasped, its dark eyes at first staring wildly at Zaifyr then blankly past him. He focused his attention on the animal's chest, watching the final rise of it with such attention that he saw a faint outline at the edges of the body, saw the shape of the stag rising. The sunlight broke through it as if it were smouldering and Zaifyr could sense the animal's confusion, hunger and cold.

The stag moved, but not far. It appeared to be waiting, but there was nothing, Zaifyr knew, that would be coming for it.

There were no more gods of death, no more gods to take the souls of the living and lead them to paradise, to rebirth, to oblivion. There was only him to bear witness, only he that could see what happened to the souls of the living, only him, who had, despite the charms he wore, the charms that had protected him from his god, found himself changed by the Wanderer's death.

Zaifyr turned and began walking back through the bare trees without the carcass, unable to bring himself to take it.

8.

'I thought I smelled something foul.'

'It's a delight, admit it.' The door closed solidly behind Bueralan. 'I found this perfume just for you.'

Across from him, Aerala wrinkled her nose in distaste. Wearing a long, thin green skirt and a brown singlet, the dark-haired, olive-skinned archer lay in a hammock, swaying slightly as her foot pushed against the rope pegged in the wall. In her lap was a half-filled parchment and as he entered she placed a quill into a small well at her side. 'It's no wonder your romances never end well.'

Bueralan chuckled and placed his axes on the weapon rack, noting with satisfaction that the weapons there had been cleaned and sharpened already. 'Where the others at?'

'Dinner.'

'I hope they don't come back drunk.'

'Mercenaries don't drink in this town,' Aerala said. 'Though your smell would make me risk the gibbet of Lady Wagan.'

He lifted an arm, sniffed. 'It's that bad?'

'You have no idea.'

Grimacing, the saboteur continued through the barracks,

picking up a cake of rough, yellow soap and a towel as he reached the end. A small room built upon a cement block with a claw-footed bath awaited him. The water he poured into the basin came from pipes in the floor, which were connected to a series of tanks beneath the city. The huge, bronze containers had originally been put in so that the city would not have its water supplies cut off in a siege, though they had since then been adapted to use the heavy summer rain falls more industriously. There were coals beneath the bath, but after thrusting his arm beneath the cold running water and feeling the freshness against his skin, he sank in straight away.

Once he had finished bathing, he drained the tub and refilled it, lighting the coals this time. As he lay in the clean, warm water, his mind drifted. He thought about the Quor'lo, the Lady Wagan, the money and the mystery that lay in Leera. That, he had to admit, he still did not like: the mystery was not one he cared to solve with the lives of Dark. But Heast had surprised him, in the last moments of their meeting.

'Samuel Orlan will be travelling with you,' the Captain of the Spine had said.

Hand on the door to his office, slants of lamp light cracking through the opening, Bueralan paused. 'That's quite an honour,' he said, finally.

'It is,' the other replied. 'He visited me this morning to tell me just that.'

The door closed. 'He told you?'

Heast was silent. When Bueralan turned, he found that the old soldier's pale gaze was not focused on him. 'In Mireea,' he said, finally, 'I watch everyone of consequence. For the most part, it is a little bit of history, investment in politics. My knowledge comes from contacts, spies and simple intuition. No one is beyond me in this city, not even Keepers. But Orlan . . . Samuel Orlan I know very little beyond his considerable reputation. Sometimes I know when he leaves the city. I know the hours he keeps when he is here and they are erratic and I do not know what changes them. I do not know who tries to win his favour or influence him. A part of me even believes he is making a game out of this knowledge, a test between two old men. If that's so, it is not a game between equals.'

'I would rather he not ride with us,' he said.

'I could not say no.' Heast's pale, cold gaze met his. 'Do you understand, Bueralan? As he stood before me, I saw a small, fat man with no military training whatsoever. I saw a man who I know intellectually will not only be deadweight to you in any fight, but who will also slow you down and put you in a greater danger. Even his knowledge of the land does not compensate for this. Yet, I could not tell him no. I hinted at it, suggested that it might not be wise of him, but he looked me in the eye and told me that he was not asking, he was telling me. I was nothing but a pause in thought. A curiosity. A kindness.'

'What game is he playing at?' he said. 'Is it vengeance? The Quor'lo did come into his shop and attack his apprentice. He lost years of work, maps of importance never to be returned to history.'

'I do not believe Samuel Orlan is a man of vengeance.'

Bueralan let the memory drift away. Heast could add no more, and it became clear that the Captain of the Spine did not want to keep him in Mireea. The awareness sat poorly, if

Bueralan was honest. The exiled Baron of Kein had once been a man of some importance, both in title and reputation. He had watched politics, taken part in it, enjoyed it. He had lost his nerve at the end when the stakes were at their highest, when a queen could have fallen, but he had never left the world of politics. He was a shadow in it, a politician made into a soldier, a saboteur who stood on the sides of other people's plans.

Before Elar, he had not lost a man or woman in seven years. He had forgotten how much it could hurt, all of Dark had, and it was part of why they had agreed to Heast's offer. The decision had not been made on facts, on money, on success: it was about forgiveness and the memory of the man they had lost. Now, however, he felt as if he had agreed to something that was verging on being large, violent and costly.

He had no doubt who would be asked, first, to pay the price.

9.

As the years progressed, Zaifyr became isolated in Kakar. His companions — once men and women of flesh and blood adorned with charms — became spectral figures, their bodies broken apart by cold light.

He recognized the change but could do nothing to stop it. In the home of his parents, haunts of the merchant and his guards walked through the walls, followed him in his chores and stood over him while he slept, murmuring in a language that he did not understand. Exhausted, he would fall asleep and awaken to their nonsensical whispers, with no beat skipped. They were angry at him, vengeful, but he could say nothing that they would understand. They left him alone only when he approached Meihir. In her lucid moments, she admitted to not knowing why they treated her so, but those moments were fleeting as the seasons changed, increasingly so.

He felt, as he stood apart from the living in the village staring up at the piles of snow around the edges of the houses, that he ought to be able to do more for the dead. He could not explain why he felt that other than a part of him, watching the reflected light pierce through their shambling bodies, felt more than his share of responsibility for what had happened. He had killed only one but had been responsible for the deaths of the others.

He discovered early that the haunts would not follow him out of the village. They were tied to the bodies that had been brought back and buried, or so he theorized. Each haunt had a range, and though it was not consistent, he knew that after a mile or two of travel, he would see none of them. Eager to find solitude, he began keeping to the caves that dotted the bases of the mountains. Lighting torches, he discovered that they were unoccupied, and he began to store dry wood and blankets there so that he could read the limited library that he owned. In the summer, he told himself he would ensure that the library grew in the hope that his intellect would one day equal the position he found himself in. He would have to leave Kakar and learn a new language to do it. Wrapped in his cloak, he felt the limitations of the world he had been born into and experienced both its inadequacies and his own. He could not explain what was happening. As he stared out of the cave and watched the faint, broken shapes of animals picking their way through the snow, he felt overwhelmed by what he was experiencing.

In the evenings, he would return to Kakar where, joined with the haunts of a witch, a merchant and the guards of the latter, that horror continued. From the moment that food was prepared, be it stag, pig, fish or whatever meat was cooked in the blackened pits of the village, he was stalked by the haunt of the beasts. Within a week, he had taken to eating his meals away from the others, pulling what he ate from the gardens that they kept. As Zaifyr trudged through the snow back to the village, he knew that unless he discovered a way soon to control what he saw and retreat to the ignorance he had only a short time ago, he would stop returning every night.

As he continued, the sound of breaking snow soon merged with words. It took a moment for him to recognize that those words were not ones that he recognized – and that they spoke loudly, commands being issued and obeyed. Stopping, he dropped into a crouch and focused, noticing for the first time that the trails of smoke that rose through the winter-stripped trees were thicker, blacker than they were, fuelled by a tartness in the air. It took another moment for him to realize what it was that he smelt, and by then he could see the broken forms of those he lived with, around the snow mounds and outlines of huts.

Slowly, he crept forward, a cold dread settling into him. The centre of Kakar was dominated by a huge fire reminiscent of the one that they had created for their families, so that he barely registered the sight of the horses, big, heavy roans covered in leather and snorting white with riders in leather and cloaks of red and gold. Soldiers, a part of him whispered; but another saw only the bodies on the fire, the bodies of his friends. There were soldiers there as well; their victory had not come lightly.

If he could have turned and left then, stalked the soldiers back to their city or run in and attacked to die with those who were his family, Zaifyr never knew. As he rose, he heard behind him a faint crunch of snow, a footstep, and he turned in time to see a dark-haired man without the red cloak leap at him. Caught off guard, he swayed, but the man had the better of him until Zaifyr slammed his head forward, crushing the man's nose, a blow he returned by jamming his knee into Zaifyr's groin. Slamming his head forward again, he pushed the man back, punching him as he rose to feel a knife touch lightly against his throat.

Words were said. Words he did not understand.

But the intention was clear, and hours after he had been tied, after he had been thrown into the back of the wagon that had belonged to the merchant, days after he spent a week next to eight bodies wrapped in red cloaks, months after he was kept in a dungeon and years after being kept on display as a savage, a man in charms who did not appear to age, thirteen years before Jae'le walked into the marble palace of the Emperor Kee to claim him, Zaifyr wished that he had not understood enough to surrender.

For thirteen years, he wished that the prophecy of Meihir had been true, and he had died at the age of twenty-nine.

10.

Ayae managed to be alone for but a moment: at the edge of the tower wall, her hand pressed against the door that led into the dimly lit hallway that flowed on to stone stairs deep in the Keep, and she took a breath to centre herself. She was more frustrated than angry, but there was no denying that it was the second emotion that urged her to act irresponsibly, to lash out. As her breath expelled, she tried to put both emotions from her mind as she pushed open the door, her low escaping breath blowing into Reila on the other side.

'The Lady Wagan,' the small woman said without pause, 'would like to meet you.'

Ayae nodded.

As they walked, Reila asked about Ayae's health – physically first, then mentally, focusing on the latter, she thought. Ayae attempted to keep the frustration she felt from being with Fo and Bau out of her voice, but noticed the more she talked, the more a small frown creased Reila's ageing face. She did not speak again until after Reila opened the door to Lady Wagan's office.

What struck Ayae immediately was the confidence and

intelligence of the large woman sitting before her. She had seen her before, of course: before the Lord Wagan returned blind and mad from Leera, the Lady had been seen in the markets, meeting merchants, holding conversations with those who had made her city the power it was. Limited as Ayae's sight of the Lady of the Spine had been, she had not been shocked Lady Wagan placed a mercenary in a gibbet for his crimes before dismissing his entire company. She had seen that in the Lady's eyes.

'You have met our Keepers,' Lady Wagan said, indicating a chair in front of her. 'A delightful pair, are they not?'

'I was charmed,' she replied evenly.

A short laugh escaped Lady Wagan. 'Did they murder small animals in front of you?' She pointed to another chair. 'Sit, Reila.'

The other nodded, easing into the chair as the Lady turned her attention back to Ayae. 'I want you to know that if I'd had it my way, I would not have you keep company with those two men. But while I may run the Spine, I do not have it my way with those two. The ties that run between Mireea and Yeflam are deep and sordid and I have to remain civil to them, especially now. Do you understand that?'

'Yes.'

'You don't like it, do you?'

Ayae hesitated, then said, 'No.'

'I don't like it either.' Lady Wagan's gaze did not leave her. 'Captain Heast tells me that the attacks on our outlying villages have stopped, that the last village they found was attacked over two weeks ago. In part, he says, the attacks have stopped because of our evacuations, but it is also his belief that with the wet season ending, a lull is being allowed to develop before the main attack begins. He suggests a month before we hear again of raids, but I think it will be half that – and I find myself in the curious position of deciding what to do with those two men in the tower.'

'You want me to spy on them?' she said.

'We already spy on them.' The light flickered across the wall behind Lady Wagan, shadows spiking sharply. 'What I want to know is how to stop them, if I need to do so.'

'They won't trust just anybody,' Reila added quietly. 'They do not see themselves as being human any more.'

'I have heard that before.'

'You're Mireean, Ayae, no matter what anyone says,' Lady Wagan said, simply. 'You may not like it some days. I certainly do not like it some days. I long to be somewhere else. Somewhere without war, without responsibility, but I am not. Neither are you. We are both Mireean. I have no doubt someone has said cruel words to you, but it will not be long until a kindness is said.'

She sighed. 'I don't know how to stop them.'

'But you may. The more you learn about yourself, the more you will learn about them.'

Silence threaded between the three women, a long, difficult silence as the implications of what Muriel Wagan asked became clearer to Ayae. She wanted the cartographer's apprentice not just to spend time with the two Keepers, but to put aside the regaining of her life. She would not be able to return to help with the rebuilding of the new shop, would not be able to continue with her studies. She was being asked to take part in politics, to put herself in danger, when all she wanted was to step back from what had – in her mind – already pulled her too far into that world.

'You're asking a lot,' she said, finally.

'I know.' Lady Wagan's gaze never left Ayae. 'But there are vital things at stake, young lady. It is not just your home, but all our homes that will be lost if we don't work to save them from the Leerans and the Keepers. That last is to be kept between us, but it is important that you understand clearly that we are caught between two forces here. As Leera draws closer and closer, internal politics in Yeflam will force the Enclave to set aside its neutrality. People will die. Mireean people will die, just as Leeran people will. This is a very real problem that we have and while I do not wish to make you spend time with these two men, it is only you that they have allowed into their world, only to you that this opportunity has been presented. Don't you agree?'

For a moment Ayae felt alone, more alone than she had felt since awakening in the hospital. She did not want this. She did not want to be drawn into conflicts, into political and physical fights. She had been content, happy with her life, and she wanted to restore that feeling, that sense of safety she had had since she had arrived in Mireea, that sense of having a purpose as her career as a cartographer's apprentice and illustrator grew. These things were important to her. She had lost too much in the fire of Orlan's shop. She had lost her sense of security, of safety. She had lost Illaan. Their relationship had not been the best, but even at its worst she had been . . . if not in love, then loved and cared for. She had seen too early in her life how the loss of all the things that defined an individual stripped them of their humanity, how it made them emotionally rough, and she did not want to become that. She wanted to restore her life. She wanted to fix what had been broken in the hours after the charm-laced man had pulled her out of the fire.

Even though she agreed with what Lady Wagan said, knew intellectually that she was in a rare position to help fight for her home, she resisted saying so. She had to think about herself. She had to get her life reorganized first, and, with the copper taste of resentment for what she began to believe was a mistake – even as the words emerged from her mouth – Ayae told the Lady Wagan that she did not agree.

11.

Once, Zaifyr had fasted for seventy-two days. It began as a whim drawn from self-reflection born of lonely travel. In the middle of the dense Gogair Forest, he stripped down, sat and waited. He estimated that he was over seventy years old, though he had not physically aged a day. Yet, he knew men and women who had died not from weapon or disease, but from age, an age he had watched creep over them from their birth until their spirits rose from their broken bodies. As the morning sun rose and fell, and then the midday sun, and the afternoon sun, he realized that it was the experience of exactly that which saw him stop, literally, his life until the gnawing hunger and exhaustion of boredom drove him to his feet, two and a half months later. He could die, he had watched gods die and knew that anything could, but his death would be a difficult one. Lack of food and water would simply not kill him. The immortality and power Jae'le had said was within him was slowly becoming something that he could rationalize in a post-god—

There was a knock at the door, soft but insistent.

Zaifyr lifted the brown bottle but found it empty and dry.

Outside, the sky was dark but for the stars and the moon. The latter was no more than a thin, broken line. The knocking sounded again and he pushed himself up, shaking off the maudlin emotion that had come across him, the feeling of cobwebs that had fallen over his mind as he had watched the afternoon fade away with his memories. It was not the first time, though it was the first in some time and, as he reached the door, he hoped that it would be the last for a long time. There was a small, grey-bearded man lit by a lantern in the doorway.

'I am Samuel Orlan,' the man said, extending his hand.

'I know who you are,' Zaifyr replied, accepting the hand. 'Is your apprentice fine?'

'For the moment.' Orlan's gaze held his, the small man's blue eyes weathered and ancient. 'I must thank you for helping her, though it will perhaps not be the last time you do so. May I come in?'

Zaifyr stepped back, allowing the cartographer to enter, his lamp illuminating the single bed, small pack and smoke- and ash-stained clothes that marked his room. Closing the door, he watched Orlan hang the lamp on the wall and, without a backward glance, turn around the chair by the window, facing it to the bed before sitting down.

'What am I to call you these days?' he asked, finally.

A small smile creased his lips. 'Zaifyr.'

'An old name, that.'

'Better than others I have been known by,' he said. 'But perhaps the old names are the best, wouldn't you say?'

Orlan's smile deepened. 'You knew the Seventy-First, yes?'

He was talking about his ancestors, the other men and

women who had shared his name over the centuries. 'And another, much earlier. I don't know which one she was.'

'The Forty-Third,' Orlan replied easily. 'But it was briefly, unlike the Seventy-First, who lived in Asila.'

'I was a different man, then.' Zaifyr perched on the edge of the bed. 'Whatever memories you have, I wouldn't put much stock in them now.'

'I don't have memories of you,' Orlan said. 'We share a name, but that is all, and I am glad for that. I doubt I could keep so many lives straight. I would be caught in them all the time and new experiences would pass me by. But, no, I know about you and the Seventy-First because I have studied history and read the books that have been written, either by ourselves or by others.'

Zaifyr refused to rise to the bait that, given the flood of his own memories, was a fair critique. 'I don't read as much as I used to.'

'Or write, either. It has been a long time since *The Godless.*'

'I thought all copies had been destroyed?'

'It is hard to destroy everything,' the other man said, shrugging. 'This is especially true of books written by a man who once said he was a god.'

'I don't believe that now.'

'Others do.'

'That has nothing to do with me.'

'Even when there is an army coming up this mountain in search of gods?'

'In search of the remains of gods,' Zaifyr corrected. 'I talked to the Quor'lo. It was not much of a conversation, I grant you, but the force coming here appears to believe that a part of the gods still exist in the remains. Since you have read the book that I wrote, then you know my thoughts on the subject.'

'Can these gods be reborn like they want?'

'You know it's nonsense, Orlan.' Zaifyr pulled his feet onto the bed, crossing them beneath him. 'Why are you here?'

'My apprentice . . .'

'Ayae?'

'Yes . . .' For a moment he hesitated, as if he knew he was crossing a boundary, and that his next words would change a part in him. 'She is a very angry young woman right now.'

'I've helped her enough.'

'With the wrong people whispering in her ear, she could believe that *she* is a god.'

Zaifyr's fingers touched a charm beneath his wrist. 'She would not be the first,' he said.

'No, she would not.'

Against the wall, the lamp sputtered, the fire rising for just a moment. 'She seemed like a smart girl. I don't think she needs me to watch her.'

'Oh, that I will not disagree with,' Orlan said. 'However, I would like to think that her introduction to whatever touch of god is inside her is not done by men who are borderline sociopaths who believe they are reborn gods, or by the priests who ride up this mountain in search of something to make into an idol.'

'Why not you?'

The small man's smile was faint. 'I have other plans.'

'Then why me?'

'The Seventy-First wrote that you were a man haunted by every man and woman you met, but yet you were a man who believed that the universe was infinite, that fate was our own, that redemption was available to us all. That is why.'

'I killed him,' Zaifyr said quietly. 'He and his family and everyone who lived in Asila. You know that.'

'As you say, you are a different man, now.'

In the Blood

There were half a dozen gods alive after Sei's death. The Wanderer fell first and, after, stories rose and fell of men and women who should have died but did not, the most infamous of these being the Siege of the Dead. The truth was much worse than the fictions created, but the stories revealed another trial for the survivors of the gods' war, in trying to retain truth. Records were tampered, eyewitness accounts influenced, the institutions of power engaged in a war to remain relevant — a war that they would soon lose to my brothers and sisters, in more ways than one.

—Qian, *The Godless*

1.

Dark returned on a mule-drawn cart before the moon had
risen fully.

'Well,' Bueralan said, stepping out of the barracks at the
sound of the wheel's clatter on the paved stones. 'This takes
me back.'

'We're not in trouble,' Zean said. 'You can see we're not
chained.'

'If you were, you would be delivered on a tumbril to a gibbet.
That's the way of Lady Wagan's empire.'

With a shrug, Zean stepped off the back of the cart lightly,
the rest of Dark following. For the first time, Bueralan thought,
they looked as if they weren't carrying the weight of Elar's
death, of the final weeks of the work in Ille. For the first time
since leaving that small kingdom, the hardness that had begun
to settle into the faces, the borderline cruelty that had come
upon them, as if an invisible barrier had been breached, had
begun to fade. He could see the relaxed stride of Kae as he
dropped off the wagon, the casual way Ruk looked around the
square they stood in, and the fact that Liaya had left her satchel
in the barracks. Approaching the driver, Zean said, 'Have you

ever noticed how prosaic the memories of your exile are?'

'Only through hard work,' Bueralan replied.

Liaya stopped in front of him. 'I think the real problem,' she said in mock seriousness, 'is that you weren't exiled for very interesting reasons.'

'There are no interesting reasons,' he said. 'You know that as well as I do.'

'It is not all about mules, either.'

As the cart began to turn across the stones before him and the others entered the barracks, Bueralan recalled the nine-day march he had made with fifteen other men, linked together not just by chains that threaded heavily around their feet, but by their failure and disgrace as well. Slouched beneath the weight of that realization, the soon to be exiled Baron of Kein trailed at the back of a line organized by rank, with only two behind him: young men who had not been able to lay claim to land or title yet. Ahead of him, the barons and lords who had been his betters made a long, ageing line that began with the fifty-two-year-old prince, Jehinar Meih. Tall and narrow, he looked as if he were made from dried wood that threatened to split in the summer.

At night, they all sank to the ground and ate the small amount of bread offered, drank the warm water from the pitcher shared between them and listened to the middle-aged prince talk of his plans, of his – of their – return. Bueralan had stopped listening on the second night. He had heard enough, and in the cooling dark when his blistered feet rested against the ground he had no time for the bitter words Jehinar Meih spoke.

We all stood on that canal wall, Bueralan thought, *and we listened to a general tell us how many people would die, how slim our chances were of survival, how we were like the butterflies he saw rise every morning just to die, and you — we —*

We lost our nerve.

There was no other word for it.

His mother had taught him when he was young that the high end of politics did not reward those who hesitated. Her words followed him, on the nine nights he lay on the hard ground. By then she had been dead for five years, having died in political isolation after his father's poisoning in the Queen's court when he was five. His mother's political exile was said, by his uncles and aunts, to have revealed a bond deeper and more intimate than any had ever suspected of them. His memories of her — frail and withered in her large bed — had become sharper and more pronounced each night, as if only now, in failure, could he recognize her wisdom.

In this regard, he was alone.

Bueralan only had to look at the guards around them to know how futile it was to plot and plan a return. Wearing the golden-edged cloak and golden-edged armour of the First Queen's Guard, the ten soldiers regarded them with flat gazes and openly laughed at their chained captives when they caught part of their conversations. Captain Pueral, who led the way on her tall grey, was the only one who did not talk. A large, middle-aged career soldier, her casual indifference served only to highlight to Bueralan just how far from relevance they had all fallen.

And then, in the cold morning of the tenth day, they were led out to the slave trader.

He was a small man huddled in furs before a fire, neither

remarkable in relation to his trade of flesh, nor his appearance, which was of a common quality. The four men who shared his camp with him were similar in their appearance as mercenaries, and none rose as the First Queen's Guard crossed the invisible line of nations; instead, they watched as the fifteen men were unhooked from the mule-drawn cart that had set their pace and lined in front of the slaver who rose, rubbing his arms for warmth, to inspect each one casually before turning to Pueral in low conversation.

'What is this?' Jehinar Meih demanded. 'Captain, you were there when our sentences were read out. We are to be released here, under our own volition, to do this is—'

'Treason,' Pueral finished. 'Have you heard of irony, Meih?'

The now exiled prince did not respond.

'The First Queen is the study of a woman who takes deep joy in irony.' She turned her horse around, facing the border and the men in chains. 'Often, I find her indulgence of it a fault. The playwrights she employs are a bore. The philosophers unwilling to answer simply and forthrightly. And the children – I will not speak of her flesh and blood, except to say that at times it can be a difficult thing to watch within the palaces. But here today, I do believe I can appreciate what the First Queen sees in irony.'

She laughed – her first laugh in nine days, loud and good-natured – as the chain erupted in complaints. Pueral responded and motioned to the men and women around her and returned across the border, not pausing even when the cruel sound of the whip rang out across the exiled prince's smooth back.

None were spared the whip, and Bueralan would bear the scars of the slaver's demonstration of power for the rest of his life. The small man told them that they would be marched down to the ocean and sold to a galley, the threat real enough by then that the exiled lords and barons promised the trader riches for another outcome. The small man shook his head and chuckled from deep within his furs. Quietly – almost as if he were sympathetic – he said, 'You have nothing, gentlemen. Nothing. You'd best understand that soon or you'll not survive the year.'

As the afternoon's sun began to sink, Bueralan had begun to appreciate the full extent of the slave trader's words. The small man set a quicker pace than the First Queen's Guard and, exhausted as he sank down to the hard ground, Bueralan listened to the others discuss their fate with an outrage that came from privilege and fear. The latter came from the knowledge that men sold to a galley left their chains only when they died or when their ship was torn apart, breaking the bolts that held them into place. The last often resulted in death, for the heavy weight would drag them down through the black water of Leviathan's Blood.

He fell asleep with the first real sense of despair he had felt, and awoke hours later to the chain's weight being pulled off his raw ankle.

At first, Bueralan did not know how to react, sure that what was happening was the herald of something worse, of a new trouble, a new violation he was in. But as he turned his gaze upon the camp, he felt his apprehension fall away. For the first time in months he sensed the lifting of a weight he had just become conscious of: all four guards lay on the ground in a neat line, with the slave trader at the head, still in his fur jacket. The morning's sun was enough to reveal the cut across his throat, the facial wounds that all had received.

A hand was extended in front of him.

'When I heard you were going to be on a galley,' a voice said, 'I almost considered waiting a month.'

'That's just like you, Zean.' Bueralan took the hand, rose. 'To make this about my weight.'

Across from him, the other man's grip was strong and warm, and he bore the weight of the man he had freed as Bueralan's blistered feet resisted his rise.

2.

From the window of his room, Zaifyr watched Samuel Orlan make his way down the cobbled street, his lamp a single, swaying beacon.

The old man shared very little in appearance with the Orlan he had known, the Seventy-First. He had been a slender man, olive-skinned and with black hair that had receded and thinned; he was soft spoken and genial. He had come to Asila in the company of his wife after the birth of his first child, wishing to avoid the fame his name provided. It was a time Zaifyr did not remember well, no more than two years before he began the ill-fated walk down the long, winding road from his tower to Asila, and to the destruction he wrought there. But he did remember the arrival of Samuel Orlan and his family.

He had greeted them in the library, a room dense with literature, with books across the walls and floors to such an extent that the dark, polished wood of his desk was in danger of being lost beneath the spines of books. He could still recall the desk clearly: its decay from order to disarray had later become a visual metaphor for his state of being. He remembered the changes in it minutely, his mind replaying images of inkwells once clean and stoppered merging into stained, overflowed ones, with quills bent and blackened, and books once ordered left open at pages he could recall no reason for being so. It was with the picking up of one such book with his ink-stained hands that Samuel Orlan had forced him to focus his attention.

'Hello,' he said.

Zaifyr had responded.

'My family and I,' said the Seventy-First Samuel Orlan, 'are moving into your city. I thought I would introduce myself.'

He had asked why, his voice hoarse with disuse.

'I was raised to be polite,' he replied. 'It is also somewhat of a ritual. Whenever one of the previous Samuel Orlans arrived in a new city, he introduced himself.'

'No, not that,' Zaifyr said, slowly. 'Why here?'

The cartographer smiled faintly. 'Asila is away from the world. It has always been that. The tribes that lived here would become lost in the mountains and disappear from civilized sight for generations before reappearing again. When they did so, it would often be so by a singular representative, by a man or a woman who emerged from the snow and ice to visit the cities along the coast, or to cross the ocean. When they appeared, they were always adorned by charms made by their family, charms said to keep them safe. I see similar pieces of silver and copper around this library – once worn but no more, I believe.' Behind the cartographer, his wife and child stood silently as he spoke. The daughter resembled her mother greatly, Zaifyr remembered, though her dark hair was longer, and she did not lower her gaze from his in fear, as did the former. 'It is for that isolation that my family and I have come. I am not like the men who have come before me. I do not like the fame that follows my name. I do not like the attention it draws to me, or to my family. I only wish to draw the maps that I can, and to ensure that the world is known by them.'

'People will come to find you, even here,' he said. 'You will find no sanctuary from your name here.'

'But the kind of people who come here will be different. Here, they will not ask me to change the shape of the world.'

For a moment, Zaifyr did not understand. He would not ask another to shape the world for him, not even one with a legacy as long as Samuel Orlan's. No, if he wanted to reshape the world, he would do so without permission. 'My brothers and sisters would not allow that, either,' he said, finally.

'No,' the cartographer said. 'But their kingdoms are larger, and the people in them are less and less beholden to those you call family.'

Zaifyr's attention drifted to the pages on the table, to the faint, half outlines of hands that pressed the pages flat, that stopped the expensive vellum from rolling. 'Settle your family in Asila if you want,' he said, softly. 'But you are not my responsibility, Samuel. My responsibilities lie with others.'

He did not hear the three leave. He remembered looking up, some time later, to find that the room was dark, and that snow had begun to drift through the open window. He could not, even now, remember if it had been snowing when they entered. He remembered rising from his seat. He could see a haunt's faint hands on the glass, looking to close it, but he did, instead. The moment was rare. Of late, he had been giving more and more of his power to the dead, allowing them tactile sensation within the world in the tower. He could feel their desire for more, could hear their whispered words, but he was still, at that stage, resisting.

When the cartographer returned, he did not bring his wife or daughter. He came alone, but, Zaifyr admitted, not unwanted. He found a chair on his third or fourth visit, and placed it in front of the desk, where the two would talk for hours. Samuel Orlan's conversation was not difficult, but it was not long until Zaifyr began to sense in the cartographer a mind that was relentless in its search for information, a mind that, despite the proclamations of neutrality and a desire to be left alone, was full of politics and agendas; here was a man who kept his own council on what took place in the borders he drew, and who believed he had ownership in what took place in them.

In that way, the Seventy-First was no different from the current Samuel Orlan.

To him, to the Samuel Orlan who had sat beneath his lamp in Mireea, Zaifyr said, 'I am not saying that I will help her.' His voice was neither slow nor disused, as it had once been. 'It may not be physically possible. I want you to understand that.'

'It is no ordinary time on this mountain,' the old cartographer said. 'You know that, yes?'

'It is not my intention to get involved in this war.'

'Of course. I would think nothing else.' Samuel Orlan rose from his chair, and turned to the door. Before opening it, however, he said, 'I often wonder how it is that your brothers and sisters define their place in the world. It is hard to walk away from what you once held as your own – hard, I think, to watch it fall to events that you disagree with so vehemently, events conducted by men and women you have little respect for.'

Zaifyr shrugged. 'That time is over.'

The cartographer inclined his head. 'Of course.'

Yet, after the old man left, his words followed Zaifyr, followed him to the window where he watched the other man disappear into the streets. Once out of his sight, Zaifyr pulled down the blankets of his bed and climbed beneath them and let the implication of Orlan's words sink in. As he began to fall asleep, he was struck by a sensation that there was a profound revelation in Orlan's words, a truth that even Zaifyr, old as he was, would be surprised by.

But as he fell asleep, he knew that the thought was but a lie, and that no such truth existed.

3.

Outside the Spine's Keep, the dark, cobbled streets of Mireea led Ayae into narrow alleys and to the cracked paving stones around the recently constructed crude walls.

Lady Wagan had been most understanding after Ayae told her no. The sympathy in her voice had come as a surprise, just as the ease in which she had said it: Ayae had expected the thread of steel in her tone to harden, for her request to become a command, one that she could argue against. She had been prepared for a fight — had been preparing for a fight since Fo and Bau — and without it, she had risen from the chair awkwardly and left. She fumbled with the door as she pulled it closed and her frustration at herself, and her expected response, was such that, by the time she had walked through the corridors and emerged at the front of the Keep, she had decided to visit the witch, Olcea.

Olcea was one of a dozen witches who lived and worked in Mireea, but was the only one of them that Ayae knew, personally. Faise had introduced her six years ago, when the two had been looking for work. Both she and Faise had been living in the orphanage at the time, aware that they could not continue to do so much longer: they were already old girls, girls whose public schooling was soon to end, and there were always new girls arriving, always a need for their beds. Neither Faise nor Ayae had much of an idea about their future, but what they did know was that they were growing tired of the long dorm that was their home, the narrow beds and slivers of personal space they shared with close to fifty others, and so they had begun what other girls (and, on another floor, boys) had begun: they searched for a way out.

The options available to them were limited, but it was Faise who found a solution first, with a job offer from the witch.

'It's not an apprenticeship,' she explained, later. The two sat out the back of the orphanage, staring at the tall, dark form of it from one of the long tables that was kept for lunches and classes. The lamps inside the building had been lit and it looked as if dozens of eyes were watching them. 'She wants me to finish the schooling here and do tasks for her. There's an older girl, a real apprentice, who is leaving and I'm going to do some of her work. Like, go to the markets, bring her groceries, keep the house clean. Maybe I'll learn some then, but who knows. She mostly wants me to travel to Yeflam. It's not great work — ' neither Faise nor Ayae could define *great* work yet ' — but it pays well enough.'

Well enough that once Ayae began accompanying her down to Yeflam, they could rent a two-bedroom apartment.

Until Ayae became Samuel Orlan's apprentice, Olcea had been the financial salvation of the two girls, a middle-aged woman moving into old age: neither Faise nor Ayae had ever known skin darker than hers. She spoke softly, a private woman who kept the palms of her hands wrapped to hide the pink skin there, as if years of work with blood and bone had worn away the pigment. On her more expansive days, Olcea told them stories of her youth, telling them that she had been born on the coast of Tinalan. She had been driven out in her mid-twenties by a series of race wars that had come from the heart of the Marble Palaces. She had lost both her children there, killed by a soldier whose head she kept in a jar at the back of her house – a head she called Hien – and on more than one occasion, as the girls finished up for the night, or arrived early, they would overhear Olcea talking to it, as if they were old friends. She was a strange woman, a witch who seemed to know more than she let on, who lived in a ramshackle house that always needed work, and who had a steady stream of girls from the orphanage to do that. She hired girls to fix the roof and tidy the garden, girls to run errands and write notes for her, a steady stream of orphans on a sliding scale of pay, learning, Ayae suspected, skills for once they were older.

According to Faise – who spent more time at the shop than Ayae – most of Olcea's customers were women, also. They came for a variety of reasons, and the two would discuss the stranger ones as they rode the witch's wagon down to Yeflam, the one-month round trip ample time to cover a range of topics. 'She has had a lot mercenaries recently,' Faise said, on one trip. 'Some of them are young, some not, but they're all armed. Guards, swordswomen, soldiers: they have a lot of cuts and scars they have her attend to. Though the other day, one of them brought in a copy of one of those cheap mercenary novels for her and told her she was in it.'

'Was she?'

Faise grinned. 'For a chapter. She said if she could do half of what it said, she'd be a queen.'

For the most part, the journeys between Yeflam and Mireea were without incident. On their first trip Olcea had begun a ritual she kept for every trip – a conversation that was a list of the dangers she knew – to ensure that they slept in the back of the wagon when on the road. After that first time, however, she need not have worried: four nights out of Mireea, Faise had pulled the wagon off the side of the road and the two had crawled into the back, tired and sore from the days of riding. Ayae had been unable to fall asleep immediately and she had lain awake, staring up at the night sky instead. Outside the city, the stars seemed so bright, so endless and, with the thought in her mind, she had stared up, lost in them until she heard a crack, followed by the grunt of a man and the sniff of an animal.

Rising, she saw not a single man, but half a dozen men. They emerged from the trees around her, grey mongrels leading the way, their noses pressed to the ground, tails levelled like lances behind.

She was unarmed, just as Faise was, and her hand tightened around her friend's arm, partly in fear, partly to warn her.

The dogs clearly had the scent of something, and for a second, Ayae had feared that it was either her, Faise, or the hulking, black ox Olcea owned; but the beast itself had made no move at the sight of the men or the animals and, as the men and dogs walked around and past it continuing down the road, it became clear that they could not see the animal, nor the two girls sitting in the back. She held her breath, and saw that Faise had done the same, and the minute that the six men stood around the cart dragged out for a year of both their young lives, for the rest of their youth passing at such speed and potential horror that, should they not have moved away and crossed the road when they did, Ayae was not sure what she would have done.

'The girl I replaced,' Faise whispered, after the men had disappeared into the dark woods on the other side of the road, 'she said Olcea paints this wagon in blood once a year.'

The same wagon Ayae saw now, the same wagon attached to the same hulking black ox, the same wagon and ox outside Olcea's shop, half filled with furniture.

4.

'I don't know why I bothered to break the chains,' Zean had said as he pulled a long coat off one of the men he had killed. Behind him, the lords and barons had gathered around their middle-aged Prince and were plotting their return. 'I don't have a wealthy blood brother any more and they would have turned a nice profit. Even the old ones.'

'But who would have thanked you back home?'

He swung the brown hide coat over his arms. 'To think, I would have missed my chance at being exiled for kindness.'

The memory still made Bueralan smile. Around him, Dark were filtering through the lower level of the barracks, passing around drinks and food, pausing only to watch when Aerala grabbed the edge of her hammock and dumped Ruk from it. He had told them about the company of Samuel Orlan, of how the cartographer had made it clear that he would accompany them, and they had taken the news well, accepting the added responsibility it put on them with a grace that he himself felt he did not have. It was a stark contrast to the hours after his rescue, when he had been the only one to find grace in the rescue. He could still remember the whispers, the hushed conversations taking place away from him and Zean, and the look of shock on Jehinar Meih's face when he said that he would not be returning to Ooila. Surrounded by those few for whom he had become a beacon to return to their privilege, the exiled prince had become leashed, and was now being driven, much like the mule that had led them across the border – though as Zean said, when Meih drew closer to them, the mule would have at least known that it was a beast of burden.

'Don't miss this opportunity, Baron Le,' Jehinar Meih said, his protective ring half a dozen paces behind him, his face steadfastly turned from Zean. 'We have been given a second chance by your man. We can still bring thought and progress to our country.'

The ten days that Bueralan had spent with the fifteen men, stripped of their positions, and their rights, had shown him that their revolution had been one built on the back of self-interest and misogyny. The last was the harshest realization, for he had not thought himself capable of such a motivation; but he had believed that the First Queen had represented a cultural and intellectual stagnation, that her statements against slavery and inequalities of wealth and gender were nothing but lies to calm her populace; he had said that her birth and feminine link to power was a gift from a dead deity. The irony that their revolution had grown out of the very thing they were born with – their rank, privilege, political strength and disrespect for the First Queen – was late in arriving, but nonetheless true.

Yet, when the exiled prince left with his court, he left with his back straight, proud and defiant. For a moment, Bueralan thought he made a mistake, one that lingered until months later when he heard of the prince's death. His execution was thanks to those who had urged him to return home, who had sold him for the promise that they would not end up like him – a promise the First Queen had kept only in terms of how they died.

By then, Bueralan and Zean were two continents to the east, crossing Leviathan's Blood as poor sailors until they reached Yeala, where no one knew his name. There, he had begun the path that would eventually lead to Dark – there, he and Zean had sold their swords in three battles and, finally, one war.

It had been a small war, a series of battles in a long chain of animosity between two families who had, in Bueralan's mind, long forgotten the reason of their feud. The opinion was shared by Serra Milai who, taller and darker than either Zean or Bueralan, had told them that was typical for most of her experiences as a mercenary. 'Feuds born from the hate children suckled on,' she said, after she and the mercenary band Sky had been dismissed by Lord Feana. They had won his small war, taken back land that had been lost two generations before. In front of them, Serra rolled a silver coin stamped with the Lord's balding head across her long, strong fingers. 'Their coin all spends the same, but their hate wears on you, sure enough.'

She had a plan to reinvent Sky. It had never been a large unit, never been defined by a single battle or event that would demand huge fees, or result in any of the fictions that had become an important part of success, but it had been loyal and long-lived. Now, though, a lot of Serra's soldiers were retiring, purchasing land that was offered by Feana at a cheap rate to seed his success around him. She hadn't been surprised: Bueralan, turning introspective as he eased onto one of the chairs in the barracks, suspected that Serra had taken the job so that her ageing soldiers would have that opportunity. It had not been for her, however.

She had offered him and Zean ('You and your boy,' she said) a job in the new Sky, a job to be intelligent with, a job to slip in and out, a job to disrupt, to step out of full pitched battles and instead work more subtly.

'It's still warfare,' she said, when she first brought it up. 'Sabotage work. It has some killing, but nothing like you've seen over the last month. None of the tent hospitals, none of the witches with pens of small animals to butcher for your healing, none of this glory shit that is becoming so popular. No one will ever need to know who you worked for.'

After she had left, Bueralan turned to Zean and asked him what he thought.

'Someone always knows,' the latter said laconically. They were sitting in a small bar, in a booth at the back. 'Which is maybe why this is not the kind of work we should be doing.'

'Not enough renown?'

Zean met his gaze. 'I know you like the sound of it, but this work is not so different from what we did for Meih.' He was *never* the Prince. 'Working weak links, plots within plots, pitting your intelligence against someone else's and seeing who comes out best.'

'You think I like it because I want redemption?'

'Do you?' he asked.

'No.'

'It was a big mistake getting involved with him.'

'It was,' Bueralan admitted. 'How'd you feel after the last battle?'

Zean leaned back, shrugged once. 'Lucky.'

'We were lucky; we're not soldiers.'

'We would learn it.'

'Would we?' he said. 'You would be happy to dig ditches, clean latrines and stitch yourself up with pig gut until you earn enough rank to pay for a witch?'

'Your privilege is showing.'

Bueralan grinned.

'But yeah,' Zean continued in a drawl, 'I'm not fond of the dog work.'

'We'd not last.'

'We won't,' he agreed, 'but you still haven't answered the question: what happens when the First Queen finds out that we're essentially revolutionaries for hire?'

5.

Ayae had not seen Olcea since the night before Faise left, but if the witch was surprised to see her arrival under the night's sky, it did not show. 'Ayae.' In the lamplight, the streaks of silver in her thick black hair shone, but her face was tired and lined, even when it smiled. 'I have heard your name spoken of a lot recently.'

At the edge of the cart, Ayae stopped. 'I can leave, if I bother you,' she said, trying to mask her frustration.

'As you can clearly see, I am the one leaving.' Olcea had been holding a box of empty jars and she placed it on the back of the cart. She sighed once the weight left her, and slid it beneath the broken-down frame of her bed, next to another pair of boxes. There was room for more, though how much more, Ayae could not say. Already, the witch had filled the cart to the brim with much of her belongings, the jumble of odds and ends and furniture that had filled her house for over two decades looking like a miniature castle. Straightening, she turned to Ayae and said, 'But I shall do it on my own terms so far as I can.'

'I hadn't heard that you planned to leave.'

'It was not my plan until recently.' She beckoned Ayae to the door. 'Come, I have a pair of chairs I have not yet packed. We can sit and discuss why I cannot help you.'

Outside, the shadowed shape of Olcea's house was, by daylight, a sagging map of repairs, as if a lifetime of work on it by children had caused its shape and consistency to be lost. On the inside, however, the witch had kept a stronger sense of herself, with the high ceiling leading to small vents, and the first two rooms being large and open and stocked – or, at least, once stocked – with glass jars of animals, bones and blood. What remained now was a vast emptiness, the internal organs of the building removed as if for embalming, leaving an echo that sounded as the witch passed through the doorways, heading deeper into her house, to the private rooms she kept, and where the rest of the boxes were stacked.

'You cannot help?' Ayae asked, following her. 'I haven't even told you why I am here.'

'You do not want to be cursed.' Olcea approached a pair of wooden chairs, stacked on each other, one upside down, with its legs in the air. 'You are not the first to visit me in the middle of the night wanting a cure.'

A hard, short laugh escaped her. 'It didn't even occur to me.'

'You cannot take it away, I am afraid.' She placed the first chair in front of Ayae and sat down on the second, her wrapped hands gripping the edge as she did. 'I could no more remove all your blood and expect you to live.'

'It has already been described to me as an infection.'

'Don't sound bitter, girl.'

'I—' She stopped herself, bit back words similar to what she had said to Lady Wagan. 'It was too much to hope for, wasn't it?'

'It always is,' Olcea said. 'But you do not look ill, or in pain.'

'I am not.'

The witch spread her hands. 'That is not the case for all,' she said. 'You should feel lucky for that, at least.'

Ayae did not feel lucky. 'Is there nothing to be done?'

'You will be able to find someone who says that there is, but it is a lie,' the witch said. 'The dead simply do not have that much to give.'

'I have seen amazing things done by others.' She was aware of how desperate she sounded. 'Done by you, as well.'

'There are limits to the blood magic.' Olcea pushed herself to her feet and moved to where the wooden boxes were. There were more, Ayae thought, than could possibly fit onto the back of her cart, each of them stacked on top of each other. As she watched, Olcea reached into one and lifted a jar from within it. 'You remember Hien, yes?'

At the bottom of the head, the spine showed from the soft, decayed edges of the neck, and it was pure and white, the only part of him that remained so. Decay and rot had set in elsewhere and pressed against the curves of the glass, the shape of his face had become distorted. His milky right eye raised itself above the dark brown of his left, the iris of which stared towards the ground. Hien had been a young man when he had been alive, and to a degree, the youth remained in the bloating of his flesh, and the gentle up-swept motion of his hair, which did not reach the briny water's top.

'Yes,' Ayae said softly.

'My oldest friend.' Olcea placed him on the ground between

them. 'He was once my most bitter enemy, but you can hold the hate for only so long inside you.'

'He was the man who killed your children.'

'He was.' Her bandaged hands reached into the folds of her clothes, returning with a small, silver knife. With a small flick, she sliced her thumb, and held it above the jar. 'If you live long enough, I've found, your enemies become your friends. Hien may think differently, but what remains of him is limited, and he is moved by the basest desires, only. He reacts only by the promise of life, and blood is life, Ayae. Within our blood is all that creation gave to us – and the nature of that should not be underestimated. It is infinite in its complexity and its repercussions.' A drop of the witch's blood hit the jar's water and, for a second, the cartographer's apprentice thought she saw a man, an outline of a soldier, his tall, lean form wearing intricate leather armour. So brief was it that Ayae doubted that she saw it until one of the boxes in the room rose and began to move, as if carried, out to the ox and cart. 'I have kept him for years,' Olcea said softly, 'his soul unable to forgo his head. He does not realize that if he could leave it, he would have nowhere to go, but that does not stop the urge. But because he cannot leave, I have used him, fed him and stolen from his very being for all that I have done in this world and will do, still. I have visited on him a horror so complete and awful that the depths of my rage are but just the start of it, the satisfaction that I demanded for the loss of my children paid a thousand times. That is the nature of what I do – the nature of my power, but it is not the nature of yours.'

In front of Ayae, the head of Hien was still, the water placid. 'Is it not?' she asked.

'No,' Olcea said softly. 'I use blood to take from the dead, but in you is creation itself, the very power that gave rise to all that we are, and that cannot be touched by the likes of me.'

6.

It was a year before Bueralan had an answer to Zean's question about the First Queen's reaction to his new role in life.

Before that, before he pushed open the cracked wooden door of the inn where Ce Pueral of the First Queen's Guard waited for him, there was the formation of Water. That was the name Serra Milai gave her newly made squad of saboteurs on the warm morning they rode from Lord Feana's kingdom. She retired the name Sky in the dirt streets and, after the waves and handshakes from her old soldiers, left it behind with the copper bracelets she had worn, the ranks that she had bestowed, and the history of success and failure she had earned as a captain over two decades of blood and violence. She did it, Bueralan thought later, with an ease that he envied at the time, without the backward glance of which he had not entirely rid himself in relation to Ooila.

He would eventually, but it would not be after he stepped out of the inn Pueral waited for him in. For years, he would be haunted by the ease and reach of the First Queen's captain.

'If you step out the door,' Ce Pueral had said as he held the old piece of wood open, 'you will be shot.'

Bueralan had let the door close behind him.

The room was empty, the half a dozen long tables of old chipped wood that filled the floor ominous in their solitude, as if they had become conspirators with the woman who waited at their end, her gold-edged armour exchanged for nondescript leathers. Before her, she had two wooden mugs, and a squat bottle of sour wine that had given the inn its name, *Second Taste*. He could not see any weapons on her, but the shadows of the alcoves and the hidden corners of the room shifted as if they were flesh, as if the dark could take a breath.

'If I wanted you dead,' the captain continued, 'you would be so already.'

'I know that.'

'I did not think you looked scared.'

'Just impressed.'

Pueral's smile was faint. 'Take a seat,' she said, pointing across the table. 'It won't be a long conversation.'

'You cleared out this whole inn?' He untied his sword from its scabbard and laid it, slowly, on the table before he seated himself on the hard bench. 'You know, I have to work in this town.'

'You were made on the street of Wisal three days ago,' the other replied easily. 'That is why you are in Venil alone, while the rest of Sky finish off their work for Aned Heast.'

'I'll still have to leave after this.'

'Consider it part of our relationship. It's healthier than the one I had with the Thousandth Prince, Jehinar Meih.'

'I do like healthy.'

'Is that why you killed two men on the streets of Wisal?'

Bueralan smiled, but said nothing. The two men had been

mercenaries, both members of the small army that merchants had hired to 'liberate' Wisal from the hands of the governor, and turn it into a free-trade port which, among other things, would allow the slave trade to gain a large perch on the corner of Wilate. The two men – both born in Ooila – had not been part of the plan that Serra Milai and Sky had devised, but they had appeared unexpectedly on a small ship to meet with the merchants, and to bring with them sample wares. The older of the two, a man named Ge, had made the exiled baron on the street and raised his hand in greeting, calling out to him as 'Baron Le!' but the destruction of Bueralan's disguise as a seller of soggy fruit had not been why he had died.

'Let me try another question,' Pueral said, her tone still light. 'What did you do with the boys that had been brought ashore?'

'I didn't sell them, and I didn't use them.' He shrugged. 'Maybe they ran away?'

'They were from Ilatte.'

'I know where they were from.'

Pueral lifted the clay pot of wine, began to pour. 'I was surprised to see Ge,' she said. 'His master has pushed very hard to expand the trade outside Ooila with the First Queen, though she has resisted. It is not to her taste, if you must know. The practice of buying the young in the wealthy families in, at least, the First Kingdom, has lost some favour, and she is happy to keep it at that. I might have had to kill Ge myself, if he had not seen you on the side of the road.' She pushed the cup to him, a courtesy that he did not fail to notice. 'Imagine if I had not come all this way to learn about the work you were now doing?'

'You're welcome to claim his death as your own, if you want.'

'I have no need for that.' A note of coolness entered her voice, yet it maintained its friendly tone. 'Please, take a drink.'

He took the cup, tasting it after Pueral had tasted her own.

'It is a strange business you find yourself in, Bueralan Le,' the captain of the First Queen's Guard continued. 'A saboteur's life is one of risk, deceit, and occasional murder – and you will not always be on the moral side of it. Your work in Hitna was very good. I had considered the war all but lost for the earl. I respected very much the part you played in the banker elections in Zoum – I had always thought democracy and capitalism went well together, but I never imagined how well until I heard that you had begun selling fake land. I won't flatter you with more tales I've heard about your exploits from the last eight months, but it is sufficient to say that I always considered that you were wasting your life with the Thousandth Prince, a point that I feel has been validated since you parted ways with him.'

'Youth is a graveyard of regrets,' the exiled Baron of Kein replied easily. 'But I leave mine in Ooila, where they're safe and quiet.'

'You could return to them.'

His hand tightened around the cup, and he almost replied immediately. Instead, he lifted it and drank, and said, eventually, 'Not even if you paid me.'

Around Pueral, the shadows shifted, as if they were alive, and impatient. 'The First Queen does not need saboteurs,' she said. 'They were the words she spoke to me. I came to Wilate on those words.'

Beneath Bueralan's grip he felt the mug weaken. 'This is not Wilate.'

'No, it is not.' She raised the cup, and drank its contents in one long drawn-out breath. 'But what the First Queen needs is exiled barons who know their title contains both those words. What she needs is the quiet acceptance of her rule that comes from that – as well as the admittance that that one was wrong. Live as an exiled baron, Bueralan.' She rose from the table, but paused before she turned to leave. She said, 'I like the tattoos, by the way.'

The first of his white inked marks was on his left arm, running from around his wrist and up his forearm, over his shoulder. 'Thank you.'

She left then and, in her wake, the shadows of six men and women emerged from the room around him. He met the gaze of each, met the flatness, the coldness of their eyes, and knew that he was a lucky man, a man who had just avoided death. In his own eyes, he would continue to do so for years after, feeling as if a power much larger than him was watching his every move. It was a feeling he would not have again until Samuel Orlan told the Captain of the Spine that he would accompany Dark into Leera.

In the barracks of Mireea, he felt a hand nudge his shoulder.

'Don't sleep in the chair,' Zean said, walking past him, leaving the empty room. 'You always bitch about that on the horse in the morning, when you do.'

7.

It was Ayae, not Hien, who helped Olcea pack the rest of the cart. It took just under three hours, the last of the boxes being packed and repacked for space, and by the time Ayae carried out the box and jar to the driver's seat, the night sky had deepened and darkened into the early hours of the next day. 'You never told me.' She pushed the last box in securely and turned to the witch, who was doing a final pass around the cart, checking the heavy tarpaulin and ropes, her wrapped hands pulling on the knots. 'Why you were leaving?'

'There is an army approaching,' the other woman replied.

Ayae did not believe it. 'You have been in fights before,' she said.

'A long time ago.' Olcea passed her on the other side of the cart and approached the black ox, her hand falling on his back. 'But you are right, I have fought before. I thought to fight here as well. Mireea has been my home for a long time.'

'But no more.'

'No more.' She scratched the ox's ear and, over the beast's head, met Ayae's gaze. 'I am leaving and you should do the same. You could even come with me, if you wanted.'

'You haven't even told me what you're running from,' she said.

'Running?' Olcea laughed ruefully and patted the ox's head. 'I am too old to run, but I am too young to stay. There is too much power in this city, now.'

'The Keepers and—'

'Another.' She left the ox and drew closer to Ayae. 'The dead have begun to *bend*.'

Ayae hesitated. In the witch's gaze was a look she had seen in Fo and Bau, a knowledge that she did not have, but unlike the two Keepers, Olcea feared what she knew. 'I don't understand that,' Ayae said, finally.

'They move towards him,' Olcea said softly. 'It is like corn in a field. The wind rises and it pushes it one way, then another, and it has not the strength to resist. I have never seen the likes of it before. The dead do not move easily, but even Hien tries to follow the call to him. He struggles to break the connection with his head, to leave the last of his flesh. I had been told before that the dead react like this to him, but to see it is another thing to experience. It is as if a myth, a tale told by witches and warlocks to their children, has emerged from the Five Kingdoms before me.'

'It ended over a thousand years ago.' Ayae wanted her voice to sound as if such a number meant nothing, but she knew that it did not. She felt dwarfed, insignificant, as if she were in the process of being consumed by horrifically large history. 'So much has been lost.'

'This has not been lost,' the witch said. 'This could never be lost. Not even for the thousand years we thought him dead, not even then could we forget. When, decades ago, he began appearing in cities and in towns, there was much panic. *Qian*, witches said. *Qian*, warlocks said. In each voice was a tremble much as you hear in mine, Ayae. They feared what he would do, and feared it even more when he did not. After a while, others began to say that he was not the same man he once was. He said the words himself to witches and warlocks and stories of him working with them began to emerge. In Faaisha, it is said he stood beside a witch who possessed a child, watched her work, and thanked her later. But in all those stories, the witches and warlocks are not like me. Each one of those has talismans made from the bones of their family, of the men and women who came before them, who taught them all they knew. Their legacy was to each other. When the witch in Faaisha dies, she will leave her own bones to her daughter, and her daughter will leave her bones for her child. Of course he would not strike her, or any of her kind. But I am not her kind. I was not given my power. I did not ask for consent. I took my power in fire and steel and the tragedy of blood.'

'He saved me,' Ayae said. 'From a Quor'lo.'

Olcea nodded, briefly. 'He found it later, and chased it beneath the city, to where all the old dead waited. Don't stay, Ayae. Don't stay for this. Come with me.'

It will not be long until a kindness is said. She heard Muriel Wagan's words again, but knew that this was not the kindness she meant. It was clear that Olcea was being driven out by her fear – fear of Qian, fear of *Zaifyr*. Her old, bandaged hands shook as she pulled herself up onto the cart and took the driver's seat. On the wooden bench, she hunched into herself as if to hide in a way that Ayae had never seen before. The witch looked, suddenly, as if she were old, much older than she was, and Ayae knew that her offer to come with her was not one born of friendship, but fear. She wanted Ayae to come with her because she was just like Zaifyr, because she was cursed.

'Are you going through Yeflam?' she asked.

The witch winced. 'For the first time in over a decade,' she said. 'I will find a boat there that will take me to Gogair, at least.'

'Drop by Faise, will you?' Ayae took a step back from the cart. 'Tell her I'll be by soon.'

Olcea's grin was without mirth. 'I would have said no too,' she said. 'But I will visit. I will tell her that – but do not wait long. Even Samuel Orlan cannot protect you from the powers that are gathering in this city now.'

Ayae watched her ride away, the black ox disappearing into the night, the witch following, the cart last. For a while, she heard the wheels move along the paved stone, but soon, she could no longer hear that. For a moment, Ayae felt her frustration rise, her anger with it but it did not peak; instead, it fell in her, and left her standing alone beside the silent, old shape of Olcea's house.

A house that was hollow inside.

8.

Scratching awoke Zaifyr, a low, dull noise that bled into the final fragments of his dream. He sat upon the edge of a trail, short grass spread out beneath him. Above, the sun was singular and sat high in the empty blue sky. He had no destination, was waiting for no one and suffered from neither situation until the noise began behind him. A scratching. Faint, but persistent. He rose, but could see nothing and the sound grew and grew until the sharp claws felt like they were beneath his skin.

When he opened his eyes, there was a large raven on the window sill, its wide, glossy back presented to him.

Reaching for the cloth trousers at the side of the bed, he pulled them on and grabbed the glass of water from the table beside him. Outside the window, morning's sun had just begun to rise.

At the window, he rinsed his mouth and spat past the raven onto the garden below. 'Good morning, Jae'le,' he said, placing the glass down.

'And to you, brother.' The raven's voice was harsh, unnatural, its vocal cords forced into positions uncommon to it. 'How do you find the Spine of Ger?'

'Interesting.'

'Oh?'

'There are two Keepers here.' He reached for the chair Orlan had sat on the night before and occupied it himself. 'Fo and Bau, the Disease and the Healer. We can assume that the Enclave does not think of this as a simple war.'

'Our sister has long ago abandoned any notions of simplicity.'

'You turn bitter, brother.'

The raven's feathers ruffled. 'You accuse the wrong one of us. Aelyn has become jealous of her corner of the world and seeks to establish firm lines.'

Zaifyr frowned. 'Is that why you asked me to come here? For her?'

'No, brother. I am, as I said, merely interested in the new power arising here. Did Samuel Orlan talk to you about that as well?'

He met the raven's black gaze. 'You smell too much.'

'Why would he visit you?'

'His apprentice was attacked by a Quor'lo.'

The raven's beak dug suddenly into its wing, tearing out a black feather, signalling that Jae'le had relaxed his grip on the animal for a moment. Zaifyr imagined the lean man in his cushioned chair over half a world away, twisting the long, dark beard that he had grown over the last century. The raven – more itself than it had been for weeks – was trying to dig him out by pulling at its body like it might a tick or a loose feather, searching for its annoyance. Then, as quickly as it began, the raven went still, its head rising.

'Perhaps,' Jae'le said, 'you are right that this is not a simple war.'

'There is also a City of Ger beneath this city.'

'That's hardly surprising. The remains of those cities are all through the mountains.'

'I thought you wanted to hear what was interesting?'

'And I found Samuel Orlan's visit—'

'I know what you are going to say.' Zaifyr reached for the glass of warm water. 'I am not interested in being chastised.'

'I was not about to do so.'

'You were,' he said firmly, ending the topic before it could reach other, older areas, where Asila could be brought up. He had done enough of that, himself. 'Now, instead, ask me about this city you have no interest in and how it links to this rising power you sent me to examine.'

Quietly, the raven said, 'Very well.'

'It is a holy war. The first in a long time, brother. The Quor'lo hinted at that and not lightly, either, which can only mean that the intention of those marching on the Spine is not meant to be a secret. We – and by we, I mean the Enclave and every other person with a touch of a god's power in them – will no doubt be their enemies, just as Mireea is for being on Ger's remains. The attack on Orlan's apprentice was most likely a chance attack on one of us – a new one without much risk, at least in the mind of the attacker. As for the city above – ' Zaifyr placed his feet on the window seal ' – Mireea cannot hold against a large army and my belief is that the city is preparing for siege while also preparing to retreat. In my ride up here, the roads from Yeflam were clear, many with rebuilt bridges. I didn't venture to the other side of the Spine, but I've heard that the mining settlements that the Spine can't protect have been forcibly shut down and the people moved. They're living in two camps on the trail when you approach the city from Yeflam, though I wouldn't say there was more than a thousand people there currently. That's Heast's work.'

'How long do you think they can hold?'

'I don't think he plans to hold, honestly. Whether the Leeran Army and those in charge of it will think the same, I don't know.'

'The priests.' Jae'le hesitated, the dark feathers on the raven ruffling. 'Do you think they are like the old ones?'

'I never saw a priest possess a dead man before.'

'The old ones had power, brother.'

'Not from blood.'

The raven's head shook. 'In this, your birth fails you. The original servants of the gods were not to be underestimated.'

Zaifyr tipped back in the chair, quiet. His brother, in this, was right: he had met none of the priests that had both terrified and inspired much of the world. Meihir had been his only connection to such figures, and she, he knew, had been a pale candle compared to the servants of other gods, or so he had gathered from Jae'le's descriptions of them. Once, the thought of meeting such figures would have driven him out of Mireea, to find them, question them and fight, but of late he struggled to recall such emotions.

In truth, he had grown tired with the intricate puzzle boxes of theories that peppered the conversations of his family since his release, conversations that he used to take part in, used to enjoy. They would begin with the idea of theft and inheritance – both theirs – but had no conclusion. The quest to know who and what they were was all that mattered to his brothers and sisters, but he was unable to share it now. It was not helped by the fact that Aelyn had not spoken to him since his release, and that the others – all but Jae'le, in truth – had been distant, managing only a handful of words. There were laws, now, and he had to admit that he did not have any interest in them, just as he had no interest in their arguments and debates any more. He could forgive them the time he had spent locked in the tower, understood it even, and agreed. He knew what he had become and the madness that lay at the centre of him . . . but there was no denying that since the door opened, he had been different: cured, yes, but changed through that, driven away by their very actions.

For all that, he had come to Mireea at his brother's request.

'The City of Ger,' Jae'le said, finally. 'Could you return to it?'

'If I wanted,' he replied, carefully.

'Would you?'

'Are you asking—'

'Yes.'

Zaifyr hesitated, then said, 'He may be protected.'

'He will.' The raven shifted, its claws scratching lightly as it did. 'But perhaps we should know in what condition Ger lies, before these priests arrive.'

'What do you think they will do?'

'I do not know, but we will learn soon enough. You need not be here for that.'

Zaifyr hesitated, then said quietly, 'I might stay. For a while.'

'People will die, brother.'

'I know.'

Unnaturally still now, as if the body of the raven were being gripped tightly by a man who had once remade the world in the image he so desired, Jae'le said, 'What did Samuel Orlan say to you?'

'Nothing that I care to share, brother.'

A Small Kindness

The last?

The last of the gods to die was the Leviathan.

She died from despair, it is said; she killed herself from the trauma of witnessing so many of her brothers and sisters at war.

Her death was witnessed by only a few, but widely reported. It was said that she sank into the ocean, turning the water black and raising the sea level permanently. For a century, only the descendants of her holy men and women travelled upon the blood of the last god. It was said that only they knew how to navigate the vast graveyard of her rot and decay safely.

—Qian, *The Godless*

1.

Though he was not given to ill omens, the morning the exiled Baron of Kein and Dark left Mireea, a deep certainty settled in him that he would not return to the city. It was a feeling that he alone had, he knew, for the lightness and ease that had settled into Dark the evening before remained, and their spirits were high as the Spine shrank behind them, despite the presence of Samuel Orlan. It was the presence of the old man that was the cause of much of Bueralan's concern. The weight of his reputation and presence sat awkwardly with the subtlety required for the job at hand – try as he might, the saboteur had not come to the view that the presence of the cartographer was a gain – and he considered briefly taking a new road with Dark and leaving the Spine to whatever fate lay at its feet after the Keepers and the Leeran Army had finished with it.

'I appreciate you allowing me to come.'

Bueralan's heels nudged his horse's flanks and he glanced at the cartographer beside him, the thought still in his head. 'That pony looks older than the sky.'

Orlan rubbed the ancient, grey beast's neck. 'You'll hurt her feelings, Baron. Age does not stop one from being useful.'

'You have to stop calling me that.' It was the third time since they had met in the early hours of the morning, outside the stables. 'And age does stop a man from running his fastest.'

'If we have to run,' the other replied, meeting his gaze, 'then we have larger problems than an old pony.'

Bueralan grunted, said nothing.

Orlan continued: 'Still, I thank you for the opportunity, and the chance to meet your friends.' He turned in his saddle, taking in all of Dark but Aerala, who rode at the front of the column as a lone sentry to guard against the raiders that had no doubt peppered the mountain with bolt-holes that the Mireean soldiers had not found. 'Usually mercenary groups are linked through a heritage – which makes sense, given that most are armies who have lost wars or are soldiers loyal to generals who have fallen out of favour. But not so Dark, I have noticed. You are a more modern group, a more eclectic collection – a reflection of the changes in our world I think. Your two sisters, Aerala and Liaya, are from the City of Marble Palaces, are they not?'

'I met them in a different city,' Bueralan replied guardedly.

'I imagine you did,' the cartographer replied. 'Men of your colour are not welcome in that part of the world. But I would argue that that is where they are from, the sharpness of their *r*s and *e*s, you see. What is more, it appears that Liaya is a trained alchemist, if I am to believe the bags I see on her horse, the herbs I smell and the clink of glass when the ground becomes uneven.'

'I did not ask for credentials,' Bueralan replied. 'Perhaps I should have you interview anyone I take on next?'

'It costs a fortune to enter the alchemist colleges there,' the

202

other continued, without rising to the bait. 'Only the wealthy can even begin to dream to sit the entrance exams.'

'People don't like questions about their past, Orlan.'

'But it is so rich!' Turning, the cartographer focused on Kae, who rode next to Zean, his back as straight as the twin swords strapped to the side of his horse. 'Here is a man from the Melian Isles who is missing two fingers on his left hand. If I was a betting man, I would say he had removed them himself fourteen years ago, one of the few soldiers to leave the ruins of Samar owned by a militant group who, adhering to the last words of the goddess Aeisha, took a vow of silence.'

The aforementioned man smiled faintly. 'Very astute, cartographer.'

The other man inclined his head. 'Next to him is a man from Ilatte.' Zean looked as if he had fallen asleep on his brown mount, but Bueralan knew otherwise. 'No real surprises there, given that Ilatte has long been the occupied territory of the Ooila, seized during the reign of the Five Queens three hundred years ago and held since then. It is quite common for young men and women upon their birth to be taken away from their parents by nobles from Ooila and raised with one of their children as a blood brother or sister, a bodyguard and whipping post, where he or she is told that their soul will be taken into the family after a life of servitude. And you, my dear, exiled B—'

'What is your point?' interrupted Bueralan.

'What you saw this morning was an old man on an old pony.' Beneath him, as if it knew it was the focus of conversation, the pony flicked its ears. 'It would be a mistake to continue to think of me in that fashion. I am not a killer, it is true. Nor do I run fast. But I am a man who has seen more of the world than any of you here present. I have seen it without a sword and I have *survived* every moment.'

'Well, I thank you for the lesson,' the saboteur said evenly. 'But—'

'Wait, wait,' interrupted Ruk from behind Zean and Kae. 'Now wait just a moment.'

Bueralan frowned. 'What?'

'The old man didn't say where I was from.'

Lips straightening – it was not a *game* – Bueralan turned to Orlan who, spreading his hands out, said, 'I have no idea where you are from, sir. Was your mother a whore?'

'*And* a fine woman,' Ruk replied hotly.

The others laughed and, despite his reservations, Bueralan allowed his horse to continue along the trail to Leera, its path unchanged.

2.

Zaifyr's second descent into the mineshaft was worse.

He had focused on the light that burnt dimly like a piece of the sun the first time, allowing it to navigate the unknown as if he were in a dream, the dark cold around him a murky promise of threat from the Quor'lo that he could ignore with the light. This time he had no globes. He was alone, having instead broken through the seal the two old men had placed over the mine entrance. Minutes before he dropped into the shaft, with the two suns warming his back, Zaifyr crouched and picked the lock securing the heavy wooden covering in place. He could have lifted it or broken it, if he were honest with himself; he certainly could have spared himself the fumbling and inaccurate pushes and twists of a skill he had not used in centuries, but he wanted to keep his second trip a secret.

His failure to quickly pop the lock spoke of a distraction in his mind, a loss of focus that would become even more apparent the moment he let go of the rotting wooden ladder he clung to. The cold, murky water was a shock, but the sudden appearance of haunts, swarming around him as he submerged was more so. Tiny and spectral, each a faint burning glow, they swarmed around him, the haunts of insects trying to catch his eye in the filthy water. Focusing on his downward strokes, Zaifyr pushed them from his mind, succeeding only as the murky dark closed over him and his hands navigated the filthy tunnel to the second ladder.

The reprieve did not last long. Out of nowhere a drowned haunt appeared in a white burn of melted, waterlogged skin, crying out in a waterlogged voice.

Zaifyr emerged with a mouthful of awful water, the haunt beneath him, its voice trapped beneath the fetid surface.

Pulling himself out, he sat on the edge of the hole and tried to regain his focus and shut out the haunt from his vision. It was Jae'le's fault. The mix of concern and chiding brought back memories, both good and bad, and undid much of the self-control he had relearned while being locked up. He had been able to command his sight, but now he was forced to wait trying to gather his focus neatly and concisely, as a fisher might drew together nets of fish. It was also why, when he stepped through the green-lit crack thinking he had done just that, he was assaulted by layers of haunts. They were a thick, burning glow: generations of men and women packed tightly together, their individual limbs merging and overlapping with others, their bodies morphing into each and every one of them in an awful tapestry of loss and sin.

Zaifyr closed his eyes.

He had not seen the sheer mass of haunts the first time he entered the City of Ger because of his focus. He needed to return to that if he did not want to be overwhelmed. He knew, from past experiences, that if he allowed that to happen, it would take him weeks, perhaps even months, to get to the point where he would not hear their entreaties to him. The solution was to focus on one of the dead, to focus his attention and power on that one so that it would overwhelm the others, and leave him with but one haunt that he could rebuild a fuller concentration around, before dismissing it from his sight.

At first he struggled to distinguish the voices, the whispering complaints of cold and hunger blurring so that it took him time to identify one that was different, that had an inflection, a sound that he could separate from the others. He had not struggled to find that edge of a voice for years and he had to return to his earliest memories on how to pick up an inflection, how to search for the roll of a vowel in a haunt's voice, an accent that they had carried in life and, now, in death. The voice he found was that of a woman. She paused between whispering the word cold and the word hunger, as if another thought persisted, as if she were trying find a way to articulate the two constants in her world.

He opened his eyes.

She was not tall. She was white, dark-haired and no taller than his chest. In appearance, she was the same age as he and the fleeting thought that he may have lost his mortality when she lost her life occurred to him. But the design of the linen gown was not one that he recognized and he put the thought and the haunt from his mind. With the sound of the river the only noise echoing around him, Zaifyr began walking down the street, in control of his sight once again but for the haunt that stood in the middle of the square, the figure he allowed himself to see to anchor his reality, to push the thoughts of the man he called his brother from his mind.

Jae'le would worry if he knew what he had done.

He would say—

'Cold,' she whispered, and paused, before saying, 'hungry.'

He would say that Zaifyr had to be careful, that he should not answer the dead, that to do so would bring him to madness again.

It had been a hundred years since he had last talked to the dead. He had reached a peace with them, an understanding that they were part of the world and that he could do nothing for them. The tower in which he had been imprisoned had been small, a tall, narrow construction twice his height and long enough for him to lie in. It had been made by hand, made from the tainted dirt and poisoned river that ran in the valley behind the Eakar Mountains. Linae, the Goddess of Fertility, had done that in her death. The horror of a god's demise had been revealed as the land, the water, the trees, the animals, and the people all followed her into her dark embrace. So scarred was the land that, even though no trace of Linae remained, no person or community had returned to it.

For a thousand years, the spirits who had died alongside her had been his companions. For a thousand years, he had their presence to teach him that his power was one of abuse, and that if he wished to leave his narrow, crooked tower, he would have to put it aside.

'A wise choice, brother,' Jae'le had said when, finally, the crude door opened. He offered his hand. 'The living are more important than the dead.'

Outside, the midday's sun had lanced painfully into Zaifyr's eyes. Placing his hand against the wall, he rose slowly, stiffly.

'Brother?'

His eyes were weeping now.

'Brother, do you understand what I am saying?'

Jae'le stood alone, dark and faceless. Despite all of what Zaifyr had thought and done to arrive at this moment, he thought of the word *jailer* involuntarily and said, 'Yes.'

'I do not need to close the door, do I?'

'I would not . . .' His voice was hoarse with disuse and he swallowed drily. 'I would not let you.'

That was not what his brother wanted to hear.

Ahead, the river crashed over the ledge, toward the violently lit Temple of Ger and the still water at the bottom. Behind him, though he had not turned once nor indicated for her to follow him, was the haunt from the city.

3.

Ayae stood before an empty leather pack and felt hollow.

The feeling had not come to her until she returned to her own home. In the dark, Ayae could only see the outlines of the damage that had been done to her house, and once she closed the door, she felt a slow crumbling inside her. It was not sudden, not as if the floor beneath her had given way, but rather it was gradual, a brick here, a piece of mortar there, and she thought to stop it by going to bed. But then she had woken, she had reached across the empty expanse of the bed for Illaan and, touching nothing, allowed herself a moment to rationalize his behaviour, to approve of his treatment of her. She could understand it just as she could understand the damage done to her property, just as she could understand the cold looks the neighbours gave her. She could. She *could* . . . but only for a moment. She felt the walls of herself continue to collapse. She knew that rationalizing Illaan's behaviour was a betrayal of herself, an admission that she was not strong enough, not old enough, to hold the curse that had been dropped on her, but yet . . .

Yet she reached out, touching the edge of the empty pack.

'I have to leave.'

Orlan had said the words to her after she had woken. He had knocked while there was still dark in the sky, before the morning's sun had risen.

'I know you want me to stay.' He stood in front of her, his ink-stained fingers holding her own. 'I would like to do so, now. Maps need to be redrawn, contracts need to be met – but first, I must see why our shop was attacked.'

'Because of me,' she whispered.

His hand tightened. 'No, not because of you. The man who entered the shop was meant for me.'

She knew he was lying. He had, she thought, always been a terrible liar. Instead, she said – because he was not Olcea, because he did not need her – she said, 'Let me come with you.'

'Ayae.'

'I don't want to feel their eyes on me like this.' Her voice was so quiet she barely recognized it, a weakness she hated. 'I have tried to get rid of it, I have tried to ignore it, I—'

'This is your home,' he said, sternly. 'Do not let them take it from you.'

But she would.

She remembered Olcea's words, remembered the sight of Samuel walking out her door, she remembered the look on Illaan's face, and she knew that it had already been taken from her. All that was left was for her to fill the leather pack and leave.

But where could she go? She wanted to be anonymous again so she crossed off Yeflam: the Keepers lived there. She would have to go beyond the sprawling city, across Leviathan's Blood, before she felt even vaguely safe to start life anew. The journey would take months and cost a fortune she did not have. She would have to find work along the way.

Going north was no better. She would have to go past Faaisha, up into the colder countries, towards Leviathan's End, before she was free. West offered Ooila and perhaps that wouldn't be so bad. Sooia was separated from Ooila by a huge expanse of ocean, but it was her birthplace's closest neighbour and untouched by war, at least so far. But what would she do while she was there? There would be no work. The moment she left Mireea she would stop being an apprentice cartographer and she would be – she would be—

'Cursed.'

Ayae shook her head, touched again the lip of the empty pack, and wondered what she could put in it. What clothes did you pack to start a new life, to begin again with nothing? With no answer coming to her, she was saved by a knock on the door.

'Hi.' The baker's apprentice, wearing his brown uniform, scratched the backs of his dirty hands nervously. 'Hi,' he repeated.

'Jaerc, I'm sorry I—'

'No, no.' He raised his hands. 'No, please. I – I came to apologize.'

Holding the door, unsure what to say, she stepped aside and let him in. Stepping past her, he glanced from the fireplace to the door to the bedroom and the empty pack that lay there. Turning to face her, his hands clasped together tightly.

'You don't have to apologize,' she said, pre-empting him. 'The mistake was mine.'

'No.' His mouth was set firmly, and his gaze never left her. 'No, it wasn't. I shouldn't have let Keallis talk to you that way.'

'She was right.' Ayae leant back against the door. 'I mean, everything she said is true. You and I both know that.'

'No.' Again, his voice was firm, sure. 'No, it's not.'

'Jaerc—'

'You're going to leave, right?' He nodded to the room. 'That's you packing, yes?'

She hesitated, then shrugged. 'Yes.'

'That's not right.' His fingers straightened, pressed against his thighs. 'I know it's not right. This is your home. I spent all night trying to sleep and couldn't because I knew when you left, you didn't think that. Keallis may have said you weren't wanted here, but that wasn't right. She has no power to tell you where you can and can't stay.'

'I am cursed,' she said softly. 'It's not about choice.'

'It is,' he said, again with that certainty. 'I don't mean to speak out of line. I don't want to tell you what to think. But this has not stopped being your home just because you're cursed.'

'What if it isn't any more?'

'I had a brother,' he said, the resolve in his tone never failing. 'He was born seven years after me. He was my little brother. When he was five he was half my height, and when he was five, flowers grew wherever he walked. Not many, and not for long, but you could see them. He thought they were funny. He would make patterns, like a kid would. He didn't understand what was going on and he didn't know that people would be frightened. My parents thought that everyone would turn on him, so they kept him inside. They locked him up. He was just a little kid and soon he was afraid of everyone and didn't ask to go outside. The flowers just followed him around the house. Until the flowers started growing on him and he got sick.' Jaerc hesitated for a moment, his flat fingers curling, then straightening, physical signs of his indecision. 'The flowers would bulge up under his skin. We tried to cut them out, but they were rooted deep like a wart, like a huge wart that was attached to the bone. It was awful.'

'Did he die?' Ayae asked, thinking of her own burning skin.

'Yes.' The apprentice baker took a deep breath, a steadying breath. 'But that's not why I'm telling you this. I'm telling you because Mum and Dad had to go to someone because they couldn't help him alone. I don't know who they talked to first, but I remember that there were people coming to see him every day, some who were scared, but all who wanted to help. People who said that it wasn't his fault. Lady Wagan said—'

'Lady Wagan?'

He nodded. 'She came at the end of the first week. She came at night and had the old healer Reila with her. She sat with Mum and Dad while her healer examined my brother and told them that she would do all that she could, that whatever we needed she would try and provide. She said that they should not have hidden it in the first place.'

It will not be long until a kindness is said. Lady Wagan's words. Quietly, Ayae said, 'Why would she say that?'

'We live on a dead god,' Jaerc said. 'She said that. I remember it so clearly. She said that Ger's remains tell us what happens when you stand alone, when you forget that you are part of a larger community. We mustn't ever do that, she said. She was so sure when she said it, I remember thinking how comforting it was, how right she was. She could have said a lot of things, like Keallis. She could have said that my brother was strange and unnatural. That the best thing would be for him to die. But she didn't. Instead, she paid for medicine for my brother, sent witches and healers and, after he died, came to the funeral and stood in the back. Afterwards, she hugged me and said I should help my parents.'

As he finished speaking, Jaerc approached Ayae. It was only then she realized that she had sunk down on the door, that she had collapsed against it. That silent tears ran down her face. *It will not be long until a kindness is said.* With a gravity that she had not thought that a baker's apprentice would have had, he reached down and pulled her to her feet.

'That's why you can't leave,' he said.

4.

The stone length of the Spine was a smudge on the horizon when Samuel Orlan's oral retelling of history began to remind Bueralan of the Lord of Ille.

Lord Alden had greeted him at the border of his small kingdom, a force of elderly knights at his side. He had gone ahead alone, as he often did on jobs that were inside a kingdom. Alden, as if age and position gave him the right, orated as he led Bueralan through the dusty streets of his small kingdom and past the old gallows that were the centre of his justice. His sense of pride grew with every word.

It had been built by two men, a father and a son, Lord Alden explained from the back of his fine horse. A tall, elderly white man with wisps of grey hair and new, but outdated clothing, he rode with an easy sway as he told how the father had made a living for forty-one years building gallows, guillotines and breaking wheels before he moved to Ille. Looking to retire, he had agreed to provide the gallows for the local government of his new home, on the condition that he himself was given a seat on the council. With such a small payment agreed upon, the father organized the pale timber to be delivered from the

Yeala Forest at his own cost. He paid the cost of ferrying it over Leviathan's Blood and along the dusty roads leading to the city by wagon and bull. His son, who was slowly inheriting his father's business, was responsible for much of the physical labour once the wood arrived. It was he who ensured that multiple trap doors opened, he who oversaw the placing of the wide deck and the beam that fell across it like the arm of a god. It was not, both men knew, an ambitious design. It would not hold forty-five bodies as the infamous gallows of Tinalan did; nor would it be as cruel as the nine-bladed guillotine that a Lord of Saan had once owned. But it was built with expertise and of expensive material and as the suns rose and fell on the day the lumber arrived, the father measured and cut, the son sank bolts and the pair laid floorboards and coated the joints with black tar.

After five days they were done, and within five years there was no council. The elderly Lord of Ille walked up on the gallows in front of Bueralan and indicated where the last of the council had dropped through the trap door, following the others, leaving the father and son as the new leaders of the small kingdom.

'It is not new.'

The words were from Elar, a small, greying man who sat in the centre of the seven members of Dark, each having taken up an awkward perch on the old furniture in the inn they had stayed in near the kingdom. Two days had passed since Lord Alden had explained the job to Bueralan, but even as he had, Elar and the rest of Dark had slipped out into the town, its inns and its people.

'It is an old familiar story: taxes and rights and death,' Elar continued. 'Crops have been bad for close to five years now, but the taxes have not altered to acknowledge that. Some people have moved, but no one will purchase the land, and Alden simply takes the rights if it is abandoned – including any cattle that are being grazed by neighbours on it. A lot of the younger people feel they're stuck and have diminishing avenues and have to decide between family and future. For a few years, the younger families petitioned to have the taxes lowered, to try and bridge the gap, but their suit fell on deaf ears, and they turned to asking for elections, democracy. Alden arrested and tortured those who raised those voices before dumping them back into the community.'

'This was supposed to be a small job,' Aerala said from her seat. 'Ille barely appears on a map.'

'It appears enough,' Zean murmured from beside her.

'What about Alden's fear of revolution?' Bueralan asked, steering the conversation back to the topic. 'How does that look?'

'There is not much talk of it, naturally.' Elar shrugged. 'The signs of it are there, though. You would need to be blind to miss it. If you take a horse in to be given a new shoe, the blacksmith will take off the current one, melt it down, and make you a new one from scrap. He will tell you the town is tapped for base materials, but he won't explain where the scrap came from. You will have the same experience when you buy a meal here. According to Liaya, the reports you brought from Alden say that the land outside the town has had a full twenty-five per cent drop in crops this year, but there hasn't been a corresponding drop in land ownership.'

'There has been a rise in stock, actually,' the dark-haired

woman added, sitting across from him, the reports in a strewn-out pile before her. 'The last two years show a five per cent growth.'

Bueralan was not surprised. Alden's guards – well fed and paid – kept a tight leash on the town and its inhabitants, their forces bolstered, from what he understood, after the first protests that had broken out. 'That leaves us with the question,' he said, 'of where we will find the leaders of this group?'

'Not inside Ille,' Kae offered. 'People there are just pieces, cogs for the large work outside. After the first protest, it is clearly professional work, run by someone like us.'

'Someone who took the better side of the job,' Zean said.

'Someone invested,' the other man corrected.

'We wear it regardless,' Bueralan said with quiet authority. 'We made the choice. We thought it would be an easy job and we took it up without the right questions. We should have listened to Sel'na when he said we needed more information, but we did not. So we wear it. We don't like it, I know that, but we've worked for crueller men and women before and we will work for worse later, one day. It is the nature of our business.'

None disagreed with him. The new recruit, Deanic, a thin white kid who read and spoke more languages at the age of six and ten than he had years of age, looked uncomfortable, the rude awakening to the reality of the work he had probably, as they all had, once romanticized. That was always the hardest of the truths to learn, that saboteur work was digging up information for people you don't like, on people you might like, on movements you sympathized with. For men and women with enough money you learned trade routes, personal connections; at other times, you broke down armies and killed men and women you did not know. The jobs were your own responsibility, your own choice, but it always paid, as Serra Milai had said, to remember who you were, to take the jobs you could believe in more than those you did not. And if, as had happened to Sky more than once, you ended up employed by a man or woman you did not like, then you were to remember that you were not being paid to have a moral objection to a man, a woman, a religion, a culture. 'Dislike who pays you if you must,' she said; 'but dislike them quietly, because to do so publicly is to ensure that you never work again.'

'We'll pay our penance when we retire,' Bueralan said to Dark, meeting their gazes. 'Before that, there are mountains, and that is where we will find our revolutionaries. They will need an encampment that will allow for stockpiling, a forge, and training if they mean to remove Alden by force. That doesn't mean that they will be easy to find. If they were, we would not have been hired. But they're out there, and they're embedded in the estate, so when the majority of us ride in tomorrow, you need to keep your eye open to learn who we can trust and who we cannot. We want to finish this before it turns sour.'

5.

Afterwards, after the baker's apprentice had guided her to the chair, Jaerc poured her a drink and sat with her until she had regained her composure.

Then he left. A part of him, Ayae knew, was older and wiser than her. She sat on her couch in the warmth of two suns — the fading morning sun and rising midday sun — and berated herself for the tears. She *knew* she was stronger than this. She had begun with nothing in the orphanage. Yes, she scratched at the burning on the back of her left arm when, later, she stood before her bed and contemplated the empty leather pack. Yes, her partner had left her. Yes, Orlan had left her. They were both different forms of abandonment, but leaving would change neither.

She passed beneath the large tree outside, the light of the two suns shining through the cut-back canopy that webbed itself in dark green across the houses around her. She would return to the Keep, to Fo and Bau and yes, she admitted as she passed a family pushing a cart full of green and yellow and red produce, to Lady Wagan. *It will not be long until a kindness is said.* She would apologize for her behaviour the night before and she would learn as much about herself as she could about the two Keepers.

At the door, she was greeted by Bau, who opened it just before she approached. 'Ah,' he said, the first word a long breath. 'I was right. You did return.'

'You should make prophecies,' she replied, her tone hiding the rapid beat of her heart.

'I have tried,' he replied, his smile easy with practice. 'When I was young, maybe fifty, sixty years of age, I spent six months attempting to write the future down. I would predict weather, trade, births and deaths. I had a very nice quill and expensive vellum.'

'But no luck?'

'No,' he admitted. 'I thought it might be a sign of divinity, should I be able to do so. That I was somehow shaping the world without my conscious knowledge.'

Crossing her arms, rubbing at the burning on her left forearm, Ayae said, 'I see this failure did not stop you from believing.'

A slight twist entered his smile. 'I am to learn patience with you, it appears. But yes, you are right. It did bother me. It suggested that there was no fate, no design at work around us, no reason for the abilities that we had. The answer suggested that we were free to do as we please. In the Enclave in particular, there was a lot of debate about it.'

'And?'

'And?' The twist deepened. 'There is no answer. That is the reason for the debate.' Before she could reply, he pulled the door behind him, and walked past her. 'Enough of that. We have work to do.'

'What about Fo?'

'Let him sleep,' Bau replied. 'He is not pleasant after an evening of failed experiments.'

'Failed?'

'You're all questions today, aren't you?'

Opening the door to the Keep, he motioned for Ayae to follow. She considered repeating the question, but decided instead to wait. Ayae retraced her earlier steps with Bau, returning to the empty courtyard. Crossing the sparse ground, the Keeper led her through a small gate to the west and into another part of the estate. The grass grew thickly around a cobbled path that ended in a squat, brown-brick smithy with the stable roofs enclosing it like ribs across a heart. It was cold and grey, unused today.

She stopped. 'What is your plan?'

'To set you on fire,' he replied easily and without stopping. 'I shouldn't worry, if I were you. You are in the company of the Healer.'

'Is that a joke?'

He laughed, but said, 'No, I'm quite serious.'

'You'd better rethink your plan.'

Holding open the gate to the smithy, he turned to her. 'You survived—'

'If you think,' she interrupted, her voice even, 'that you can even touch me, then you should think again.'

Bau's eyebrows rose slightly.

'*Think* again.'

'Don't think like a mortal,' he said, as if he were talking to a child. 'You cannot—'

'You will not burn me.' There was no give in her voice.

He moved the gate back and forth, a touch irritated, until he finally said, 'Let us see how you light a fire then, shall we?'

Pushing past him, Ayae stepped into the smithy. There were horses standing on either side of the building and not one of them paid attention to the new arrivals. The ground was covered in fresh sawdust that had become soggy and dark at the edges. It clung to the soles of her boots as she walked to the tool rack and picked up a shovel. She drove the shovel into the coal beside the furnace, kicked the door open, and dropped it in there.

As she dug in for a second time, his hand closed around her wrist. 'You should not play me for a fool, child,' he said softly.

She met his gaze. 'I am not a child.'

His gaze flickered, fell to the floor. 'No?'

To the pile of coal which was suddenly, and without explanation, on fire.

6.

As if to spite Bueralan, the job in Ille dragged out and turned sour.

He remembered standing outside an empty brick and wood farmhouse next to Aerala, the afternoon's sun high in the empty sky above. Inside, Liaya, Zean and Kae were moving through the building slowly, working through the traps that had been left within, in the hope that they – on the 'tip' they had received anonymously – would run in and be killed. Now, they would comb the building for clues, for the pieces that they were missing in the identity and location of those who were in charge. 'It was clumsy,' he said to Aerala, following her gaze to the edge of the forested skyline. 'I assume they did it to make us, to figure out who we had in hiding, but all they've done is give us something. It might not be much, but after two months, it is more than we had.'

'Silence would have been their best choice,' the dark-haired archer said. 'They were close to starving us out on information before this. Another month like this and we would have no choice but to walk away, to leave Alden to his own fate. It would have been a failure on our part, but it would have been

225

a clean one. Surely, whoever is organizing this must be young, must be someone who hasn't yet learned patience – someone for who this means more than it does to us.'

'Someone emotionally invested?'

'Yes,' she said without pause, 'someone just so.'

Two nights later, Bueralan met with Lord Alden to give his weekly report. He and Liaya had worked up a hypothesis of the number that opposed the lord, a month of maths and estimates that he presented without the evidence of a confession, or sighting by his own people. Yet, he planned to maintain belief that Alden and his small army were outnumbered five to one. Even allowing for the difference in training, that left the Lord of Ille at a disadvantage. In his planned responses to the information, the saboteur had included the option of leaving, a choice that he was going to steer Alden towards before hiring mercenaries, if he could.

He wanted, as well, to pull in Deanic, Ruk and Elar. All three had filtered into the town and farms at the end of their first meeting, but little had come of it. Deanic had found nothing and Bueralan knew he wouldn't last a second job. Ruk, working a whorehouse as security, had turned up a few men and women, but none led back to the centre of the movement and he was of the opinion that the job had run dry. Only Elar had had some luck: he had re-entered Ille on a mule, head shaved and a two-week beard grown, looking for a dead cousin – the irony of it now struck hard as Bueralan rode away from Mireea – and found himself working on farms. He felt that one of the farmhands led back to the chain of the revolutions command, but he had not broken him yet. It was the closest any of them got to being in a position of power, but it did not change Bueralan's opinion about the situation.

Lord Alden disagreed.

'It is one or two men at the heart of it, I am sure,' he said, sitting on the long leather couch that ran opposite the glass window of his office. 'Disgruntled soldiers, a wayward child from across the river. I have given you names.'

'All of which have turned up nothing.'

'Like your hypothesis.' The lord lifted his left leg across his right. 'Let me ask you, Captain, do you sympathize with these men and women who plot against me?'

A low sigh escaped Bueralan. 'I do not take sides,' he said.

'Everyone takes sides, even if they shouldn't.' Alden nodded to the window, to where a long garden of green, red, and yellow was kept. 'Take my grounds keeper, for example. He has worked for me for close to twenty years but I doubt he would be upset if a rebellion took my head off. He may even cheer as the sword came down. He had a sister who had been caught stealing from here and I was forced to punish her for it.'

The woman had been flogged, her fingers cut off after, one each day until there were none left. Bueralan had heard the story.

'I can't fault him for that,' Alden continued. 'But if I were to die, he would lose the money that has paid for his fine house, the money by which he lives now, caring for his sister and her child. None of the men and women who behead me would concern themselves with his welfare afterwards, a fact that may or may not escape his attention. He would have no work, no prospects and because he was still working for me when the rebellion broke my gates down, he would have very little chance to turn those fortunes around. But I have no doubt that still he sides with those men and women more than he sides with me, and I would be a poor man if I did not realize that. I would also, I hesitate to admit, have a much less beautiful garden if I did not understand it.'

'And your garden is quite beautiful,' Bueralan said. 'But it does not change the fact that you have a much deeper and much better organized rebellion than you believe.'

'Whereas I believe, Captain, that you and yours lack the proper desire to see this through.' Alden rose slowly, his knees cracking as he did. 'I have watched you and your team develop a dislike for me, for my *cruelty*, as it is popularly reported. If my gardener were in my place, I wonder, would he be different? I do not know and it does not matter – but it has led me to believe that there lacks a desire in Dark to finish this. Please, follow me.'

Alden led the saboteur out of his office and down a dark, warm hallway. The walk was not long, but had enough distance that by the time he approached the door, Bueralan had begun to suspect what was going to be revealed.

He was not wrong.

In the centre of the room, on a low table covered in a dark cloth, lay Elar. The afternoon's sun lay thickly across his still, wet form, while puddles of water pooled beneath him, laced with faint traces of red. Most of the blood, however, had already been drained out of him – drained through the cuts, punctures and amputations that had taken place.

'He washed up in the river this morning,' Alden said, closing the door behind Bueralan. 'He was found by a farmer who brought him here.'

228

Elar's right hand was gone, two fingers remained on his left, crooked like bent wheat. Tar had been used on the ends, burning the skin; from them, his arms and chest were mostly whole, marred by cuts and slashes, half a dozen holding lumps that had been stitched over. With his knife, the saboteur cut open the stitches and found small bags. Lord Alden, standing on the other side of Elar, informed him that they most probably held flesh-eating grubs, given the depth of the wounds when he lifted the cloth away. Following the flow of his body, Bueralan saw the mutilation of Elar's genitals, the stitched cuts down his legs, the shattered kneecap and the amputated toes that ended in hard black tar.

Reaching up, he tilted the face – the face he knew, the face untouched but for the lines that spoke of his death – to him.

'You may dislike me as you feel fit, Captain,' Lord Alden said quietly. 'But there are only villains in revolutions.'

7.

The Temple of Ger had no door.

It sat as it had the day before, half submerged in the lake with the water moving slowly around it, the red light filtering over it and illuminating the smooth walls. Zaifyr contemplated the sight while he stood on the shore next to the cold remains of the Quor'lo, untouched by any insect or animal since he and Bueralan had left. That was not a surprise: what was left after possession was always shunned and ignored by scavengers.

In comparison to the scavengers, Zaifyr had little knowledge of the temple before him. Most priests had turned to sacrifices, had turned to a poor understanding of blood magic, and Ger's priests had been no different.

Stepping into the cool water, Zaifyr waded out to the temple, swimming the last few metres as the rock and dirt floor dropped away. His hands touched the smooth building, feeling the cool stone that, he imagined, would be a sandy colour, if not awash with the rude light from above. But as he swam around the building gently, his searches above water, then beneath, he only proved what it was that he had thought as he stood on the shore: complete and without a break.

When he emerged from the water the haunt awaited him, having finally made its way down the rocks.

'Cold,' she whispered. 'I am cold.'

He faced the temple.

Perhaps, he thought, the reason that there was no door was due to magic. The people who lived in the City of Ger had reached a violent end at the hand of the first Mireean people, but the light in the ceiling lent itself easily to the idea that someone in their community had had power.

'You're old today,' he said to himself quietly. 'Your head is in the past, too much time thinking about things you cannot change.'

'Old,' the haunt whispered.

Slowly, he turned to her.

'Old,' she repeated. 'You are very old.'

After a moment – in which all his senses rebelled against him – he said, 'So we both are. Do you remember here?'

'Yes.' The red from the ceiling mixed with her, leaving splotches of colour throughout her body, wounds that would not dry. 'It was the first temple in the Spine of Ger. People would travel throughout the world to it. None of the other temples were as well attended as this one, but the priests would only allow people in on the holiest of days. They were allowed to see Ger here, to see the burns that did not stop blackening, the water that poured from his mouth and the soil that ground against him and the wind. The wind that tore at him.'

Zaifyr frowned. 'When was it sealed?'

'When the soldiers came.' The haunt stepped past him, her pale feet touching the water, the shadows of her falling like roots that sank deeply. 'They did not care for Ger, they did not honour the people who had built a life in the caverns. Economics, greed: that was what drove their army into the mountains and began the slaughter of peaceful men and women and their children.'

'You are much too lucid to be born here,' Zaifyr said quietly. 'Much too young for this war you talk of.'

The haunt stood silently over the water.

'You overplayed your hand,' he said.

Finally, the haunt of the woman who had possessed the Quor'lo whispered, 'I have never before been so hungry.'

'It will only get worse.'

'I have faith.'

'You cannot see it,' he said, 'but all around you are the dead, the souls of all the people who ever lived in these caves. There are so many that I cannot tell where an arm ends, where a foot begins, where the individual remains. There is no reason for faith.'

The haunt shook her head, the lines from her feet deep, but broken in the water's reflection.

'If I could help you, I would,' he admitted, his voice not yet a whisper. 'I would help all the dead if I could. I would continue their journey if I knew but how.'

'I *feel* him.'

'You do.' Zaifyr ran a hand through his wet hair. 'I feel Ger too, but it is simply a trick of time. We do not share the same passing of it that they did.'

'Yours are the words of the faithless,' she said.

He did not reply.

'Faithless,' she repeated, her voice rising.

Still, he did not speak.

'I can pass to him.'

'You cannot.'

'Lies!'

Turning, the haunt ran to the temple. The water showed no ripple as she leapt up, her body awash in red, a scarred, tragic figure that threw herself at the smooth wall—

—and burst across it.

Heavy of heart, the man who had left his charms in his hotel room and felt suddenly naked without them, eased himself onto the hard ground. It would take a while for the haunt to return to shape, to step from the water to the shore, and by then he would be ready to talk to her again. To draw from her what she knew about the temple. It was possible that this – the smooth shell around the building – had been put up by Ger, but Zaifyr doubted it. For the most part, the defences of the gods were servants, immortal beings who had been created for the purpose of standing guard for eternity. By and large they were violent, held by oaths that could not be broken, longing for escape as much as they longed for entertainment, for a break in their endless service.

Mostly, Zaifyr knew, they were mad.

Like him, once.

8.

Though in hindsight it was obvious, Ayae was surprised when Bau theorized aloud that her ability to set the coal on fire and her survival in the shop were due to her loss of emotional control. She did not like what he said, nor the way he stared at the burning coal, nor how he turned the conversation to what god or element curled inside her. 'Ger's wards,' he said softly, stepping back from the fire before him. 'The four elements – fire, earth, wind and water – that were chained to him, that were guided by his strength, his control.'

'I don't—'

'Please, just listen,' he said. 'Tell me, are you uncomfortable in this city?'

She hesitated. 'You mean, am I comfortable now?'

'Not with me.' His tone held a trace of contempt, a hint, nothing more. 'In general, are you uncomfortable in the city?'

'No.'

'I am,' he admitted, leaning against the wooden beam opposite her. 'I feel as if something is standing beside me, trying to shape my thoughts. What I feel is Ger, the last of Ger, struggling to announce himself and to continue the war that the gods were involved in. At least, that is my belief.'

'Your belief?'

'*Our* belief, I should say.' The contempt was gone, replaced with a serious yet excited tone. 'Before the fall of the Five Kingdoms, Qian wrote a book that argued the gods were not dead, but dying. The presence that we felt when around one of their corpses was allowable because time moved differently there – but while we felt that, the gods, having experienced time in a different fashion, were already dead. They could not interact with us, even if they so desired. It was very controversial among us, though the publication of it in cities for mortals to read was more of one, and a great deal of what it said went unremarked for years. It is generally considered now that Qian was right, that our ability to feel the gods in their fashion revealed a connection between them and us, an unseen cord that tied us together. Qian argued it differently, of course – he argued that the power that bled from them was undefined, random, unpredictable, but his own state of mind refused to acknowledge anything but the most unhealthy conclusion.'

'I don't feel Ger at all.' Ayae stepped away from the coal, the flames fading through no work of her own. 'Maybe that means I am not what you think I am?'

'No, you are. You have fire in you, I am sure of it. But as to feeling . . .' He shrugged. 'To be honest, I would be surprised if you could. With everything you have experienced in the last few days, and the changes you are going through, your senses are probably in overload as we speak. I know I was.'

'Maybe I'm not like you. No one ever talks about the

elements bound to Ger,' she argued. 'They're not even on the pyres.'

'The elements were not worshipped individually.' He glanced at the cooling coals. 'They were not considered gods by most people. Some old images show that Ger had them chained, as if they were animals. I suspect that they were more than that, that they were talismans, really, a way to focus and trap the wildness of the elements. It would explain why he broke his chains upon his death, freeing them.'

'Doesn't that make me right?'

His hands fell open before him. 'I don't know.'

'You don't know?'

'No.' His smile was humourless. 'And neither do you.'

Over the next hour, Ayae endured Bau talking about the elements, about Ger and about what he felt in Mireea. She was increasingly aware of his verbal slights, his comments that became more personal, more direct in trying to control her emotions and make her angry. She likened it to his attempt to get her to hold a hot coal in her hand: blatant, pointless and easy to ignore. Eventually she grew tired of him. After he tried to bring Illaan up, she said, 'What happened to the people working here?'

'I told them I needed it for the day,' he said.

He had known she would come back. 'I think they can have it back.'

'You do?'

She met his gaze.

'Your eyes flashed,' he said, quietly. 'Like they were on fire.'

The gate was warm beneath her touch, and she looked down

at her boots, half expecting to see sooty footprints left in the grass.

By the time Ayae entered the overrun gardens of the Keep's courtyard, she had regained her composure, though that earlier, frightened part of her that had stared at the empty leather pack threatened to return. She quietened the urge, though, focusing instead on the fact that she had walked away, that she could be in control, and the fact that he knew nothing. It was becoming clear that she would never get simple answers from Bau. To a degree, he was making it up as he went along, throwing out ideas to see what would stick. Bau would not be able to help her any more than Lady Wagan and Reila had been able to help Jaerc's brother.

There was only one person who could help her.

9.

Zaifyr was dry by the time the haunt rose from the water. With her gaze upon him, she drew closer, the splotches of red throughout her shrinking, diminishing to tiny points. 'What is your name?' he said to her.

'What happened to me?' the haunt asked, instead.

He did not reply.

'Tell me,' she insisted.

For a moment he was silent, uncomfortable. He could not reply. He could stand and leave. It would be what Jae'le would want. It would— 'You cannot leave here. This is where you died – where the Quor'lo died. Before today, I might have said that you would be where your body lay, but I would have been wrong. Your soul died here. This is where you will remain until the world is no more. As to what happened to you when you hit that wall?' He shrugged. 'You can't pass through walls.'

'I'm cold,' she whispered.

'I know.'

'I'm hungry.'

She was not fully restored. It would take days, not hours, for every part of herself to thread back into her soul. It was as if parts of her immortal being were seeking a way to pass on to another existence, to find what the gods had promised at the creation of the world. 'What is your name?' he asked.

The haunt hesitated, a troubled look stealing across her face. 'Oyia,' she said finally.

Zaifyr had thought that her appearance would change as she pulled herself together, that the modest, dated dress she wore would disappear. His cynicism prompted an image of wealth, of a modernity that opposed the ideals of equality and humility that he knew priests spoke of with a rhetorical joy. He found instead that the dress remained reminiscent of an older culture, that its simple cut and modest angles were a truth.

'I feel as if I should not have said that,' the haunt said, her voice confused with regret. 'My name is power to the likes of you.'

'It is.' His fingers touched the skin beneath his wrist, seeking out the absent charm as he reached out for her, not physically, but with a touch that, while unseen, was still tangible. Oyia would feel the weight in her mind, as if a solid object had pressed against her skull and was looking into her following the trail of memories back to her origins.

At first, he saw a room no larger than a cell: a bed stood along the left side with a table to the right. A basin of water sat on it, books next to it.

Applying pressure took him outside the room. A long hallway greeted him, rooms lining both sides. The doors made from white ash wood. Inside, the spartan living standards of the first room were repeated and men and women, each wearing simple robes of brown, were within. They knelt, stood, prayed, their faces turned away from the door and hidden from him. Zaifyr did not push against her resolve.

Yet, the stone hallway felt like it never ended and Zaifyr briefly considered turning around, returning to the rooms he had passed. But a sense of anticipation had begun to fill him, the emotion drawn from the haunt. He had loosened his pressure and she was lost in her memories, unaware that he was there, unaware that he felt not just her love but her respect for the person who stood in a long, high-roofed auditorium, surrounded by rows of benches.

A man. A single man, militarily attired.

He wore not leather, nor chain, but a uniform of white and red, the former colour dominating while the latter ran in lines down the chest and connected to a long, flowing cloak. A peace knot was looped around the long sword at his side. He wore the weapon uneasily, as if he were unaccustomed to its weight. His bearing, the way his hands clasped behind his back and the tilt of his head, spoke neither of a military background nor a religious one. Yet he commanded the kind of respect that Zaifyr had connected with leaders, with kings and generals – but even as he thought that, he realized that while the man was respected he was not the object of love that Zaifyr had felt upon entering the room.

The true object of the haunt's love lay behind him, in a small room made from brick and empty of anything else.

A child. A girl, no older than seven.

She was pale-haired and pale-skinned and wore a robe of purest white. Her eyes were green, like his, but they held nothing of importance, nothing to suggest that the child was anything more than that – until she lifted her gaze and met his.

Zaifyr blinked.

In front of him, the haunt whispered, 'Cold.'

There was a chill in him as well, born from what he had seen, what he had done. From the recognition that both, he knew, would have to be confessed to his brother.

'Can you . . .' She hesitated. 'Can you stop the cold?'

'No,' he lied.

10.

After Bueralan organized for Elar's ashes to be shipped back to his children — he could not bear to send them his body — the job took another two months. As the morning's sun rose nearly five months after Bueralan had first ridden across the border, Dark rode out of Ille, leaving one hundred and twenty-three men and women to be executed, their pound of flesh bitter black.

Deanic had not ridden to the coast with them. He had parted from them two days after they left Ille, and the rest headed, tired and broke, to the small town of Asli. There, they would spend a single night in a cheap inn before finding a ship to take them to Yeflam. After that, they would ride up to Mireea, where the work offered by Captain Heast waited. The job had come in the final days of the revolution against Lord Alden and there was no mention of his cousin in the short note, but Bueralan had not expected there to be: Heast's letter alone said that he knew.

Now, one night out from Mireea, one night and seven months after Ille, the camp Dark made was a quiet affair, Bueralan the sombre heart of it.

'You have been quiet all day, Baron.' Samuel Orlan was seated across from him, on the other side of the smouldering camp fire, an old man who had missed nothing. 'Does something about this work bother you?'

'I told you not to call me that.'

'So you did.'

A thin trail of smoke rose between the two, the smell of cooked meat clinging to it. 'Why are you here, Samuel?' Bueralan asked, after a moment. 'Why are you not back in Mireea?'

'My shop has been burnt down,' he replied. 'My apprentice attacked. I would like to know why.'

'Revenge?'

'Don't you feel as if something is not quite right in these mountains, Baron?' Between the two men, the rest of Dark watched silently. Bueralan saw Zean shift slightly, so that his body was turned towards the cartographer. Kae's three-fingered hand placed the plate he had been eating off on the ground, near the hilt of his sword. Aerala fed a long stick into the ash, heating the embers, while Liaya's hand dropped slightly to the outstretched body of Ruk, whose steady breathing altered to her touch. Without concern, Samuel Orlan continued, 'You have been beneath the city, you have seen the temple, you know what I know.'

'Which is?'

Orlan's smile was faint in reply.

Bueralan thought of the presence he had felt before the temple. He picked a piece of fat from the plate beside him, cut from the meat provided by Lady Wagan, the first and last of the fresh meat they had been given. He flicked it onto the dying fire, and said, 'Do you know what happened to the last man who thought he could play us?'

'I heard that the Lord of Ille was hanged on the gallows his grandfather and father made,' the small man replied. 'I had heard that you were employed by him.'

'We were,' Bueralan admitted. 'He had an armed revolution building, one that he believed we were not motivated enough to stop. He did not doubt our loyalty to our word. We have earned that in our work. But he did doubt our dedication to our word, and he thought he could motivate us if something personal was at stake. He killed one of us and it did motivate us all, but not in the way he had hoped. See, he overplayed his hand. Lord Alden was a man who loved detail. He kept records of stock, land ownership, taxes, population, all of which fell under his control – including the details of life and death. He revelled in the details a little too much.'

'So you took him to his family gallows?'

Aerala's stick snapped, sending up a cloud of dying cinders.

'No,' Bueralan said. 'The people of Ille did that. We found the head of his revolution a week after Elar died. The young woman responsible had made a mistake earlier, and that led to her. She was quite an intelligent individual and, after introducing ourselves, we made sure that within the next two months, all of Lord Alden's finances were directed to her, from his investments, to the land that he owned. More importantly, we made sure the neighbouring kingdoms recognized her and her new government. Then we helped organize the night that she and her friends could enter Ille and take Lord Alden and his remaining loyalists, including, you will be surprised to learn, his gardener. In the morning, they were all led onto the floorboards of the gallows that his father had laid.'

'If the moral of that story, Baron, is that you are not to be trifled with – ' Orlan held up his empty hands ' – rest assured, it never crossed my mind.'

'Take your mule back to Mireea, Samuel.'

'He is a pony.'

'I could have my soldiers stake you down in the dirt, leave you here until the morning.' Bueralan saw Zean shift straighter, the movement mirrored by Kae; in his periphery, he saw the remains of Aerala's stick drop, saw Ruk's legs shift slightly and heard Liaya's bag clink, once, but loudly through the silence of the camp, as if it were a bell, announcing the start of a race. 'You should not doubt it.'

'I do not. Nor should you doubt that after I freed myself, I would ruin you,' the cartographer said with no trace of anger in his voice. 'All of you. In many ways, I am similar to all of you, and I can do what you did so well in Ille. But I would do it in all the cities you have been to, in the places where your reputation matters, where you ply your trade. I would do it where you were born, and where you lived now, and I would be able to do it because, my dear, exiled Baron of Kein, I am the eighty-second Samuel Orlan and I am not a common man, nor even a lowly lord like the late Alden of Ille. I am something else entirely.'

Across the dying fire, the saboteur met the other man's gaze and held it for such a time that when he blinked, his eyes stung.

'I once had trouble imagining what Heast thought when you stood in his office,' Bueralan said quietly. 'Once.'

'I *do* like you, Captain,' Samuel Orlan said, smiling as he did. 'I do hope, sincerely, that you do not die any time soon.'

11.

Two days after she left Bau, Ayae walked up the three creaking steps at the front of *Red Moon*, the hotel where Zaifyr was living.

The information had been delivered to her the evening before by a thin, neatly attired sandy-haired man who had knocked upon her door. He held an envelope in his hand and, after handing it to her, said, 'Compliments of Lady Wagan through Captain Heast.' Inside, in neat handwriting, was all the information she needed. She had not spoken with the Lady Wagan directly, but it appeared that no conversation – no apology – was necessary.

Inside the hotel, a large man sat behind a long desk. A painting of a naked, dancing white woman was on the wall above him, reds and blacks swirling around her. As Ayae drew closer, the man placed down a block of wood, a carving knife following it, and smiled, revealing the empty left side of his mouth. 'Welcome,' he said, pleasantly. 'We have rooms to rent, at discount prices if you are hired under Captain Heast and if you are part of the mercenary units here to defend the city.'

'I'm not here for a room,' she said. 'I'm here for the man in room nine.'

'That's a man who smells of awful things, if I may say so.' The man picked up his shapeless block of wood, revealing knife cuts across his hand. 'If you're looking for him at this moment, you'll find him down in the public bathroom, but I cannot promise that he is alone there.'

She smiled despite herself. 'That's very subtle of you.'

'We get all kinds here.' His unharmed hand picked up the carving knife. 'I take it you're not here on business?'

'Not that kind.'

He nodded to the hall to his left. 'There's a sofa on the second floor. He'll pass it on the way to his room.'

She thanked him and began climbing the stairs.

She did not have to wait long. Zaifyr appeared after she had found the old leather sofa and sank into its dented cushions. He was wearing black linen trousers and his bare feet moved lightly on the wooden floor. A faint half smile creased his lips as he approached her, towel and soap in hand. 'This is a surprise,' he said.

'Is it?' she countered.

'It has been a while since a woman called upon me.'

'Do you remember your manners, then, and are you going to invite me in?'

He held out his hand.

Ignoring it, she pushed herself up. After a brief walk down the hall, she stepped into his room. There was a bed, a table next to it, a chair, and an open window. There was a smell, also, a ripe one that was a blend of rotten garbage and burnt clothing. It was strong enough that she glanced at him with an upraised eyebrow. With his faint smile turning embarrassed, he said, 'I was wondering if there was a smell.'

'It's why women don't call on you often.'

'Thank you,' he said drily. 'The last few days have been rough on my clothing.'

'Have you been rolling around in garbage?'

'To a degree.' He motioned to the chair before the window, the moon's pale light held back by the lamp hanging there. 'You're best to sit here while we discuss why you're willing to make enemies out of Fo and Bau so quickly.'

At the open window, the smell was barely noticeable. Easing into the chair, she said, 'Is that what I've done?'

'Perhaps.'

'Perhaps?'

'The Keepers have their own way of doing things.' Zaifyr sat on the edge of his bed and, from the table next to it, took a copper chain and began to wind it around his wrist. 'The evolutionary path of a god is not one that you can find in a book, after all.'

'Do you believe that?'

'That I can find it in a book?'

'That you're a god.'

His thumb pressed against the end of the chain. 'No.'

She leaned back in the chair, her fingers lacing together in her lap. 'I don't know what to think,' she admitted. 'I have been told so many things – about curses, about gods, about life. Even you. They told me your name was Qian.'

'Once.'

'And that you were mad.'

He picked up a long copper chain and repeated, 'Once.'

'Should I discount what they say?'

'If you want.' The chain wrapped around his knuckles. 'I

don't have any answers either, if that is what you're looking for. I don't know why you're cursed. I don't know why the man at the front desk isn't. All I know is what time taught me: I will live a long time, which I am thankful for. As for the rest, well, I was once Qian, I once ruled one of the Five Kingdoms, and at the end of it, my brothers and sisters locked me in a madhouse for a thousand years. After that—'

'You will tell me there are no answers?'

'No, there are answers.' His green eyes met her own. 'But you come by them by removing every other choice, until there is only this choice for this moment.'

'Will you help me?'

She saw his hesitation, as if the bluntness of her question and the unadorned way she presented it surprised him. It surprised her as well. He was not the opposite of Bau: he was no more sure of his creation or his purpose than the Healer was. But neither was he Bau. When she met his gaze she saw her youth, her innocence and potential, and her promises that lingered like the smouldering beneath her skin. But she saw too his age, that length of a life that was so long that she could not begin to understand what he had seen, the changes he had lived through and the tiredness it had borne. As she held his gaze and felt on the verge of knowing a small, vital part of the man who, having once been a god, now wrapped himself in the ancient charms of the long dead, he smiled his half smile and the sly, cynic's humour returned, leaving her with but a glimpse of him.

'Yes,' he said.

In a Town Called Dirtwater

For a long time, there was nothing, nothing but the fading religions, the old rituals, the empty words. Nothing, until Jae'le, until myself—

Nothing until the first of the 'children'.

—Qian, *The Godless*

1.

For a week, Zaifyr did not leave *Red Moon.*

It had not been his plan to stay. He had meant to return to the foul-watered shaft and, with a long-handled hammer, begin breaking through the stone around the Temple of Ger.

Instead, he allowed Ayae to keep his attention. Her presence in the beer garden at the back of the hotel became a world that he and she occupied beneath the rise and fall of the three suns. At night, when she was gone, he would return to his room and note the progression of thick boards being erected across shopfront windows and doors. Slowly, Mireea was becoming uniform: a city of shut buildings and empty lanes, the divisions of economy washed away and falling into memory like the sprawl of markets. Each new building shut up was a part of Mireea lost, and soon he would also be gone. If he was not, he ran the risk of being drawn into the units that the Mireean Guard were making from citizens. That he had no desire for. He awoke to see their painful morning jog through the empty, cobbled streets, struggling beneath the weight of mismatched armour and swords they had been given, with either a bucket of water in each hand or a stretcher full of bricks between two. They followed the streets throughout the city all day, passing beneath all the wooden gates and crude wooden walls that divided the city, carrying out mock exercises that Heast issued from his position on the roof of *The Pale House*.

He might have stayed longer in the garden and forgotten his responsibilities were it not for the explosions that began to punctuate the day. Neither he nor Ayae knew what they were, but after she had left, he saw First – or was it Second? – carrying an empty pack covered in dirt walking along the streets. The small man squinted at him as he crossed the road, grunted a greeting and told him that Heast had ordered the tunnels down the mountain caved in and the road broken up. There appeared to be no immediate threat to Zaifyr's foul tunnel – it was too close to the city to be a defensive weakness, except to anyone who fell in – but still, before the first light of the morning's sun, he walked through the city gates with the weight of the hammer over his back, leaving his charms inside his hotel room.

The night before, he had told Ayae he would be gone for a few days. They had sat at the back of her house at a small wooden table, the light from the night sky piercing strongly through the cut-back trees.

'You should probably prepare yourself,' he said. 'I know you won't leave, but your preparations—'

'I have tidied my garden,' she said. 'I washed my walls down. I don't need to shut my windows up, lock myself away.'

'You've not fought in a war before.'

'But you have?'

'Many,' he admitted. 'After the gods had died, we had our own wars to divide up what they had left.'

'What was it like?'

'Eventually, it was terrible.'

'Eventually?'

He placed the empty glass he held on the table, the juice pulp a dark pattern to the lip. 'The first war I fought in was about survival. We were the Children of the Gods before we were anything else, and there were many who contested us. We fought for five hundred years, if you include the standoffs that were not peace. It mostly felt like years of survival, of making sure the people around me did not starve, had homes and weren't killed in streets or in fields.'

She struggled with his age, with the breadth of it. He knew that and tried to imagine it from her point of view, but couldn't. 'How did you manage with your – your—'

'Curse?' he finished.

'I am trying not to use the word,' she admitted, flushing.

He shrugged. 'Describe it how you want. Eventually you'll stop thinking of it as a different part of you. It changes you, yeah: and some more than others. For some, it kills them before they can experience it. For others, it makes them immortal. No one has known why, or why not, in either case. It's fickle. Random. And no matter what it does to you, you're left to manage it like everything else in your life.'

'Discipline.' She said the word slowly, as if tasting it. 'Everything is about discipline to you. You rely on nobody but yourself, do you realize that?'

At the mining shaft, Zaifyr lifted the wooden seal and dropped into the foul water. It was cool, not yet warmed by the three suns. The wooden shaft of the hammer caught on the ceiling of the tunnel twice, forcing him to push his fingers through the muddy silt to pull himself down.

'You're responsible for yourself,' he had replied, turning the pulp-splattered glass around in his hand. 'You tell me I speak of discipline and I tell you that I try, but fail regularly. That is how I ended up in a madhouse, because I failed at that. I thought I could do something for the dead, that I could bring them peace, but that was not what I could do for them. What I could do was to bear witness, to acknowledge their pain, and to acknowledge that I could do nothing. Why would I be given power for that? I struggled with that question for a long time, until I realized that the question itself was one that was flawed. I was not chosen. None of us are, and that is the hardest thing to accept. But it is what we must do, what I especially must do. That is the sacrifice that the world has demanded from me.'

Half a smile crossed her face. 'You speak as if the world was alive.'

'It is.' He leaned back, looked up at the sky. 'Look at everything around us, everything that is sustained without a god. We live on a giant living creature, so old it makes me feel young.'

'Could it not be a god itself?'

'It could.'

'But?' The other half of her smile emerged. 'There's always a but.'

He laughed, enjoying himself. 'But if so, why did it not take its place in the war?'

'I don't know.' She too looked up at the sky. 'Are there more worlds alive out there, do you think?'

'Not that I can feel.'

She turned her gaze to him.

'I can see it in the moon.' He touched the charm beneath

his wrist, once, twice. 'The moon is what remains of Sei. The shattered suns are his kingdom, but the moon, the moon is his form, huge and curled into a ball. If I focus on it, I can feel his pain and his anger. He is caught in a slow death, like all the gods – while, at the same time, being dead. What I sense is the haunt and the last parts of his life, merged together. At least, that is what I think. I know there is nothing left of his mind, just as there is nothing left of the others. Constant pain has destroyed any consciousness. They lash out at the only thing they can, the sense of another god, of another power – that being us.'

'I don't feel anything.'

'Sei is too far for any but me.'

'I don't feel Ger.'

One of the rungs in the ladder crumbled beneath his grasp, plunging him back into the water. Slowly, spitting out the foul liquid, Zaifyr pulled himself onto the stones and ran a hand through his hair, shaking it out. Ahead, the green light shone through the sliver in the wall, a hint that would grow until it illuminated the entire forgotten, haunted city.

'Bau said my senses were just overloaded. That he wasn't surprised, but – well, it makes me believe that you are all wrong.' Ayae let out a low breath after her words. 'That I am something else, something more or less.'

'The elements were not considered gods,' he replied. 'But in this, Bau has a point. The changes that you've gone through, that we all go through, do not happen in an empty space. He is overlooking the fact that you've lived here for so long that you simply may have grown used to the sensation of Ger around you. For most of us, we live with our power before we're aware of it. The lucky ones have it dawn on them, slowly. The unlucky ones – well, they're more like you. In a moment of danger, they emerge, and they lash out. That is why so many people fear the curses. But if you cannot feel another god, later, then your questions will be important and perhaps the answer will reveal more about Ger than we thought.'

'Like?'

'Understanding. With it, awareness.'

'But you just said—'

He smiled. 'I know.'

She shook her head, her smile rueful, and said, 'Would others think that? Is that why a Quor'lo would want to kill me?'

He told her he had no answer and the subject had changed, though this time it did so with his help. He had a lot to talk to her about: ideas, rules, stories. He told her what he knew of the others who had come before her. He did not hold back as he told them, nor encounter any of the cynicism and tiredness that he felt when conversing with his brothers and sisters. But he was conscious of the choice he made, the chill he felt and the questions that it opened up.

Questions that in the depths of the old, crumbling city, the haunt of a woman who was a new priest might know the answers for.

2.

The bread was two days old and it would be another three before she received a ration card to buy a new loaf, but despite that Ayae was content, if not yet happy.

A large part of it was due to Zaifyr. He had not been able to explain her curse – no, not her curse, *her*, it was her now – and said it was more than likely that Bau was right, that inside her was the remains of Fire, the elemental charge of Ger. 'What literature I have read said that he was considered the Warden of the Elements,' the charm-laced man said. 'He did not create them, but before him, the elements were wild. There were storms of fire and wind and water, all of which would hammer the land, and earthquakes that swallowed nations. After his death, there was some of that, but mostly, the elements continued as they had before, and the mystery of what exactly Ger did was born.' The ease with which he answered her questions, the honesty he spoke with – in relation not just to her, but to the gods, the Keepers, and all other immortals – had left her with her first sense of normality since Orlan's shop had caught fire.

She had even gained a small semblance of control over her

curse – over her*self* – and the burning sensation beneath her skin.

'I can't make a flame,' she said to him the day before he left as they sat in the garden behind his hotel, the midday's sun shining through the cut-back branches. 'But I can heat myself up. I can change my body temperature without changing my emotions. That's all, though. I feel like I should be able to do more, that I should have more control. It's frustrating. I feel like I could prove something to myself, to everyone, if I could just say for certain what I could do.'

'It takes time.' He used his lazy, mocking smile. 'But maybe you could ask Bau for some of his special help? I'm sure he'd do it, if you used that charm of yours.'

To demonstrate her charm, Ayae made a rude gesture.

Yet for all that she enjoyed his company, there were times when she felt out of her depth, as if she were standing beside an object so large that she could not view it all at once. She felt that way when he talked of his incarceration, his madness, and when he talked of the gods. Zaifyr had told her that Ger had sunk to his knees and began building the mountain, his cairn, after he had suffered a dying blow. She was struck not by how melancholy he sounded, but how the green of his gaze showed tiny lines across his iris like the fractures of a giant jigsaw puzzle; pieces of such a diverse set of experiences, lives and moments that she felt no more than a child.

'Ger spoke for fifty-seven years as he built his burial mound. Priests gathered in tent cities around him and recorded every word he spoke. They wrote and rewrote and translated his words for hundreds of years, turning them into prophecies and morals,' he told her. 'The Temples of Ger came later, during the Five Kingdoms. There were always the remains of the gods, and always the remains of their belief, and no matter how hard we fought to stamp it out, to remove it, it would remain. Eventually, we learned to turn a blind eye to the edges of it, and that is when the Cities of Ger were built. The priests and their followers cut through the rock, down to his body, to listen for his voice again, to wait for when he arose. He had said that he would speak once more, before the end, apparently.'

'But he hasn't?'

'None have.'

There was a knocking on the door behind her. Bread knife in hand, she crossed the floor and found Reila standing in the morning's sun. 'May I come in?' the healer said.

She stepped back. 'Of course.'

'Do you mind if I sit?' The healer was pale outside the sun. 'I am afraid that all this running around lately has worn me out.'

'You don't look well,' Ayae said.

'Just late nights and early mornings.' The small woman settled herself in Ayae's chair. 'But you, my dear, look positively lovely — and I am pleased to see that your house has been repaired as well. Have you had any troubles?'

She had not. At best, her neighbours were withdrawn, silent to her where they had once not been, but given the preparations going on in the city she was not surprised, and said so as she returned the bread knife to the kitchen. She opened her ice chute and pulled out a bottle of water, the cold drifting off her hand as she poured a glass. The faint wisps still trailed off her as she handed it to Reila.

'I have been meaning to come and see both you and Lady Wagan,' Ayae said. 'I wanted to both thank you and apologize for my behaviour the other week.'

Taking the glass, Reila waved her free hand. 'You were going through a lot.'

'Still.'

'Still,' the healer repeated, 'I do hear that you have made friends with another in the city, since then.'

'Thank you for the letter.'

'It was Captain Heast.' The kindness in Reila's tone remained, though with her words a slow awareness began to dawn in Ayae that she wanted something from her. 'The captain speaks well of him, though he claims he is not much of a fighter.'

'His name is Zaifyr.'

'The captain has wanted to speak to you for two days about your friendship with him,' she continued. 'Heast says that Zaifyr often leaves before a battle, that it is near impossible to make him stay, but we would like him to do so. I know it puts you in a difficult position, however. I understand that. So does Lady Wagan. But we wanted to help you, and he — I fear he is the best for that at the moment, and he is helping, yes?'

She hesitated. 'Yes.'

'Good, for we all need help.'

Caught off guard and surprised by the naked need in Reila's voice, Ayae did not know how to respond. She had assumed that the Mireean Army and the mercenaries would be able to wait out the siege, would be able to wear down the force that was coming. It would be difficult: the memories of her childhood had broken walls scattered across Sooia, broken by the Innocent, left with the corpses, left with the desecration of land and flesh that could be attributed only to him, and she knew what those memories did to people behind the walls, to those fighting to stay alive.

The glass in Reila's hand began to tremble. Raising her free hand, she wrapped it round the glass. 'Do you know,' she said, finally, 'that Fo and Bau refer to him as Qian?'

'Yes,' Ayae said softly.

'It is an old name,' the other woman continued. 'I have only the smallest knowledge of it myself, but once it was said he was powerful. So powerful that he outlawed the use of blood magic and killed those who practised it – for a brief time, at any rate. Since then the practice has grown stronger, though there are some who refuse to kill any creature to use it.'

'I—'

'I'm sorry, this makes you uncomfortable.'

'Yes, but . . .' She hesitated. 'I don't think that the memories of that time give him any pleasure.'

'Anything he could do would be *very* appreciated.'

Ayae hesitated, then said. 'He will not fight for us.'

Reila nodded but said nothing, and Ayae, her earlier happiness tarnished, watched as the slick dew of the glass fell to her floor.

3.

The Leeran Army lay across the humid marshland, its tall wooden siege towers stretching stunted fingers above the canopies while heavy catapults, horses, cattle, camp fires and people sprawled like debris around the fifty buildings.

It was the largest army that Bueralan had seen. Standing on a muddy rise and with a metal spyglass in his hand, he shifted his gaze from tower to tower, observing not the people, but the material, the mismatched wood and the paint that tried to create a sense of unity, to hide what they had cannibalized to make all fifty structures. Some were obviously parts from houses, but others were the sides of factories, barns, silos. 'Three years without trade,' he said to Zean. 'That's what Lady Wagan told me. You think two years of stockpiling, then a year of breaking everything down to make these?'

'And the catapults.'

He hadn't looked at those. His glass eye slid down the long tail of the army, where bulls were being used to pull the siege weapons. He counted eleven, made similarly. 'They won't do much damage going up the side of Ger's Spine.' Behind the catapults were livestock: pigs and cattle and sheep, penned at the moment, kept in place by dog and man. 'But once there . . .'

Beside him, Zean lowered his spyglass. 'How did Heast not know more?'

Bueralan thought the same thing. Two days ago, they had encountered the razor-wire chain fence that ran across the border of Leera and that had, as Heast said, gone some way to explaining why they knew so little. A long string of dignitaries and their guards were strapped to the fence, most with their throats slit. On each of them, wilted letters of introduction had been sewn into the skin. It was difficult to tell how long they had been strung up on the country's border but Liaya, poking at each with her long fingers, said that they were at most three months old. 'The humidity makes it hard to be sure,' she had said. 'But they've not joined the bones on the ground, yet.'

That was the best answer any of them had, but it was not enough. 'Bad magic,' Ruk muttered sleepily as they sat around their cold camp the night before and discussed the fires on the horizon. 'Why are we even discussing it? It has the smell of blood all over it.'

'It's easy to make a country look like it is experiencing a civil war,' Bueralan said, lowering his own spyglass. 'It's easy to hide what people are hearing.'

'That's a big army in front of us. You spill a lot of blood in a nation to hide that, and more to hide that you spilt it.'

'You don't have to spill blood. Every revolution we have been part of, or broken up, has been spread out among the city as if it was nothing out of the ordinary. Bits here and there, nothing too suspicious, a bit of misdirection. You know that as well as I do. The patrols we've come across returning to the main body could be nothing but that.'

For the week after they had left the Mireea and entered Leera, Dark had not seen much. Beside the corpses on the border it had mostly been heat, still bodies of water and insects. On the third day of the second week, however, they came across a small band of raiders: six men, none of them worth much of a fight. They didn't have much in the way of belongings, but their teeth had been filed down to points, a self-mutilation that spoke of cannibalism. They avoided two more groups after that: Aerala picked up the trails early and led Dark around the raiders or into a quiet corner to let them pass. In those groups there was nothing to suggest a wildness, a departure from the morals that all men and women shared or the degeneration of a civilized mind. There had been, instead, a stillness and a quiet as they rode back into Leera.

If that wasn't enough, the first village that they rode into with marshland mist clinging to them helped Bueralan's argument. In the morning's sun, Dark had ridden past stripped houses, their frames bare like browned skeletons, the grass long and untended, the vegetable and garden patches overgrown and smelling of ripe, rotten fruit and vegetables. But for all that, there was no sense of destruction, no bones, no marks of fire.

'A civilian army.' Zean spat. 'That's the last thing you want to walk into.'

Bueralan did not reply. It would take years to train an entire nation, years to fashion them into a military force, but if they had done it . . . There were between thirty and forty thousand people throughout the countryside, three times what he believed Mireea held, and that was men and women of fighting age. But Bueralan had seen not just young men and women, but older ones; in his glass eye he had tracked an elderly man wearing a green-and-brown-streaked cloak with a matching tabard walking around a siege tower, examining the wheels.

'Nothing changes,' he said, finally. 'I want you to start back-tracking, seeing to the wells and water holes, the bridges that they will likely take.'

'And you still mean to go to Dirtwater?'

'I know you don't like the idea.'

'Does anyone like it?'

No.

Bueralan pushed his way through the grey brush, moving slowly down the muddy decline to the cold camp Dark kept. Kae and Aerala had removed as much of their tracks as best they could, though it would not stop a decent tracker, but not much would. Before him, Liaya sat on a log, working through her bags, while behind her slept Ruk. On the edge of the camp stood Samuel Orlan and his ancient pony, his mouth still wearing the frown that had appeared last night after he had heard the saboteur's plan.

'Well?' Aerala asked.

'Nothing has changed.' He pushed the spyglass together. 'Orlan and I will head down to Dirtwater and the rest of you can start working. Don't worry, I've done this before.'

'Why not me instead?' Kae asked in his quiet, assured voice. 'I could go alone. I would be less of a loss if this general is a powerful warlock.'

'You would not be less of a loss,' he replied. 'Now, I know

none of you like it, but we are being paid to find out who is leading this army – and there is not a better way for us to do it.'

'We should already know, Bueralan.'

That was the real problem. General Waalstan was an empty name, one step above being no name at all, with all the descriptions of him or who he was nothing more than rumours. It had been a problem when he had spoken first to Lady Wagan, when he had seen the Quor'lo. It had not changed since they had entered Leera and not one member of Dark liked the idea of being blind. They liked it even less when there was no clear way out if things turned sour. He had taught them too well, taught them risk and reward, and they saw no reward for the risk in this particular plan.

But he did.

Before Orlan had joined them, he had planned to sneak into the army, to find a way to slip into the back of it, a member of Dark here and there, learning what they could from the unranked end of the army. It was a risky plan, but with Orlan, Bueralan could be brought into the camp and introduced to the general, perhaps given dinner, and then sent on his way in the morning to rejoin the others. The reputation of Samuel Orlan would protect him, would ensure his safety: the cartographer was such a prize that no general would look critically at the horse he rode in on.

Not even one who had made an army from a nation.

'You don't have to like it,' he told them. 'I don't like it much either, but we have questions we need answers for. Now, wake up Ruk, and start moving. You all have a lot of ground to cover.'

4.

After they had left, Bueralan pulled himself onto his horse and waited for Orlan. The cartographer's pale-blue gaze had watched the others leave, following each into the marsh. He had stared into the trees long after they had gone.

'It'll be fine,' Bueralan said. 'They worry about nothing.'

'I did not agree to this,' the old man said quietly.

'You want to ride with us, then you don't get to avoid the risks. Besides, this is just a bait and switch. We drop you in and later we pull you out. If it gets to be a problem, we'll pay your ransom.'

'And if there is none?'

'There's always a ransom.'

'In an ordinary army, yes.'

Bueralan did not reply. Orlan's barb came on the heels of his own doubt, but he did not plan to discuss it with the cartographer. There was little other choice anyway, he told himself as he nudged his horse toward the start of the thin trail leading out of their camp. After a moment, Orlan pulled himself into the pony's saddle and they made their way down the trail.

In truth, Samuel Orlan had not proved to be a difficult companion, not even after the first night when Bueralan had asked him to leave. He had gone out of his way to be of use, providing quiet trails, knowledge of the area, and doing his fair share of the cooking and watch. Indeed, until the night before when Bueralan had said that he planned to use him as bait to meet the commander, the cartographer had been easygoing and witty. The sisters took to him immediately, Ruk shortly after. Kae and Zean had been won over before they led the horses carefully over the barbed-wire fence that marked the Leeran border, and that had surprised him. Both had been uneasy with the inclusion of the man when he told them. Yet now it seemed to Bueralan that he was the only one who retained a healthy distance from the man.

They reached Dirtwater before the second sun had reached its zenith. It was easy to find. A large trading town, the first of three stops on the way to Ranan, the capital of Leera. According to Orlan, the town had been founded by the first settlers. They had built it believing that they were close to a fresh water supply only to find that the river behind was stagnant, more bog than stream. According to the old cartographer, enough bodies lay in there that if you drained it, you would find entire generations stretching back to the War of the Gods. Despite that, a town had sprung up with a huge wooden wall encircling it.

Not any more, though. On first sight it was clear that the wall had been stripped, leaving only the skeleton to form a ring, like a warped halo, around the overgrown village. The buildings had suffered a similar fate, though three had been made from solid logs that must have proved too thick and heavy to move, for they stood complete in lonely positions through the town, dark and immovable. On the peaked roofs of each sat black swamp crows, the murder the thickest there, though they were by no means sparse on the warped skeletons of the stripped buildings.

The road had been left in place. Made from thick stones and weaving through the village, it was the only sign left that Dirtwater had been a sizeable or even successful town. Their slow ride through the village did not reveal any other signs of wealth: no livestock, no silos, no blacksmith, no stables, absolutely nothing but the husks of what had once been a life, now overgrown and owned by silent, watching crows.

'Bueralan,' Orlan said softly. 'To your right.'

A man.

An old white man, more bones than skin, more grey hair than bones or skin. 'You ain't got no business here!' He stood half in the doorway, his face pressed against the door frame of one of the three solid houses, the second sun's light barely reaching past his bare toes, bony knees, thin chest, and matted beard. 'You need to leave! You both need to leave!'

'Why don't you come out.' Bueralan swung off the horse. 'Tell me what happened in this town.'

The old man shrank into the darkness of the building.

'Do you have anyone in there with you, old man?'

'Soldiers!'

Behind him, Orlan said, 'Let it be. You'll get nothing from this one.'

Bueralan didn't reply. Instead, he stepped closer to the building. 'If there are soldiers in there, they should come out.' He dropped a hand to the hilt of his axe. 'I have a man to sell.'

'No one,' came the old man's scream, 'sells Samuel Orlan!' Bueralan glanced back.

'Why are you persisting in this?' the cartographer asked, disgust evident in his tone.

'He knows you.' Bueralan took another step forward, then another. On his third step, the old man inside the hut screamed, but before he could get deeper into the hut the saboteur was there, his fingers snatching the tattered remains of his shirt, ripping it until the old man broke free with a harsh thud on the floor and scampered further into the darkness.

With his eyes adjusting to the light, Bueralan could make out faint shapes across the floor, shapes that became ridged, became bones: bird bones, swamp crows. Black feathers littered the ground around each pile and, as his eyes grew more accustomed to the light, he saw not a few piles, which the old man broke through as he scampered to the back of the building, but hundreds.

The old man had been eating them for months, for a year, for longer.

'Have you no place to go?' Bueralan asked. 'The army doesn't want you?'

'I have to hide!' He was shouting, had not even heard the words. 'I can't be seen! If Samuel can find me, then the general can! Then *she* can!'

'Who can?'

With a wordless scream, the old man launched himself forward. He caught the saboteur off guard, pushed him to the ground, then leapt up and burst out of the door. Bueralan was quick to follow him. His fitness was enough to bridge the gap, but as he leaned forward to crash into the old man, he heard

Orlan's voice. Heard him call his name, heard him shout it with so much force he stopped and turned.

Turned to the eight soldiers who had just entered Dirtwater. Five white men and three white women. They each wore the same green-and-brown cloak, each had their hand on a sword or a crossbow.

Leeran soldiers.

It was not the first impression he had hoped for.

5.

The haunt Oyia circled the Temple of Ger slowly, her body lit by the violent light above.

Zaifyr could hear her voice, softly repeating that she was cold and hungry as he swam out to the half-submerged structure but lost track of it — and her — after he hooked his first metal spike into the wall. It was a much more difficult job than he had thought: the smooth rock had to be broken by a hammer too awkward and too big to easily slam in the spike. Still, he managed a first, then a second and third. But rather than hang from the wall to hammer in a fourth, he pulled himself gracelessly onto the top.

The once charm-laced man lay beneath the red light and raised his hand, holding it up against it. It sank into the skin, colouring him, changing him. A child who had been born in the City of Ger would have spent years without knowing the natural colour of their own skin. It reminded him strongly of the early years of his life, where children were raised on the faltering beliefs of their parents. In the company of Jae'le, Zaifyr had passed ocean-side villages where children were born in the settling black blood of the Leviathan and a series of small cities where the left hand of a child was maimed in deference to Aeisha, the goddess of literature. As he rose from his position, the memory of them did not remove the queerness of light above him, nor leave him feeling less apprehensive about what he would find when he broke open the shell. Still, with his hand curling around the wooden shaft of the hammer, it did not stop him from striking the stone either.

After the third strike, he heard the haunt beneath him: 'You think to break it open like a clumsy child with a coin jar?'

'Yes,' he admitted.

'This will anger Ger,' she said. 'Are you not afraid?'

'No.'

But he was afraid, though his fear had nothing to do with Ger. It came from the ease with which he spoke to the haunt, by the familiarity of it and the whisper of his soul that said to do otherwise was to deny his very being.

He swung the hammer a fourth time.

That strike left a mark, a faint crack, but it was long and arduous work for more to appear, for a spider's web of crafts to emerge around his bare feet. Strong as he was − stronger than most − Zaifyr was not his brother, Eidan. The huge man's patient and methodical mind hid the strength that would have broken through the stone in half the time that it would take Zaifyr. It had been he who carried Zaifyr to the crooked tower, to his prison. He who had held him as the others built. He had not been aware of that − he could remember only constraint − but the haunts had told him so, had murmured in their brief moments of lucidity about his captivity without and within. They had said that Eidan stood still for five days, that he held Zaifyr in his grasp like a child, both unmoving, both silent.

Zaifyr had seen him only once since he was released from his tower, travelling to where the huge man lived in the ruins of his birth, rebuilding it painstakingly like a model.

Easing the hammer down, he stepped close to the edge and gazed down. 'Oyia.' The haunt returned his stare. 'Why did you attack Orlan's shop?'

'I did not know it was his shop,' she said. 'I would not have wanted to anger *him*.'

'Few would, but you did because . . . ?'

'I was told to do so. There was a girl inside.'

'Who told you?'

'*She* did.'

The nameless girl, the child in Oyia's memory. There could be no one else for the haunt. But who was she? Zaifyr remembered her gaze, how it had not been new, but not yet ancient. *Like me. Like me when I was young.* 'How did she know Ayae was there?'

'She *knew*.'

He went down on his knees, his hand reaching for the charm that was not beneath his wrist. 'Did she know I was there?'

'I do not know.' A ripple in the water passed beneath the haunt's body, distorting her for but a moment. 'She did not say so, if she did. My first awareness of you was when I lay on the pyre, trying to remove myself strand by strand from that body. I felt you and the Keepers, then, as well as her.'

'You were fractured,' he explained. 'Your awareness was drifting between two states of being—'

'I could sense Ger, as well.'

'You would have, yes.'

He had begun to tell her that it was the transcendence of flesh to spirit that had done it, that she had glimpsed the part of the world that had been made in the War of the Gods, but he stopped. She would struggle to understand him. It was difficult to convey that in absence there existed the definable sense of the world, the universe and them. But she would not retain what he said. He would tell her the same words again an hour later, and the hour after that.

Instead, he asked, 'Why did you attack the girl in Orlan's shop?'

'She said I could defeat the girl.' She was uncomfortable, shifting from foot to foot in the water, her tread without mark. 'She said that she did not even know about her power.'

'That does not explain why.'

She did not reply.

'Oyia.'

'I do not know,' she whispered.

'Oyia,' Zaifyr replied softly. 'A name *does* have power.'

Her mouth twisted, firmly shut.

'Oyia.' Persuasive, a hint of pressure on her being. 'Oyia, tell me, what did you plan to do with the girl?'

'She wanted me to bring her back!' she snarled. 'She said there were many like her, many who just didn't know – and she wanted to know if I had the power to take her!'

Zaifyr's hand touched the part of his wrist where a charm had rested only hours before. He went to press another question – to ask why *she* wanted her back (and where back was, exactly) – but the words did not emerge. As quickly as Oyia's anger had risen, it had gone, drained from her frail form and lost in the dark water beneath her feet. She turned and began to circle the placid lake, her words faint whispers of hunger and cold, her mind taken by the need inside her, a need that would consume her, unless he wanted to use his own power – power he was already uncomfortable with having used.

Lifting the hammer, Zaifyr returned to work.

6.

Heast wanted to speak to her. Before she had left her house, before she had parted ways with the healer, and in an attempt to divert the conversation away from Zaifyr, Ayae had asked Reila who the captain had sent to her, though she knew the answer. Deep in her stomach, she knew it. 'It was a mistake,' the elderly woman said. 'Heast makes them rarely, and this one was a man's mistake. Do not hold it against him.'

She replayed the words as she approached Illaan, two blocks from her house.

He sat behind a wooden table in the middle of a cobbled road, surrounded by ration booklets and boxes of canned and dried food. He had not shaved since she had last seen him, but the stubble on his jaw did not lend him the air of a veteran soldier. Rather, she thought him the parody of one. He was too tall, his facial features too neat. Ayae had always thought of him as a man with an air of culture about him, a soldier who did not draw his sword but fought with laws and politics and economics. But seeing him now, she realized that the opposite was true: that Illaan did not fight with knowledge or intelligence, but with fear and with force.

She had always thought well of him, from the first time she had met him, in Mireea's large, sprawling Saturday market. She had been standing with Faise, listening to her friend haggle over a brown- and gold-flecked dress. Lost in people watching, Ayae saw Illaan emerge onto the narrow path that weaved between the stalls, but it was not until he greeted the merchant by name and, with a few words, cut in half the price Faise had been bargaining over that she gave him more attention than she had anyone else. Later, he told her that he had made up the price with the merchant, had used it only to meet her.

He knew everything and everyone within Mireea and within months his knowledge of her was just as complete. He knew not to ask about the memories of her parents, about if she had seen the Innocent, about the orphanage or Samuel Orlan; but he knew how to spell her name, how to pronounce it and how to make her laugh. It was his own background that taught him that: he was the third son from a family of wine merchants in Yeflam, the son whose father had purchased him a commission in the trade capital of the world on his sixteenth birthday, to educate him and prepare him a place in the family business a decade later.

He saw her now, as she approached his table, but did not rise. He held her gaze, then turned to the two guards behind him, the first tall and young, the second older, solid, grey going to fat. She did not hear his words, but they were about her. The latter man shook his head. To that, Illaan said, 'You'll do as I say.'

'He'll do what?' she asked.

He did not turn.

'I don't want to fight, Illaan.' The words surprised her, the ease of them suggesting a truth. 'I was told you were meant to find me.'

He kept his back to her.

Finally, the older guard said, 'Sergeant, the girl—'

'You're wrong, Corporal. She's not a girl.'

'Look at me when you say that,' Ayae said.

'She is *cursed*.' He turned and, for a moment, she did not recognize the man before her. But just for a moment. 'And we need not help those who defy the natural laws of the world.'

'I didn't know that you had begun defining what was natural and what was not.'

'The world is not unknown to me.'

Despite herself, she laughed.

He spat.

Her hand, when she lifted it to her face, when her index finger caught the spittle that ran down her cheek, was warm.

'Sergeant—'

'I am really,' Illaan said in a quiet, controlled voice, 'really not interested in what you have to say, Corporal. Look into her eyes. Look and you will see what she is.'

'Can I do the same for *you*, Sergeant?'

The voice came from a newcomer. A woman stepped past Ayae, tall, strikingly pale with short black hair. She wore a mix of boiled leather and chain mail, the dye a faded black. At her side she wore a long sword, the scabbard one of simple, aged leather. Behind her came two men, both of a similar age to the corporal, but where he had begun to run to fat, these men, twice his size, were as much muscle and greying beard as they were leather and chain. Over their backs they held

281

large weapons, the one on the left a huge two-handed sword, the one on the right an equally large axe.

'It is amazing what comes out of the son of a Traders Union official from Yeflam,' she continued. 'You would almost think that fear had become a political currency to be used against a ruling class.'

'This is none of your concern, Meina,' Illaan growled. 'It's no concern to any mercenary.'

'I outrank you considerably, Sergeant,' the woman said. 'You would do well to remember that when addressing me.'

He spat on the ground.

Ayae's flat palm connected with his chest.

Illaan hit the wall behind him.

The mercenary crossed to where Illaan lay and crouched over the smouldering remains of his leather chest piece. The imprint of Ayae's palm was deeply burnt into the armour. Meeting her gaze, the tall woman said, 'I think I like you.'

Beneath her, Illaan groaned. Meina's hand slapped his bruised chest. 'I would stay down, if I were you, Sergeant,' she said pleasantly. 'In fact, I wouldn't get up until myself and your girl are gone. Even then I might consider staying down. I can only imagine what your captain will say after he hears about this.'

7.

'Just a mercenary,' the exiled Baron of Kein said. 'That's all.'

He had not given up his weapons, but he had not been asked to do so. Nor was he chained or guarded, though the eight soldiers circled both Orlan and himself. But they did so loosely, informally.

Bueralan understood why. Unlike the raiders, the five men and three women around him had armour made from polished chain mail and oiled leather, all of it well cared for and sitting with a seasoned ease on each. And, while there were no bars of rank on any of them, it was clear that the seven took their orders from a brown-haired man of indeterminate age, whose tanned face could be at any point past his youth, but who moved with a swiftness and ease that suggested that the activities of those in the summer of their strength were not beyond him.

He called himself Dural and offered no rank and no affiliation. 'A mercenary with Samuel Orlan?' He was the only one of the eight to have dismounted and he stood before the saboteur, a full head shorter. 'For ransom.'

The way the word *ransom* emerged from his thin lips did not sit well with the saboteur. 'I was hired in Mireea.' However, he could not change his lie now. 'I didn't think much of the work, but there is not a lot for men like me in Mireea.'

'Men like you?'

'I don't know how to fight in a siege.' He shrugged nonchalantly. 'I don't want no trouble. This is just a simple transaction to me.'

'Do you always betray your employers so quickly?'

'I am always honest to myself, first.'

That was a mercenary's answer, an answer Dural could accept with a grunt. Glancing around the saboteur's shoulder to the cartographer, he said, 'Not your day, old man.'

Orlan was silent.

'Will I need irons?'

'No,' he said, finally.

The soldier nodded. 'Both of you on your horses, then. We'll take you to the general.'

It was not right. Bueralan pulled himself into the saddle, glanced at Orlan, but the old man did not meet his gaze. He knew as well, the saboteur was sure of that. He knew there was something wrong with this, a gut-level reaction, but he knew that the die was cast now. Bueralan's horse moved slowly along the road, Orlan and his old pony behind him, the silence of Dirtwater lingering until they rode through the dismantled fence, and the swamp crows lifted into the air in a series of screeching calls.

The soldiers did not react to the sound. They followed the trail as it narrowed into single file and became overgrown, two hours of a solid pace until the trail ballooned and the sound of people began to emerge. It was a growing susurration of voices and pots being packed, of the stamps of horses and the bark of dogs, of pigs and cows and more.

The Leeran Army soon appeared as he was led through low, green-grey trees, and it defied his gaze. He could not take the size of it in easily: it was too much for a single man, too large, too complex to make a quick appraisal of. It was much larger, much more diverse than what he had seen in the morning, but riding through it there was no sense of disorganization. There was a sense of everything being where it should. A hundred horses greeted him first, lightly armoured soldiers feeding and rubbing them down. Lean, young, eager. They saluted Dural as he passed and he greeted them by name, with nods and smiles. Wagons followed, more than Bueralan could clearly identify in the density that grew around him. The livestock was similar, but here the saboteur could count the stockhands easily, since they numbered three. Two men and one woman, each with whips and dogs.

More soldiers followed.

Bueralan's hand tightened on his reins. Around him, the cannibalized building materials were clear: long fence palings, thatches from roofs, doors, and more. But for all that the siege towers and wagons and catapults were an uneven collection, the men and women he passed were not. Not one was of a skin colour other than white, and in most the saboteur saw a commonality that suggested a nationalism – surely they were bonded by more than military organization? They were, he was sure, a civilian army and more. As he was led deeper and deeper into the press, he thought it possible that they may well be a nation, but the organization and discipline that defined them did not sit well with him. He had not yet seen anyone who, through armour or insignia, revealed themselves to be part of the chain of command.

Until he was led into a small opening. It was dominated by a large, solid-oak map table, the size of it suggesting that it would take four or more people to move it, and not the tall, middle-aged man who stood over it.

In appearance, he was not a distinctive man. Much like Dural, the man at the table was a white man with brown eyes and brown hair; his face was neither blessed nor cursed with a trait that left it memorable in either grace or ugliness. There was no sense, either, that the man was a warlock, that blood had ever stained his hands. There was a quality about the men and women who used such power, a blemish in their gaze, as if each had seen a part of the world that those who did not draw from the dying could not possibly begin to understand, and there was no such look in the eyes of the man before him. If anything, his was the face of a clear and honest man.

Dural stepped from his mount. 'My General.'

'Lieutenant.' The man wore a white shirt and brown leather trousers, with no weapon in sight. 'What do you have there?'

'A mercenary — ' Bueralan's hands refused to release the reins ' — who has brought us Samuel Orlan.'

The general's smile was faint. 'Is that true, Samuel?'

Behind him, Bueralan heard Orlan slide from his saddle. On either side of him, the horses of Dural's soldiers shifted and the weight of their riders, followed by their steel grasps, closed in on his still limbs. 'I am afraid my hand has been played early,' the cartographer said, walking up to the man before him. 'For that I do apologize.'

'You are unharmed?'

'But for my pride.' Orlan turned, his cold blue eyes meeting Bueralan's. 'The cost of it does present a small gift though. Perhaps you have heard of Captain Bueralan Le, of the saboteur group Dark?'

8.

He pushed the stone, felt it give and heard it hit the water. A cascade of smaller stones followed, sounding in hollow splashes that tore a jagged line down the side of the Temple of Ger.

The building was rotten, both in appearance and smell. Made from brick and wood, the latter having turned black, decay leaving its grasp like a handprint on the stone where the two met. In a crack not wide enough for him to drop through, Zaifyr saw that the tall windows had broken inwards, the discoloured glass shattering across the ground on impact.

'You are about to violate something very holy, Qian.'

'A haunt does not learn.' Zaifyr settled his gaze on her. 'Once, I wanted to explain to the dead what was happening to them. I thought it would be easier to do so. But the truth is your kind will take in no more after you have died. Every idea, every belief, every moral is trapped in you, like a bug caught in amber. You will not remember this conversation, just as you will not remember the one before.'

'I remember all that is important.'

He hooked his hand around a sharp edge of stone. 'Look inside and tell me that Ger is alive.'

She did not move. 'Your kind has always lied.'

'If you were capable of learning you would ask why it is that you barely felt Ger, why he was so faint, here in his mountain.' The stone broke, fell into the water. 'You have more ability now to know that than you ever did in life.'

'I have faith.'

'Faith is a very subjective emotion.'

Standing, Zaifyr picked up the hammer. It felt heavy in his hands. He was tired, but he brought the end down on the weakening edge of the stone. After another two blows enough of the rotting window was revealed that he could carefully drop into the building, a prospect that did not excite him. He felt no threat from within, either from Ger or from anything else that might live within the darkness, and it was exactly that absence which troubled him.

He lowered himself from the ledge slowly, using his wedges as handholds as his bare feet searched for a perch on the window and finding none until his toes touched glass-covered stone. Wet, slippery. He dislodged the shards before letting it take his weight, his tired arms trembling from the effort.

The haunt drew closer to him, the red from her chest rising and diminishing as she stepped out of the ceiling's crude light. She did not make a move to speak and Zaifyr, his hands searching for holds that were not crumbling, did not try. Once he had secured himself, he used her light to stare into the darkness of the temple.

There were rotting pews and, to the left, a broken dais. He could make out only the edges of other items, shapes hinted at in the dark that teased the imagination.

Pushing himself forward, Zaifyr dropped to the ground, the

momentum carrying him to his knees. His hands pressed deep into cold, slippery mud.

There was glass beneath his feet and he tried to avoid it, but did not succeed. Within two steps, his left foot had two shallow cuts. Ignoring the wounds he stared ahead at the dark that, with the faint light of the haunt no longer being blocked by his body, revealed more to him than it had previously done.

'You are not welcome.'

From the dark: guttural, barely understandable.

'You are not welcome.'

He approached the voice, the mud sliding between his toes, the edges of glass threatening to cut him again. He passed the outline of a rotting pew. Before him, a figure began to take shape. He saw a bestial head that could have once belonged to any canine creature, but which was defined by the length of a wolf's nose and the dull, bared teeth of the same animal. It was made from steel, however, a suit of armour cast for a figure much larger than human.

'You are not—'

Zaifyr's hand touched the cold metal mid-sentence and the helmet toppled, landing to his left with a clatter. The suit followed, sprawling across the ground. Whoever – whatever – had owned the ancient armour was gone, dead. Perhaps. Perhaps it had fled, leaving once it realized that Ger had no power over it, that the binds that once held it in place as a guardian were broken, that after servitude for millions of years it was free.

9.

His eyes adjusted to the dark, easier now that the haunt had drifted into the temple behind him. She had pushed through the shattered remains of the shell that she had broken apart against earlier, but he knew that she would not appreciate the feat. Zaifyr wondered if the sight of the decay, the crumbling remains of everything that had been enclosed, was a shock to her – but this, he did not ask. He wanted to keep her glow as light, so that he was not forced to resort to using the haunts that were trapped inside.

He could feel them brushing against his skin, dozens, hundreds. Yet the strength of Ger remained the same.

Thousands of years ago, in the twilight of the Five Kingdoms, the God of Truth, Wehwe, had inspired a cult. Blame – the name his followers had adopted after his fall – had come to the edges of Asila and tried to move the slim, brown-skinned god from where he knelt, but had discovered that Wehwe's skin burnt at their touch. It scalded them, but did more: it created a heat without fire beneath their skin, a heat that consumed them. In response, they had purged the land of settlements a hundred miles in every direction around him.

291

By the time Zaifyr walked into the dense forest, Blame was long dead, torn apart by Aela Ren, the Innocent. It had been that act that had finally drawn Zaifyr to investigate, for Ren had been a man who had spent the years after the gods' deaths without a single death being attributed to him. Zaifyr had never met him – the Innocent had gone to some lengths to avoid the Five Kingdoms – but in the rare moments that he heard about the man, he heard stories that were more myth than reality. He heard of scars, of wounds that wept, of one man, and of half a dozen men with one name. What was consistent was that he claimed to be the inheritor of Wehwe's power. But until Blame, he'd shown nothing of it. Zaifyr had returned to his brothers and sisters with the story of how the cult had been murdered, having laid down arms first. Since it had been so isolated, and Aela Ren such a notoriously difficult figure to find, they had agreed to do nothing, to watch, to wait. Perhaps they had been wrong to do that, since later, Zaifyr learned that the Innocent had begun his war in Sooia shortly after he had been locked in his crooked tower for three hundred years.

But on the day he had approached Wehwe, as he walked the rough road to his still form, Zaifyr had felt the god's awareness, the primal acknowledgement.

It was difficult to explain just what the dying god felt towards him. When Zaifyr reached out to touch him there was pain, but there was always pain. In that, all the gods were the same, though he had yet to reach any understanding as to why that was. He did not understand how it was that time could move differently for them and him. He knew only that there did not exist behind the pain a series of rational thought. What existed was animosity and hatred, a bitter venom that he would not have thought to ascribe to the God of Truth, if he had not already felt it before.

It was such a powerful hatred that by the time Zaifyr stepped into the empty, sun-drenched clearing where the slender god knelt, he could barely stand.

But with Ger, it was different.

With the giant god, Zaifyr felt the presence, but it was faint, nothing more than a whisper of disquiet or resentment. At first, he had been unsure what to make of it. Was it because of his time in the tower? Had that changed him? If so, how did Fo and Bau feel? But then he had met Ayae and listened as she told him that she felt nothing; for a time, he had not known what to think. But now, as he moved to the front of the church, past the still skeletons and paintings that held nothing but the smear of faded colour, he wondered if it was just that there was not much of Ger left.

That the god was almost dead.

He stopped at the dais and looked across the ruined temple. At the broken entrance the faint outline of Oyia stood. He could hear faint murmurs, but the words were indistinct and it was clear that she would not be following him.

Closing his eyes, a part of him shifted. When he lifted his eyelids, the light in the room had grown, the haunts of children appearing between broken pews, walls and around the fallen armour. They were all boys, not one of them older than fourteen, most young and each of them wearing old robes that dragged across the floor. They had been sealed inside, Zaifyr knew. Sealed with the men he saw at the edges of the room and in the doorways.

Behind one middle-aged man was a set of stairs. Leaving the dais, Zaifyr made his way to the rotting door and began walking down the narrow, slippery steps. The wooden railing on the left crumbled as his hand touched it, but the light was strong enough that he did not need it.

At the end of the stairs, the mud stopped, though he was well below the lake. Zaifyr's feet left wet tracks across the dusty corridor. There were cells on either side of him, and inside the haunts of men and young boys stood individually. Halfway along the short passage he closed his eyes and focused again, to see if he could add a layer to those who had been sealed in, and how strongly the generations ran. But when he opened his eyes nothing had changed.

Another set of stairs took him downwards.

A crude red light filled the room, revealing skeletons around a dirty glass dome in the centre where another skeleton lay.

On the floor, among the bones, were stones and dusty cups, the latter mostly intact. They had not been knocked over by falling bodies, however, but by earthquakes and explosions from miners. Neither of whom would have known or cared about the sanctity of the quiet chamber at the bottom of the Temple of Ger, where men and boys had taken their own lives – and where one man had stood in the centre on a large glass dome and brought the stone walls up, until the temple was sealed from the soldiers who were destroying the cities throughout the mountains.

'And that,' Zaifyr whispered, 'is how they sealed the temple, with their blood to fuel what power can be stolen from the dead.'

Edging past the skeletons, he approached the glass dome.

He pushed the remains of the lead priest away – he could see him, a large, pale, bearded man – and bent down beside the glass, his hand reaching out to scratch away the dried blood and dust.

Beneath it, he saw dark wounded flesh, though just what part of Ger it was, Zaifyr could not tell. But it was flesh, just a hint of it. If he broke through the glass, he would be able to lower himself through the hole, his entire body, but the flesh he stood upon would be only the smallest patch of the entire being, the skin weeping blood, the wounds inflamed and infected, how much pain there must be spread out for miles beneath the city above.

And then he was touched. A faint, frail, light touch, akin to how he could reach out to the dead. A faint touch that was there for but a moment and then gone, a touch that looked at him and then moved on, dismissing him.

Zaifyr was not left with a feeling of hatred or animosity; nor was he left with kindness or love. He was left with indifference, of not mattering. He felt the barest acknowledgement of his existence, a brief glance from the figure whose huge form he stood over, the god who was moving in the opposite direction from him, the god that knew he was not moving towards life but to oblivion, to nothing.

And who was looking not for salvation, but for *someone*.

The General

When I first knew Jae'le, the Animal Lord, he did not have a church, a priest, a home.

He would, eventually: a sprawling, intricate city built around rivers, a beacon of warmth and light after the wars, a city of safety, of beauty, of nature. He would have brothers and sisters as well, their relationships like the rivers and light he created.

But when I first met him, he was a killer, a murderer, a man who ate only the flesh of those he killed.

—Qian, *The Godless*

1.

'If you don't mind a piece of advice,' Queila Meina said with easy humour, 'a man is only as good as the coin you put down for him. Put down nothing, you'll get nothing.'

The three mercenaries led Ayae alongside the Spine, the work on top forcing each to raise and lower their voices accordingly. As they passed a steel barrier being bolted into the wall, Meina had raised her voice and asked Ayae how long she had lived in Mireea. When they had walked around a group of men and women hauling barrels of oil up by rope, the captain had asked quietly how long she and Illaan had been together.

'I wouldn't listen to my niece if I were you.' Behind them, the large man with the axe spoke; his name was Bael. 'She hasn't met a man she hasn't paid for in over a decade.'

'You make it sound like a terrible thing, Uncle.'

'Your father would be horrified.'

'My father?' Meina turned to face him, her dark, leather boots moving backwards without a hint of doubt. 'My father did the exact same thing with men, as you well know.'

'He didn't try to carry out meaningful relationships with them.'

'Neither do I.'

Her second uncle – Maalen – chuckled. 'The entire company waits for the day you meet a fine man. We bet on it.'

'That never happened to my father.'

'No, he met a woman.'

'And did that make him happy?'

Maalen made a face. 'It was a poor choice.'

'But a choice still.' Meina spread her hands. 'If he had kept to his rules and simply paid for her, he would have been much happier.'

Laughter stole into the air with an ease that surprised and shamed Ayae. She had left Illaan lying on the ground, the elderly corporal bending over him. He had been hurt, by *her*, but not ten minutes later she was laughing as she walked down the street, aware that the words of Queila Meina were for her benefit. She – even she, who knew nothing of mercenaries – knew the reputation of the former Captain of Steel, Wayan Meina. He had built the mercenary unit up from the remains of others, a young man with a vision that saw the group gain fame as quickly as they had contracts. He had been one of the first mercenary captains to really embrace the use of cheap fictions, which until then had been used mostly by retired soldiers to supplement their income. Wayan Meina had been the first captain to bring bards and authors into his unit, with the express desire that they produce the fictions that would make heroes out of his soldiers. He had wrapped the truth of a mercenary's life in a lie and, when news of his death on a small farm emerged, it was followed by a slim novel detailing his exploits of defending it for four days against a band of twenty-three raiders, the woman he stood beside the mother of his only daughter.

Meina and her two uncles stopped outside *The Pale House*. One of the tallest buildings in the city, it was constructed from large, white bricks that the original owner had brought in at great expense from across the Leviathan's Throat. When Captain Heast had taken its roof as his command post, Ayae had heard that the current owner had closed down the rest of the hotel and told his staff that they were now, in an unofficial capacity, the servants of the city.

'You'll find Heast on the roof with his table,' Meina said. 'He's expecting you. He has been expecting you for days, but don't let him push you around. Once you are done there, come by Steel and share a meal.'

Ayae grasped the other woman's hand, her palms warm. 'Thank you.'

Then she was alone.

She had been inside *The Pale House* twice before. The hotel – despite its current use by Captain Heast – was an establishment for the wealthy. The first time she had entered with Faise, and the two of them had promptly learned that a pair of girls from an orphanage had neither the money nor the contacts to be treated properly in the open, ashwood bar that dominated the ground floor after reception. On the following occasion, she had accompanied Illaan, and met two of his brothers and their wives in the elaborate, second-floor dining room, where she had sat quietly and awkwardly throughout the evening. On her third visit, she crossed the empty, pale-stained floor and approached one of the staff, asking for Captain Heast. She was directed to one of the narrow, spiralling staircases that were like tubes throughout the building, and climbed four flights of stairs with only the echo of her steps for company.

At the end of the stairs, a guard held the door open for her. The light that followed was so bright that she squinted at the empty sky first, before noticing the cut-back branches and trunks that ringed the roof of *The Pale House*. It was at the far end of the roof that she saw Captain Heast, standing with a small, heavily scarred man before a large, heavy table. On the top of it she could make out a detailed, miniature model of Mireea, the Spine of Ger and the surrounding land.

'I have company,' she heard Heast say, 'but I think that should cover us for the time being.'

The other man nodded and said, 'I'll make sure that it's done,' but it was not until his heavy steps had faded from the stairwell that Heast spoke to her.

'Drink?'

'No,' she replied. 'But thank you.'

'I asked for you two days ago.' His voice was even, controlled, with no hint of emotion. 'I am to take it that my sergeant did not pass on that information?'

She started to apologize, but the Captain of the Spine held up his hand. 'Please, it isn't necessary. I was hoping for a different response from him.'

'He is a good soldier.'

'In peace, yes.' Heast's hand touched the table before him. 'Now? He is like brittle metal, continually cracking beneath the surface. It is not just the situation that he finds difficult, but the news that comes from Yeflam and his father. It appears that a power shift in the Traders Union has left him uncertain of his father's future. But the question I am faced with is one that any smith faces in the same situation.'

'To reforge or to abandon,' she said softly. 'What did you want to see me for?'

'To discuss what I am to do with *you*.'

On the table before her, the Spine of Ger ran from end to end of the map, the cartographer using the form of a giant to give shape and depth to the mountains around it. She was not surprised to see Orlan's signature at the bottom, as the brush-work and modelling were without doubt his – but what did surprise her was how the signature repeated, echoing an earlier one, suggesting that the table she stood before was much, much older than she would otherwise have thought.

'I don't believe in calling it a curse,' Heast continued. 'Maybe here in the heat, on the Spine, it can only be that – but not with me.'

There was nothing friendly or unfriendly in Heast's gaze. It felt calculated. There was an honesty in that, she realized.

She had not met Heast before in any personal capacity. He did not attend the functions that the soldiers organized. She had heard stories of him when he arrived – even young as she had been, then – but the hope that he would be of as much interest as the stories of Meina's father had fled within weeks. What books there were about him were about strategies, about the details of battles that, Ayae had heard, were dry and humourless. He was a man, the Mireean Guard said, who only worked – and though this single-mindedness had more than won their loyalty, it had not won him the adoration of the city.

'In a tower above the Keep, there are two men who are a curse to me,' he continued. 'If asked, they will say that laws keep them bound, that their neutrality is fundamental to them, but it is not to be believed. With them, I could heal an army, poison another. I could end the war before it began. Instead, I am left to fight — to watch not just my soldiers die, but those of a nation I have traded with and fought before. Fo and Bau think nothing of that, which is why their neutrality is but lip service.'

'I have little skill to fight either, if that is what you're asking me,' she said. 'All I can offer is the talents I do have. I can tell you your map is off.'

He turned, slightly. 'Where?'

'The western edge.' She ran her finger down the hard edge of the mountain. 'Here. That was cleared of bush for six new settlements over a year ago. Miners, if I remember right.'

'Thank you,' he murmured.

A loud knocking broke their conversation, followed by a sweating, young guard.

'Sir — Sergeant Illaan!' He caught his breath in gasps. 'The healer wants you to know that you're needed, that you should come and see the sergeant immediately!'

2.

He had introduced himself as Ekar Waalstan, any title unspoken, his authority unquestioned. 'If I had been asked what I thought of you, Baron Le, I believe I would have said that you were a man moments away from panic.' He spoke conversationally, friendly, as if an army did not lie behind him. 'But now I have the unpleasant experience of feeling the opposite: that you are exactly where you want to be, that you planned this and knew Samuel would betray you. I commend you on that.'

'That's very civilized of you.' The saboteur raised his chained wrists in a salute. 'Thank you.'

The general's brown eyes held a faint amusement. He sat across from Bueralan, right foot folded gently across his left knee, a gentleman in his chair with his long fingers laced before him. He was calm and relaxed, his body language one of control. Despite the general's words, Bueralan *was* caught flat footed. He had not suspected Orlan's betrayal: he had believed in the fire of his shop, had not considered that Samuel Orlan – the famously neutral Samuel Orlan – might have been involved. Not that he had much time to ponder the betrayal. The saboteur knew keenly that his life could end before he rose from the hard wooden chair he sat on, that his body could be left on the dark green grass to be trampled over by thousands of soldiers, his wrists still chained tightly. Lieutenant Dural stood on the edge of the conversation, attentive and still, his hand never far from his sword. Waiting for the moment that he could provide this service.

'I have heard of you, of course,' General Waalstan continued. 'There is one particular story that interests me, a most recent one where you were hired by a man known as Lord Alden. From what I understand, you and Dark were hired to root out civil war beginning in his own yard. It is said that you spent six months eating his stale bread to compile a list of one hundred and twenty-three men that you did not even send to the gallows.'

'You know more of me than I you,' Bueralan said, feigning ease. 'I believed that King Rakun led his armies. If the king remained in Leera, then his son led the army.'

'True.'

'But no more?'

'Yes, I do believe you are exactly where you wish to be.' He turned towards the elderly man beside him. 'He reminds me of you, Samuel.'

The cartographer sat on the third chair provided and though he had been subdued since his arrival, his bright blue eyes told the lie of his body. 'Am I to be complimented?' Orlan asked. 'Or is it to him that you are paying the compliment?'

'To both of you?' the general asked.

'It is a dangerous game,' the cartographer replied. 'You should decide either to kill him or buy him now and be done with it.'

Waalstan's long fingers pointed to Bueralan. 'Can I buy you?'

'I have a price,' he said. 'I don't know if you would meet it, though. It might be high for a soldier whose army feeds itself through cannibalism.'

'A regrettable task that some of my soldiers have been forced into.' His fingers were without callus or scar; this was not the hand of a man who wielded a sword. 'There are times I thought we went too far, that the illusions we created have been largely unnecessary and will come back to haunt us in the following years.'

'Your soldiers aren't eating other people?' Bueralan asked.

'No, they are.' The humour in his eyes was gone, now. 'They have orders and they have belief.'

'Belief?' he began.

'We believe.' He glanced to his left, to the force that sprawled around him, to the silent soldiers who stood in a perimeter around where the three talked, watching, waiting. 'There is a purpose to all that we do.'

'Your war is holy?'

'That is what others will call it, yes.'

'And yourself?'

'Enough.' The man's right hand rose. 'This is not an interview.'

'It is if you want to employ me.'

'We both know that is a lie,' Ekar Waalstan replied. 'You cannot afford to, either morally or professionally. Many will understand why you turned on the Lord of Ille once he killed your man, but the question will hang over you and the rest of Dark if you now betray Lady Wagan. Not that you plan to do so, of course — the money that you are being paid is nothing in comparison to the moral need that you all have to prove yourselves to the family of one of your own you feel you let down.'

Bueralan made no reply. He did all that he could to keep his face still, to not let the surprise he felt show in any way, but he felt—

'Now that,' said the man of whom he knew nothing, 'caught you off guard.'

—that he failed.

'Who are you?' Bueralan whispered.

'Merely a humble servant.' Waalstan stood slowly. 'Samuel, what do you think my chances are of finding the rest of Dark before every well of drinking water is sabotaged from here to Mireea?'

'I would say none.' From his chair, the cartographer had become still, as if he were surprised by the sudden display of knowledge that the general had revealed. 'A group of raiders stumbled over them when we entered Leera and they were most efficient.'

'Lieutenant Dural, please inform the men that they are to drink only from what is rationed by their superiors.' He moved before Bueralan, an unarmed man who radiated confidence and surety and was all the more dangerous because of the natural way it fitted him. 'If I killed you,' he said quietly, 'I would have five assassins to deal with, would I not?'

Weakly, the saboteur tried to brush it off. 'They're not assassins.'

The general's smile was fleeting and humourless. With a nod, he signalled for Bueralan to be taken away.

3.

As the carriage rattled over the cobbled stones to the hospital, Ayae was quiet.

In her mind's eye, she saw Illaan lying on a stained sheet, his skin burnt black and cracking with his every movement. Blood — boiling blood — seeped through the worst of the wounds, the indents around her palm on his chest. She wanted desperately to push the image from her mind, but Heast's silence offered no support. His metal leg acted like a bar before the door, though she could not decide if it was intentional or not. Not that it mattered: with her hands like lumps of ice in her lap she was moments away from an admission of guilt.

When the carriage stopped and the door opened, Heast's leg moved stiffly, and he gave a short nod for her to follow.

Outside, there were no guards or chains, nothing but the sound of the birds in the cut-back branches, their lurid green bodies suddenly exposed when presented against the empty sky.

Wordlessly, she followed Heast and the Mireean Guard up the warm path to the hospital and inside. A middle-aged man sat at the front desk, but he did not speak. There was no sound until the three of them had passed through another door and Heast's leg began to stamp loudly down the hall, as if to announce his arrival to those who stood at the end of it, Reila and Bau.

Both stood outside the final, closed door, their voices rising and falling in conversation. The handsome, ageless man said, 'No,' repeating the word again before he said, 'There's very little that I can do.' He intended to say more, but was interrupted by Heast.

'Keeper,' he said evenly. 'I'm surprised to see you here.'

'I am sure very little shocks you, Captain,' Bau replied easily. 'My visits have no doubt been well documented by your men. I hope, of course, that they detail—'

'Your occupation of a hallway?'

'—my work here,' he finished.

Ayae tried to hide her reaction at Heast's dry disregard for the Keeper, though she need not have bothered. Bau was neither surprised nor bothered: his casual, left-shouldered shrug was clear in its opinion of the Captain of the Spine.

'If it would please the two of you,' Reila said tiredly, 'we might discuss our patient before we bicker.'

'What has happened?' Heast asked.

'We haven't decided, yet.'

Beyond the door was a long dormitory of beds divided by narrow paths, similar to the one that Ayae had been in earlier. As they had been then, the majority of the white-linen beds were empty, except for one by the wall. Illaan lay covered in a single, light sheet. As she drew closer, Ayae could see that the cloth was weighed down by a dampness that showed his tall outline. He was sleeping, but fitfully, his lips twitching. At the foot of the bed lay a silver bowl. Around it were stains of blood.

No one spoke and it was not until their silence dragged out to become noticeable that Ayae realized they were waiting for her.

'Did *I* do this?'

'No, child,' Reila replied.

'I hit him.'

His armour lay behind the bed, a collection of burnt leather.

'While I sympathize with the desire,' Bau said, 'unless your touch now has the ability to cause a fever that also results in vomit laced with blood, you have nothing to worry about.'

Heast stepped past her and approached Illaan's side. With a surprisingly gentle touch from his calloused hands, he rearranged the edge of the blanket. 'You're not going to tell me it is natural, either, are you?'

'No,' Reila replied.

'Saboteurs?'

'We know that they're in the city.' Gently, the elderly woman eased herself onto the bed opposite her patient, a sigh escaping her as she settled into place. 'When the sergeant first arrived he was fine, but for the damage to his armour and his pride. I examined him myself, and there was nothing to note of ill will. He took a drink of water and then, a minute later, he was vomiting with such force that I was forced to sedate him. The water he drank was fine – I had some myself, as did Bau, and neither of us could taste anything different.'

'You don't look well,' he said bluntly.

Reila smiled wanly. 'I am afraid I am getting too old for war, Captain—'

'She is merely exhausted from using her own blood for simple spells,' Bau interrupted. 'If she used it as most others did, if she killed even the smallest creature, she would be fine. But rest will cure her. It is quite different with your sergeant. I believe this is the first sign that your guards are not as honest as you think.'

'There have been seven saboteurs in Mireea for three weeks,' Heast said, with his back to them. 'We have watched them very carefully to know where they have been, and I have had no new reports. Obviously, this is evidence that suggests otherwise and I will look into that, Keeper. Why don't you tell me what will happen to the sergeant?'

'We don't know,' Reila said. 'As of this moment, we do not know what afflicts him. Illaan looks like he has been infected by a poison known as semodyle, which is rare in this part of the world, but not fatal. On the other hand, there are diseases—'

'It is semodyle,' Bau interrupted. 'I told you that.'

'And I *told you*,' she replied, 'that it is a common poison with an antidote that has had no effect on him. If you keep insisting it is something that you *clearly* know it isn't, I will have you removed.'

The Keeper's smile was light, but strained.

'I see.' Heast straightened, turning awkwardly on his metal leg to face them. 'Do you know how it was contracted, at the least?'

'Nothing, as yet.'

'You'll find none, if it is semodyle as I have said,' the Keeper answered. 'It is easy to use a dosage of the poison that is not fatal in one sitting. Its effect can be cumulative, having been digested over lengthy periods of time from, say, a water source.'

The captain glanced at Reila, and the small woman nodded. 'He's right, but ignoring all the other evidence.'

They continued to talk, but Ayae had nothing to offer, either in relation to the question of poison or those who might have used it. She found herself staring at the still form of Illaan, watching him shift and twitch, watching pain flit across his face for but a moment. A part of her wished that she felt more responsive to it. That would be proper, she thought. Despite everything that had happened, he had been a part of her life for over two years and she had loved him. But she felt only the sadness she would feel towards anyone in his situation, to anyone who was in such pain.

'Bau.'

The conversation stopped, and the Keeper met her gaze. 'Yes?'

'Could you not just help him?'

'To do what I do requires a very extensive knowledge,' he said. 'To know exactly how things react in the human body, to know what it does to blood, to organs, to all that is in the body. On the day you met me, I knitted a man's throat together, but that was a very simple thing, for it was just tissue damage. If the diagnosis here is wrong . . .'

He let the sentence hang, but, wearily, Reila finished it. 'If he is wrong, he will do more damage to Illaan than the poison itself. That is why it is important to know that it is semodyle first, before we do more harm than good.'

'Is that right?' she asked the Keeper.

Bau's smile was faint, but without humour. 'Sadly, even I have limitations,' he said.

4.

The cage was not new: made from old, black iron, it was tall enough for him to stand if he hunched and square enough for him to sit if he did not stretch his legs.

He had seen other men and women in cells like this before, had in fact used a pair when he was not yet the *exiled* Captain of Kein. It was an easy form of torture, a slow way to cramp and waste muscle, to weaken the body and erode the sharpness of the mind with exhaustion.

General Waalstan did not want to be far from him as that happened. As if the idea were new and Bueralan the first man he had the chance to witness it on, the general kept the saboteur's cage in the same slow, bumpy cart as his map table, a podium and leather-bound booklets. All but one of the latter were empty, the marred one half filled to judge by the leather marker down the middle. The twenty books did not look like the treasured tomes of warlocks and witches, where spells and potions were noted alongside experiments, but rather like personal diaries. That slotted neatly into Bueralan's emerging knowledge of the man ahead of him, however, building into an analysis of both innocence and arrogance, similar to that of a young unbeaten swordsman.

Bueralan believed that Waalstan was not a soldier who had risen through the ranks. Neither did he believe that Waalstan had earned the loyalty of his soldiers through acts of bravery or skill on the battlefield.

What, then, could he say about the man that rode easily on a dark-brown horse next to the old pony that carried Samuel Orlan?

Was he a man who had entered the ranks of the military late in life?

A reluctant, yet genius general, drawn from the civilian population of Leera?

Or had he been a priest, educated and raised for this one purpose?

There was more evidence for the last: after Bueralan had been pushed into the cage, after the lock sealing him had closed with a heavy thunk, the army had remained in camp for another twenty minutes, finishing meals and performing a short prayer before they broke. He had not heard the words – the prayer had been silent, the bowed heads the only indication – but the general had led them, that was sure.

Allowing his mind to turn over the question, Bueralan stretched the cramps in his legs and rose. As he did that, Waalstan leaned over his saddle and shook the hand of Samuel Orlan. Words passed between the two and then the cartographer turned and disappeared into the ring of soldiers around them. Soon, the small, elderly forms of both him and his pony were lost in the leather and chain and the drooping, leaning, dark-green-leafed branches that tinted the midday's sunlight.

Having noticed his attention, the general halted and waited for the cart and cage to draw alongside him. 'I could spare you the curiosity,' he said without malice. 'If you would like?'

The saboteur nodded.

'He is off to find Dark.' His hand dropped to the side of the horse's neck. 'Though he told me he was off to the city, to the capital of Leera, which I also don't doubt. He has a strong interest in the cathedral there. But first he will try to convince Dark to follow him to it, in exchange for your freedom later.'

Bueralan reached out with his left hand, steadying himself as the cage jolted.

'If he plans what I think he does, then he will die, and Dark will die with him. I won't lose much in such an inevitability, but—' Ekar Waalstan's gaze met his. 'Only a fool would trust Samuel Orlan: he has his own agenda, and sees us all as pawns to be played.'

'But you play him?'

'Within my limits.' The admission was easy. 'It is difficult to understand what Samuel truly desires, until you begin to consider him a man like those who claim to be the children of gods. A mortal he may well be, but he is a moral man who wants for very little and owes no loyalty but to himself, a man for whom the affairs of those like you and me are an indulgence.'

The saboteur remembered Heast's words. With hindsight, he realized that the Captain of the Spine had woven his doubts about Orlan into his conversation, one that Bueralan had not paid enough attention to. The realization hurt. He should have noticed it, would have if he had been clear-headed and was not as tired as the rest of Dark; if the fatigue of Ille and Elar's death had not set into his bones. And as much as he wanted to believe that the others would not believe Orlan, he knew otherwise: the cartographer had already won them over.

'How do you think,' the general asked quietly, as if reading his mind, 'your soldiers will fare without you, Captain?'

The saboteur offered no reply and the general nudged his horse forward, leaving him to fall into a hunched crouch, one hand curled tightly around the dark bar, the other curled in on itself. If the man leaving noticed and was concerned by the violence it suggested, he gave no evidence of it.

5.

'I have a task for you, now.'

Ayae did not reply to Heast. Instead, she walked beside him, her agreement given through her silent company as the Captain of the Spine limped heavily over the cobbled ground. Behind them, the hospital was lost beneath the glare of the midday's sun, as if the light itself were trying to obscure their trail and hide from what happened in the room where Illaan lay.

'Where is Fo?' Before they left, Heast had turned to Bau. 'He would be able to tell you what this was, yes?'

The Keeper's shrug was easy, nonchalant. 'He comes to the hospital only when required.'

'He is required.'

'I will tell him that he has been ordered then.'

'Do so,' the Captain of the Spine said, a hint of steel entering his tone. 'I have no place for either of you if you will not work for me.'

'Captain.' Reila pushed herself hurriedly up from the white linen she sat upon. 'We don't need this right now.'

'I believe what she is trying to tell you,' Bau said, his smile as easy and as confident as his shrug, 'is that you do not want to pursue this line if you wish to maintain Yeflam's support.'

'Yeflam is not supporting me.'

'Not in the way you want, no,' he admitted. 'You want Keeper intervention, but you and I both know that will not happen. Yeflam does not go to war. The rules that stop immortal men and women from fighting each other keep the country neutral. Yet we are both interested in the Leeran Army. We have both heard the rumours of priests, and that is why we are here, and why we are sympathetic to your plight. However, if you send Fo and me back because we will not intervene on your behalf with violence, I assure you that you will not have a welcome for your refugees when this city is overrun.'

'*If* this city is overrun, I would march through those hallowed gates regardless of what you or your kind *want*.' The Captain of the Spine's voice did not rise, but behind him Illaan's body flinched, as if the words pierced him in his delirium.

'I believe you would.' The Keeper's smile faded. 'But before you got there, the roads you carefully cleared and the bridges you quietly mended and reinforced would be returned to their previous state and you would fight a long rearguard action without reinforcement. You would do well to remember that our assistance might not be what you want, but we have not stopped your retreat. And though the following concession is small on my part, you should be pleased Fo is not here to look over your sergeant. The methods he would have used would likely have killed him.'

'You are the Healer, are you not?' Heast replied, still controlled. 'What does a man fear with you around?'

'Only death.'

Reila's hand settled on the captain's arm. 'We should focus on what has made Illaan sick, first,' she said.

'If it is a saboteur responsible for the poisoning, there will be more.' The ease with which Bau changed the subject caught Ayae's attention, though she could not explain why as she walked down the street. 'And while your healer does not agree with me in her diagnosis, we both agree that you will need to find the source of it quickly before it infects others.'

Heast grunted in reply and when he turned, Ayae believed that she could see a hint of cold satisfaction in him.

Later, outside, Heast – silent after Bau's words but for nods and grunts – waved away the driver of the carriage who turned on the road and returned to *The Pale House* without its owner.

'Did you hear me, girl?'

She nodded. 'Yes,' she said, when she realized he was not looking at her.

'The Keepers have their own game,' he continued. 'The heart of it is in Yeflam, but we are a part of it, now.'

She thought of the caged animals that Fo had kept, the mouse he had fed to the snake. Despite that, she said, 'Surely they are concerned with the Leeran Army?'

'This is not a battle fought on one side alone.'

She remembered Lady Wagan and Reila and their words to her.

'The Keepers don't want us in Yeflam, but that is not surprising,' he continued. 'No one wants us on their doorsteps.'

The Spine of Ger emerged, an empty tower rising to the left. Months ago, a merchant had run a stall out of the building, banners falling colourfully on each side. Now only a narrow spiral of stairs was there to greet them.

'Mireea has never had an official conflict with Yeflam, nor with any of the other kingdoms, but the loss of our independence would please them more than it would Faaisha. We have been too strong in Yeflam's eyes since the day the kingdom was established; whereas for Faaisha we are but a trade port on the way to the ocean.' With awkward movements, Heast began to climb the stairs, his metal leg striking harshly with each new step as he lifted it up. 'Unfortunately, I do not think that the Enclave wishes to claim Mireea. They are in a struggle for political dominance against the Traders Union and, if it is true that a leadership change has been effected there, then it will no longer be fought in terms of propaganda on the streets.'

'Then that is not our conflict,' she said. 'I don't see why it would impact on us, not now, of all times.'

On the wall, the captain paused, his hand drifting down to the part of his leg where steel and flesh met. A thin sheen of perspiration showed on his face, the exertion of the climb impossible to hide though he made no mention of the toll. Heast was not the kind of man to speak of weakness, to give it voice and strength. Neither did he ignore it. His slow walk to the edge of the wall, to the construction material, where the wooden balustrades and cauldrons of oil had yet to be placed, was an acknowledgement of what he was and was not capable of.

'When we reached out to Yeflam, the first response we received was from the Traders Union,' he said. 'They were prepared to offer us aid, to provide refuge for us. Illaan's father is who responded to us. No doubt, his response had some influence in Fo and Bau coming here, but it was not all. They are naturally curious. Priests are like a red flag. But when the son of a high official is poisoned, the questions it raises are many.'

She stood next to him, her hands on the stone blocks. 'If it is the Keepers—'

'It may be the Enclave.' The tone of his voice did not change. 'It may be that the political fallout in the Traders Union is larger than we think. If the latter, I doubt either Fo or Bau would lament that, or go out of their way to solve it, which means that we must rely upon ourselves to learn that. You will have to be careful: Illaan's house will be watched and you will as well. I cannot spare you soldiers at the moment. More so, I cannot spare their gossip, not in this matter. You will have to protect yourself, though, perhaps, I can enlist some help.'

Below, Ayae saw a figure emerge from the trail that led to the funeral pyres. Half naked and with wet hair, she was not sure at first who it was, though Heast's straightening of his back indicated that he knew. As the figure drew closer and she could see his features, she glanced at Heast and saw that a thin line of dark amusement had creased his lips.

'To think,' the Captain of the Spine said, more to himself than to her, 'he only asked for half of a corporal's daily pay.'

6.

Zaifyr returned to the hotel and washed. Behind the large desk, Ari, a new, thin bandage around the tip of his left finger and a block of wood in his hand, informed him that he smelt worse than ever. After he had washed and dried, Zaifyr picked up the loose trousers he had worn and sniffed. Fit to burn, he told himself, though he feared he would be out of clothes – it was bad enough that he had only one pair of boots and they had holes in both soles. He hadn't had that pair for long, either: a year at most. But he did a lot more walking, now. He made his way barefoot along the wooden floor to his room, having already found a bin for the trousers.

Inside, the faint smell of smoke lingered and he doubted it would ever leave. Zaifyr eased himself down on the one chair, spreading his charms and chains on the bed before him. He had begun attaching each to himself in the slow ritual he had learned as a child – *the copper vi'a first,* his father said; *vi'a is a minor protective charm, but it is always the base* – when behind him sounded a soft flap, followed by the faint scratch of claws on the window ledge. He hooked the thin clasp of the chain around his wrist into place, the chain that had been blessed by the witch Meihir for luck, and looked at the window.

'Hello, brother.'

The raven stared at him, its head tilted. 'And to you,' the Animal Lord, Jaele said in its thin, hard voice. 'I saw you return. Smelt, too.'

'I've been told.' His smile was faint. 'What else did you smell?'

'Meat.' His wings ruffled and he glided from the ledge to the bed. 'I also smelt oil, steel, sweat and a city preparing itself.'

'When was the last time you were in a siege, brother?'

The raven watched as he picked up a piece of leather threaded with silver, tiny orbs laden with old symbols of life and fertility. 'A long time,' Jae'le's bird voice croaked. 'In Seomar, on the Eastern Coast, I believe.'

Nine hundred years ago. Zaifyr began to wind the charm into his damp hair. 'The last of the Animal Kingdoms,' he murmured.

'I wept when men swept in.'

Jae'le had given five animals a voice and a kingdom origin-ally. It had been in the heart of Kuinia, a tiny world near his capital, a decree from a man who saw himself as a god. For every following decade – and there had been many decades in the Five Kingdoms – Jae'le had given another animal the power of speech, of an upright stance. No longer animals, but never men or women despite their ability to communicate, the chosen ones of the Animal Lord had been feared throughout the Five Kingdoms.

In Jae'le's home, in the elaborate building that curled like fingers around tree branches, there was a leopard who, Zaifyr was sure, the dark hand of the Jae'le had dropped to. A leopard whose head he stroked with more than a casual touch.

'I saw Ger,' he said, finally.

'And?'

'Dying.' He tightened the charm in his hair. 'He has no protector, no defences and time has almost caught up to him.'

'So soon he will be dead?'

'And aware of the fact.' The raven's gaze no longer followed the silver pieces as he lifted them from the bed.

'Do you think he has drawn the Leerans here?'

Zaifyr shook his head. 'He is different to the other gods, that's for sure. There is not the hate and the anger—'

'And the pain,' Jae'le said. 'I feel the lack of that, as well.'

'He doesn't like us here,' the other said. 'You can still feel that, but it's instinct, I believe, a reaction to what is in us. But he accepts us — something, I think, that the Keepers might not be fully aware of.'

'They are not that young.'

'Perhaps.' He reached for a new charm, this one a mix of silver and copper, symbols to turn away swords and arrows. 'But he is looking for someone.'

'He has seen something in the final moments of his death?'

'I do not want to argue for fate, but — ' He shrugged. 'But in this case, it appears he has seen something in the future.'

The raven moved, claws picking at the cover. 'I do not like this line of argument.'

'I do not either.' Lifting his right foot, he wound it around his ankle. 'But you and I have learned that there are no truths, not in our world. The truly worrying idea is that he is looking for someone in the Leerans. I was shown a child, though I do not wish to trust the sight.'

'The sight, brother?'

Zaifyr's smile was faint. 'The sight of memory. Of the haunt's memory.'

'You rode the mind of the dead?'

'It was necessary,' he insisted.

'The others will not be happy to hear.'

He shrugged.

'Do not shrug, brother.' The raven's thin voice struggled with Jae'le's emotion. 'We must be careful. *You* must be careful.'

'You're ignoring what I told you.'

'Yes, I am.' The bird drifted to the edge of the bed, where the midday's sun cut across the faded frame. 'If Ger has a presentiment, then it will emerge, and it will be something that we are either forced to deal with or not. But you – you brother, this is how it began, with the visions given to you by the dead.'

Instead of replying Zaifyr wound another silver and copper strap into his hair, this one with a simple prayer for safety written on it from when he was a child. He said nothing to the bird. He was right, of course; but whereas before he had been struck by his own fear on the top of the temple, he did not feel that now. Instead, he felt the desire to argue, to tell Jae'le that it was nothing, that it had simply been what was required. If he had not done it, he would not have seen the girl, he would not have felt her power – power, he was sure, that rivalled their own. Besides which, if Jae'le had not wanted him to speak with the dead, why had he asked Zaifyr to return to the temple itself, where the largest, most troubling of corpses lay?

He said, 'I think——' before three knocks on his door interrupted him, and it was pushed open to reveal Ayae.

326

7.

'Your bird is talking,' she said.

'No matter how hard I try to stop him,' Zaifyr replied, closing the door behind her. 'May I present to you Jae'le, my brother.'

She had heard them speaking in the warm hallway, the voices muffled but with enough clarity that she could distinguish both. The second voice — Jae'le's voice — had chilled her, struck a nerve within her for its harshness, for the torture of broken vocal cords. The chill continued as she stepped through the door and into the stare of the raven.

'Hello,' she said.

The raven's head inclined shallowly.

'Don't make friends all at once.' Zaifyr's fingers ran across the silver and copper charm in his grip. 'We were discussing Ger.'

'I heard some of it.'

'What's your opinion?'

She leaned against the wall opposite him. 'You will know more than me.'

'We must not forget that economy is always a part of war,' the raven said, moving from the bed frame to Zaifyr's shoulder. 'You have to feed soldiers, establish treaties, maintain alliances.

We must assume that this army will want to do that, especially if it wishes to build an empire. My first army was one built without any currency: we made our treasury out of what we sacked, leaving little behind. It fuelled us for a while, but it strung us out in the end, left us hungry and fatigued. Our final battle was with a garrison a quarter our size, but well fed and well rested. We shattered against their small walls.'

'A good thing you were a bird.'

'Then, I was not.' His feathers ruffled. 'I survived, but just.'

'Did Heast see me come in?' Zaifyr asked, reaching for his smoke-stained boots. When Ayae nodded, he said, 'Did he know where I was?'

'No, but – ' She reached into her trousers, drew out a letter. 'He has orders for you.'

He took the short note. 'Should I salute?' he asked, folding it again after he read it.

'If you would.'

He smiled. 'He doesn't mention what you are doing.'

'Illaan has been poisoned.' It felt strange to say the words, to say his name like that of a stranger. 'Heast wants us to look in his house.'

'For saboteurs?'

'Or an indication of the Keepers' involvement.'

Zaifyr's smile deepened, but she felt that the raven on his shoulder was not as pleased. The bird said nothing, lifting itself off its perch to drift to the ledge of the window as Zaifyr rose and stomped his feet, settling them into the boots he wore. He looked much as he had the first time she had seen him, dressed in blacks and reds and seemingly unarmed, but with holes in his boots and the odour of smoke about him.

It was a sight that comforted her, strangely, as they left the room and walked downstairs, past the large man who was winding a new cloth around his finger.

Despite that, Ayae did not speak much as she and Zaifyr made their way to Illaan's house, the midday's sun beginning to set while the afternoon's sun rose. She was unsure of what she would find, though there would not be much of hers there. Having her own house after the orphanage had been important to her; and Illaan, in the early stages of their relationship when he had given more of himself, had understood. He understood that she had something, finally – a tangible, physical piece of property that was her own, even if the money had come from another. But the deeds were in her name, the responsibility to furnish and repair was hers, and after growing up in a narrow dorm with a bed that three other girls had slept on – their names carved on the headboard – and with blankets shared and handed down, that had been terribly important to her.

Illaan's house was different. It was his third since she had known him, each a new purchase moved into after a pay raise, the last in a rich neighbourhood defined by narrow lanes that limited the sprawl of Mireea's markets. All the buildings were on two levels, with each having roof terraces that were hidden by ancient, elderly trees with roots sunk deep into Ger's Spine. She remembered him complaining, with a touch of irony, about the Mireean Guards who had climbed into the trees to cut them back. He had joked about writing a letter to Captain Heast and Lady Wagan about the injustice.

At the polished wooden door, Ayae pulled the key from her pocket. She had not asked for one from Heast, and he had not offered.

'Will we find terrible secrets inside?' Zaifyr asked lightly beside her. 'Invitations to underground markets, perhaps?'

She turned the key, pushed on the door. 'Just—'

'—birds,' he finished.

Inside, two large cages lay on the floor, the bars bent and broken, as if trampled on. There were no birds.

'He had about a dozen,' Ayae said, approaching the fallen cages. 'He would let them out when he was home and they would fly between both levels.'

'What kind were they?'

He had told her, but she couldn't remember. 'Green coloured,' she said lamely. Slowly, she crouched down over the remains, pulling the bars away and revealing the crushed feeders beneath. A few green feathers lay on the rug, but there was no other sign of the creatures.

The rest of the floor did not look as if it had been touched. The fireplace had a small pile of wood, threaded with grey lines over the black. The pale-grey couch sat away from it, a torn-up book on its left side. The book did not look as if it had suffered like the cages, but rather that someone had torn long strips down the middle. Zaifyr was already there, leaning over to pick it up, but she knew that Illaan had destroyed it. After the mercenary companies began to arrive, he had purchased a popular military series to learn about them, or so he had told her. With the yellow cover and the hint of swords that she could see, Ayae guessed that was what it was. Upstairs were different books, military studies, serious pieces that he would not have kept beside the other. Downstairs, there only remained the kitchen table, and behind it cupboards and drawers, as well as a series of rolled-up pictures.

Her pictures.

Pictures she had drawn for him, taken down.

She turned, facing Zaifyr, who was looking up at the ceiling. 'What—'

He held up his hand for silence.

She began to speak again, then stopped, hearing a faint movement.

Zaifyr was moving up the stairs before her; she followed, the knife in her hand, though she did not know what she would do with it.

Not that it mattered. As Zaifyr pushed open the door, revealing Illaan's bedroom and office, Ayae realized what the faint noise was that she had heard: a window opening. At the far end of the room, a rope fell from it. The charm-laced man in front of her made his way to the window, picking his steps carefully, making his way around the small, frail forms of the dead birds.

They had flown up here when whoever had broken in opened the cages. Frightened, they had gone straight for safety, but there was none. Indents on the bed, and the pillow case that was stained with blood, showed how the intruder had killed them. She bent down slowly, intent on picking them up.

Zaifyr stopped her. 'That's probably what infected him.'

Her hand balled into a fist.

'You see the money?' He pointed to what lay on the floor beside the bed, beneath a pair of the birds.

'He wouldn't leave money like that.'

'No.' Zaifyr approached the bed, pulled off the second case. 'We must have interrupted her before she could get it properly stashed away.'

'Her?'

'The perfume.'

It was there, a faint, delicate fragrance already disintegrating. Zaifyr bent down and, using the case, picked up one of the birds. 'Should you do that?' she asked.

'It should be fine.' He glanced up, looking at something that she could not see. 'They are looking for him.'

The birds. She realized with a chill that he was looking at the dead birds.

'Here.' Holding the bird, he approached the bookshelf against the wall. Books had tumbled from it, scattered across the floor, but the debris was only half complete. A pair lay open, their pages ripped, as if something had been held inside. 'Did he keep treats for the birds here?'

'They had liked to perch there.'

His hand reached out, and he turned, revealing a small piece of twine. 'Something for their legs, perhaps.'

'We can take the bird to Reila,' she said, quietly. The implication that Illaan was using his birds to send messages was not surprising. He had always been proud of his training of the green creatures. But the fact that someone had killed them, that someone had come in search of the messages that they carried, and that they had seemingly found them, even as Zaifyr and Ayae entered his house, left her strangely empty. 'Maybe their bodies will tell her more.'

8.

He watched the sprawling Leeran Army stop from his perch on the back of the cart:

It began in hand signals, the general lifting his right fist after the afternoon's sun had peaked. Two young boys and one girl began running back through the lines from beside him. As they did, others in position raised their hands and silently the army ground to a halt. It left the saboteur with a strange feeling in his stomach not estranged from awe, watching as picket lines were struck, horses and cattle watered and rubbed down, tents and camps unrolled. He had never seen an army of its size move with such synchronization, such cohesion.

He had not been spoken to after Waalstan left him, neither by the general or others, but he had been fed twice as his cell warmed. Warm water and cold food, both delivered by silent soldiers, neither of them offering him conversation. That did not bother him, but he knew it would in time. Samuel Orlan would have reached Dark and, while Bueralan believed that they would find him and sight him from a distance before they agreed to go anywhere with him, he knew that they would eventually agree to his plan. The old cartographer held the key that would unlock his cage, allow him to step out of it.

At least, that was what he would tell Zean and the others.

Bueralan had to free himself, and right now it looked impossible. There was no weak link in the guards, no immediate chink in their armour that he could exploit, but patience would be a virtue in relation to that. However, the longer he remained in the cage, the less likely he would be to keep his patience. That, he knew, was his immediate danger.

As the afternoon's sun sank behind the dense treetops and the humidity began to recede, poles were erected around an empty patch of muddy grass. They were lit, but differently to the fires that had begun to emerge through the camp, the fire burning brighter, cleaner, fuelled by oil rather than wood, Bueralan assumed. As they burned, soldiers approached the cart that he was in and, stepping past him, lifted the podium out. He watched them wordlessly position it in the middle of the grass.

Later, a shadow emerged beside him, pushing a plate of food through the bottom of the cage. 'You look like a man with urges to stand upright, saboteur.'

Bueralan took the plate. 'Let me out for a walk, Lieutenant?'

'I don't have a leash.' Dural, still in his leather and chain, pulled himself onto the back of the cart and eased himself down before the map table, his legs stretched out. 'If I let you out now, I would just have to kill you.'

The old leather boots were within reach. 'We couldn't have that,' he said, picking a piece of barely cooked meat from the plate. 'I don't suppose this is one of your men?'

Dural's smile twisted one side of his face. 'One of our cattle, freshly slaughtered for tonight. The general wants your strength to remain.'

'So kind of him.' Beneath the meat there was mashed potato, awash with blood and fat. 'How does he plan to talk to the entire army from here?'

'Patience, saboteur. All will be revealed soon enough. When he speaks, you will be the first foreigner to hear him. I hope you appreciate that.'

Bueralan scooped a piece of meat through the mash. 'That why you're here?'

'Everyone must be attentive.'

The saboteur smiled and shook his head. Both he and Dural knew that he would not interrupt the speech, just as both knew that the presence of the soldier had nothing to do with security and everything to do with gauging his response. Dural lifted a canteen of water and took a drink, his feet crossing before the cage.

The lieutenant was a career soldier, a man Bueralan suspected had volunteered at a young age, leaving the farm, or one of five children with no family future available to him. His unassuming, easy bearing, the chain mail old but well cared for and the speech with its slight roughness told the saboteur that he was not a man who had purchased his position. In Bueralan's experience, Dural as he was now was a soldier who would not want to progress further, a man who believed he had enough responsibility one step up from sergeant, and did not seek to add to his burdens with rank and privilege.

Soon, a silence fell over the camp, amplifying the snap of fire and the movement of animals around him as the general stepped up to his podium.

At first, Bueralan did not recognize Waalstan. Whereas before he had appeared as an affluent man with a sword purchased by or gifted to him, he now appeared in a heavy suit of ceremonial plate armour. Polished until it shone, the steel verged on being liquid white beneath the fires that surrounded him, while the fine sword he had worn earlier hung at his side by a clean, but well-worn leather strap that held both the weight of it and the bright, heavy gauntlet hands that rested upon its hilt.

'My friends.' His voice was clear, carried easily. 'My friends, we are drawing closer to our destination, to the start of our crusade.

'I have said before that when you look beside you, when you look at the brother or sister who stands beside you, who will fight with you, that you must cherish them now. There is a sad truth about war, whether it be for the noblest of intentions such as ours, or the basest, and that truth is that no man or woman is safe from death. When we are done, your brothers, your sisters, your family, could very well be gone.'

The audience was attentive, solemn. In the back of his throat, the greasy taste of the bloody meat grew, but when Bueralan spat to the ground, his spittle was clean.

'It is a risk we take. We are faithful. *The Faithful.* That is how we will be known soon, not as Leeran, not as men and women who worked this land, who toiled, who struggled, no. We will be known as those who have faith. Those who do not enter battles to take, or to steal, but to bring a truth. To bring *the* truth.

'Tomorrow, we will cross the border and march on the trails that lead to Mireea, to the city beneath which Ger lies entombed, a city of capital and greed. Tomorrow, we will leave our homeland. Our true tests will begin there – for we will be tempted, first by our own fear, by the threat of battle, and then by our bodies as we endure what has been asked of us, as we embark on making not just an empire but on saving the divine and freeing it from the shackles about it.

'Our enemy anticipates us. They have sent spies into our forces. One, as no doubt you have heard, is kept in a cage beside me.' Uncomfortably, Bueralan lowered his plate as the gaze of all those around him turned. Infamy as a symbol, as a representation of what they fought, a grounding for the new recruits. The saboteur had a grudging admiration for Waalstan. 'He is a man who works for money, whose loyalty is bought, who can be your friend one day, your enemy another. He is a symbol of those that you must be vigilant against, brothers and sisters. Do not underestimate him and do not mistake him for the men and women you march against. Yes, he is hired by those who perch above us, but as we approach their majestic wall, know that at their core they are not purchased men and women.

'They are people who have made their homes on the back of a god and that god will soon die. Without us, without our faith, all of him will be lost. The people on that mountain will allow that to happen. They will continue in this world that we find ourselves in, never truly aware of what has been lost.

'But we will know what has been lost.

'We are the Faithful.'

Behind General Waalstan, a white stallion emerged. It was drawn out of the shadows by a soldier, but the animal moved slowly and majestically, as if it knew that every eye had turned to it, that it was now the centre of all attention.

The taste of blood in the back of Bueralan's mouth grew as Waalstan drew his sword.

'Brothers and sisters, we make a sacrifice now, on the eve of our war. It is a sacrifice not to her, not to She who has given us so much, but a sacrifice to us from Her. We make it with the eight stallions that she sent with us, that she blessed for this moment, that she gave, to reinforce the faith that moves us.'

With one swift move, he drove his sword into the neck of the horse.

Bueralan expected it to cry out, but it was silent, even when the Faithful's general withdrew his sword and drove it into the ground. Even then, the horse did not fall. The killing blow bled profusely and, after a moment, the greasy taste of blood in Bueralan's mouth grew stronger, as if his own blood threatened to spill out of his mouth. Yet he knew immediately that what he was tasting was neither the meat, or his own blood, but the magic in the air, the display of power that was unlike anything the saboteur had ever felt. Raw, and without finesse, it washed over him, over the camp around him, and over the entire army as General Ekar Waalstan sank to his knees before the still standing horse.

There, he cupped his hands, and drank.

As all the Faithful did.

Blood Ties

There were five of us, five to form a family, five to fight and squabble, to love and hate. Jae'le and myself were the oldest, and Aelyn and Eidan, the youngest. The middle sibling was Tinh Tu, quiet, dangerous Tinh Tu. She was the connective tissue for us, the bridge for generations, the mediator for our arguments, our fights. We required her to be that, for we were the children of the gods. We had come to claim what our parents had left. We came to claim land, to claim people, to claim minds – and, like so many children of a worthy inheritance, we did not plan to take what was ours in terms of equity.

—Qian, *The Godless*

1.

From the roof of *The Pale House*, Heast's view of Mireea was that of a misshapen scar connected to the stone line of Ger's Spine. Throughout it, the streets, houses and markets were divided by the tissue of heavy wooden gates. After months of work, the gates rose across the skyline in blocks of shadow, complete with a busy network of builders and soldiers. Secured into place, they tightened, checked and rechecked, before reporting to him.

And it was in one of those reports, closest to the Spine itself, that he learned that the Leeran Army had begun to make its way up the mountain.

2.

Feeling ill, and pressed against the black bars of his cage in an attempt to stretch out as much as he could, Bueralan watched the Leeran Army as if he had not seen it before.

After the ritual with the white horse, the soldiers who had drunk from it – who had drunk more blood than he believed could be in a beast – had butchered the remains of the animal, mincing it in the remaining blood before putting it into the feed of their animals. The power of the ritual had continued to hang over the long, sprawling camp of the army. The beasts had eaten the meal in eerie silence, watched by their silent owners, their hands stroking their necks, holding the bags for the most part, but at times bringing them to the mouths much like a parent to a child. The camp's silence kept until the morning, when the buzz of insects announced the return of a sense of normality, but just the sense of it. The morning's sun rose and a strangeness – connected, he knew, with the blood magic he had been witness to – gripped Bueralan as he gazed at the soldiers around him, seeing the discipline that was at their core, but now with a darker edge. He watched dogs vomit blood only to lick it up, horses shift awkwardly, pigs lie panting, and soldiers offer food and items to each other without words, their understanding and knowledge of each other an intangible part of their world, reaching such an extent that he watched a young man and woman begin to file each other's teeth, a damaged courtship ritual. He'd been left to his own devices once the ritual had begun, Dural had left him, and since then it had been as if he did not exist. Even his greasy, bloodstained plate remained on the wooden slats of the wagon.

It was that plate that moved first when the cart lurched, lodging itself in one of Waalstan's blank books.

Bueralan was not a man who avoided blood magic philosophically, though he had no talent for it himself. The witches of his homeland promised much when a mother came to them with a new pregnancy, and though he had little time for the politics of rebirth, the women who held tiny bottles of kept souls were not without power. At a young age he had broken his arm – he had, like most children, been adventurous when he should not have been – and his mother had taken him to a witch who had cut open her thumb and, after smearing blood across his arm, mended the bone in one of the most painful moments of his young life. It was not until he was older that he realized his mother had allowed the pain to be caused deliberately, to instil in him a sense of personal self-preservation.

Yet, he had never seen blood magic on the scale that he had seen it the night before. He had never seen it so raw, as if it were a child's fist, smashing across an arrangement of toys. If he had been able to step outside his cage, to follow Dural to the white horse, Bueralan knew that he would have. The knowledge that he would have drunk the horse's blood appalled him, yet, he did not believe that General Waalstan was the originator of the power. It would be easy to fall back upon the assertion that the unknown man was a warlock, that he held the Leeran Army – and indeed, the Leeran nation – in his thrall, but Bueralan believed that the man had no more power other than the one he exerted from rank. Waalstan was as much a victim of last night's magic as he was, though admittedly a much more willing one. As Bueralan's stomach began to rebel beneath the hot day and rough journey, he remembered how had seen Waalstan rise at first light, his body coated in a thin sheen of sweat; for a moment, Bueralan had thought he was confused by what he saw before him, that as he stood before thousands of men and women, he did not recognize a single one of them, nor the land he stood upon, and the direction he was marching. It did not last long, for the hunch of Waalstan's shoulders had straightened as he took a second and third step, and the ease with which he held himself returned, but Bueralan thought he had glimpsed an important revelation in regards to the general.

It was the *She* of Waalstan's speech that Bueralan returned to as the cart made its rough way across the ground, drawing closer to the Spine of Ger, his body uncomfortable against the warming bars, the meal from the night before sitting worse and worse in his stomach. Pushing it aside, he focused on the nameless figure who was the cause of such inspiration, who had sent the white horses to be slaughtered. She could be a witch, perhaps, or one of the men and women who had woken to find that what had been contained within the bodies of the gods had found its way into her own. Both would be rare, but neither would be unheard of, especially the latter. No 'cursed' figure intent on violence and conquest had emerged in Bueralan's lifetime, but he had grown up in Ooila, where the Five Queens modelled their power after the Five Kingdoms, after the men and women who had conquered much of this part of the world, believing they were gods.

Before him, the cart hit a ditch. His stomach heaved and he reached for the bars on either side of him, hearing a voice as he did.

'I am afraid, mother.'

A man's voice, but a voice he did not recognize, a voice that did not come from around him. The cart pulled itself slowly out of the ditch, rocking his cage as it did.

'You have no need to be afraid.' It was a woman's voice, strong and confident. 'We are not people who fear death, for whom the unknown is but darkness. We are watched and cared for, soldier. We are known and held. We are loved, like no other human has been loved. You must never forget this as you approach battle. You must wear it proudly. You must wear it without doubt.'

There was no reply and, in an attempt to still his protesting stomach, Bueralan lowered his head between his knees and breathed deeply and slowly.

3.

After taking the birds to Reila, Ayae and Zaifyr had returned to Illaan's house to wait and watch for whoever had been in it. They did the same the next day, but after picking up the cages, cleaning the bedroom and watching Zaifyr read from various books, it became clear to Ayae that no one would come. Uncomfortable in the house and with Zaifyr – the sight of him reading blended with her memory of better times with Illaan – she suggested that they leave. With nothing new to report to Heast, they returned to the beer garden of *Red Moon* and sat in the empty, hot square, listening to the sound of the city and discussing what they had seen distractedly. It was, she thought, as if her discomfort had spread to all around her, and she left early.

When Ayae returned the next day, she found the charm-laced man already in the garden, but this time he was not alone. With him was Reila. The small, old Healer had her hair pinned back by a simple clip made from silver and jade. In front of her was a small package.

'One of our birds?' Ayae asked, taking a seat from the table next to theirs and placing it between the two. 'You have news?'

'She hasn't said,' Zaifyr replied. 'We were discussing the news, the new news.'

Reila's fingers threaded between each other. 'The Leeran Army has been spotted.'

'The lady was asking me my opinion of that,' he said. 'I told her that I was just paid to be here, nothing more.'

The elderly woman nodded slightly, her left hand untangling itself to touch the wrapped form in front of her. 'It is a bird,' she said. 'One of the birds that you brought from Illaan's house, but I have nothing to say beyond that. I am still analysing it – the solutions take time, I am afraid. But it is time that I may not have. I was going to ask Zaifyr if he may take it to Fo, to ask him his opinion.'

He was silent for a moment, the woman before him clearly uncomfortable. She looked to Ayae, who had no answer.

'It's okay,' he said, finally.

'No, I—'

'I'll do it.' Zaifyr's smile was faint, tired. 'But understand: it is the only favour a humble mercenary will give.'

After Reila had left, Ayae reached for the bird. It had been wrapped in a green cloth, twine circling around it to secure it shut. As she drew it to her, she said, 'She came to me earlier about you. She's desperate.'

'They're all desperate.'

She glanced at him, surprised by the sadness in his tone.

'This is how it begins,' he said, rising. 'People work on your sympathy and you are asked for favours. You are manipulated emotionally or intellectually, or that's the intention; you can see when it's happening most of the time. But even when you do it remains flattery, a tip to your ego, because you have more power than they. In the end, you do it because of that. You solve their problem. But a new one arises, and another, and they ask again and again and eventually – because you tire of doing it for free all the time – you ask a small token from them to somehow even out the equation. It's then that your relationship changes, that the power you have alters how you appear to them and they appear to you.

'Some days, I imagine it is how the gods found themselves to be gods, to be worshipped, and why they became distant like they did.'

She thought about his words as the two made their way along the cobbled streets. A sense of urgency had emerged from the soldiers on the Spine and the gates mapped across the city. She felt it around her as she walked, felt it melt into Zaifyr's words and emerge into a feeling that, if she had been the kind to do so, she might have called a premonition: one that spoke to her of pain, of power, of a tangible part of the world being altered for ever.

They passed beneath the gate of the Spine's Keep without speaking and made their way up to the tower where Fo and Bau lived. As they made their way through the large hall, it slowly dawned on Ayae how quiet it was, how both their steps appeared to echo, and how the glass shades of the lamps were the only gaze that watched them as they pushed open the door and crossed the wall to their tower.

Transferring the bird to her left hand, Ayae knocked.

Fo's scarred eyes did not reveal surprise when he saw her, though when his gaze drifted over her shoulder, the muscles in his hairless face hardened; but he greeted them both – Zaifyr as Qian – and stepped back. Inside, his benches were empty of animals and the flowing test tubes, cages and burners had been packed into boxes that were stacked upon the ground.

'You're leaving?' she asked.

'With the news of the morning, my work is done,' the Keeper said. 'Both Bau and I will be expected home soon. Won't you, Madman?'

Zaifyr was running his fingers along the edge of the bench. 'I'm really not at the beck and call of another like a dog,' he said. 'Speaking of which, we have a request.'

'About this bird,' Ayae added quickly, hoping to distract from his words. 'It was found in Sergeant Illaan Alahn's house, after he fell ill.'

She failed.

'I am not a dog,' Fo replied, crossing his arms.

'Aren't all you Keepers Aelyn's dogs?' When the other man did not reply, Zaifyr continued. 'I have never met you, Fo, but I know her and the kind of men she keeps about her. And I can see what has died on your bench.' He ran his fingers together, rubbing away the dust he had collected. 'Snakes and mice.'

'But not dogs,' the Keeper growled. 'Nor a bird.'

'Aren't you curious about the bird?'

The bald man did not turn his attention to the wrapped body in Ayae's hand. 'There is not much to be gained from the dead.'

Zaifyr brushed off the insult with a shrug. Ayae, trying to defuse the situation, did not know what to do: she had not expected Zaifyr to be so antagonistic.

Before she could think of anything, Fo spoke:

'You have met me, Madman,' he said quietly, intensely.

'Though I doubt that you remember the day. I was born in a city you once ruled and, as part of the tradition there, I took my first son to the Temples of Night. You were said to visit them, though I had never seen you, only your priests. The men and women who wore black and tattooed their faces with ink made from your blood. It was those men that gave the first drink to my son, a drink from a cup of poison that would kill him. It was an honour that every parent gave, a blessing that their firstborn would speak to you of their love and the honour of their family when they were dead. I trained my son to say the most beautiful words.

'My son did not die beautifully, though. He died in pain, screaming, and I could not forget the sight, or the sound. In desperation, I sought to make amends, and took a poison to be with my son. My wife and second child did as well, and while they died, I did not. My hair fell out and my eyes were damaged and, after your priests came for my family, I was left in my house, and then in the street. My last sight of everything I cared for was of their bodies being carried away. *Your* priests told me that my death was being forbidden for my failure of faith.' The hairless man's scarred hands came together tightly. '*My* failure.'

'I was a different man, then,' Zaifyr replied, meeting his gaze. 'I have no desire to return to him.'

'And I do not forgive shadows.'

Ayae began to speak, but Fo shook his head and spoke over her. 'Take your bird and leave. I will do nothing for either of you.'

4.

Bueralan gripped the bars of his cage tightly as the cart moved unevenly along the rough road, his eyes closed, his breathing steady.

The mother's voice had returned. For the last hour, her voice had come to him unbidden in snatches of conversation, brief responses to a prayer by a soldier, a comfort she gave before she fell back into silence, only to return again minutes later. Her voice came loud and small and she drifted in and out of his hearing with the beat of his heart. To hear it, he believed, was an outcome from the night's ritual. To be comforted and assured, to be personally spoken to each time you needed to be, to ensure that the Leeran Army was not a force of individuals, but a nation: that had been the reason for the ritual with the horse. But the power — the brutal, undisciplined power — had hooked into the blood of his meal, into the near raw meat he had eaten, and included him. It was accidental, he was sure, and would not last.

He came to this conclusion gradually over the hour. He watched as the voices of the army returned around him, at first in half conversations, as if they spoke internally and externally, and then only with the latter. When they finally did speak only with their voices, they were calm, serene, in complete opposition to how Bueralan felt. To a certain extent, his pain was self-inflicted: at one point, the cramps in the saboteur's stomach became so painful that the urge to turn his head and vomit out the side of the cage was overpowering. It had been during one such moment that he had felt bile rise in his throat while the mother spoke and as he turned, ready to be sick, her voice had cut off in mid-sentence. Instinctively, part of him had swallowed and the sharp, acidic taste of his stomach had left a hot trail down his throat as the mother's voice returned to him, still in mid-sentence.

Bueralan did not know what would come from hearing the mother's voice. She said nothing of military value, either in tactics or chains of command, offered no insight into the general, but yet he nursed the illness in his stomach, nursed it long after the voices of the soldiers returned, despite the mother's continued conversation, and ensured that the blood he had swallowed – the catalyst to what he heard – did not leave his stomach. At the very least, he hoped, she would reveal a soldier he could draw into his confidence.

What he did not expect was to hear a voice that he recognized.

'I have no desire to follow you into Ranan, Orlan.' Zean sounded as if he was next to him, as if he stood outside the cage, but only the stained plate lodged in the diaries waited when he opened his eyes. His blood brother said, 'None of us do. In fact, if I was to be honest, it's only your casual admission of betrayal that keeps you alive at this moment.'

Another voice spoke – it did not *feel* like the mother, in fact, he could not sense her presence at all — but the words were a murmur, too indistinct for him to hear clearly.

'My response is always the knife,' Zean said, coldly. 'I have no problem with the blood of men on my hands, even very famous men.'

Again, the murmur — Bueralan squeezed his eyes shut and his hand tightened around the bar as he strained to focus on it: '. . . is regrettable, I know,' Samuel Orlan said, his tone as confident and easy as it had always been. 'But I assure you that your captain is the safest of us all, right now. What concerns us is—'

'Ranan,' the other man finished. 'As you said before.'

He heard the cartographer sigh.

In that breath, a breath that curled around in Bueralan's mind, a scene began to build itself. He could see a series of buildings with incomplete walls, standing on overgrown, empty grass. The walls of the buildings had not been torn off, nor had they been damaged by a storm; instead they had been pulled off with care, a ritual that spoke of a town in Leera, though how far from the chain-wire border it was, the saboteur had no idea. The town's people who had taken the buildings apart had, however, left long strips still in place, and the buildings had the look of a broken shell, as if a series of giant children had been birthed inside, only to break out through the walls and roof like a bird's egg. It was in those empty walls that he saw Dark seated: Ruk had his hands wrapped around the edges of the floor tightly, his gaze intently on Zean and Orlan, while the sisters, Aerala and Liaya, sat beside each other with a sombre look upon both their faces. Only Kae, standing behind them, a shadowed figure with a hand on his sword, was not watching — though Bueralan knew he was listening.

'Much is at stake here,' Orlan continued, his voice sounding quiet and far away. 'Much more than you could possibly imagine.'

'There is always something at stake,' Zean replied. 'Everyone who has ever hired us has said that.'

'We are not talking of the simple power struggles that you are paid to intervene in.'

'Of course we're talking of them.' The coldness in his voice was like a wall of ice, thick and impenetrable, and with an indistinct, ugly shape on the other side. 'Men and women like you are always talking of power. You gnaw on it, as if to do so would let the juices of it soak into your very being, so that it could never be taken from you. You ignore that it is a construct that we make. A set of rules we adhere to, an order to give meaning to ourselves.'

'I am talking of power that does not exist any more. Look at our history, Zean – look at it all of you!' Orlan's voice pitched up, appealing to the rest of Dark. 'There is a certain power that has shaped the world you and I live in, a power that we are largely free of, but which now threatens to return.'

'In Ranan?'

'In a cathedral in Ranan.'

'There are no cathedrals in Ranan,' Zean said.

'There is now,' the cartographer replied. 'One was built for a girl, a child that must be—'

His voice choked off, brought to an abrupt end by Zean slamming his foot between Orlan's legs. Yet, the final word, the proclamation of what Orlan wanted – *killed* was what he had meant to say – was spoken. It was a dark desire, the cause of his betrayal of Bueralan. Gripping the bars tighter as his stomach and emotions rebelled, he watched as Zean turned in cold fury, leaving the old man sagging to the ground, clutching his genitals, the old pony bending its head in concern, the cartographer's only doctor.

Ahead of him, Dark emerged from the broken shell of the building.

'We'll stay with the plan that we had before,' Zean said as he drew closer. 'It does not change except that the job will be over for us. We'll find the general and we'll pay his ransom for Bueralan and then we'll leave this continent. The Leerans have maybe half a day on us, but we can make up that time.'

'What about Orlan?' Kae asked evenly.

'Liaya will dope him up,' the other replied. 'Ruk can stay here with him.'

'I'd rather go.' He spat. 'Fuck the old man, let's just bleed him and leave him.'

'Yeah, that is the temptation,' Zean began. 'I'd rather still have him alive though, just in case he is part of the ransom.'

'General Waalstan will not accept a ransom.' Raggedly, Orlan had pulled himself to his feet. 'I have known this man for two years. It has taken me that long to earn his trust, to learn what is at the heart of the Leeran rising.' He paused and took a deep breath. 'I know you do not like what I have done. I wish that I had not had to do it, but the blood has already been spilt, and I will not see it spilt again. Ranan cannot be ignored.'

'I don't fight god-touched people, old man.' Zean stalked towards the cartographer. 'Let the Keepers of Yeflam do that blood work.'

And, before Orlan could reply, his fist smashed into the man's temple.

355

5.

On top of *The Pale House*, Heast stood on the edge of the roof and listened to reports. He was told the early numbers of the force approaching, about the Spine's preparation, Steel, the Brotherhood and his own guard. He heard from the hospital and from the Keep. Flares were delivered, supplies counted. As the day wore on, it felt as if his visitors and their reports were one endless shape, but he knew their names and worth.

All but one.

6.

Zaifyr had stood outside the Spine's Keep with Ayae and, when he realized that she was not speaking to him, he said, 'I'm sorry. My mind is all over the place.' He did not have to explain why: he did not have to repeat Fo's words, or re-create the horror of his worship again.

'It's okay.' She was distant, both physically and emotionally. 'I can find you tomorrow, if you would like?'

'Yes,' he replied. 'Please.'

As he walked away, he chided himself internally. It had never occurred to him that Fo could have been born in Asila. It could be no other city for the Keeper was not, as Zaifyr understood, that old. It was said that he was twelve hundred at most, which meant it had been during the time that Zaifyr had become reclusive. He spent centuries lurking in the towers of his castle, attended by a handful of servants and a host of haunts. He travelled down the steep incline of his home only when the Ritual of Child had taken place and he did so with trepidation. He could still remember the final century of walks, the spiralling staircases and the dark nights, the roads lined by torches and the temples that were now nocturnal.

And the children.

He remembered the children most of all.

It was difficult for Zaifyr to reconcile the actions that had been done in his name with the person he was, but it was not impossible. For all that he had changed, he could still see the man he had been, the man who had become lost in the demands of the dead. The ritual was all that had brought him down to his people in the last centuries. He could not remember the living, the men and women who worked in his name, the families that had sought to gain his favour. He remembered only the dead and he had reached out and pushed his hands through the haunts that had been created – and in so doing, blessed the ritual.

'Jae'le.'

The door to his hotel room closed gently behind him.

'Brother,' the raven said from the window seal. 'How did your meeting with Fo go?'

'You saw?'

'Not inside.'

'He was born in Asila, if that's an answer,' he said. 'Did our sister tell you that?'

'No. We speak very little and even then, it is only if I visit her Enclave.'

'I have not spoken to her . . .' He hesitated. 'In a long time.'

'She knew you were to come here.'

'You told her?'

'I thought it best not to further upset her.'

'I knew we had our difficulties,' said Zaifyr as he sat. 'Out of respect, I did not enter Yeflam, but now . . .'

'Aelyn did not take the loss of her godhood well. She knew it was not true, as we all did. But to stand outside Asila and tell the thousands who gathered that she was just mortal was damaging to her pride.' The raven's feathers ruffled sourly. 'She never thought the tower sufficient punishment.'

Her remembered her hard, blunt hands and how she reached for his neck, intent on using her strength in that final moment. Shaking his head, he said, 'That is why her law is a farce.'

'It was born in the final moments of Asila, brother. The actual decree came a decade later, but I assure you, it was born then, in her rage.'

'Was Yeflam born then, as well?'

'The Enclave was a long time in birth,' the Animal Lord said. 'She disagreed with a lot of what we thought, what we proposed, and others joined her. They all thought it a mistake telling our followers we were not gods. Aelyn argued that since we would be, eventually, there was no need. When her opinion was not shared, the split was inevitable. You had no real influence on that other than to hasten it. But the presence of Fo? I cannot assume it is a coincidence. He may believe that it is — and I have heard her warn him against you, but she cannot have sent him innocently.'

'Which means she still wants to—'

He meant to say, *kill me*. But instead he lashed out with his arm, slamming Jae'le off the window sill a moment before an arrow punched into it.

Squawking and turning in mid-air, the raven rose high. As Zaifyr spotted a glint of light through a window off a street, so did the Animal Lord. Stepping out of the window frame for safety and thinking to follow the bird, he did not at first hear the heavy steps to his door. But he heard and saw the kick that splintered the lock.

It revealed a man and a woman, dressed in loose clothes. They had wrapped scarves around their heads, but neither hid the paleness of their skin; nor did the loose dark-blue cloth they wore hide the hard-boiled leather beneath.

'No scream?' said the man. 'At very least pleading? I like a man who begs, not a man who fights.'

'Are there even words worth saying?'

'None that I've heard.'

In the room where Zaifyr lived, there were two haunts. He had chosen it because they were old. Their deaths had happened so long ago that he could not know the details without pushing deep into the hungry and cold subconscious of each and that suited him fine. He knew only that they were both men and that they had been middle-aged and anything else was quickly lost as Zaifyr flushed his power through them. His attacker screamed as a cold, spectral hand curled through his chest.

A moment later he heard the woman's knife drop and a low moan escape her.

Zaifyr turned back to the window. He did not need to watch the haunts tear the pair apart, rip into the bodies for warmth and food, take their first comfort with the substance he had given them. He did not need to watch and think about how easy it was for them, and how easy it had been for him to do it. *An old life – like putting on an old mask.* Or taking an old one off.

Their physical presence in the room was temporary, he would see to that. When they became insubstantial again, there would be four in the room, not two.

Staring at the empty sky, he waited for the raven to return. When he did, his beak was bloody and his claws held scraps of skin.

'Brother,' Jae'le said quietly.

'You can't stop them,' he replied. 'Look elsewhere.'

'How can I?'

'You turn your head.'

'*Zaifyr!* You cannot be doing this!'

He met the bird's dark gaze. He imagined the concern in Jae'le's real eyes, the fear that he knew was there; the fear that was born from the experience of Asila, of the quiet horror he had felt as he walked along the cold roads, knowing that the dead were around him, but unable to see them. 'I am not doing anything,' he said. 'I acted to protect myself, nothing more. Did you kill your man?'

'No.' The raven's claw scratched at the shaft of the arrow, as if it were the cause of a wound that none could see. 'An eye I might have blinded, but she was prepared – there was no animal around her, nothing I could use to follow her. I lost her a block later in a series of houses.'

'Someone knew you were here.'

'There is something else.'

'Ayae?'

'I do not know, but there have been other attacks,' Jae'le said quietly. 'I can hear the noises, the alarms. There is smoke from the keep, soldiers are running to the hospital, and on the roof that Captain Heast has set himself upon, a man has died.'

7.

He lost Zean outside the town as he walked towards his horse, Aerala, Liaya and Kae behind him. It was sudden, a painful clench of his stomach, made worse by a sudden spasm in his legs. Bueralan fell forward onto his knees, his head pressed against the black bars, and hoped that no one around noticed his obvious illness. He wanted to throw up and he felt a sense of delirium in repressing it, as if his consciousness was being hurtled around the border of Leera and the Mountains of Ger. He was startled, momentarily, by a voice, a mother's voice, who said, 'Don't panic.' But she was not talking to him, he knew. She could not sense him. She said, 'The darkness is not your enemy.' He took a deep breath and felt his stomach settle, aware that he was reaching the end of his ability to keep the blood and meat within him. 'Soon you will join the others,' the mother's voice said, before falling silent.

If Bueralan could reach Zean again, he might be able to talk to him, might be able to advise him . . . to what? Even captured, he would not suggest that Dark come to the Leeran Army and rescue him. Bueralan did not believe a ransom would work – that, if nothing else, Orlan was right about – and neither did he think a desperate act of violence and liberation was likely to succeed. Both were futile. Nor would he tell Zean to go to Ranan, either: whatever loyalty Samuel Orlan's neutrality kept, the killing that he wanted was one the old man would have to do himself, and one he would have to bear the burden of afterwards. Dead children bore their own weight, heavier than dead friends. No, if he could reach out to Zean and speak to him as the mother did to the Leeran soldiers, he would tell Zean to stop his horse, to pull hard on the reins, to pull the horse's head back, to stop the ride he and the others were taking, to not pass the grisly fence of the border, to go quiet and to wait for him.

'You must not panic,' the mother's voice said, suddenly.

Bueralan saw darkness.

A deep, impenetrable darkness, a darkness that felt as if it were smothering him.

He opened his eyes and saw the black bars of his cage, the broad back of the cart driver, and the mounted soldiers around him.

Closing his eyes, Bueralan tried to focus on Zean, again. He had almost reconnected to Zean, had been able to see him, hunched low in his saddle, his face set in a grim mask of determination. Bueralan *knew* that look. He had seen it the first night that the two of them, as children, had been introduced. Zean had stood beside a low, stone table, beside an ugly, short-bladed knife that his father would use to cut deep into the palm of the boy he had purchased, followed by his only son. It was a look that Bueralan mirrored as he focused on the bond he had with Dark, on the bond he had with Zean in particular, to use what little of the blood magic was in him in a way similar to how the mother was using it to talk to the Leeran soldiers.

Zean would be using the back roads, Bueralan assumed. Orlan had known the bandit trails, hunter traps and switchbacks down the mountain and into Leera, and had taken delight in showing them to Dark as a way to win their trust. If they wanted to skirt the army first, to see exactly where Bueralan was, where the general was, then they would have to use them. The risk was that the Leeran soldiers, the Faithful, would not bring Zean and the others in as they had with Bueralan and Orlan, and the saboteur was not sure what choice his blood brother would make in regard to that.

He could see Zean now, riding point, Liaya and Kae following, Aerala at the rear. The sight of them gave him no answer to the question of how they'd approach, and in truth, Bueralan did not know if they had crossed the border yet. They would be close to it, either way. He still had time – enough time, he believed, until the cart slid across dirt and rock in the road and caused his cage to slide, his stomach lurching with it, a heavy lump of bile rising in his throat.

His fingers dug into the bars and he used his weight to steady it, but without luck. After the lurch, the road rose, the start of an incline up to Mireea and Bueralan overcompensated for the way he wanted to lean and the cage, finally, tipped.

His stomach fell with it.

When he hit the ground, the blood and meat came up, painfully, out to the side of the cage, and over himself.

8.

After, the cage was lifted, water thrust at him. He ignored it and spat bile and vomit out of the cage, further disgracing himself, though in the eyes of the Leeran soldiers and himself, the reasons were different. Bueralan had been close: he had needed but another hour, perhaps not even that, to speak to Zean, he was sure of it. That he had no idea how he would speak – that he might have drawn the attention of the mother to him by doing so, and if she had been responsible for the ritual and the power, he would be in trouble – occurred only to him later, as the day's heat wore on, and the saboteur settled in to wait for news of Zean and the others.

By the time the afternoon's sun had risen, Bueralan had accepted a second offer of water from a soldier near the cart, enough to wash his mouth of the taste, to clean away the remnants of the vomit on him. He had begun to gather himself as well, letting the logic of what he saw come to him – the ritual, its implication for communication, the jubilant mood of the soldiers as their own voices returned to them fully – and he began to move around in his cell as much as he could. It had not been damaged in the fall, and he had gained no new room in it, yet he still tried to stretch his back. The muscles of his stomach ached, but it was the muscles on the lower half of his back that were protesting with more regularity, just as the muscles along his shoulder blades were beginning to do. There was little he could do to relieve the pain of either, he knew, but he tried the little he could. Falling into a crouch – the pressure on his calves was coming quicker and he knew that they would soon begin to complain as regularly as his back – the captive saboteur stared ahead of him, trying to catch sight of General Waalstan.

Instead, he saw Dural.

The lieutenant was walking towards him, chains and shackles thrown over his right shoulder. The long, winding length of the Leeran force had begun to stop, and Bueralan's cart was just doing that when he arrived, nodding to the soldiers on either side. They were not the ones who had picked him up, or shared water with him later. Waalstan was very careful to ensure that Bueralan did not have an individual guard who took responsibility for his food and care. He knew the danger in giving him a single individual, a man or woman to talk to regularly who was not him, or the lieutenant.

'I thought you said there would be no walks?' Bueralan said to Dural as the cage door swung open. 'But you found your leash, I see.'

'You've been sick. You're not walking anywhere.' He tossed the shackles onto the floor. 'Put them on.'

Ignoring the open door, ignoring the urge to grab the iron and swing it, ignoring the dozens of eyes that watched him, Bueralan clamped the pieces around his ankles and wrists. Once he had, Dural closed the door and dragged the chains out through the bars, hooking them onto the edge of the cart. He pulled on them and stepped up next to the driver, where he ordered him down the hard-packed main road that led further up the mountain.

Bueralan crouched down as the cart moved and quelled a rising panic. He was not surprised when the cart broke through a ring of soldiers towards the front of the force to reveal not just General Waalstan, but Zean.

His blood brother leaned casually against the side of his mount, the brown mare pawing at the ground and breaking up dirt beneath her hooves. He was unarmed and unconcerned by the soldiers who stood around him, watching only the cart, watching only him. Bueralan saw a flicker of concern and anger in the other man's eyes, emotions drawn from the flecks of vomit, the confines of the cage, and whatever else the saboteur had not noticed about himself. Finally, after a long, drawn-out silence, Zean straightened and turned to the general. 'Now we can talk,' he said.

'Captain Le.' Ekar Waalstan was as he had first seen him: the brown civilian trousers and white shirt, and unarmed. 'I was impressed when I met you, but I am doubly impressed by your man. I want you to know that. Half an hour ago, he caught one of my scouts and informed her that he had poisoned the rivers ahead of us, but was willing to discuss the treatment of those same waters if I met him to talk about your fate.'

'I am here to pay his ransom,' Zean said. 'There are no other conversations to be had.'

'Did Samuel not tell you? I do not ransom.'

'He said that.'

'You did not believe him?'

'No.'

'Believe him.' Waalstan turned and indicated the cage. 'Your captain belongs to me now. He is my spoil of the war, though a slightly ill one, as you can see. In many ways, it should make you think of the poisons you have been laying down for my men, for he will drink the water before any of my men. He will not die, of course, for he is my assurance that you and the rest of Dark, who I assume are spread out around me and are hearing these words just as you are, do as Samuel Orlan has requested of you. That you take him to the cathedral in Ranan.'

'Do you know what he promised us?'

'That he would free your man.'

In his cage, Bueralan pulled on his chains, trying to catch the eye of his blood brother. *Don't listen to him, Zean. Just step back and go. You can't stay.*

'Do you know what he wants us to do?' the other man asked.

'I believe so.'

'He wants us to kill a girl.'

Waalstan smiled.

'A child, in fact,' he added. 'Does that not bother you?'

'Does it not bother you?' Turning, the general approached Bueralan's cell. 'He will not listen to you, Captain. Do you think he will listen to me?' He spoke softly, raising his voice to readdress Zean. 'Have you ever had faith, soldier? Real faith, I mean? I suspect not. A lot of men and women haven't, and in this day and age, who is surprised by that? But the men and women in front of you have faith. They know what it means for there to exist something better than you, for there to be a being, a deity who is more powerful, more knowing, more moral than themselves. Through their faith they acknowledge the care of another, they believe in fate, in a path that has been inscribed on the soul of each and every one of us.'

He reached the cell and, wrapping a hand around the bars, pulled himself onto the back of the cart. He was within easy reach of Bueralan's chained hands.

'I do not fear the man beside me, nor you, nor Samuel Orlan, because I have faith in the fate my god has given.' He leaned on the top of the cage as he spoke while, beneath him, Bueralan tried to catch Zean's gaze. 'But fear drives Samuel to Ranan, to a pair of large doors at the front of a cathedral and the child that is behind them. What awaits him there is the same fate that awaits Captain Le, I promise you.'

'Without us, Orlan would not go to Ranan. Have you considered that?'

'He will go, regardless. He must,' Waalstan said. 'So must you. It is the only chance that you have to save your dear captain's life.'

Don't go to Ranan. Bueralan caught Zean's gaze and held it, trying desperately to impart his words to him. *I will find a way out of here. None of you have to take risks. Following Orlan is a bad choice. Whatever waits in that cathedral will be blood gorged — it doesn't matter if it is a 'child' or a 'mother' — the risk is one you shouldn't take. It is too dark a gamble on our set of weary souls. Don't take that risk. Not now. Not here. Take the others, take them away—*

Zean shrugged. With a swift movement, he pulled himself onto his horse. 'None of us wins in this, General. I will tell you about Ranan when I see you next.'

After he had gone, Waalstan bent his head, met Bueralan's gaze through the bars. 'He may be just as dangerous as you.'

'He'll kill you before your war is done.'

It was bravado, a hint of defiance, a reaction to the situation that saw him caged and ill and knowing that Dark would, once they returned to the town where they had left Orlan and Ruk, begin to ride to Ranan. They would not like it; they would know instinctively to cut the head off the army, would not stop it, not even if the head was figurative.

Yet he could offer them no alternative but to leave him.

Outside the cage, General Waalstan smiled sadly. 'I know I will not see the end of this war. In that regard, however, I will not be alone.'

9.

By the time the afternoon's sun had begun to set, Ayae knew she was being watched.

After leaving Zaifyr, she had not returned to her home. At first her steps had been without direction. Fo's words replayed in her mind, the horror she felt was strong; but when the sense of being followed emerged she realized that she did not want to bring whoever it was into *her* home. The thought was a surprising and sad one. As she passed along the Spine, lined with men and women who had not spoken to her since the fire in Orlan's shop and who now sought to catch sight of the approaching army, she knew the thought was untenable. The wooden walls around her had begun to look more and more like the walls of the camp in Sooia and she knew that the war would come to her home no matter what she wished; but she told herself that it could wait.

Two blocks to her left, where *The Pale House* rose like a thick, white gravestone, there was the sound of a horn and the Mireean Guard began moving quickly to the building, passing her with grim faces. She did not follow. No matter what drew them – and she believed that it was nothing more than a training exercise – it did not have anything to do with her, but the sudden appearance of the guard did put a thought in her mind, and she began the slow circuit that took her looping around Mireea to where Steel were encamped.

The mercenary army was camped on the western edge of the city, in a timber yard that had been closed shortly after their arrival. The wood from the company had been used for the gates that stood in rough attention around the city, while what remained in offcuts had been taken by Steel and turned into barricades throughout the western part of the city. The camp was located near the Spine, but to reach it Ayae had to pass through three guard checkpoints and at the second, with two lean mercenaries nodding her through, she heard a woman calling her name out.

The Captain of Steel – Queila Meina, shadowed by her two uncles – lifted her hand in greeting when she turned.

'You missed all the fun,' the dark-haired woman said, drawing closer. When Ayae made no response, she added, 'Heast was attacked on the top of his building. Well, attacked is too strong a word: he killed an assassin who had slipped in at the back of a meeting. I was there and I still can barely believe he walked up to an unassuming-looking man, grabbed the back of his head, and slit his throat all while talking about supplies. Before the man hit the ground, Heast had reached for his horn to call the guard to send them to the hospital and the Keep.'

'How did he know?'

'He had never seen the man before. I would not have had the confidence to do it myself, but by the time we were leaving, reports of men and women breaking into both the Keep and hospital were being carried to him. No one was hurt, by all accounts.' Meina shook her head and laughed, a quiet sense of disbelief in both. 'If that's the opening gambit of the Leerans, it's going to be a short war, I tell you that. Now, what brings you here?'

Ayae hesitated, then said, 'I'm being followed.'

'Still?'

She nodded, though she could not have explained how she knew, other than the warmth that had begun to spread throughout her body, a sensation so different to what she had felt before that she could only explain it as a warning.

'It would make sense,' Bael murmured quietly. 'Heast, the Lady Wagan, that Healer and the Keepers. They're the power in this city.'

And Zaifyr?

'We'll have to trust that the Keepers can take care of themselves.' To Ayae, she said, 'Let's head in and see if we can't draw whoever this is out.'

Ayae doubted that whoever was following her would do so as all four walked deeper into Steel's camp, but the sensation of being followed did not leave her.

Steel's camp was the timber mill itself, located deep in the poor working-class district of the city. Past a thick wooden wall and gate, the mill nestled against the Spine, dominating the expanse of land it owned with a large building that had housed the timber that had been brought in, not by river, but by human and animal muscle. Ayae had been told by Orlan it was a business that defied the usual practice, forcing loggers to pay the price of hauling their merchandise up the mountain rather than using a river as was traditional. But even located at the edge of Mireea as it was, it was a mill that was in the centre of numerous trade routes, a mill whose owners took pride in having a variety of wood available for those who came to it – wood now, Ayae knew, that dominated the city's skyline, taken at a quarter of the going price under the order of Captain Heast.

The large warehouse was being used as Steel's sleeping quarters. As she walked past the mercenaries with Meina greeting most she passed, Ayae was told that the other two buildings in the yard – both large offices – were used by herself and her officers for meetings and as a storage facility for their food and water, rations that she said would be important if the siege began to drag on, or if they were forced into retreat.

At the door to her new office, Meina – free from her uncles – sat herself down on the stairs, leaving room for Ayae. 'You don't appear that impressed.'

She took the offered place next to her. 'Memories,' she admitted.

'You've been in sieges before?'

'I was born in a village called Iqua, in Sooia.'

'We're competing against the memory of Aela Ren? I will be happy to come in second.'

'I never saw him.'

'Few have,' Meina said. 'One of the advantages of genocide, I imagine.'

She nodded.

'There are rumours that he has left Sooia,' Meina continued. 'A lot of gold has started to come out of Ooila, and with it the rumours that he is there.'

'It was said that the armies of Sooia rose up against him, at first. That they were huge, nearly equal to the armies of the Five Kingdoms, but they did nothing. In the camps they would talk about those old battlefields, and men and women would dig in them for weapons.' She spread her warm hands out in front of her. 'It is not the same, but—'

'This is all too familiar,' Meina finished.

Ayae nodded.

'It's home to me,' the mercenary said. 'My family is here, the memories of my family and the business I was raised to inherit.'

And she would die for it as well, but neither she nor Ayae said the words.

Instead Ayae let her gaze drift over the paved ground, the afternoon's sun having risen to start baking the stone. The mercenaries of Steel came and went beneath her gaze, half a dozen entering the provisions building and emerging with freshly slaughtered meat.

The mercenary began to speak again, but her voice was stolen by a sudden explosion that shook the ground and the Spine, that caused the base of the wall to fall inwards. A cloud of debris rose and it fell like a curtain across the mill.

And from it emerged armed men and women.

The Woman Made from Fire

It was agreed that we would make our own kingdoms. We had conquered enough. We had fought long enough. We had to lead, to teach, to love. We had half the world and we needed rest. We needed to consolidate. We needed to show our armies that their faith was not misplaced.

In the heart of the Five Kingdoms, Jae'le built his domain, and gave voice to the creatures that had none. To the west, Aelyn's intricate, beautiful cities rose over forests and rivers, and her gaze, as now, as then, was ever upward. In the east, Eidan dug beneath for iron, for gold, for gems, for wealth. He dug for what is locked beneath us. In the south, Tinh Tu took in those with crippled hands and built libraries of such wealth, such knowledge, that she now begins to deny the opening of her gates, while in the north . . .

In the north, there were cities dedicated to those who spoke, but could not be heard.

—Qian, *The Godless*

1.

At first, Ayae did not react.

She remained on the stairs as Queila Meina rose, her voice ripping out through the dust and silence, her response immediate, seasoned, commanding. Her orders cut out the shapes of the men and women rising from the debris and drew the eye of those under her command to the leather they wore, the steel they carried. But beneath Meina's voice – 'Archers! Defensive positions!' – Ayae could hear a dull, repetitious thudding, the sound of something solid hitting a wooden ramp at a great speed and weight and her breath caught when she realized what it was—

'Horses!' Queila Meina cried. 'Steel! Fall back to the streets! *Fall back, Steel!'*

The first horse burst from the dust as her final words tore across the mill's now broken lot, its rider crouched low, a short, hard blade held at his side. Ayae could make out little else, for he was a shadow wreathed in dirt, a dark and terrifying figure followed by a second and third, each unfolding like a fan around the first.

'*Archers!'*

Ayae was wrenched to her feet as the mercenary grabbed her, dragged her off the stairs as she ran towards the entrance of the yard.

A small group of men and women from Steel were running towards them, armed with heavy crossbows. Releasing her, Meina pushed Ayae forward, pushed her past the mercenaries to take one of the weapons. Stumbling, Ayae turned to see her and the mercenaries drop into position as more riders swept through the yard. Emerging from the dust, she could see their mouths split into vicious, sharp-toothed grins as they cut off small groups of mercenaries, rode down those who did not move fast enough and hacked down with their swords.

'*Fire!*'

The first volley of crossbow bolts punched into riders and horses, but drew the attention of a group to Ayae and those around her.

This time, she moved of her own accord, sprinting to the left as the riders thundered towards her. She saw Meina hurl her unloaded crossbow at one, saw the other members of Steel drop the heavy weapons and pull out swords; then a rider bore down on her. More out of instinct than any conscious choice, the cartographer's apprentice ducked beneath the wild swing aimed at her head, trying desperately to grab her attacker—

Who screamed suddenly.

His sword hit the ground before he did, and Ayae snatched it from the dirt. His screaming had not stopped when she turned on him, his sword-wielding hand clutched at his face. Blood was seeping from the ruined right eye his fingers were desperately trying to keep in the socket.

She heard shouts and screams and horses around her, but

there was no indication of what had attacked him; but, with no time, Ayae gritted her teeth and slammed the sharp end of the sword into her attacker's neck. The blade cut deep, but not all the way through, and she left it there in the man as she turned back to where she had last seen Meina.

The mercenary captain was pushing herself up from beneath the rider who had attacked her, the other man's stomach a bloody mess from the dagger that Meina had thrust into him. She stumbled as she straightened and Ayae, moving quickly now, ran to her side.

'I'm fine,' she said, but leaned on the other woman's shoulder. 'Really, I'm fine. Better than most.'

The charge had broken against the small group, but half of the twenty members of Steel that had stood against the attack lay on the ground, injured or dead, surrounded by the remains of the small charge. Of the mercenaries, a middle-aged man had the worst wound, his hands holding his stomach together as he muttered to himself and tried to move backwards with his legs. His killer was bloody from where she had driven her sword into him, her leather armour untouched but held together in strips, while through her hair were twists of twine and feather. The mercenary had crushed her face with the stock of a crossbow, but Ayae could still make out a tattoo that went from her left eye to her cheek.

'Raiders,' she whispered.

'Leeran raiders.' Meina limped over to the middle-aged mercenary, dropping down next to him. 'You were a good man, Rel.'

The fallen man did not respond, and a second later could not.

'Gather up those you can.' The Captain of Steel rose. 'We need to be at the gate, and we need to be there, now. Is your protector going to come with us?'

Ayae glanced to her right, following Meina's gaze, and found a raven perched on the body of a horse.

'He'll go where he wants to go,' she said, finally. 'But – thank you.'

The bird's head tilted slightly and then lifted into the air with an easy jump and glided to her shoulder.

'I should be so lucky,' the mercenary captain said beside her.

Ayae did not reply. For a moment, she doubted that she could. The memories – the distorted memories of her childhood – were rushing in against the reality before her. At the wall, the dirt had settled, and she could see the barracks surrounded, the closed doors holding, but under threat. Mounted raiders and others on foot moved through the lot in small groups, riding down soldiers and using the remaining two buildings to provide cover from archers who shot arrows and bolts towards them. In the middle of the yard, where there was no cover and where the men and women of Steel had been standing for the start of dinner, lay the bodies of three dozen men and women, not all dead. Their screams would not be easily forgotten.

Not by her.

2.

From his place on top of *The Pale House*, the Captain of the Spine gazed intently through his eyepiece, counting horses, raiders and the hole they had emerged from. 'Move the Fifth to the gate, and the Eighth to the wall,' he said quietly. 'Then cauterize it.'

From his roof, a mournful note rose over the city.

3.

Ayae had eased herself to the floor when she heard the alarm sound, the dull horn rolling through the streets. She and the half of Steel that were neither trapped in the barracks nor lying on the dirty ground of the mill had filtered into the streets and separated, slipping into the narrowest lanes they could find, which the raiders were not keen to follow them down. It was in one of those, a handful of Steel around her and Jae'le silently sitting in the empty, stripped branch of a tree above, that she heard the horn blast. She believed that it was a sign that Heast was moving his soldiers into position, but the mercenaries' reaction – swearing and laughing bitterly – caused her to turn to Queila Meina.

'What did you expect he would do?' She addressed her soldiers from the top of an overturned crate, her injured left leg pushed out before her. 'They dug *through* the Spine.'

That Ayae understood: the Spine sank deep into the ground, deep enough that many believed that it was fused to the vertebrae of Ger himself. The sheer enormity of the task for a force to push through centuries of stone and dirt packed into the ground was not lost on her.

'And they did it,' the Captain of Steel continued, 'quietly, with none of us – not to mention the Captain or Lady of the Spine – knowing it was taking place. If you stop and think about the fact that we've been there for over two months now, the implications are not pleasant.'

'The mill was bought out a year ago.' Ayae pushed herself up from where she was sitting and approached the mercenary. 'Everyone in the city knew. Heast is going to close one of the gates, isn't he?'

Behind her, a loud shuddering, wooden creaking began to emerge.

'He'll do more than that,' Meina said.

'More?'

Her smile was sour as her good foot tapped the ground. 'He'll collapse part of the city. This part. He'll crash it into the tunnels below.'

Ayae could not respond.

'That's what the gates are for,' the other woman continued. 'You were all told that they form catchments, that they let Heast box in soldiers in parts of Mireea when they are over-run, and it's true. What you weren't told was that he has spent months restructuring and lining the underground passages so that he could collapse each part of the city safely without causing a chain reaction. He had the idea years ago when he realized portions of Mireea were built over empty caverns, but it wasn't until this threat that he was given reason to do it.'

'How long?' Her voice failed her. 'How long do we have?'

'Until the morning. We have some time, though whether it will be enough to regroup and pull half of Steel out of the mill, I don't know.'

She stepped back behind the mercenaries as Meina talked to them and organized them despite their protests. She had two concerns, Ayae heard: those they had left behind and the split of their forces. To free those in the mill would require all of them, more than the dozen listening to her now; they would need a small force to draw the attention of the raiders and another to go in; and then they would have to fight a rearguard action to the gate. Ayae was not sure that they would be allowed through the shut gate if they arrived with a force, but she did not question it. Captain Heast had laid much of his plans in advance and told the people of Mireea very little of them, but she did not doubt that he and those under him had contingencies to ensure that their own soldiers would be evacuated safely.

It was clearer now than ever before that neither the Captain of the Spine nor those who knew the full extent of his plan expected to win once the siege began against Mireea. Until that moment she had nursed the belief that they had a chance, that Heast and the others she spoke to were pessimists and pragmatists, paid to plan for the worst. But that was not true, and the weight of that realization settled heavily on her, coupled with the knowledge that Heast planned to demolish all of Mireea as it was overrun, leaving nothing but rubble and debris for those who claimed it. Partly, she knew that he was doing it to ensure that he would not have to fight a retreat in the form of a long, bloody chain, spending the lives of mercenaries and soldiers and civilians as he made his way to Yeflam . . .

But.

But her *home*.

Her home would be gone.

Not lost, not stolen but *gone*.

Devastated, she walked down the narrow lane, closing her eyes to centre herself.

'You have nothing to fear.'

She felt the raven's claws pierce the fabric of her shirt.

'Head to the gate now,' Jae'le continued. 'None here will stop you. You're not a soldier. Once you are past it, find my brother. Find him and the two of you can be gone before the fighting starts. Before you are both forced to take part in this conflict.'

'Before we're forced to take responsibility?' She spoke quickly, bitterly. 'That's what you really mean, isn't it?'

She brushed the raven from her shoulder before he could reply and returned to where Meina was giving out orders. Her uncle — Bael, to judge by the axe he wore — had begun to argue, and as she drew closer, Ayae heard his voice: '—in no condition to lead anything that requires speed, and you know it,' and saw Meina shake her head. It became clear that she was alone in her opinion, for much of Steel were in agreement with the large man. Soon, she capitulated to their demands.

'Fine, uncle. Start gathering as many as we can, and prepare to move. We can't stay in this alley much longer.' She turned to Ayae. 'I can have someone take you to the gate, if you want?'

'Have them take the bird,' Ayae, who had once been a cartographer's apprentice, replied. 'I'll go where I can help the most.'

4.

As Zaifyr approached the third village, the afternoon's sun began to truly set, leaving hand-printed smudges of orange and red on the horizon, a child's painted sky.

He had been outside Mireea for over an hour, having dropped down the Spine and into the cooling brush while the sun still remained. Before the light had begun to fade, he passed through two villages, finding them empty. No more than two dozen cheaply made buildings accounted for the two towns, but they were all bigger and better kept than those in the third settlement. This was smaller than the two before it, and he suspected it was the oldest, but from the silence that greeted him it did not promise to be any different than those he had already searched.

Earlier, after the first gate within Mireea had been lowered, Zaifyr had found himself on the roof of *The Pale House*. He was drawn to a large tabletop map where he, the Captain of the Spine, and the two old miners whom he still referred to as the First and Second circled half a dozen villages that were along the western edge of the Spine. There, they believed, a tunnel had been made. 'A difficult tunnel,' First insisted.

'A dangerous tunnel,' the Second added. 'Finished with an explosion.'

'That explosion was structurally unsound,' the First muttered. 'Never mind that they dug between two caverns with two cities and had only metres of rock and dirt to separate them.'

'It's just one large city,' said the Second. 'But I bet they broke through. I bet if we look we can see holes.'

'There's no town there on your map.' Zaifyr tapped the mountain area that they had circled. 'Are you sure I'll find something there?'

'According to my report, the villages were cleared with all the others,' Heast replied. 'They are the newest settlements, though, which is why they're not on the map. They're our best guess as to where the tunnel begins.'

Zaifyr briefly considered telling him no, that he should send someone else. The illusion of their relationship – that one had hired the other and that the positions of power they occupied were based on such a transaction – did not need to be preserved; but he thought of the haunts in his hotel room and of Ayae, who was on the other side of the gate, and he said nothing. Of the last, he had only found that out after Heast's corporal had located him outside Ayae's house, peering through her window determined to explain himself to her.

'It is entirely possible,' the Captain of the Spine continued, 'that all these towns are part of the one force we are currently dealing with. If that turns out to be true, I will be sending out a force to deal with them, but I need to know first. I leave the east of the city nothing more than a skeleton if I do that and

I would rather not take the risk if I am to collapse the western part of Mireea anyway.'

'There's no one from these towns inside Mireea?'

'No.'

Privately, he had thought that Heast and the old men were overreacting, but after he had discovered the traps he'd changed his mind.

It was only luck that kept him from serious injury when he pushed the first door open. A crossbow bolt had sat poorly in its cradle, the winch having broken from the strain earlier. If it had not, the short black bolt would have punched into his leg or stomach. Since then, he had found another twenty crossbows, and left each of them alone.

The third village was no different than the previous two. Its silence echoed his steps, the movement through scrub around him. The similarity of it to those before gave more credence to Heast's claim that all six villages were connected, for he could find no sign of living inhabitant either through tracks or haunt. As he progressed, he began to think that a deep stillness lurked within the village, and the ones before it, as if it had been preserved, sanctified somehow, by the men and women who had lived there before.

Leaving the third, he made his way to the fourth village, careful not to use the trail.

'I do not want to show my hand early,' Heast had said to him. The First and the Second had left minutes before, given the task of examining all of the Spine that Mireea was built against. 'Collapsing the roads is inevitable, but I had hoped that the Keepers would have left by then.'

'They would still be against you retreating to Yeflam,' he replied.

'But they would be unable to stop me.'

Zaifyr had almost said that they would not, but the words died on his tongue.

At the fourth village, Zaifyr stopped suddenly, a lancing brightness startling him. It was not a natural brightness, but rather the frail light of a haunt magnified by tens upon tens that milled in and through the dirt before him. A dirt that was threaded by lines of collapse in the final smudges of light, and the light of the dead. Dirt that had given way and sunk suddenly into a depression.

He did not need to reach out to the dead around him to know the shock, the fear and the unforeseen deaths that they had experienced after the explosion erupted on the Spine's foundation.

5.

Crouched in his cell, Bueralan stared at the Spine and watched the fires. They were small, isolated, and looked to be more for purposes of light than signals of destruction. He had heard that they had been created by raiders who were attacking the city, but none of the soldiers he overheard were sure what they signalled. There had been a lot of excitement when the first line of smoke emerged, but emotions had tempered as the moon rose and the flames remained at the foot of the sky.

If it was an attack led by raiders, Bueralan believed that the general had played his hand too early. The army was two days' solid ride from being in a position to deploy their catapults, and that did not take into account the soldiers digging in, building trenches, fences and fortifying their camp. It surely would have been better to wait until they were in a position to do that to launch a surprise attack on the back of whatever they'd set up. But as he stretched his back against the bars, he was reminded of the pitch darkness he saw when the mother was speaking, and the brief sense that he had of being all round the Mountains of Ger.

'Do you watch our fire?' The general emerged from behind the cart, holding a plate in his left hand, a cup in his right.

'I was told a long time ago that in war fire is not your friend.' The plate was pushed through to Bueralan's unshackled hands. 'Do you not subscribe to that?'

'The grunt's perspective. Spoken by a soldier who liked the spoils of war, but had very little interest in battle.' Waalstan leaned against the side of the wagon. 'Do you know that they are our raiders up there?'

'Your cannibals?' The meal was cold, barely cooked meat, the bread beneath pink from the juice. His stomach rebelled at the sight of it, despite what his mind said. 'Did they dig through the ground with their filed teeth?' he asked.

'Over a year ago, I organized the purchase of a mill within the city. At the same time, I purchased a series of land lots, half a dozen close to the Spine and another four further down the mountain. The raiders that we sent out had three jobs: to create a small series of skirmishes, to ensure that the villages followed a specific design and—'

'—to dig the tunnel.' The mother's voice *had* spoken to the men and women who had hidden in the tunnel, in the dark. In searching for Zean and Dark, he had seen that – heard briefly her words to them, to soothe their concern. 'To live in it.'

Waalstan's smile mirrored Bueralan's feeling of confidence. 'We'll come up on the other villages within two days. By then, I will have a good measure of Lady Wagan and the Mireean defences.'

'At the expense of your soldiers.'

'I do not expect to lose them.'

Bueralan shook his head and poked at the piece of meat — with it, might he be able to ride on another wave of Leeran magic? — while the general's smile faded.

'She has never seen battle,' he said, finally.

'No, you've never seen battle.' Bueralan gazed at him through the iron bars, the plate held tightly in his hand. 'Muriel Wagan has ruled over the trading capital of the world since she was thirty-two, a city she was born into, unlike her Lord. She married him: Elan Wagan was only Captain Jeal of the Mireean Army before, a man with no family name or history. He took her name and became the public head of the city, but anyone who met Lady Wagan would not believe that she gave control over her home to anyone, not even a man she loved.'

'I met Lord Wagan when he rode into Leera over six months ago, his treaty with us in his satchel. He was a proud man.'

'Was that before or after you gouged his eyes out?'

Waalstan shrugged off the comment. 'He had been good friends with Rakun—'

'And is your king alive?' Bueralan forced a laugh before he could reply. 'You know, before you came here, I was thinking that you had made a mistake, that you sent your raiders in early. But that's not quite what happened, is it? Your raiders have made a mistake. They panicked.'

'Everything is as it is.'

'That's why you're here, asking about Wagan, trying to figure out how she will exploit your weakness? General, I tell lies for a living and you have much to learn. You will learn from her, as well, but not in the way you think. She's an intelligent woman who knows she has never faced battle like this before.

But so what? She made the Captain of the Spine for that purpose.'

Waalstan pushed himself off the wagon. 'Are you finished with your meal?'

'Did you ever wonder why he took the job in Mireea?' As much as his stomach rebelled, Bueralan wanted to eat the raw meat, to see if any of the raw power remained for him, if he could force the same reaction as before and reach Zean and the others before they reached Ranan. He curled the plate against his stomach and continued speaking. 'Aned Heast could have demanded more coin on any side of Leviathan's Throat.'

'But he did not.'

'No, he did not. In another kingdom, Heast would be a general. Perhaps he would have been more. In any kingdom where he worked, he would have demanded respect and got it. But in any other kingdom than Mireea's, he would never have been anything but a man of low birth, who had made his name as a mercenary and built his reputation on a series of ugly battles doing what few would. In a time of peace, the people of the kingdom he was in would ask why he was there, why their king or queen kept him. That never happened in Mireea. Up on that mountain – on the back of a dead god – he is the Captain of the Spine, and that title is his legacy and his dream, the piece of him that he will leave behind long after you and I are dust.

'You ask of Lady Wagan, General, and I know why you ask, and you misjudge her. She has ensured that for you to take her home, you have to go through the man she has given status and respect to, who was as infamous as he was famous for how he won his battles. She knows that. She knows the nature of the man and how it reflects on her.

'And before this war is done, so will you.'

6.

After he gave his verbal report to Heast, Zaifyr climbed the stairs of the Spine and made his way down to the western edge of the city. Mireean soldiers had erected metal barricades to stop their attackers from scaling the wall and breaking into other parts of the city, but it was unnecessary. No such attempt had been made. Fires had been lit instead, causing thick, pungent smoke to run up the walls and into the sky.

'We have misunderstood the nature of our enemy,' the Captain of the Spine had said as the two stood on the roof of *The Pale House*, earlier. 'We were deceived by stories of crop failure, poverty and rebellion. We saw the filed teeth on the bodies of those we killed and thought nothing of the nature of a person who would submit to such pain. We heard of priests, but knew nothing of their god and did not ask. We thought we knew the answers and characterized the Leeran Army as a religious crusade, one directed by madness and desperation, but it is not. They have dug through the Spine while we watched the show they provided. We have, in short, been complete and utter fools.'

Zaifyr nodded to where the fires trailed into the night sky. 'How many made it through?'

'We estimate two hundred and fifty. Even a conservative take on the number of men and women in the towns you saw would suggest that they have lost around forty per cent of their force.'

'You were lucky.'

'We were.' Heast's pale gaze turned to him. 'Imagine how much worse it would be if it happened in two days' time, when the siege engines are in place.'

He did not disagree. After he had told Heast what he had seen, the other suggested that the collapse of the tunnel had forced the hand of those in it rather than the collapse being a result of overeagerness.

'A handful of people were cleared out of each town two weeks ago,' Heast said. 'We've been unable to account for them in the camps and my belief is that most returned to the villages and joined those living in the tunnel. It's more luck than anything else that a part of it collapsed and they were forced to play their hand early, or risk suffocation, or worse. Still, we do not want to be fighting in the streets when the rest of the Leeran Army is within range of their catapults.'

'How long are you giving Steel?' he asked.

'Until the morning's first sun,' the captain replied.

And until then, Zaifyr knew, he could only wait.

'How you stand apart from them, apart from those mortals,' a voice said from behind him. 'It is very symbolic.'

Bau.

'I want to avoid smoke in my eyes,' he replied lightly.

'Also symbolic?'

'You tell me.'

Dressed in his clean, white robes, the Healer walked around

Zaifyr, stopping well before the smoke and the line of soldiers who lurked around the barricade, their faces covered by cloths and longbows held in their grasp as they waited for a target to appear. 'You are not what I had imagined, Qian,' Bau said, turning his back to them. 'Aelyn had described you to be passionate, emotional, whereas I find you . . . much more disaffected. Tell me, what do you think of all this?'

'Of this?' He glanced at the soldiers, at the fire and smoke behind them. 'Nothing much. People have died and fought for centuries.'

'But you remain.'

'So do you.'

'We should have left already.' Wood cracked in the fire and a sudden burst of smoke arose along the Spine. 'But there is some work to finish first. Would you believe, however, that it grates on me to leave? There is much I can do here, and more I could do if I was not forbidden. The world would be a different place in the span of five days if I had free rein to do as I please.'

'Nothing would truly change. At best you would just re-create the immediate world in an image you believe in, but it would just be your creation about your morals, your life. And it would not stop war and famine and cruelty around the world. You would realize soon enough that you need an army just like the one around us, and what you stopped would only begin again.'

'Aelyn said that such thoughts made her realize that our laws were a necessity.'

Zaifyr replied blandly, 'I have heard it said before.'

'Doesn't the hypocrisy of it bother you? I mean, here we are, both of us sent to learn what is happening. Our very presence is representative of larger forces and ideologies of dominance.'

'You are only describing the Enclave, Bau.'

A sudden burst of flame lit the Keeper's face, revealing his smile fully. 'I have often thought the same.'

'Do your brothers and sisters share that thought?'

'Some.' He turned and pointed to the trails of smoke rising. 'Like all organizations, opinions range from one side to another. Certainly, some laws have had a positive impact, but in others, such monsters like the Innocent thrive because of it. Personally, I think of the Enclave as a cage hanging over a fire. When our evolution is complete, when we are the divine and our power has finished rebuilding us, it will be then that the fire is at its strongest. Those that we have ignored will have evolved just as we have and our reluctance to engage them will only fuel that which we have been trying to avoid. When the floor drops away and plunges all of us into the fire below, I will not be surprised.'

'Your fire is just another word for war. Nothing else.'

'I know.' Ash began to settle on Bau's white robe, discolouring it. 'But that is nothing new for you and me, either.'

7.

Ayae was in control of her breathing and herself when she closed her eyes, but was hard pressed to maintain her calm upon opening them.

Before her were the smouldering remains of a street two blocks back from the mill, a line of burnt husks with fires lurking within, as if the hearts of the houses — the emotion, the love that was attached to the building — was revealed through destruction. That destruction had been set by the raiders. After an hour of chasing Steel through alleys with little success they had set the streets around the mill alight, destroying any advantage the mercenaries may have had in their hiding places and knowledge of the streets, and erecting a barrier between themselves and any support they may have received from the Mireean Guard who stood along the wall. For Ayae the fires had been so much more debilitating, bringing back memories not just of her attack in Orlan's shop, but of Sooia, of the primal memory of childhood, of the fire that had consumed familiar buildings she would see years later in their blackened state, surrounded by the stone cairns that had been laid months after the destruction.

Staying in control of her emotions had rendered her more than taciturn, had turned her mute, to the point where her replies to Bael were no more than nods.

If the large, axe-wielding uncle of Queila Meina was bothered by that, it did not show. He accepted her nods and stepped only outside his role of leadership to point to the large raven that shadowed her, jumping from standing building to fallen, never out of sight. For her part, she did her best to ignore the bird, following the quick pace through the narrow streets and steeling herself as she passed burning buildings, being led towards the untouched, silent form of the mill that loomed before them.

A skinny youth with short red hair had asked Bael why the raiders had not already torched the building, burning those trapped inside.

'They've been careful with their fires around the mill,' the mercenary replied. 'There's lots of space between the set fires and where they are. My guess is they're digging in.'

Ayae did not understand why they were doing so. If Bael had a theory, he did not voice it. 'Deal with what we have, not the why. The why can wait until later.' There was no point arguing with him: for every two mercenaries from Steel that they met and drew into their group or directed back to Meina, they found another dead or near death. Already Ayae had seen Bael run his blade along the throat of two of his men, witness to the passing of a man and woman whose names she never learned.

As the moon entered the final quarter of the night, at times hidden by smoke, Ayae began to think that she herself would soon join those who had died. Her control was slipping, and

402

when she closed her eyes she could imagine Bael's large hand around her mouth. When she touched her face she rubbed at the invisible impression his fingers would never make, and could feel the warmth of his impressions on her skin. She had become so consumed by her own fear that, as the large mercenary began to explain to those around him what was required of them, she missed what he said. It was only when he began to pass out the long-stemmed torches that she realized that they were to begin their attack.

Yet, when it came time to cross the road, to follow the others and light her torch from the dying flames of a building she had tensely passed through, Ayae did not hesitate.

When they began to climb the wall that surrounded the mill, her panic flared again. Yet, for the first time she was able to take it and place it apart from her. She was not in Sooia. The memories, the emotions she felt, were part of a different time, a time of terror, in part because of her own lack of authority over the situation. She had been a child. Her parents had been lost. She had been at the mercy of the goodwill of others in the camp, and that was not always forthcoming. Against the Innocent, they too were without authority. But the soldiers before her were not the unseen, almost mythical troops of a merciless man who had spent centuries destroying all life in the country of her birth.

They were just men and women.

And when the raiders emerged she was able to run through the smouldering buildings, charred wood crunching beneath her feet, without hesitation.

8.

Soon, she was separated from the others.

It had always been the plan. 'After you've drawn them out of the mill yard, you will split up,' Queila Meina had instructed them earlier. 'Don't go alone: break into pairs, three at the most. Give the raiders a lot of targets to follow, enough that they will need to send two to three for every one of you that they see. This is a big area – an industrial area. The streets are wide, the buildings are big and empty, so run them around as much as you can as you make your way back to the gate. The rest of us will be there as quickly as we can, but you are responsible for yourself. Do not – I repeat, do *not* – hole up for the night. By the time the morning's sun has begun to rise, we need to be out of this area.'

Ayae ran through the remains of two buildings, following the young man who had spoken earlier. She did not know his name, couldn't remember it being spoken. He had joined when Bael found him in the second storey of an empty house, holed up and waiting for other members of Steel to find him. He had elected to stay with them, to help them draw out those inside. 'The easier of the two suicide options,' he had said, getting a laugh from those around him. He ran quickly now, skidding around a blackened wall, one of the few still standing, glancing behind him as he did. He grinned at her and made his way through another building – this one with flames licking at its frame.

Ayae did not hesitate. She moved quickly, clearing the gutter after the smouldering building, never pausing as he led her down to the lanes where the warehouses burned most strongly.

She heard hooves crunch through cinders behind her, a look behind confirming that there were two riders: but the second horse had shied and refused to run through the low flames. The first showed no such caution, and its rider rose in his saddle as he closed in on her. His short-bladed sword slid out, but he missed her as the stride of the horse took both beast and rider too far over the gutter, landing closer to the young man. He was barely able to spin out of the reach of the length of the blade.

Turning his horse, the raider began to move on Ayae and she drew her sword, stepping into the gutter; but he had moved only a handful of steps before a scream erupted from behind, stopping them both. The second horse had thrown its rider and reared on its hind legs, its front hooves crashing down with a sickening crunch. There was a curse from the living rider as his horse began to buck and rear, seemingly determined to throw him off and deal with him as its companion had its own rider.

A pair of claws settled on Ayae's shoulder.

'I fear,' Jae'le said in his inhuman voice, 'that you misunderstood my earlier words.'

Now quiet, the horse milled around its rider, directionless.

Ayae slid her sword away. 'You could have done that during the first attack.'

'No,' he replied. 'I am greatly limited here. Most of my concentration is spent on keeping control of this bird. One horse is fatiguing enough – I had only the smallest influence over the jump that one made while I controlled the other. Also, I would not attempt to approach either: both are loyal to their riders and will not willingly leave their bodies. I would recommend you do, though.'

Slowly, she began to jog down the road, using the line of burning warehouses as her guide to the gate. 'You wanted me to leave.'

'Yes, but you misunderstand: I want you to leave with Zaifyr.'

'He can take care of himself.'

'He *cannot.*' The raven's claws were not as strong on her shoulder as before, the only sign of Jae'le's weariness. 'You do not understand what is going to happen. Soon, people will die. Many people. You will see their corpses and you will weep over those you know. But for you, just as for me, there will be nothing else. Not so my brother. Soon, the dead will begin to form a ring at his side, will seek him out, as they seek no one else, searching for answers. It does not matter what side of this conflict they were on, they will seek him and demand answers from him, and he will be unable to provide them.'

She heard a beam snap and fall, the start of a roof collapsing. 'What will happen then?'

The raven let out a squawk, not in response to her question, but rather to the sudden appearance before her of three raiders on foot. For a moment, all three were as surprised to see her as she was them. Only Jae'le reacted: he leapt off her shoulder, flinging his black form at the face of the first man, beak and claws striking the tall man's eyes; had Ayae followed his attack with one of her own, it would have been swiftly over. But she fumbled, her hands suddenly clumsy on the hilt of her sword, and the tall raider battered the raven aside, kicking it viciously as it hit the ground.

Then Ayae was upon them.

Her sword moved more quickly than she had ever seen it, and she thrust it into the man's stomach. The momentum of her attack carried her forward and through the defences of the two raiders — one bald, one not — behind him. Yet, for all her speed — a speed that was unnatural, that was the fire manifested inside her without her consent — one of the blades caught her shoulder and left a long, shallow gash along her back. The pain caused her to lash out with her foot and drive it into the bald man's knee, to use that leverage to turn and confront the final raider.

He did not hesitate, thrusting and slashing even as she, unarmed, stepped to the left, then the right, then right again and forward, slamming the palm of her hand into his midriff. It did not result in the forceful hurl that had picked Illaan off the ground, but she heard a series of cracks as if the left side of his ribcage had suddenly caved in. As he fell, she grabbed the hilt of her buried sword and, wrenching it from the body of the first raider, brought it around to block the thrust from the bald man. He leaned heavily on his uninjured leg, the knee hurt. She dropped the block suddenly, putting him off balance and quickly battered his blade to the side. With a speed that was growing in her, a speed she felt impossible, she slashed the tip of her sword through the man's neck.

Turning to the man with the broken ribs, she plunged her blade into his chest.

Catching her breath, Ayae searched for the raven and found it behind the three bodies. It was clear from the angle that it lay, from the outstretched wing across the stones, that it would not rise again.

'But you, Jae'le?' she murmured. 'How did you fare?'

9.

Lieutenant Mills, a short, middle-aged woman with close-cropped, greying hair, reported to Heast after he arrived on the roof of *The Pale House*: 'Steel suffered light losses in the attack on the mill, sir,' she said. 'They are now fighting in a retreat up the main street and taking more losses there. They're not yet within range of our archers, but will be shortly.'

'Tell the Fifth Division to be ready.' He took the eyepiece off her, limped to the edge of the building, and placed it against his eye. 'Then send up the first flare.'

10.

She had — thankfully, *thankfully* — left the street of burning warehouses behind when an orange line of light erupted in the sky.

Ayae picked up her pace. She would have asked Meina or Bael, had they been near her, what the flare was for, but the question would have been rhetorical. She knew. All of Steel knew, but as she made her way through a narrow lane — the main street a silent, broad lane a block away — she saw none of the mercenaries hurrying to the gate as she had expected.

She had not gotten lost. Ahead, she could see the rough wooden beams that for months had held builders and now held archers and torches. But yet, the gate had not risen and there was no sense of movement at it. The only sound she could hear that indicated any action was the clamour of fighting behind her — but she had heard that periodically since she had passed the burning streets, the noise struggling to raise itself over the roar of flames, the crash of roofs collapsing, and her pumping adrenalin.

Yet now she made her way to the main street, despite her better judgement, using the dark buildings to cover her as she edged her way to the corner.

Ahead was an empty road leading to the gate. At a slow jog, it was no more than two minutes away.

Behind her—

Behind her, Steel fought.

The mercenary group had been divided into two groups, each with large, round shields as tall as she was, and each part of a chained defensive position. She could see, even though the lines of fire that they were passing threatened to obscure her vision with smoke, that the free group moved up the road to form a defensive line that curled around the already existing defence when it passed, freeing those mercenaries to move up to a new position.

She tried to imagine what Meina's attack on the mill yard had been like, to reconcile what she saw now with the mental image of desperation that she had believed the mercenary captain and her fifty mercenaries would have experienced when they first attacked. Lacking the shields they held now, they had been armed only with swords and crossbows, the latter without enough bolts to load all. But she could not match her thoughts with the smoothness of the movements before her, the way in which Steel held the larger force of the raiders in place and those without the shields struck through gaps, reinforced by those who did carry the large pieces of wood and steel and together withstood the men and women and horses that hurled themselves at the wall.

And watching them as they made their way through the final line of burning buildings, Ayae at last glimpsed the other mercenaries.

They left the shadows of the warehouses past the fire, making their way back to it to join the larger force, to take their place among the other members of their unit and lend their sword and axe. She saw Bael slap his equally large brother on the back, the brother who had been caught in the mill during the attack.

Before she could think otherwise, Ayae left the corner of her building and made her way down the street to follow suit. As she drew closer, she heard Meina crying out – 'The left! The left!' – and saw three mercenaries, two with shields, one without, rush to the front line in that direction, while a cacophony of sound – swords on shields, horses' hooves striking the cobbled ground, men and women shouting – enveloped her as she stepped into the back of the retreating mercenary unit.

'Aren't you supposed to be at the gate?' Meina called to her. 'Didn't I give you all specific orders?'

'I'm almost there,' she replied. 'Just look behind you!'

She laughed and, for a moment – despite the situation – Ayae did as well, but then Steel moved backwards and she found herself bending down to help another pull a shield with a young woman on it. Then a large hand was on her shoulder, and she found herself pushing forward beside Bael and Maalen, reinforcing the new shield wall that had just erected itself, following their lead as they thrust above the rims of the shields, calling out attacks, doing what she could to help keep the raiders at bay. It was, she realized, much more about delaying by pushing back than stopping those who followed them, and she did not score a particularly well-timed hit at all. But stopping the raiders was going to be the job of the Mireean Guard when Steel brought the force within range of their archers.

A second flare, this one red, burst into the air.

'One line!' Queila Meina's voice ricocheted among them. 'One line and move, now!'

The urgency that consumed Steel was an answer to the question Ayae did not ask. She turned to face the gate that they were approaching, and saw that it had lifted – but only just, the gap being large enough only for the mercenaries to dive and crawl through. Around her, others saw the opening and the Mireean Guard rising around the gate, bows raised and arrows notched, but it was not until Meina's voice shouted 'Break!' that the shield wall that had been holding the raiders broke apart in twos and threes and they began a rapid retreat to the gate, using the fire of the archers as cover.

The raiders pushed their attack regardless.

At the gate, Ayae found herself urging those around her through the gap, standing beside a tall man with a shield. As a raider drew closer, she stepped out, her sword striking quickly, cutting through his face: a stroke that she had, she realized, more than ample time to make, as if everything happening around her was suddenly in slow motion. She could see arrows moving through the sky, could see the raiders urging their horses and themselves on, could see mouths open, see them shape individual words –

– and she could see a faint light beneath the cobbled road, as if a lantern had been lit behind a curtain and the silhouette of a person was revealed. She heard a dim roar that grew and grew, as if a giant furnace had erupted and she thought *this is how the gods felt before they died.* She heard her name shouted, and then strong arms were around her and she was thrown to the

413

ground, dragged through the gate, the last person beneath as it slammed shut and the roar formed an explosion and all of Mireea shook around her.

11.

The dead came to Zaifyr as he walked through the living, searching for her.

They did not come in a rush, for which he was thankful. Once — before Asila, before his home for thousands of years had even begun to take shape in his mind, but shortly after he and Jae'le had begun their wars — he had happened upon the ruins of a coastal village. A tsunami had risen from the ocean a week before. The water still remained, though it was only in the large pools that had formed from the broken clay roads and fallen buildings and trees. Lines of silt and mud marked the height of its passage across the shattered roofs and walls that lay all around him as he slowly negotiated a path through the ruins. He had picked his way through half the village before he came across a stone wall lined with bloated, rotting corpses and with haunts that lingered over their bodies. At the sight of him, the hundreds of dead echoed the wave that had lifted from the ocean and swept upon him.

He had done his best to help, but he had been young, young enough that the name Qian was not yet his, and he had only been able to leave when his brother, two days later, found him.

Older, a different man now to then, he ignored the dead that approached from the ruins of Mireea. He paid no heed to their questions and their confusion, and searched for Ayae in the makeshift hospital that had been erected beside the wooden gate to tend the mercenaries who had escaped.

'He's gone.'

She sat alone on the edge of a brick wall, her sword beside her, its hilt warped. Her shirt was dirty, stained with ash and grime and blood.

'Your brother, that is,' she continued. 'Jae'le. I tried to help, but . . .'

'How is your shoulder?' he asked.

'I couldn't save the raven.'

'Jae'le is fine. He has lost his conduits before.' He sat on the wall next to her, the sword between them. 'He'll have a headache, nothing more. Now, your shoulder?'

'It hurts,' she admitted. 'It will need stitches, Meina said, but I'm waiting for those. There are people who need attention more than me.'

And there were: across the street, the survivors of Steel — no more than a hundred and fifty, he suspected — were being attended by Reila's staff. The worst had been taken to the hospital itself, but already haunts lingered in the area, standing over the bodies that had once been their own as their lips moved with questions only he could hear. Questions he ignored.

'It was strange.' Ayae picked up the warped hilt of her sword. 'I wasn't even aware that this had happened, but — but there was so much else I was aware of, right at the end. I could see things as they happened. It was as if everything was moving through a wall, a wall of water, and that the very passage of time was slowed by it. Afterward, though, I was told that the world I was watching had not changed, but rather, I had. Meina told me that I had become so fast that it was hard to see me.'

'Is that when your sword melted?'

She placed it on the ground, placed it clearly between them. 'Yes.'

'It was said that Air was fastest of Ger's wards,' he said. 'But, truthfully, all the Elements had speed, one that defied an ordinary understanding of it. Even Earth, said to be the slowest and largest of the four, was swift.'

'Will it hurt me, do you think?'

'It hasn't so far.'

Reila made her way towards the pair, a satchel draped over shoulder and chest. She moved slowly, pausing to examine the mercenaries who lay upon the ground. Twice she called over one of the doctors that were working around her and left instructions, corrections, before she was returned to making her own, slow walk to the two on the stone wall.

'Let me have a look at this shoulder.' She took Ayae's place on the wall, setting the bag beside her. As Zaifyr watched, she lifted the thin bandage that had been placed over the wound, the discoloured linen lifting parts of her shirt as well. 'At least it's clean,' she murmured, but even as she said the words, she pulled a bottle of alcohol from her bag and rubbed it over the long cut. 'It's not too deep, but it will need some stitches.'

'Will Lady Wagan be down here?' Ayae asked.

'I imagine so.' Reila began to thread the needle. 'Now that it has been revealed what the gates are for, she will have to speak to people, to reassure them.'

'Reassure them of victory?' Zaifyr's tone did not hide his cynicism. 'The way you all speak, I would be surprised if they didn't ask you why you hadn't evacuated yet.'

'They will not ask, not those who have stayed.'

'He does have a point.' Ayae winced as the needle pierced her skin. 'If we don't believe that we can win, why stay?'

'Do you want to leave?'

'No, but—'

'You think others will?' Reila's fingers worked confidently, pulling the skin together. 'I do not wish to speak ill of you, dear, but that is unkind of you. No one wants to give up their home. Few are content to just give it up, to let someone, anyone, simply take it because they wish it, or because they believe they have a right to it. Many would rather die than do that.'

'They would be wrong to do so.' Zaifyr's hand touched the copper charm beneath his wrist, his thumb and forefinger rubbing it lightly. 'There is no pride in death.'

'But no shame, either,' the healer replied. 'Death is a natural thing in our world, Zaifyr. It is nothing we need fear.'

'You are wrong.' A pair of haunts began to approach him, their voices joining a growing murmur of conversation that saturated the air around the man who had, once, been called the God of Death. 'There is much to fear.'

The Important Garden

The voiceless demand me to take responsibility for each and every one of them. Yet, every action I take does not. I have shed blood in their name, I have sacrificed, I have honoured, but it is not enough. It has never been enough to sate their demands, never enough to grant them peace.

—Qian, *The Godless*

1.

The priests visited General Waalstan the day after the siege officially began.

Crouched in his cage outside the general's house, Bueralan watched them approach in a quiet and sombre line. He had been sick again the night Waalstan had talked to him, the raw meat only offering that as a return experience. Unable to reach Zean and the others, he had been forced to give up the idea of piggybacking the blood magic of the army and to eat more conservatively, more for his strength. On the following night, he had asked for the meat to be cooked, but he had been ignored and, after leaving two plates of the meat untouched (the bread and potatoes eaten), Bueralan had been given slightly more cooked meat and left in silence to watch the Faithful set up camp at the first of the four villages they intended to occupy.

Consisting of just over fifty buildings, the town had been constructed as if it followed a spiral, with each line of houses and shops part of a circular wall. As the midday's sun rose into the empty sky, barbed wire was stretched between each of the buildings while outside the centre of the town, guards were posted upon a large wooden wall that encircled the whole village, and, in front, trenches were dug. The priests had not taken part in any of that work and, in truth, the saboteur could not think of a single time he had seen them during the Faithful's march. It was possible that they had been kept away from him — his cell was a small state in the country of the army — but it was just as possible, he thought, that they had kept to themselves, away from the soldiers, a division of privileges that could be used to prise the tongues of common men and women around him open.

His attention did not linger on Waalstan's modest house, however. Earlier, as he struggled to stretch his limbs, the catapults had moved slowly up the mountain, dragged by bulls along a narrow trail cut through the trees that had once grown between the four villages. But the raiders who had cut that trail had not made one all the way to the Spine, and the dense thicket of trees standing before the village was the cause of a problem. Dural had informed the general that, beyond the trees, the Mireeans had constructed a killing ground of around a thousand metres. 'It will take two days to cut through, sir,' the soldier had said, speaking within earshot of Bueralan's cage, ironically the only part of the village not thronged with heavy traffic. 'Once the trees are cut down, I'll have the logs turned into debris we can hurl across the ground, to provide our units with some cover as they charge.'

'Keep the logging tight, we don't want to expose ourselves.' Waalstan spoke easily, his confident, assured manner revealing nothing of the man who had talked to the saboteur the night before. 'I doubt we have much to concern ourselves with. Mireea will hide behind their wall, but it can only defend them against us for so long. Once we've established a foothold, our sheer numbers will win us the battle. Tell that to the men, Lieutenant. Reassure them that what happened the other night was just an unfortunate circumstance.'

Bueralan's cage was being lifted from the back of the general's cart when he overheard what had taken place the other night. He had been curious: the explosion that had rolled like thunder down the mountain, as if brought by the morning's light, had been inexplicable until the scouts had returned to the village. They reported collapsed mineshafts and that the western half of Mireea had been turned to rubble, which had shocked all who heard. No one had expected that Heast would collapse part of the city. Bueralan felt a small click, the final piece of a puzzle he had not known he was trying to solve slotting into position, upon hearing the news. But for the others around him, the truth of the matter was not that they had just lost three hundred soldiers, but that they had been handed their first defeat by an enemy they had obviously underestimated. Bueralan had felt no small sense of satisfaction at their dismay.

Bueralan heard nothing more from Dural and Waalstan: the two moved away shortly after, leaving him to watch the felling of trees and listen to the soldiers talk.

'Get ready.'

A pile of chains fell to the ground in front of him.

'Do you finally plan to take me out for a walk?' he said to Dural. 'Or do you plan to wheel me in my cage?'

'This time, you're on the lead.' The lieutenant motioned to one of the soldiers beside him; both were large, pale-skinned men who might have been twins, if not for the very distinct and ugly nose that was squashed against the face of the one who approached the cage. He named that one Handsome, the other, Ugly. 'You have an audience, so be on your best behaviour.'

Outside the cell the saboteur stretched to his full height, feeling the deep protest of his muscles as he did so. Quietly, he waited as the more handsome of the two men hooked a chain between the restraints on his ankles and wrists, and refrained from telling him that he needn't have bothered. Bueralan stumbled to the door of Waalstan's house in such a state that stepping over the wooden frame almost sent him sprawling to the ground. He caught himself, but only just, and did not miss Dural's thin smile as he straightened.

The inside of the house was as modest as the exterior and dominated by Waalstan's large map, which had been carefully moved in before Bueralan's cage had been placed outside. A second, smaller table sat at the back of the room, before a narrow kitchen. To the left was a single doorway and it was there that two male priests stood, while three female priests were spread around the room, two looking at the intricate map, and the last — the oldest — sitting at the small table beside the general, whose hand rested gently on her knee.

'Captain Le.' Waalstan rose. 'I trust you're enjoying being out of your cage?'

'I could positively sing.'

'While I enjoy your banter, please understand that it is not wanted at the moment. I have the pleasure of introducing you to Mother Estalia.'

The woman who rose from the chair next to him was on the other side of fifty, the thickness that she had gathered in the latter part of her life threatening to verge into fat. White-skinned, her hair was a grey silver and cut short. Her face was a series of hard lines around her mouth, but it was her eyes that told him the most, for in the depth of their dark colour, there was a coldness born of horrors that had robbed her of any joy. For a long moment she regarded him steadily, as if she knew all the terrible things Bueralan had done in life.

'He is the one,' she said, finally. Her voice was familiar, and for a moment, he did not realize that what he heard was the mother's voice. Here before him was the woman who had tried to calm the soldiers in the tunnel – the woman who had spoken to all of the Leeran Army, not as a figure of worship, but as a servant. 'Our God has shown me truth once again. He knows where the temple lies.'

'In the City of Ger, Captain Le,' the general elaborated.

'There's a number through the Spine—'

'The one you have been to,' Mother Estalia broke in. 'I do not have time for the games that Ekar does. Please remember that.'

He would. 'There is a temple beneath us.' With his chained hands, he pointed to the floor of the house. 'The only way to it that I know is through a flooded mining tunnel. But I guess you already knew that.'

'Oh?'

'The Quor'lo.'

'I did not control it, if that's what you think.'

'I don't. But someone cleaned up the blood of whoever did. Blood has power. You ask any witch.'

The hit was to his stomach. It came from Ugly, hard enough that it would have doubled him over if he had not already been weak; as it was, he fell to the hard dirt ground, and thought that he would vomit.

But he had done enough of that, lately.

Mother Estalia turned to the general. 'I see your point, Ekar,' she said. 'I will take the two guards, but I will leave your Lieutenant Dural here. You will need him.'

'He will command a small force to guard you until you're in this mineshaft,' the general said. 'This is not the time to take risks, Mother. We have been surprised once and we need to be wary of it a second time. With that in mind, I must ask you again: do you truly need this man to accompany you?'

'I do, and you should trust that he was given to us for a reason. More practically, I must admit that I do not know exactly where this entrance is, nor the directions that were taken once inside. It has been very difficult to see what is in Oyia's blood since her death.'

'That shaft is flooded with water.' Bueralan rose slowly. 'I'll never make that swim. Neither will you.'

'Trust in God, Captain.'

'What if I don't?'

'You'll drown.'

2.

Zaifyr spent the night in her house. Despite the fact that Ayae had invited him – that in itself was a surprise to her – he was the first man besides Illaan to have spent the night in her home and when she awoke, she felt a strange sense of guilt that she could not justify. In the first, drifting moments of her consciousness she believed it was the chasteness of the night, that fact that he slept on the couch in the living room that was the cause for her feelings.

'What now?' he had asked her the night before, when they were finally left alone. 'Would you like me to leave you alone? I would understand that.'

'I—' She winced as she moved her shoulder. 'Did you really do what Fo said?'

He did not hesitate in his reply. 'I gave form to all the dead in Asila. Not just the city by its name, but the entire kingdom. I had listened to them for far too long and I gave them their desire. I gave them food and warmth. If I had not stopped, I would have given all the dead such a grace.'

'It was monstrous.'

'Yes.' He reached for the warped hilt of the sword, lifting it

427

from between them. 'And I live with that, just as I live with sights much worse. Now, if you will forgive me.' He handed her the sword, hilt first. 'I need to find a place where the dead will be unable to locate me. Where I can be quiet, before I leave.'

'My house?' The words surprised her, shocked her, and she thought to take them back the moment they emerged. Instead, she added, 'You're welcome to stay there.'

'Me, you and the elderly woman who was buried beneath your kitchen.' He smiled as he said the words. 'But I would appreciate it, thank you.'

As they began walking, Ayae thought of the old woman's grandson from whom she had bought the house. He had been born in Mireea, born in a different house that his mother had sold after the death of his father, a house she had used to buy the one he was now selling. 'The grandson spread her ashes around the house,' she said. 'He said that she had loved the house in the last half of her life more than anything else – but I don't think that he ever thought her spirit would actually be there. Rather, it was symbolic.'

'It has never been symbolic,' Zaifyr said. 'In literature, the Wanderer was said to take the souls of the dead, to guide them to a place of peace, a place of rebirth. His priests would recite the story of him and a farmer. In it, the latter is honest and giving and known as a man who honours both the living and the dead of his family. He does it to such a point that he talks to the dead at night, every night, though they never answer him.

'One day, the Wanderer arrives at his farm, appearing as an old beggar, looking for dinner. He is given a place at the table and, after all have gone to bed, the farmer tells the god that he feels blessed, that because of this, he is happy to share with those less fortunate than himself. He says that it is his family that makes him feel this way. That he can feel his father and mother about him all the time, just as he can feel his son and daughter. He tells the god that he honours the living and the dead equally because of this.

'In response, the Wanderer tells him that it is true, that his family is around him, but that it is nothing to be proud of. Against the farmer's anger, he explains that the presence of his ancestors means that they are lost, that they are suffering, and that they watch him out of envy and hate.

'The farmer is distraught by this thought, but he doesn't believe it. He argues with the god, but even though he appears as an old, homeless man, there is something undeniable about the words he speaks. That night, the farmer kills himself. It's an extreme response, but the story is a parable and all the parables of the gods had violent extremes.

'At any rate, after the farmer dies, he knows that the Wanderer is right. He can see his parents and their parents and he can sense their hate and envy. He begins to weep and it is then that the god appears, no longer in the form of an old man but as a shadow, a spectre more detailed than any around him, as if the souls of all the dead dwell within his form. He tells the farmer that it was his fault what had happened. He says that because he loved his family so strongly, so deeply, so obsessively, they could not leave him.

'From there, the story drifts into the moral, the lesson that the priests would impart, which was that you must accept death, that it is a natural part of existence. The story is all but forgotten now, and so is the truth it speaks, the truth of a world without the God of Death — and it is a truth that will be on show in the following week, when the fighting begins.'

'That's why you will leave,' she said. 'Your brother agreed with that. He is worried about you.'

'He is right to be,' Zaifyr admitted. 'My days of warfare are long gone.'

'How did you live with it when you did take part?'

'Take part?' He smiled half a smile, a cynic's smile. 'I did not take part: I made war. I made it and I believed in it. I could rationalize a terrible thing and claim it as normal when I was younger. I suppose that part of it is that it is difficult to see what I see and feel every day and to always think of it as abnormal. But it is no longer that time, for which I am grateful. I do not wish to watch men and women die, just as I do not want for them to come to me afterwards, searching for answers I do not have.'

Then they had arrived at her quiet home, a dark square among other silent, dark blocks. For a while they had talked, and then parted for the night, the house silent until Ayae pushed herself out of bed and dressed slowly. She pulled the hard leather armour on over her clothes, wincing as it rubbed against her injured shoulder.

Before she and Zaifyr had left to come to her house, the day after Steel had escaped and the floor of the city had erupted, Lady Wagan had delivered her speech. Dressed in sombre greens and whites, with the Captain of the Spine at her side, she stood in front of the Western Gate. It had not been a long speech: she began by telling them all that she would be honest and forthright. 'This will not be a short war, though the battle before us will be,' she said to the crowd before her. 'You have seen the size of the force approaching us. You have no doubt asked what is it that we can do against them. You ask, not just how can we survive, but how can we triumph? We cannot do either if we are conventional. We cannot engage the Leeran force in the way they wish us to do. Neither I, nor the man beside me, plan to do so. Trust both of us on this, trust that Mireea is a wealthy nation, and trust that what we leave behind we can rebuild once our debts are settled.'

Ayae's hand lingered on her door frame as she stepped onto the narrow back veranda that looked over her small, empty garden plots. Zaifyr sat at a table to her right, a still figure next to a glass jug of juice trailing lines of moisture. A plate with cut sandwiches was also there. 'Just simple food,' he said, as she eased herself into the chair opposite, thanking him. As she poured herself a drink, he added, 'Heast has sent for me. The same messenger informed me that you have been requested to attend Lady Wagan.'

'When?'

He shrugged. 'I said you would be there once you were awake.'

'You could have woken me. It's probably important.'

'It is always important,' he said drily. 'Tell me, can you hear anything unusual?'

She could not and said so.

'I could, earlier. We will hear it again, I am sure, but it is only the sound of the Leeran Army cutting down trees. They want to talk to us about this, I imagine.'

She wanted to rise, to head to the Keep, but instead she remained seated. 'The other day, before the Leerans attacked,' she said slowly, picking her words. 'Captain Heast told me that he could end this war before it began if he had the powers of Fo, Bau, or you.'

'I do not know about the others.' Zaifyr ran his hand through his hair, shaking the silver and copper charms throughout. 'Maybe Fo could.'

'You could, couldn't you?'

'No.'

'Not . . .' She realized her mistake, stumbled with it. 'If you could – if there was no past.'

'There is never no history.' His smile was faint. 'But I understand what you are asking. In Mireea you are emotionally connected: it is your home, your life. Your future was in it, in all ways, and you haven't left that yet. But last night you rightly spoke to me about the horrors I have done – and yes, I could end this war. But it would be done violently, awfully, with thousands of deaths. I am one of the first, Ayae. There are few who could stand against me. But after – after I would have to live with it, and I live with so much, already.

'It is an experience that Fo and Bau have never encountered. They have never seen the destruction that can be caused by a man or woman, by a "god" who believes he or she has a moral superiority over another. But they will, soon enough. If the Leeran Army has come for Ger, for the power of the gods, it will move on to Yeflam after this, it will follow the refugee train of Mireea, and it will lay siege to a nation where men and women believe they will, one day, be gods. And on that day you will see the awful things your peers can do, and you will be thankful that neither I nor my brothers or sisters rose up to defend your home.'

3.

His words lingered, following her along the cobbled streets and past the activity on the Spine, beneath the arch of the gate to the Spine's Keep. If the content of Zaifyr's words surprised her, the effect they had on her did not: part of the reason for her guilt this morning was that she did not shrink from him after he had admitted to the horrors that she knew he had committed. She knew that he was, by turns, arrogant, cynical, and fatalistic, but yet . . .

Yet, she thought, *yet he is a human.*

Would she think the same if she ever met Aela Ren, the man who had the temerity to call himself the Innocent?

Beyond the gate of the Spine's Keep, she experienced a surprise. Where before the gardens had been cleared, the ground reduced to dirt, she now found the Keep's staff digging with shovel and hoe. It was not half a dozen, or even a dozen who did this, but rather the entire staff, from maids, to cooks, to guards, each stripped down to simple clothes and creating neat, orderly lines for which they would take one of the hundreds of small, potted plants behind them. The plants themselves were succulents, an array of greens and reds and

433

purples, each as hardy as the next, and each being lifted and passed by Lady Wagan, who stood in the middle of it, while behind her sat the blind Lord Wagan.

To Ayae's knowledge, this was the first she — or anyone outside the Keep — had seen of the Lord since his return, with reason.

Before he rode into Leera, Lord Wagan had been a tall, distinctively featured man who had gained a degree of gravitas about his face as he aged that had not been reflected in his intellect. Generally, the inhabitants of Mireea viewed Lord Elan Wagan as an attractive accessory to his politically minded wife, her trophy in a world where, on either side of Ger's Spine, women were more often than not there to be seen, not heard. Lord Wagan, after fifteen years of marriage, was not as silent as the youngest and newest of those wives and was generally considered to be a capable horseman and superb host. He was even aware of the place he occupied in the city, taking a great pride in his ability as a host and its importance in a city built on trade. But of all that, there was no longer any indication: Lord Elan was a shrunken man in his wheelchair, his long frame and bones held together by the brown-and-white robe he wore and the white cloth that was bound over his torn eye sockets. His hair, still full, looked as if it threatened to overpower his face, the skin below having sunk into his cheekbones and following with the rest of his body in presenting a diminished appearance.

As Ayae approached Lady Wagan, it was also clear to her that her husband was unaware of where he was. Both he and his chair were surrounded by a faint odour of opiates and when he moved, slowly, it was as if parts of him were reacting to commands conveyed five to ten minutes beforehand.

'Lady Wagan,' she said, stepping through the rows of tiny potted plants. 'You asked to see me?'

The Lady of the Spine bent down, lifting a plant that was predominantly red, but with swirls of black running through it. 'Yes, though I was given the impression that I would be lucky if I did. Some men are best disabused of their power, quickly.' She smiled and passed the plant to a guard. 'The pot is a little broken, Gerard, so be careful with it. With any luck, we will be done before the day is finished – before any of the fighting begins.'

Before she could stop herself, Ayae said, 'But why?'

'Why plant?'

'Yes.'

'Is it not obvious?' Lady Wagan indicated the already half-filled garden before her. 'No? The truth is, I have always liked my gardens. I have taken great pride in them, though they are not the finest in any land and the time I devote to them makes me an easy target of mockery for those who are my detractors. But still. It fills me with joy. It is life, creation, nurturing. A garden is not similar to childbirth, or even being a parent – something I can attest to, I assure you, but there is a pleasurable work in it. It does not have the darkness or the intellectual terror that being a parent can, especially in this world we find ourselves in. It is about growth. About life. And that is why we are planting – and planting a world that is difficult to kill, a world that will live in anything, even debris.'

The look on Ayae's face caused the other woman to chuckle. 'Look around. Are they not happy because of it?'

She admitted that they were and, with that, Ayae realized, the Lady of the Spine was also sending a second message, one coded through to the people around her, through the large amount of staff that worked the field.

'I do have things I wish to discuss with you, but not here.' She turned to the Mireean guard who stood behind Lord Wagan, a tall, young woman whose startling blue eyes gazed at the work in front of her flatly. 'Caeli, bring him in within the hour, please. The drugs will have begun to wear off by then.'

The guard made no reply, but Wagan had already stepped through the line of pots before her, and called out to those working. She offered her apologies and left the guard she had spoken to in charge of the pot arrangement, before turning and motioning for Ayae to follow her up to the entrance of the Keep.

Neither spoke until they had begun to walk down the long hall, towards the unused throne room. Then, quietly, Lady Wagan said, 'He is gone. The man I loved, that is. He has been gone since they tore his eyes out, since whatever happened to him in Leera. When not drugged, he remembers what they did, and screams.' Ayae remained silent. 'Some days, I have the deepest sympathy for him. On others, I resent him for it,' she went on. 'They are the only emotions I have, now – love and arousal are gone. Do you know that feeling?'

'Yes,' she replied, thinking of Illaan, of how she felt about him in the hospital, of how little she felt, both before and after she entered his house.

'It is unfortunate, is it not?' The Lady of the Spine stopped them before the throne. The midday's sun fell through the room, illuminating the silver arms. 'To experience love and then to lose it, to feel at the same time betrayed by it. For you, it is perhaps worse than for me, because your youth will keep now. Thousands of years from now, the hollowed feeling you have will be gone and other memories will have replaced it. But for myself? I can only watch and wait for the remains of my love to die.'

'Why are you telling me this?'

'Why?' She laughed good-naturedly. 'Because I am going to ask you a favour and this time I do not want to be denied.'

4.

The Captain of the Spine delayed the start of his meeting for fifteen minutes, a rarity. He delayed it for Zaifyr, waiting for the charm-laced man to open the door across from him, though he knew that he would not. Still, he waited. From the roof of *The Pale House* he watched the Leeran Army, his first real sight of it, his first chance to see for himself the sprawling, shifting mass of bodies, the nation that had been raised and armed. He had not even begun to suspect its real size, a mistake he had not made for over a decade; still, he had known that it would be large, and did not believe his plans would change greatly. His only true alteration would be once he received word of a solitary mercenary leaving the front gate, walking through the camps that stretched either side of the road to Yeflam.

Walking away.

After fifteen minutes, he began to speak to those around him.

5.

If a chance to escape was ever to be offered to him, it would be soon.

Bueralan, chained to both Ugly and Handsome, followed Mother Estalia through a series of narrow, overgrown paths in what he believed was a slim road that ended close to the back of the funeral pyres. An illegal road, an unofficial road, a child's road: the saboteur had no idea who had made the path, but it was as old as the villages that the tireless Estalia left behind with her soldier's pace. Beside her were her four priests and a fifth, the odd man out, Lieutenant Dural. The latter had fanned a small regiment of soldiers around all of them, including Bueralan. 'My preference with the prisoner,' he had said to Estalia before they set out, 'is to cut the tendons in his heels now.'

'How would he swim?' she asked.

'He wouldn't,' he replied. 'He would be forced to stay with me, where he would not be a danger.'

'That won't be necessary, Lieutenant.'

She started down the path before he could object, leaving the Leeran Army, the sound of trees being felled, the sight of soldiers in orderly lines being moved across four villages and the newly erected pens of livestock that had just been constructed. Considering himself lucky, Bueralan followed her at a reasonable pace, not wishing to give Dural a chance to cripple him.

Still, the walk was not easy for Bueralan. He struggled to keep up with the pace that was set, the wasted muscles in his legs and back protesting, especially when he went up inclines, of which there were more than one to varying degrees in the Mountains of Ger. Without any other choice, he pushed through the pain, reminding himself that if he fell, he would be taken back to the cage — or simply not get up again. Both would take away his chance to reach Leera, to reach Dark — both of which were in the opposite direction of the wall that rose in front of him and the people within. The images he had seen after the sacrifice of the pale horse had stayed with him, and he had no doubt of the truth of what he had seen. He was running out of time to reach them before they pushed the cathedral doors open, he knew.

He had no choice. Mireea was just a payment, but Dark . . . *Dark. They will take their time.* He repeated the words like a mantra as the midday's sun began to sink. They would not rush. It was three days' ride to Leera, at a push, and they would not push. He was safe, in as much as anyone in an army was safe, and Dark would know that they had time. They would discover an empty city, a city stripped to make siege engines, to fuel a war. There would be only one part of it with people, one whole, and that would be the church. The very building Orlan wanted them to enter, the building that held the child he wanted them to kill, a murder that none of them wanted to be part of.

They'll wait.

They'll watch.

They must.

As the afternoon's sun rose, Mother Estalia called a stop. Of herself and the four priests, only she spoke, though he was sure that all five communicated with each other. The small force came to a halt in a small clearing, a shallow stream to the side that ran downhill, a flow well enough now to drink from, but which would evaporate as the dry season set in. From it, the priests took water in silent turns and took it around to the soldiers, though not Bueralan. After a moment, the saboteur sighed and, despite the chains, sank to the ground and lay on his back, staring at the fragmented orb that passed above him as he rested his muscles.

Shortly, he saw Dural approach, holding a canteen of water.

'How is he?' asked the soldier.

'We'll probably be carrying him by the end of the day, sir,' Handsome said to him. 'I doubt that he has the strength for much more.'

'There isn't much more,' Dural replied. 'Just watch him.'

He drank what the lieutenant left for him and, soon after he had finished, Estalia rose and set the pace again.

How long would they watch the church? The building would be large, difficult to map from the outside, impossible to know every corner and room and hard to know how many people it held. A week, he answered. They would watch it for a week. A week would allow them to understand the daily routine of the building. Kae would argue for a second week, would argue more caution, but it would not be given. Zean would argue that there were other considerations and the others would agree with him, even the older swordsman. But if there was enough variation . . .

There would not be.

Ahead, up a steep incline, the pyres appeared, their metal structures barely visible. Looking at it now, Bueralan wondered how it was that he had survived the chase off the ledge: not only did it drop more sharply than he had thought, but the tall green grass looked more dangerous than it had when he had followed, hiding the shape of the land, the holes and the trees and the creatures that lived in both. But he had survived to follow a Quor'lo down the mountain, to where it stretched out gently and men and women had dug shafts to find a fortune to last generations, the openings of which were now peppered with wooden covers.

One of them was open.

Without being asked, the saboteur approached it, Ugly and Handsome behind him. He was aware, as his naked foot pushed at the cover to reveal the inky darkness beneath, that others had gathered around him, that they watched him and followed his gaze down the broken ladder into the darkness, where—

'There is no water,' Mother Estalia said. 'You said the mines were flooded.'

The ladder continued, broken in places, but more intact than Bueralan had previously thought. 'It was,' he said. 'But look at the wall. There is a crack running through it. Something has caused the wall to fracture.'

'The explosion, I would imagine.' She peered down at the wooden covering. 'The lock has clearly been broken.'

Bueralan did not reply. Instead, he watched as Estalia turned to those around her and began issuing orders for ropes to be set, for a path down the shaft to be made. She wanted it to be strong enough to take herself, her four priests, Ugly and Handsome and himself.

'Won't you please reconsider,' Dural said, as the men around him began to move, to prepare what she asked. 'Any of our men would gladly take his place.'

'They are needed up here,' she replied. 'Lieutenant, he has been given to us for a reason. Do not doubt that.'

One week, Bueralan thought. *I have a week to reach Dark before they enter the church. They reached Ranan this morning.*

6.

If Lady Wagan's office was a measure of her intelligence, her strengths and her weaknesses, then it was an office that presented a woman with a mind that held both disarray and order within it equally. Paper was strewn across her table, scrawled notes and an array of knick-knacks. Yet each of the items on her desk had an order, a place: that much was clear. Through it all was a thread of control, of an underlying structure that was known to the woman who sat behind the table, who held all before her in a glance that did not require a rigid structure, but who was happy to allow overlaps and meshes.

And then there was the drink.

'Good laq is the work of an artist.' The near-finished bottle sat before the Lady of the Spine, while she passed one to Ayae and poured one for herself. 'All liquor is, truly, but it is laq that I find has the most variety in its creation, the most room between the good, the excellent, and the brilliant. In part, it is the difference in how it is made. Take this, for example: this expensive bottle was made in ice. It is the work of a brewer in Faaisha. Once a year, he and a crew of fifty sail up into the cold north, to where the ground is made from ice, where, if there was no ice, there would be no ground, and where your exposed skin dies from cold if you are not careful. He stays there for three months and he and his men – they are all men, incidentally – freeze the start of the liquor, and spend the remaining three months removing the ice from it.'

'Why would they do that?' she asked.

'To make a fine drink.' Behind her, midday's sun had begun to set, the afternoon's rising in the empty sky. 'Is that not reason enough?'

'I have had laq before,' Ayae said. 'This isn't that different.'

'But it *is* different.' The Lady finished her drink, poured a second. 'Sometimes, a big act only results in a small difference, but it can be the difference between greatness and success.'

'Is that what is happening here?' She was only halfway through her own, but did not intend to drink a second; she had never overly enjoyed laq. 'What you and Heast have planned with the gates is a big act that will only make a small difference at the end? We will still be driven out of our home.'

'There are large differences. Sadly, I might add. Perhaps it would be as you said if we could leave before the fighting started. If Yeflam would open its gate to refugees who were not bloodied, both you and I would be on the road now. But the Keepers will not help us unless we are in dire need. The social pressure of seeing men and women in terror is the only thing that will move them into real action and see them break their shallow neutrality and publicly align themselves against the Leerans. If I could, I would negotiate a peace with the Leerans that I could undermine and erode, but they are interested only in what is beneath us. That leaves few options in either direction. The truth is, we are an empire of finance and if we fall, there will be people lined up to pick our carcass clean – so when you say that our act is big, yes, you are right; but when you say the difference is small, you are wrong.'

'Our homes will be lost.'

'Our homes will still be here. I will give up nothing.'

'And your favour?' Ayae placed the half-empty glass on the table. 'Do you plan to explain it to me yet?'

'When Reila—' A knock on the door interrupted the Lady of the Spine, but she smiled when it was pushed open. 'Who is here.'

The elderly healer smiled, fatigue straining the edges of her lips. With a greeting to the Lady and Ayae, she pulled a chair from the side of the room and seated herself before the table, taking the glass of laq that was poured for her. 'You'll have to accept my apologies. I had to attend a meeting with Heast at the last minute.'

'Any problems?'

'None you have not already heard. An army is in front of us, Steel is half its strength and the saboteurs have been a complete failure.' She hesitated. 'However, Qian was not there.'

The Lady shifted her gaze to Ayae who responded, uncomfortably. 'He said that he might not go,' she said.

No more was required from her, for which she was thankful. Instead, Muriel Wagan nodded to Reila, who pulled out a wrapped bundle from the satchel she carried. Small, the size of a bird, it was wrapped in green cloth, and was followed by a notebook, half of the pages used.

'You recognize the bird that was found in Sergeant Illaan Alahn's house, no doubt,' Lady Wagan began. 'With it are the notes comparing what was found in the bird with what has been found in Illaan, a compound that caused a scandal two hundred and seventy-two years ago when the recipe was sold to a black-market apothecary in Yeflam by the Keeper Fo.'

'It caused a scandal,' Reila continued, 'because it was seen as an attempt by Fo to move into the underworld, to take not just a financial stake but to claim all who worked in it as his own, as his province. It was the first time that any of the Keepers had tried anything like that and the scandal that came from it was not about the poison itself, but rather the idea that anyone would seek to lay claim to a group of people, to start appearing before them as a divinity. The result was a loss of power for the Keepers. As a result, the poison became known as Divinities Facade.'

'Will it — is there an antidote?' Ayae asked.

'In a day, maybe two,' she said. 'Hopefully it will be in time for Illaan.'

She said nothing.

'The book and the bird are our evidence against Yeflam,' Lady Wagan said quietly. 'It is leverage that shows the Keepers were not sent here to help us, but to stop us from retreating. It is not much leverage for us against them, but it is leverage for the Traders Union. That conflict I would prefer to avoid, but it is from the Union that we are receiving what little help we are, and not the Enclave. Furthermore, the change in leadership in the Union has meant that we have to offer more now than we did before. To the previous leader, Lian Alahn, a battered and bruised brave band of refugees who have fled their destroyed city was an event that he believed he could use to erode the power of the Enclave. Under his leadership, the Union were not interested in destroying the men and women who ruled over them, but rather about sharing. Their new leader, Benan Le'ta, is a much more radical man. He does not believe that battered refugees are worth much.'

Ayae's voice cracked on the first word, but the second was strong, clear. 'What . . . what do you want from me?'

'It is said that a Keeper will not attack a Keeper, that to do so invites the wrath of all the cursed upon you.' She lifted up the drink in a salute. 'Because of that, I would like you to carry our evidence through the gates of Yeflam to Benan Le'ta, to ensure that when we fall back, there is someone waiting for us at the gate of Yeflam.'

7.

Bueralan descended last, watching the unmoving silhouette of Dural as he was lowered slowly into the darkness.

Once his feet touched mud he released the rope, leaving it slack while his eyesight adjusted to the frail light at the bottom of the shaft. Constantly under threat from shadow, he could make out the shapes of those around him, but their details – their expressions – eluded him. Yet he could see that one of the priests had lifted the glass orb that had been used to light the path he'd swum earlier with Zaifyr and that either Handsome or Ugly was crouched before the crawlspace that led deeper into the mine.

'You are going to say into the smell, aren't you?' said the latter. 'That's what you're going to say to me, isn't it?'

'Take a deep breath.'

It was hard going, more so for Bueralan whose hands were still handcuffed together, forcing him to move like a three-legged dog. Yet, it was better than when he had swum before: the sense of being crushed by stone had abated, though it still lingered on the edge of his consciousness. Halfway through the crawlspace he realized that enough mud had worked its way up between his wrists and chains that he could pull his hands out, if he twisted and turned enough. It would not be easy, but he could do it, given enough time; but with Ugly behind and Handsome in front, and priests both in front and behind, the saboteur did not have the time and plodded on slowly, smiling grimly as those in front of him gagged on the putrid air ahead.

Once in the bolt-hole himself, he held his breath and quickly pushed through the fissure into the City of Ger.

Or what remained of it.

A part of the stone roof had fractured, resulting in a large part of the cavern collapsing. No doubt the same explosion that had cleared out the rancid water had left its mark here. Standing on the path to the temple, his gaze adjusting to the pale light, Bueralan located the break point: the newly drilled holes in the ceiling. Those around him would have difficulty recognizing that, and he was caught in two minds about it: firstly, he believed it better not to explain it, not to tip the extent of Heast's plan; but he realized that it offered him an easy opportunity to thin out the numbers around him, an opportunity for either one of his guards to be sent back to the rope, to Dural, the general, the Faithful and their war.

'Tell me, Captain, how did this look before?' Mother Estalia stepped around him, the muddy priestess gazing up at the ruined ceiling. 'Was it complete?'

'Mostly,' he replied. 'The paths had eroded and houses crumbled. But there was destruction as well, evidence of fighting.'

'Yes, of course.' Slowly, she began walking down the street, the ruined buildings on either side shadowed crypts, their open doors dark depths that held bones and little else. 'The people who lived in Ger's tomb were eventually killed by the first of the Mireean people, most of whom came in search of gold. What they panned from rivers and dug from the ground laid the foundation for the city that they built around the Spine, the original base of the city above us. But they first had to murder the people who lived beneath, who saw everything in it as sacred to Ger himself and the Spine of Ger as a holy artefact, a walk they took in birth and death, a journey across their god to celebrate and mourn. At their peak, those people numbered twenty thousand if I recall correctly.'

'They were eradicated.'

'They did not have a standing army,' she said. 'They were a fractured community, divided by their cities and temples, with no centralized government. They fought a guerilla campaign with intermittent attempts at suing for peace for over three decades. Their enemy was similar in that it had no central government, but their wealth eventually demanded that they come together and form one, which resulted in the building of the first Mireea. It was there that the People of Ger destroyed their last chance for peace, when they burnt the city to the ground. The Mireeans hired an army to clear out the caves, a campaign that took eight bloody years but which saw the end of a people and their holy work.'

'And that is why you're marching on Mireea now?' Ahead of him, Bueralan could hear the rush of water, the start of the river. 'Because of that work that was stopped?'

'Always the spy, I see.'

He shrugged. 'It's mostly curiosity.'

'The Mireeans are a faithless people, that much is true, and their deaths are a firm statement in this new world, but . . .

no, that is not the reason.' Ahead, the river appeared, the violent red light of it brighter the second time, stronger, as if in response to the destruction around it. 'Within this tomb there are twenty-three temples. That is what is recorded, at any rate, but I would not be surprised if there were more. Each of the buildings was built over a fissure directly over Ger's body. It gave the priests access to the wounds that he had sustained against his brothers. For the centuries that they lived here the priests tended his wounds, attempting to heal him. It was their belief that he would rise again. Which way, Captain?'

Bueralan indicated to the left and, slowly, they began to follow the river.

'We do not wish to heal Ger.' Estalia raised her voice over the water. 'His time is done, as is the case with all the old gods. Very few will argue with that. But there is power still in him, power that we have been sent to take and to return.'

'To return to who?'

'To the gods' child.' The red light mixed with her smile, stained her teeth. 'Why do you think the gods went to war, Captain?'

8.

Zaifyr remained seated for longer than he intended, his mind adrift.

He had not attended Heast's meeting, but that had not surprised him. After the messenger had been and gone, leaving a written note to both him and Ayae, Zaifyr had known that he would not set foot onto the roof of *The Pale House*. There had been no insult. No demand. In truth, the letter had contained nothing out of the ordinary. It was a simple request by the Captain of the Spine and, while Zaifyr did not dislike the ageing soldier, the illusion that he was a cheaply paid mercenary at the other's call was only that and he had no desire to perpetuate it.

Truthfully, he had lost his desire to do so shortly after his arrival. The Quor'lo had been of enough interest for him to ignore the presence of the Keepers. But Samuel Orlan, followed by Ayae, had ensured that he'd never been able to assume the role he had sought to play. He should have recognized it when he had stepped into the burning building, drawn by the presence of Ayae, the feel of her power, and reached through the fire to slit the throat of the Quor'lo.

'Why shouldn't we be interested?' Jae'le said, months earlier. Zaifyr had been living in his house, a huge, sprawling, three-levelled building that twisted through two ancient trees, bent to the will of the man who had lived in it for a century, hidden deep within the Qarli jungle. 'It is some distance from us, I allow that, but Mireea is built upon the body of Ger and if an army led by priests does truly march on it, shouldn't we be interested?'

'You don't even know if this is true.'

But he did.

Zaifyr should have known as well. He should have looked at his brother − the Animal Lord, the First Immortal − and known that he was not a man given to fancy.

Yet, it was also true that Jae'le had become solitary, a hermit who had, for centuries, only left his home to travel a narrow path that snaked through the broken peaks of the Eakar Mountains, to sit outside the crooked madhouse he had built. It was he who had opened it and offered to take him in, to care for him. That was why Zaifyr had always returned to the house, to its twisted limbs, slow heat and animals that spoke no words to him.

What did his brother know? The question was one he repeated as the suns rose and set. Why had he insisted that Zaifyr leave shortly after his arrival? What game was being played?

No answer was forthcoming. The afternoon's sun rose, the heat sinking into his bones, and he felt fatigue seep into him. He knew that Jae'le had kept information from him, but that was not unusual: all five brothers and sisters had done so in the past, himself included. He kept his secrets partly as a by-product of his desire not to be judged, and partly because he had grown disinterested in the debates and squabbles of his siblings. He had not, as he had said to Jae'le, visited Aelyn once his ship had been pulled into dock outside Yeflam; not because of their past, but because he did not wish to be drawn into the squabble that existed between her and the others regarding her Keepers and their ideologies.

He had only his own apathy to blame, a fact he could recognize now, after having spent time with Ayae.

He ran a hand through his hair, shaking the charms, and rose. Her life was so strongly tied to Mireea and the war upon Ger's corpse that she would not be free of it for a time, if ever. Some wars malingered – he knew that, certainly. They dug beneath the skin to bury in the veins and blood, to become new muscles, new pulses. Zaifyr had seen men and women become entrenched in history, unwilling to leave at first, and unable to do so later: Aela Ren, the Innocent, was one such man, and his war would only end when another killed him.

If another killed him.

The comparison between Ayae and Ren was an uncomfortable one and Zaifyr let it fall from his mind as he left Ayae's house. He walked the streets, looping two blocks around *The Pale House* to his empty hotel, in case one of the Mireean Guard or Heast saw him. Not that he suspected the old soldier would say a word to him; they would glance at each other, one would nod, but no words would be exchanged. Still, it was easier – and a cynical curve to his lips emerged at the thought – to take the longer road and mingle with the people there.

While doing exactly that he spied a woman, her left eye damaged and scarred by a bird's claws, emerging from a simple house.

Apart from for the injury, there was nothing about the woman that would have drawn his eye: she was of medium height, wearing the mismatched leather armour that nearly all Mireeans wore now. By her side was a short sword, the pommel plain, the scabbard likewise. Her hair was short, brown with grey flecked through it, and Zaifyr thought that she was no older than forty, a tanned white like many of the men and women who lived in Mireea.

Slowing his pace, the charm-laced man followed her, though it soon became apparent to him that he need not have worried. From over the shoulder of two large men ('How many are there? All I see is a sea of them,' said one; 'I've heard ten thousand,' said one to the other) he could have reached out, could have taken the discoloured cloth she raised to her wounded eye, to the pus and blood that further stained it, that caused her to wince.

She turned at a T-junction, her objective seemingly the hospital at the end. Zaifyr moved around two men between them, quickening his pace, but waited until she had pushed open the door to close the gap, catching the door as it swung shut. The lack of sound caused her to turn.

Her face, tightly drawn in pain, revealed its recognition. She turned and sprinted deeper into the hospital and Zaifyr, momentarily startled by a quality of desperation, of need, in her expression, hesitated. He gave her four to five steps, time enough to burst through a door that he shouldered through, time enough to find her in a room full of occupied beds, each holding a mercenary from Steel, with a pair of healers working through the ranks.

'What is this?'

One of the latter called out as Zaifyr reached the woman, as he grabbed her shoulder and felt it give beneath his hand, felt it crumble with fragility, as if something were rotten beneath.

Then, blood splattered across his face.

He stepped back, momentarily confused. He had not hit her, had not attacked her – and then he saw, wiping the blood from his eyes, her smile, her bloody smile, as she stepped away from him, as she stumbled to the ground. A wave of nausea followed and he staggered, surprised, shocked. He had not – he could not – he raised his bloody hand to the approaching healers, attempting to call out—

He fell to the hard, white-tiled floor.

The Circumstances of Birth

For many years, I have looked upon the city beneath me, trying to see how its dark towers and lamp-lit streets could help the voiceless. I performed terrible acts and allowed for terrible acts to be done in my name. Worse, the men and women who perform these acts thank me for the privilege, for the moral certainty, for the frames I have given them that absolve all from their cruelty. They thank me though they need not, they thank me because they believe I am the child of a god.

But I am not.

I am not, no, and the terrible truth is that everything my brothers and sisters and I have done has been with a belief in an absolute authority that we do not have.

—Qian, *The Godless*

1.

He was not dead, but neither was he alive, not as he knew it.

Zaifyr's body lay on the floor beneath him, familiar yet not. He could feel a chill in his spine, but it was dull, the pain hidden behind another's. That pain, in contrast, was a full-body chill, of empty veins and lungs, of cold, cold emptiness sharply accentuated around the shoulder and the eye, the echo of brittle bones frozen deeply within him. Within *her.*

He felt the woman who had died in front of him as clearly as he did himself, the second presence surrounding him as he gazed not just at his prone form, but at hers as well.

She was dead.

Just as he promised, she was dead.

Zaifyr's will leashed her panic, stopping her thoughts before they overwhelmed him. It was the same expression of power he had used to flesh out the haunts in his hotel room. But the result was different. Her awareness formed an undefined tether, threatening to bond her to his being and trap him in her. A witch and the dead felt the same, a warlock and his blood rites, the bonding of the living to the dead. If she were dead, then he was alive: and he applied pressure over her being, bent her will until he felt calm, controlled, and could look about the room.

All were dead.

The haunts of mercenaries and healers lingered over the prone, empty forms of their bodies, lying in beds and on the ground, while half a dozen had fallen at the door of the ward.

It was clear to Zaifyr that he had lost time after he had fallen, that the separation of his spirit from his body had not taken place quickly. He was not yet sure how it had happened; it was a new experience for him, one he did not feel comfortable with. It did not feel right. The world had a faint grey taint to it, as if it were slowly being petrified. Is this what the gods felt as they died? The slow, torturous death? Did that mean he *was* dying, that their power over him had rendered him a death centuries in length?

Forcing the haunt of the assassin to move out of the ward he entered the hallway, and found more bodies there.

None had made it out of the hospital, thankfully. Instead, a bar lay on the floor, the last of the mercenaries to reach it attempting to barricade the door, to stop anyone from entering.

The door opened.

He said—

Fo.

He said, 'Saet, did you not think I would notice you in Mireea? You have done too much for me to walk down a street unnoticed. No, don't speak. I don't want to hear your defence. You are a paid assassin. You need no excuse. But did you truly think I would not smell my own poison on Illaan Alahn's birds? And then, later, on him? That old healer here knows. When I went into her hospital to look at the sergeant, I thought she would attack me, that she would order the soldiers in their beds to pick up their weapons. It wasn't until I stood beside him that I could understand her fury. Then to have the evidence presented to me by another shortly after by the Madman himself!'

The door closed behind the Keeper. Slowly, he made his way down the hall, pausing at each body, turning each over, running his scarred hands over each, before rising and continuing.

'The Enclave sent us here to learn about the Leerans, that is all.' Fo's hand fell heavily onto her shoulder, his fingers digging painfully into her skin. *'But who, I imagine, will believe that back home? I think that is what offends me the most, right now, that I will be blamed for assassination plans I consider beneath me. After all, if I had wanted Illaan Alahn dead, I would not have given a poison that lingers. Nor would I have ordered assassination attempts on the Captain and Lady of the Spine, much less the Madman. I can only imagine that the money that was offered to you by the Benan Le'ta to enrage his rival and frame me was of such an amount that your common sense was abandoned.'*

It was clear that Fo could not sense Zaifyr or any of the dead. If so, he would have noticed how the latter lingered around him, their chilled presence drawn by his power and the heat of him.

'Do you feel the cold in your shoulder?' She nodded beneath his scarred gaze, unable to do anything but. *'Good. I have a simple task for you, Saet, one that will serve to remind the Traders Union of what will await them when I return to Yeflam.'*

'I will—'

'You will die.' Beneath Fo's fingers, Zaifyr could feel the bones of her shoulder fracture. *'The plague you unleash here will leave nothing but the gods' chosen to return to Yeflam, a plague that will ravage the men and women who believe that I could be framed so easily.'*

He approached Zaifyr's fallen body, the expressionless calm

of his face breaking, a slight smile emerging across his pale features. 'Now, this is a gift, Madman. Are you dead?' The Keeper's fingers pressed down on his neck, feeling the pulse. 'Not quite, but it is a shallow coil that ties you to this world and it will break soon enough.'

Zaifyr could not return to his body.

He searched deep within himself, pulled his awareness from the assassin's haunt, separated all parts of his being forcibly, harshly, the actions disorientating, damaging to his awareness —

— and which resulted in his awareness in another.

A man, a young man, a mercenary. A chill seeped into his arm, where it had been broken and rebroken, before being set.

'Your eyes are open, but you do not see. How apt.' Fo rose. 'Can you hear me, Madman? I have often wondered if the gods could understand us as they die. If they could hear our words and rage at what we said. Now, I ask, do you? I did not plan this, but I will not walk from it, either. The sounds of Asila have never left me. If, when I return home, Aelyn seeks to punish me for what has happened here, then so be it. I will gladly own the price for your death.'

2.

It was not until late in the day that news of the outbreak reached Ayae. By then, she had returned to her house, to the quiet of it, to the stillness that lay at its core. She sat down, feeling not the moral responsibility of documents that she held upon herself. Zaifyr was not there. He had left her a note and she believed that he had made good on his earlier words, and left the city, the result of which left her feeling oddly weighted as if she had lost a part of herself and she drifted into a restless sleep.

She was woken by her neighbours talking and the story of the outbreak that none would bring to her.

She made her way quickly through the dimly lit streets, the crowds thickening as she reached the hospital. It was a terrible parody of the people who had usually swarmed around them for the markets, complete with members of the Mireean Guard and wooden barriers around long lamps, closing off the path that led to the building but leaving it in a burnished light – a bubble tainted by fire and smoke. The guards did not help her though: they stopped all from approaching, but their gaze never fell from the closed door of the building.

Queila Meina stood at the back of the crowd, her arms folded across the chest of her clean, dark stained leather. Beside her stood Bael and Maalen, large, silent shadows, the hilts of their weapons flared against the wall behind.

'Do you know what has happened?' Ayae asked, approaching.

'No.' The mercenary's voice was cold, her gaze on the hospital. 'We know only the story that has been spread around: that a guard approached the building and found patients at the door, who had died trying to barricade it shut. No one knows if he died before he alerted others or if he is still alive. Based upon the look of the Healer and the frustration she feels at Lieutenant Mills for not allowing her to pass, I suspect that he did.'

'I heard it was a Keeper who found it,' Bael said. 'That he entered after dismissing the guards at the door.'

'Did you speak to one of the guards?'

'No.'

'Then we still know nothing,' Meina coldly continued. 'Not even how our men fare.'

She had begun to say, 'I'll ask—' when another voice spoke over her. It was a voice that she knew well, one that was casual in tone, but not intent, and whose inflection revealed not just a lack of care on his part, but a purposeful baiting. 'They're dead,' said Bau, not pausing in his walk past any of them. 'Why trouble yourself over questions you already know the answer to, Captain?'

'You should hope you are wrong, Keeper.'

He turned. 'Little Flame,' he said blandly. 'You best remind your friend who she talks to.'

'I know who you are,' the Captain of Steel said.

466

'She knows,' Ayae told him. 'Do you need an introduction to her?'

Bau's smile was fleeting, a quick cut between his lips before he continued to make his way to the side of Lieutenant Mills and Reila. Both stood at the front of the crowd, and neither made an indication of greeting as the Keeper stepped through the barricade.

'I only left there this morning,' Meina said quietly. 'Only this morning.'

'Let me ask.' Before she could respond, Ayae pushed through the crowd, following the path left by Bau. As she did she heard Reila's voice, rising with each step she took. 'You go in and you retrieve your companion.' Gone was the fatigue, the tiredness; gone also was any semblance of compromise, of peace. 'You bring him out here right now! I will not tolerate what he has done!'

'Consider your words, please,' Bau replied with the same inoffensive blandness. 'If you are accusing—'

'You know very well I speak with authority,' she returned. 'If I find that you charlatans have been respon—'

'Charlatans?' Cracks in his voice appeared, fractures of contempt revealed. 'We are both diplomats from a city you hope to find refuge in, and both of us are children of the gods, with more knowledge than you have obtained in your entire life!'

'Ma'am,' said Lieutenant Mills, her leather-clad hand on Reila's shoulder. 'Fo has emerged.'

In contrast to his companion the Keeper Fo, who had moments before gently closed the door to the hospital behind him, was a figure that radiated certainty. His scarred eyes appraised the scene as the path drew him closer to not just

Reila, but the crowd that had formed. The crowd, Ayae thought, that had no love for him or Bau.

Or her.

'They're dead,' Fo said, speaking to the crowd as much as he did to Reila. 'Your staff. The patients. You can go in, if you wish – the risk is minimal. There is only one man alive in there and the disease but lingers docile in him.'

Illaan?

The thought was unbidden, unwanted.

'What have you done?' asked the elderly healer.

The Keeper's quiet, half laugh was clear to all. 'You seek to blame me for this? When the only man who lives in there is a man that both Bau and I warned you against?'

'Zaifyr,' Ayae whispered.

'His real name is Qian. A name that anyone who has studied history will find in the corners. He is death—'

'You *know* he would not kill.' Behind her, Meina and her two uncles approached, their shadows falling across her own. 'What have you *done* to him?'

'You have no right to ask anything of me, child.' Fo's scarred gaze met hers evenly. 'You made your alliances.'

She had taken one step when the horn sounded. One step, her hands beginning to burn. One step, responding to Fo's smile. One step, her warming hands falling to the hilts of both her new swords. One step, but that was all before a horn released in a lone, urgent note across Mireea, a deep call that resonated through all who stood before the hospital.

'Positions!' Lieutenant Mills' voice rang out before a second step could be taken. 'All to defensive positions!'

The Faithful had arrived.

3.

'To understand why the concept of a child was frightening to the gods, you first have to understand how they lived,' said Mother Estalia. 'In our post-divine world, we no longer ask that question. We have stopped asking how gods saw us, what our purpose was, how we are part of their plan. Instead, we ask, what existed before them? A foolish question, especially since the answer that is put forth by philosophers and alchemists and astrologers . . . is nothing. They write in countless books that before a large, cataclysmic event, there was absence. There was nothing. Life, these men and women argue, was born out of whatever this event was, the force of it awakening a spark that over millennia allowed for the creation of all life. It is the wrong question and the wrong answer, but it is an understandable mistake, born from watching the world around us and its growth.'

She had begun speaking on the rocky shoreline before the broken Temple of Ger, though Bueralan had not asked her to do so.

He had not spoken to her, or to anyone else, since they had begun the narrow, treacherous walk along the red-lit river. No one had asked if they were going in the right direction, but the temple was easily visible. Instead, he remained quiet, fearing that if he lost his concentration, he might stumble. The muscles in his legs already ached not just from the journey, but from having to balance himself against the slippery wall with chained hands. He was keenly aware that every misstep he took, every strain on his body, saw his ability to escape gradually slip away.

And so he was silent as he weighed his options.

'The truth, however, is that time is not linear,' she continued. 'While you and I experience it as a concept that has a beginning, middle and end, that structure is merely a product of our life, of mortality, and the time that we have constructed to measure it. When, in discussing the world, we begin at the "start" we do so in a flawed position, for the "beginning" of anything is a construct, a narrative distinction that you and I have been taught to recognize as a social one. For the gods, however, that concept of time does not — and did not, for some — exist.

'It is not disagreed that the divine experienced time differently than you and I. Earlier histories report stories of the gods being slow to react to prayers, of intervening on disasters decades after the fact; of curses put on dead men and women for failings long gone; of rewarding success that had turned into disaster. Eventually, it was agreed that the way by which we could understand how a god saw us, was by understanding that they existed in a singular moment that was defined by the past, the present and the future, and all its possible outcomes and permutations. One priest wrote that all elements of time were merged together in a constant awareness for a god, with no sense of causality.'

The climb down the jagged wall had been just as difficult for Bueralan. His fingers, without the strength to hold his weight, slipped multiple times. For all but the last, he was able to judge where he landed, ending on a narrow ledge or a small path. For the last of these falls, he misjudged the direction and ended in a two-foot drop that saw him arrive at the base in a dirty, injured mess, his knuckles skinned, his shoulder bruised and a mix of both on the left side of his head.

'It is difficult to find many people who hold this awareness of the world, now. There are a few, the surviving servants of the gods, and one of the new immortals.' Mother Estalia stood beside the decaying corpse of the Quor'lo as if it were a talisman, a truth. 'The latter theorized that the gods were dying, that they had been dying for thousands of years while they fought, while they were alive and while they were dead. He offered a frightening vision of gods who saw multiple strands of time, who were always dying, always alive, always in war, always at peace.

'But he did not know about the child.'

She paused as, across the lake, the four silent priests rose from the water like strange newborn to the fissure that ran down the temple.

'Very few outside the gods knew about the child. She was the creation of the Goddess of Fertility, of Linae. It was perhaps fitting that a god who fashioned herself as a woman gave birth, but she did not do it in the way that you or I understand. Rather than use her own form, she dug into the earth and created a womb from soil, from mineral, from blood, from bone, and infused it with part of her life. She gave a part of her divinity to the ground, so that it would pulse, breathe and incubate the child she had created, though she would be unable to explain why. Perhaps the reason for it is as simple as her death, for she made the womb as she experienced her death at the hands of the Sun God, Sei. Or, perhaps the reason is different, and if so it is lost to us now.

'For Sei, who would be called the Murderer by us, the reasons were written down. He told his priests that he struck Linae because that was what he had always done. Everything existed as one and once the child was born – and the child always existed – he killed Linae. He had always done so. He would always do so. There had never been a time when he did not kill Linae. It was, he said, a truth.'

She turned to Bueralan, but there was no kindness in her gaze, only dedication, commitment and an obvious, belief.

'It was fate, a single, unalterable fate,' she said. 'With the child, all other time was lost. No more would there be multiple strands, multiple outcomes, and with it, the gods lost their self-determination, their freedom. They no longer saw possibilities, they saw facts, and the gods feared it.'

4.

'Runner, find Lieutenant Mills and have her report to me.' On the roof of *The Pale House*, a boy and a girl stood attentively behind the Captain of the Spine. Heast's copper-and-silver eye-piece ran along the wall, pausing like a scavenger on debris, on oil that lay slick on the stonework, on the dead. 'Runner, inform Captain Meina that Steel will be reinforcing the Sixth. She will also be taking command from the fallen Sergeant Pael. Then find Sergeant Eran from the Eighth and inform him that he is to support Steel and the Sixth if the fighting continues. Also—'

He stopped, his mirrored gaze falling from the Spine, and into the dark that pooled around the fighting. He could not say why he ran his gaze to the edge of the trees and had stopped speaking, other than instinct. There was nothing but languid darkness. Nothing until— 'Runner, my previous order is altered. Inform Captain Meina that she will need to prepare for catapults.'

5.

'That story.' Bueralan stopped speaking as he stretched his back, attempting to ease the cramped muscles and only partly succeeding. 'The witches from my home bottle the souls of the dead, for a price. You sound just like them when they say that the family will want to pay a prosperous pregnant woman to drink it, to ensure that their kin's next life is good.'

'Are you accusing me of lying?' Mother Estalia did not appear bothered. 'I have just explained to you one of the great mysteries of the world. I explained to you why the gods went to war, as explained to me—'

'—by a child,' he finished.

Her smile was benign, condescending in its every curve. 'Follow me, Captain.' Her first step took her to the edge of the still lake, where a small knife appeared in her hand. She sliced the tip of a finger, letting the blood fall – and took a second step onto the water as it did, where her feet found a hard surface, similar to board. 'It is not difficult for me to understand your scepticism,' she said. 'I was young, myself, when we found our god. So young that the two men behind you were not yet born, nor were their parents. They find it difficult to stomach your words, but only because they do not remember a time without the gaze of a god in their heart. But I remember the emptiness of my youth. The fear I had when I heard stories of cursed men and women. The terror when I saw them.

'I watched a childhood friend of mine die as her skin shed itself daily, similar to a snake, but without the grace of nature. My friend was five at the time, and the shedding left her bloody and raw and in constant pain. She cried out to a god, any god, but there were only the cures promised by witches and shamans, cures that dulled pain and nothing else. To watch that was to understand not just that there were no gods, but why no man or woman desired to hear of divinity again.'

Beneath his feet, the water was cold but solid. A display of power she had not shown to those beneath her, who had swum the length.

'But then, I also remember the visions of my childhood. They began a week after the death of my friend, dreams of such vitality and strength that were impossible to ignore. We were called like the prophets of the old in our dreams, given tasks to attend, bent to obedience. Once we had accepted that, we joined each other in travel to the Eakar Mountains in search of our God. There, they found a forgotten valley that lay between the broken crown of a range. In it, the remains of empty villages and white bones were threaded by poisonous rivers and toxic soil.

'Of the twenty who made the journey only half reached the middle of the valley. Three died while crossing the ocean, in fights, in sickness, but the greatest toll were the seven who died in the valley. Three men and four women fell to the toxicity there as they made their way to the centre, their skin drying and their breath fading until they crumbled into dust. My mother was one of these women and, even though I mourned her passing for years, I eventually came to understand that she perished because she did not have the faith to continue. She had followed my father and me in our journey, having had the same vision as us, but I believe now that the longer it took – and I had aged two years since we left Leera – the more the vision diluted, turned watery for her. She had lost her faith by the time we stepped into the valley and wasted away, while the faithful among us remained strong.

'If she had not lost her faith, my mother would have been witness to the sight of her vision, to the spherical husk of soil that floated in the middle of the valley. I can still remember how it felt as we approached it. It was a power unlike anything I had felt before, yet it was not complete. What was in the soil was both perfect and flawed and as we stood before that, we were humbled.

'We broke through the soil slowly, each crack revealing a warmth, a soft inside of roots that encircled the arms, legs and body of a girl. Gazing upon her, we saw only divinity, though she was not yet awake. My father, who carried her from the earthen womb, said she at first weighed nothing – but as we returned to Leera that changed. She became a solid weight, too heavy for arms at first, then for a single donkey to carry. It was a team of bulls who pulled her into our country after four years of travel, still asleep. My father said she gathered the weight of the world about her as we went.'

Ahead was the broken opening of the Temple of Ger. To Bueralan's gaze, the shadows within were a dark stain that could not be removed.

'He never did see her awake. My father died at the age of sixty-seven, the proud caretaker of the church he had placed his God within. With the aid of the King Anann, he designed and built the huge structure upon his return, ensuring that a chamber was built deep into the ground beneath it, and it was there that he laid her sleeping body. He claimed that she needed to be near to the soil, to be nurtured by the earth itself. He harboured a belief that Linae had infused the very ground with her power, but it was twenty-three years after his death before we could ask such a question, before we could hear her agree, in part. There, she taught us about how the gods saw time, how even as they died they were alive, how with her creation, an infinite number of possibilities had collapsed and that they struggled with that, still. She could herself, however, only see one future, could experience time in only one fashion.'

'And then she told you that you would have to change that.' Before Bueralan, Estalia drifted through the opening, leaving him with his cold toes to navigate the stone and broken glass along the edge of the temple. 'How long before she said you would have to go to war?'

'War is a certainty in life.'

'Death and taxes are a certainty. War is something we create, we strive for.'

'So are taxes,' she replied drily. 'But to answer your question, Captain, we knew from the start.'

After a small jab from behind, the saboteur eased himself through the broken frame and to the cold, slippery floor. 'Why is that?'

'She is an incomplete god.' Mother Estalia followed the tracks left by the priests, light blooming in her every footstep, illuminating faded murals, creeping mould, broken pews and rusted, broken armour. Soon, a stairwell appeared before her. 'The war ensured that, Captain. As the gods died, their bodies broke. Their power spilled from them, and spills still. It is responsible for every cursed person you have ever seen, from those who function to those who do not. It is a power seeking its owner, its rightful place – a power that our god is here to reclaim, first from the bodies of her parents.'

'Why not the cursed first? You would even find support in this part of the world.'

'We tried.' The stairwell was long and slippery, but Mother Estalia did not take the rail. 'We found one of the youngest in Mireea but it was beyond us. It was chance, truly, nothing more. The Quor'lo had been sent to find the temples of Ger, but when that girl's power awoke, we sent it after her. We thought to kill her and bring the body to our god. The power was hers by right, after all, but we learned quickly that a single cursed is a difficult enemy for us, and that to find one isolated is impossible.'

6.

When Steel moved to reinforce the Sixth Division of the Mireean Guard, Ayae was with them.

She had not been assigned a place on the Spine, had not been given a place to stand in the defence and, as the horn's call had faded into the night's cooling air, she was without direction. She wanted to go into the hospital: inside were both Zaifyr and Illaan, and despite all that had happened with the latter, she felt an unexpected grief opening inside her, made by the memories of the good times and of their loss. Yet she could not go into the hospital. As the horn faded, Reila ordered the guards to erect a makeshift tent for the injured and then gave one final order — an order for no one else to follow — before she walked through the hospital doors.

Meina's hand fell on her shoulder, breaking her thoughts as the dark-haired mercenary inclined her head to the right. The horn let its deep bellow out again and Ayae nodded. Without words, she accepted the invitation, following Meina and her uncles to Steel's new camp.

After Lady Wagan had praised their escape, their bravery, their survival, Heast had ordered the mercenary unit into a reinforcement position, settling them on the western side of Mireea. For the surviving members of Steel, it had felt like a judgment on the battle they had fought, the losses they had taken and the real measure of their success. They had gone from a large and spacious compound with bunks, cooking fires and storage sheds for arms, to weathered tents stretched across a narrow lane, their weapons kept within. Forced to sleep on bedrolls over hard stone with no fires, the men and women of Steel felt as if they had been judged to have failed, to have not met the challenge given to them.

'Survival,' Queila Meina explained later, 'is not victory.'

Having been part of that survival herself, Ayae felt the verdict unnecessary and harsh, but she remained silent.

In part she did so because she acknowledged that the criticism had little to do with Heast — who she did not believe had a similar complaint — and more with how Steel viewed themselves after the battle.

Slowly, Ayae began to distinguish the sounds of fighting on the wall before her. Swords and axes rang out against steel, against flesh, against stone, against wood. She heard orders shouted. She heard screams. She heard sobbing as well. Among the bodies she could see fire that had sprung up from spilt oil, but so far it lined the edges of the wall, hindering those climbing more than those defending. As she drew closer, she could also see the dead and the injured, and with each step her muscles knitted tight together, threatening to render her motionless in their tension.

Then Steel was on the wall.

They did not charge, yell or announce their arrival. They fanned out and moved beside the Mireean Guards, reinforcing their position to help to push back the Leeran soldiers who had climbed to the top of the wall. Ayae found herself lunging forward, her short swords thrusting at the face of a young man, a man whose face she did not remember, not even after he had fallen. That would only come later, in her dreams: she would remember the smoothness of his white skin, the brown of his eyes, the shaven head, and she would dream of his name, a name she would make up. She would awake after her time on the Spine, surprised at the detail she did remember, at the clarity of it, and would wonder if it was a trick of her subconscious. But at the time, he fell, her blade hacking up through his jaw, and after she, drawing her breath, feeling the rapid beat of her pulse, tried to spy the catapults from her position.

'The push is to draw more of us in.' Meina had explained it to a fanned-out Steel before the runner had left. 'You all know how it works: hit a section hard, force them to reinforce and make a better target. This target will even have fire on the wall. Not that it matters, because the result will be the same: you thin out the rest of the defensive positions for a second push or you thin out the strongpoint with the catapults. The downside for those attacking is the risk that it runs to their own soldiers – but if they don't care about that we will take heavy casualties if we don't fight smart.'

There: on the edge of the cleared kill zone.

She lost sight of it quickly as another wave of Leeran attackers came over the edge of the Spine. Standing next to a Mireean guard, Ayae parried and dodged and slashed and found herself before a tall woman who pulled a long, two-handed sword off her back after clearing the wall and, seeing Ayae, swung it in a straight arc. The guard beside her tumbled to the ground, catching the blade in his chest. A second swing of the now bloody blade saw Ayae back up a second step, the length of her sword not enough to press a hard counter-attack.

Behind the woman another two, then three Leerans appeared.

'Incoming!'

She heard the shout as the boulder hit the ground, too far from the Spine to damage it.

The woman's sword swung again and Ayae rocked back, but only slightly. Pushing herself forward, she caught the return sweep of the sword with her left blade, her arm shuddering from the impact. Her right blade thrust forward quickly, pushing the woman backwards and forcing her to raise her blade above her head – only to find Ayae's sword slashing messily across her throat. And easily. How easy it had become, how easy and—

'Incoming!'

This time she recognized Meina's voice, and saw the dark arc of solid rock bearing down on the Spine.

It crashed solidly into it.

The debris sprayed harshly and she turned her head, feeling whips of rock stinging across her cheek even though she was a good ten lengths away from the impact. At the point of impact, she could see two of the guards had caught chunks of stone and lay on the ground. A Leeran soldier lay between them, his body crushed by the rock. To her horror, Ayae watched the top of a ladder hit the wall and a trio of Leerans filled the gap that had been made.

They were not retreating. That was clear. The Leerans were going to fight through—

The ground shook.

At first she thought it was another boulder, that it had come down where she could not see. But then the ground shook again, her balance wavered, her arms going wide to keep upright, even as the soldiers before her and around her did — and as she managed that, a third shock cost her her stance, saw her fall to her knees as the Spine itself shifted, tilted and—

—*and*—

—straightened, just as the killing ground burst open, showering dirt, mud and rock into the night sky as the ground gave way, as it buckled and crumbled and the siege engines that had come onto it sank forward, devoured by the hungry, angry ground.

'*Steel!*' In the silence, Queila Meina's voice rang out. 'No one leaves alive!'

7.

'Are you sure he will die?'

'It was the faintest pulse, Bau. A death rattle, nothing more. But I can return to cut his throat if that would please you.'

'You know it would not.'

'It would please me. It was all I could do to stop myself, but I did.' The scarred Keeper sat himself down. 'But you must control yourself. It has been long believed that he would never abide by the laws, and Aelyn will not punish us for his death.'

'If he is dead. You said the disease had burnt itself out. If he isn't dead, that means he is now the vaccine to your prized creation.'

'There is enough in him that he will not survive.'

'Reila will be at him now.'

'You believe she can do anything?'

'Do not underestimate her.'

'Do not underestimate *me*,' Fo replied. 'Now, sit. You're making me miss the battle.'

Zaifyr heard Bau grunt, but the white-robed man did sit next to the other and face the Spine. From the second floor of the tower it was lit by fire, the smoke blowing away from their gaze. The Keepers had retreated to the tower after leaving the hospital, unconcerned by the sparseness of it, the emptiness. The Healer had asked Fo three times if Zaifyr was truly dead, until the Keeper began to suggest snappishly that the only way to be sure was to take a knife to Zaifyr's throat. All three knew it was a hollow idea: regardless of where he died, or what he believed, his brothers and sisters would demand to see his body. Despite his bravado, if Fo was found to be responsible, the response from Jae'le at the least would be terrifying.

But I am not dead.

He might as well be.

He had suppressed the haunt of the mercenary he found himself in, turned the voice of the young man into a tiny whisper, and had put aside the pain he had felt when he died. He could move, also, much further than any other haunt he had seen. He suspected that if he wanted, he could walk the haunt into Leera, and feel nothing of the pull that the dead felt to their bodies. Still, there would be no reason to do that, for he could touch nothing, and a creeping cold had begun to settle into him that did not belong to the mercenary.

'Look at their numbers,' Fo said, leaning forward. 'How much of their nation has emerged from the darkness for this war?'

After a moment of study, Bau said, 'More than we estimated.'

'It does appear that way.' He pointed out a part of the Spine where, as if it were a thick, flat snake made from stone, it crawled out into the dark of trees and bush. 'They will push that edge soon, I believe. Work the edges to weaken the middle.'

'Will they come into contact with your plague?'

'Soon enough. Those that Saet infected during her travels will show soon enough.'

Zaifyr had followed the Keeper in the hope of learning more of what had happened to him, but he had heard nothing. Fo did not discuss the details of his poison, how it affected the body, and he left Zaifyr with no idea of how he could cure his body – a body that, like Fo, he believed would not survive the poison inside it.

Approaching the window, he gazed down at the box-like shape of the hospital and focused on the tether of his own body. He had felt it since he left the building, as if it were an echo through a tunnel. He had felt an ache inside him at the call, but it was sickly and he was reluctant to focus on it without knowing how to cure the last of what was in him.

But it was all that would lead him back to his body.

Like a cord, he thought. *A deathly trail by which I can return. What choice do I have?*

He felt it, as if it were in his hands. Around him the haunt – the mercenary who sent his pay to his mother, to his sister, to his family who lived in a small town – dropped from him as he began to follow it. His senses changed and he felt a chill about him.

His very being was suddenly assaulted. Hundreds of haunts lifted into the air about him, each of them launched from the ground in a pale-grey haze, bursting from the battle that was taking place. The haunts came straight to him, drawn to the cord of his life. They saw in it a way to return to life, to end their suffering. They did not fear him, nor consider that – rightly or wrongly – the body he was returning to was his own. They were driven only by their fear, their horror at being dead and their need to return.

Unable to do anything else, Zaifyr released his grip.

The haunts crashed into his being, hit him with a shock so profound and deep that he lost himself.

Zaifyr did not know for how long he drifted, but when he felt his own being again it was not alone. The echo of the earth closing in on him was strong, and for a moment he felt that he was buried – though he knew that this could not possibly be true, for the people of Mireea did not bury their dead, but burned them. Shortly, it became clear to him that, in his loss of awareness, his subconscious had gone in search of another haunt, one whose body also lay in the mountains, who had been lost, and found himself buried alive. He had a vision of rising in one of the narrow caves that the Cities of Ger threaded through, a lost gold digger, his ancient bones the force by which Zaifyr would have to return to the hospital that held his body.

But as his consciousness took more shape and he regained more and more of himself, he realized that he was wrong. He was not solid, not in terms of bone or flesh. Instead, a freezing crush began to emerge across his chest, as if his ribs had been shattered, and he began to become aware of another presence, that of a woman, no older than the mercenary whose haunt he had inhabited before. This woman was not from the Mireean Guard, nor the mercenaries, but rather from the Leeran Army. Memories of a march up the mountain reached him, a woman in search of conquest, a soldier directed by her god.

She searches for that being now. The realization saddened him. *She searches for a god that will deliver her to paradise and care for her immortal soul and she thinks she has found her.*

But she was wrong.

There was only him.

8.

Bueralan had struggled to reach the bottom of the temple stairs without falling but managed to do so twice. In this he was not alone, as both Handsome and Ugly, gripping the rotting railing tightly, caused it to break. It was possible that none of them would have fallen if they had not tried to keep pace with the sure steps of Mother Estalia and her light.

He had decided that his best chance of escape would be when they were leaving. When they had done what they wanted and were distracted by their success, he was confident that was when his opportunity would come.

'It is an incredibly sad place, this,' Estalia said, speaking to the battered three who limped along the dry corridor behind her. 'I had thought that it would not be so, at least not for me. When I was told that there was a temple here I longed to see inside it, to experience the sanctity of it. Imagine the secrets we could learn, I said. The artefacts we could find! I was like a child, at first. But now – now I know why I was cautioned: the temple is like a rotten egg, with nothing of sustenance on the inside.'

The rooms on either side were empty cells, small squares

dominated by narrow bunks that were covered by threadbare blankets. Small tables sat next to each in ancient contemplation.

In contrast to Mother Estalia, Bueralan felt the earlier sense of being watched, that he had fallen beneath a gaze so complete and utter that a chill began to seep into his bones. He was aware of his skin contracting, of goosebumps emerging. He could take nothing friendly or reassuring from the gaze. Instead, he felt a strange lack of passion, as if the gaze watching him had seen it before, as if the hobbled steps he made had been done so a thousand times, not by a person like him, but by him.

Another set of stairs emerged. At the bottom of the steps, a red light washed out the glow by Mother Estalia.

'And here,' she said, 'here is the saddest part of all.'

Bones littered the floor, chalk symbols surrounding them, patterns that had been made by the four priests who had entered before them. They stood now in positions that were spaced evenly around the room, their cardinal locations protected by circles they had drawn, patterns that extended into loops and arcs, each directed to the centre of the room, where the dirty, bloodstained glass sat like a dead eye.

'Do you feel it?' she asked, following Bueralan's gaze.

He did.

He could sense the presence of another standing next to him.

'It is Ger.'

He knew before she spoke. He moved up to the glass, and through the streaked grime, he saw the wounds, the burns, the breaks, the trauma healing itself only to break open a moment later.

'The people who live on this mountain have forgotten that a god lies dying beneath them.' Quietly, she approached the dome beside him. 'I do not blame them. It is easy to forget, when your day-to-day life has no need for a deity. When you believe only in commerce. Eventually, when you look up from your ledgers, all you see are the rocks and the rough way that they have welded themselves together over the centuries. You see the trees stretching out to form that thick canopy. You travel that winding, steep road, where animals move around you. You see that life every day beneath our fractured suns and you forget that beneath your every step there lies a giant, a figure of such immense size that the mountain is his cairn, fitted to his divine being.'

It was the first time he had seen the remains of a god. It did not strike him as strange that such was the case, or that he had been brought there in chains.

'You're mistaken,' he said, finally. 'You think people have forgotten, but that is not the truth of it.'

Behind Estalia and the faint condescending smile that she wore once again, the chalk began to glow in faint, phosphorescent lines.

'What you will not admit,' he continued, 'is that Ger is no longer relevant. No god is. They neither have the power to alter the world we live in, nor the presence to issue commands. Where you believe that people have simply forgotten them – that they have somehow let their modern life ignore the corpses beneath them, the shattered suns above, or the black seas and countless other ways in which the gods have changed the world – I see people who have simply moved on. People who have adapted. People who have grown. There was grief – the city we have just walked through is evidence of that. But it was grief from thousands of years ago and we have ended now in independence – we are children who have outgrown the need for parents. The gods are no longer wanted or *needed*—'

His voice stopped suddenly.

At his feet, the chalk lines had lifted from the ground and wrapped, in thick, fleshy tentacles around his legs. His own tattoos were a faded white in comparison. After a moment, he began to feel tiny bites on his skin, as if the tentacles possessed thousands of tiny, suckling mouths that were trying to draw blood from his flesh, but were unable to do so.

'Enough from you, Captain.' Mother Estalia held his gaze. 'I have heard these protestations from others previously, as the cry of the faithless. It is not just the Mireeans who have left behind the keeping of their souls and chosen to abandon what in their heart they know is right – it is all of us. That is why what we do is so very important, why the remains of Ger must be taken back to his child – my God. It is why she must be allowed to grow. In a fashion, you are going to be part of that. The four who have come with us will be the containers of what remains of Ger, and they will bear him back to our god. It is a great honour that they will do, but it is not an easy task. You have seen what the power of a god can do to those who are weak, who are flesh, and to take it this way is no easy feat. It must be done at such a moment that our time and Ger's experience of it meet, where death is imminent for him. It must be done right and it requires an entire body's worth of blood to do so – and for that, you are being given that honour, and though you do not wish to do it, I thank you for what you will give to make our world whole again.'

No.

He would not die here, he would not be used for her ritual. He would head to Leera. He would find Dark. He tried to repeat no, aware that the first had not emerged from his throat. He realized that he could not move or speak, and his breath was shallow and struggling, resulting in a light-headedness. He protested against it, but he was aware that he was losing consciousness. The red light around him faltered. The floor shook. He heard a loud, splitting crack, as if something had broken open. He felt the floor move, sure that it was rising to him —

— and his chained hands snapped up, grabbed Estalia's head, and twisted with a suddenness that surprised even him.

The elderly woman fell in a crumbling heap. She made a solid sound as she hit the ground, her neck bent at a strange angle. He felt detached from that for a moment, as if he were watching it from a distance. Then he felt a surge of energy as the chalky bindings released his legs, leaving him without pain, without fatigue as he turned to both Ugly and Handsome.

He ducked the first's swing, sidestepped the second's thrust. The saboteur moved fluidly, feeling twenty years younger. He drove his foot into the back of Handsome's leg, brought him to his knees to crash his manacled hands against the side of his head. He wrenched the sword from the man's grasp, bringing it up to block Ugly's slash. He felt euphoric, nothing but pure adrenalin, and he knew, *knew*, that it was not his, that his body was too tired, too tortured and beaten to perform any of what he did.

He knew that even as he parried a second slash from Ugly. He used the momentum to bring his new sword up in a two-handed grip and hack into the man's chest. It was as if he had felled a tree: the blade dug deep, through leather armour, bone and skin, forcing him to wrench the notched blade out. He had just freed it when Handsome barrelled into him from behind; but he twisted out of the fall, slamming the hilt down on the side of the man's head to break the grasp, to step out of his reach.

In response, the soldier growled and came to his feet. Around him, Bueralan felt a streak of pleasure, of appreciation in the tenacity and fighting spirit that Handsome showed. Yet there was more pleasure — a bloodthirsty joy — as the saboteur brought his two-handed sword down in a vicious arc when Handsome leapt for Ugly's sword. The cut took off the lower half of his left arm, which dropped to the floor in a clutching, bloody mess, while the second swing buried the large blade into the man's face, caving it in with a strength that Bueralan knew he did not possess.

Lifting the bloody blade up, he turned to the four priests.

He had no need. They lay on the floor, their bodies impaled on sharp shafts of earth that had spiked out of the temple floor, breaking through the chalk lines the priests had drawn.

They had died as silently as they had lived — though he was not sure that the other priests in the Leeran Army would have agreed.

It was then that Bueralan felt the presence of another being, the same being that had watched him when he stepped into the temple, the same being who had lowered his gaze onto him when he had followed the Quor'lo to the rocky shore. It was a presence that could not be explained, that had no emotion he could easily understand, that was alien.

He walked slowly to the glass dome.

Beneath was the flesh of Ger, the devastated and inhuman, dark-red flesh that, when he had looked upon it before, had been healing itself, caught in a constant battle against its wounds. But now, as he sunk down to his haunches, as he laid the sword on the ground, Bueralan saw the wounds expand, the flesh give way beneath the damage and the fatality that had been part of them for so long.

Alone now, the pain of his body returned.

9.

It was a slow, dark crawl from the bottom of the temple.

Bueralan moved in pitch dark navigating up the dark stairwell; the faint light from fissures in the temple was like the midday's sun. The strength that he had felt before was gone and the returning pain had almost made him sink to the floor among the dead. He had fallen to his knees before the images of Dark came to him, before the sight of them in Ranan came to him – real or imagined, he did not know. He had groaned as he rose, but had not stopped as he began to walk. His feet touched cold mud before the second set of stairs and he smeared it over his wrists. Scraping his hands and wrists, he pulled himself free from the cuffs that he had worn, cuffs that he wished he had broken when the strength flushed through his body. Slowly, his feet shifting through the glass-ridden mud, he found a broken pew and took a seat. It groaned from his weight, but held. It was not until a moment later that he noticed – thanks to the position of the seat – that the temple had sunk. As he grew accustomed to the light, he saw that faded paintings had fallen, bones shifted and rusted, broken armour had rolled down to the wall. Only the pews, bolted to the floor, had resisted the call and remained perfect in the broken lines.

'Should I thank you, Ger?' His ragged voice echoed, its own answer. 'I don't understand any of what just happened, but I don't like it. I feel like I was used, that you thrust yourself inside me, that you saw everything about me, everything I've done and will do. But I have my freedom and I don't know that I would have it without you. So I'll thank you for that, and will be glad that this is the only time a god showed interest in me.'

The temple groaned and sank, the movement startling him.

It was not until he pulled himself out of the temple that he saw the damage around him. The once-placid lake was riddled with stalagmites, the red-lit ceiling having fractured and fallen, leaving lurid lights in the water. The destruction had broken open other parts of the temple, threatening to reveal the rotten wood and cracked brick building, its glass windows broken eyes throughout. But the real damage had been done not to it, but to the floor of the lake beneath. Gazing down as he swam, Bueralan saw the wide, thick fractures in the ground and felt the faint pull of the water as it seeped downwards around the building, as the weight of the lake threatened to take both the temple and river downwards – down to Ger's body itself.

There was nothing divine about the destruction. As the saboteur pulled himself up, he saw the top of the cave threaded with cracks and breaks, could smell the powder of explosives: the work of Heast and the two midgets he'd had prepare a series of explosions in the killing ground.

The path he had followed to the temple was impossible now.

It had been difficult to climb the first time, but now, with the ceiling fallen over it, Bueralan knew that he would not be able to make his way to the river. Not that he was confident that that was the way he should leave; following the river took him back through the city, through the mining tunnel and to the shaft. If there had been no major damage done to any of those steps before, as there was with the wall he had to climb, there still remained one important fact. Dural had drawn the rope up.

That left him with following the caves out. In the opposite direction he had entered, a dark exit was his only choice.

'I'm keen not to do that swim again,' he had said weeks ago, while standing beside Zaifyr. 'But I have no idea where on the mountain this will leave us. It could be anywhere.'

'It could be nowhere,' the other man had replied.

No choice now.

The walk was slow, dark. The only light to guide him came from the carapaces of bugs and stones that glowed red, then green, and which lost their luminosity shortly after he lifted them. It was a barely lit trail, revealing nothing to him of his surroundings, resulting in sharp stones cutting his bare feet, his toes stubbing on rises. But worse were the ditches, the sudden impacts on his spine that he could not avoid. Two ditches dropped him so suddenly that for a moment he thought he was in free fall . . .

Only to land, hard.

After a while, the need to drink drove him to small recesses of water. He drank from those he could see in the pale light, avoided those he could not. Still, some of what he consumed was fresh, some not. His thirst, his hunger and his muscles kept time, but it was imperfect. He knew he had slept twice, but had no idea for how long. A third time was interrupted by ants crawling over him, biting him. As with the previous times he had slept, he had only sat to gather his strength before rising and continuing onwards.

He did not know which sun he saw when he emerged from a cave. Nor did he know where he was. The brightness of the sun blinded him at first, left his sight washed out in grey and white and black, as he adjusted. But when colour returned with the heat, there was nothing to indicate how far along the mountain he had gone, or how far down. He assumed he'd come some way, and not just because of the strain on his body. Around him the trees and grass dropped downwards, falling in a series of declines that were lost in the thickness of the forest around him.

'You will need shoes to rescue Samuel Orlan.'

He spun to his left, aware that he did not have the strength to fight—

'You should have chased me more.' The old, ragged man from Dirtwater grinned, revealing a mouth of missing teeth. 'I would never have led you deep into Ger's tomb, I promise. But on the other hand, you would not have been touched by a god, and how unique a thing is that now? And by a dead god! A dead god's touch!'

Dry, raspy, Bueralan muttered, 'What are you doing here?'

'I brought you shoes.' The worn but good boots sat next to the old man's dirty bare feet. 'Though I do wonder why I didn't steal a second pair – I took two horses, after all.' He pushed himself off the fallen tree that he had been sitting on and beckoned for Bueralan to follow. 'But maybe there is a system to all of this. One pair of shoes is really two shoes, and two horses are eight legs, and two swords are many deaths. The maths really does make complete and utter sense.'

The saboteur said nothing, followed the old man as he rose, holding the boots and leading him through the trees.

'The important thing, however, is that you can now rescue Samuel.' Ahead of the ragged old man, a small clearing appeared. Two horses were staked to the ground, near a saddle, a bedroll, and a bag of supplies. 'It's really against my better nature to do this. I warned him, you know. I told him that we could not engage her. That we had to step away. She was inevitable, of course, the last bit of fate, but he – he said enough of that – '

'Enough of him.' Bueralan opened the pack, found it full of food, water. 'He can live or die, it's of no interest to me. I care only for my own.'

'Your own? Well, I suppose you might save them, as well. But.' The old man shrugged and dropped to the ground, cross-legged. 'But unlikely.'

He ate a piece of dried meat, slowly. 'How'd you get here?'

'Oh, you know. Here, there. The wind whispered.' He gave Bueralan a benign smile. 'He said to me, after Linae died, he said that I should be here. He said I would meet the last of the god-touched here. He promised to deliver unto us a man by whom we could be free.'

'Ger.'

'And so here I am, one last task. But that's life, is it not? You work for one business faithfully and get a satisfying retirement and suddenly you have to do a favour.'

'Is that second horse for you?'

'Oh, no.' The old man's smile faded and his gaze grew troubled and frightened. 'I will not go near her, no matter who orders it.'

The Dead

I will demand that my brothers and sisters admit that
they are not gods . . .

—Qian, *The Godless*

1.

After two days of fighting, a sense of loss had grown in Ayae.

It was difficult to explain. In the lull between attacks on the Spine, she tried to reason it through. She stared across the broken ground from the stone wall, the shattered soil littered with bodies and, at the end, three huge catapults, half sunk into the ground. It was not a scene she felt was familiar with her home: it felt like an obscenity, an artist's work intended to frighten and a horrifying warning for a choice she had to make in life. Every day a new element emerged. On the first day, unable to bring their remaining siege engines onto the field, the Leeran general had ordered boulders thrown to litter the approach and provide solid cover for his soldiers. It had proved a mixed success, and those who made it to the stone wall did so with heavy casualties, only to be driven back into the field.

The general and his soldiers must have expected that, and today the green-and-white Leeran flag had begun to emerge in the killing field, planted by those who had begun to establish small defensive positions behind stone.

None of that explained Ayae's sense of loss.

Nor was it drawn from any person around her. The grief that she felt from Illaan's death was different, personal, and as others died around her, abstract.

She had seen his corpse once, out the back of the tent hospital, and she had barely been able to recognize him. It was not just damage that had been done to his body, but the stillness, the emptiness of his remains. The man she had loved was, now, truly gone, an acknowledgement that struck her deeply when she walked back into the hospital, where the sick and dying lay. Though the real hospital had been cleared no injured soldier had felt comfortable entering it, so Reila had ordered makeshift series of tents strung up outside. The block itself looked like a series of giant, white sails, and she had heard a man say that if a strong wind came along, it would lift the city from the ground and allow them all to float to Yeflam in safety.

Zaifyr had been laid in a private corner of Reila's makeshift office. When Ayae first visited him, she had found the elderly healer sitting by his side, her narrow fingers tracing his left arm.

'I cannot explain why he does not wake up,' she said quietly as Ayae slipped into the fabric chair across from her. 'He has no signs of illness. There are no breaks, no welts, no burns, nothing. In comparison, a man and a woman who came in today show signs of rot in their bones. It is similar to the rot that was in those who died in the hospital. A rot that he is without any sign of. Yet here he lies.'

She had said nothing.

'I need to work on a serum. An antidote. On something to help those people.' Next to her hand was a syringe and three vials. 'Do you think he would let me take his blood to help with that?'

'I do not know.'

'Do you agree?'

She was taken aback by the question. 'Me?'

'Who else can speak for him at this moment?'

She said yes, he would agree, even though she was not sure. She had no idea what would come from it, but she could see little else that could be done and rightly feared that if an outbreak spread, such as was in the hospital, they would all be in a dire situation. As the afternoon's sun began to set on the second day of fighting, her gaze drifted over the standards on the field, letting her sight settle on the movements around, a glint of steel. Tonight, tomorrow, any one of the people out there could die. It would happen easily. It could happen as it had done so earlier today, with archers picking the movements first, their arrows hitting shields and limbs, until the ladders hit the stone blocks and the Leeran soldiers began to climb. To climb into a wall of shields and swords. To be thrust back to the dirt at the base of the Spine, blood soaking into—

'Bring back memories?'

Meina.

'Not as much as it did before. I see less of Sooia every hour, and more of Mireea,' Ayae said. 'You?'

The mercenary leaned against the wall. 'I never believed that idea that all battlefields were the same. Some of it is all familiar. The smell of the dead. The flies. The crying. None of that is new. But each city has its own scars that make it unique.'

She pointed to the killing field, to the siege engines. 'Especially with Heast's plan.'

'It certainly will make sure the Leerans remember him, if not the rest of us.'

In contrast to her words, Steel had performed well over the last two days. They had held their section of the Spine with the lowest losses of any company along its length. Word had it that the Mireean Guards in Meina's charge had already asked Heast if they could work under her command until the end of the siege.

It was easy to see why. The shields the mercenaries had used to escape the mill had also come to the wall and created a second terrifying and mobile defence that parted to reveal swords and pikes. So far it had broken only once, during the morning's surge over the wall: a dozen soldiers had thrown themselves at the shields, using their combined weight to crash through, though it had cost all their lives. Ayae – further down – had heard Bael's shout and turned to see the collapse just as he charged into the break, three soldiers behind him. For a moment the line of shields looked as if it threatened to break: it flexed and curled, soldiers shuffling, stringing the line out while they adjusted their position, but it quickly strengthened to cover where it had been broken. Bael formed the new centre, bloody and roaring, his huge axe in one hand and the fallen shield in the other – the latter as deadly as the former.

Once the breach was driven back, it was revealed that only one of Steel had died. Meina's uncle had saved the others who had fallen beneath the push, though two had gone to the hospital.

'It sounds melancholy considering our current state,' Meina said, as if guessing the other woman's thoughts. 'I don't mean it quite that way, though. You become very matter-of-fact about the dead after a while. You start to treat them like a sword, in that you have favourites that you keep close and you try your best not to get too attached when one breaks.'

'Try to rationalize it when it does?'

'No, don't do that. Don't make excuses. My father always said that justification always made a mercenary weak. If it breaks, if you lose it, accept it. Take responsibility for it.'

'Do you believe that?'

'Some days.' She shrugged. 'We have been requested by Lady Wagan, the two of us.'

'What for?'

'I was not told, but since more people are showing up sick at the hospital and neither Keeper has been seen attending, we can let our imaginations go wild.'

2.

There was a terrible calm. It lay across the haunt-infested killing ground, familiar in some emotions, unfamiliar in others.

Zaifyr had drifted across the torn-up ground for an indeterminate amount of time. He was no longer aware of day or night and the living were becoming difficult to see. He knew they were there, lurking around the boulders, beneath the flags and behind the sunken siege engines. To him they were like the bones on a dig site, the unseen promise of horror. Even though he could not see them, he was unable to forget them entirely because of the suppressed Leeran soldier he was in. She wanted him to follow the living, to walk through the barricades that her army had built and rejoin them there. Drawn by duty and faith: the urge was easy to resist, but he was without an alternative. He could not return to his body. He feared that when he took hold of the thread to lead him back to himself, the haunts would see their chance to live and swarm him again.

Or so he assumed. It was difficult to know what would happen, since Ger's death.

The awareness of the god's death came to him in a wave. It

washed over him, invisible yet tangible. It had lifted the incorporeal body of the soldier upwards before dropping both to the ground and leaving him caught in a calm that settled around him uncomfortably. There was an expectancy to it, as if he was waiting for something important to begin – a calm born unnaturally and dangerously.

He had felt the same in Asila over a thousand years ago, the night before the fires had been lit, three days before his brothers and sisters had arrived.

That night he walked down the twisting path from his castle, the long, dark road to the city below him. He remembered being struck by how much of a metaphor it was, how the physical form of his home and kingdom had become an apt representation of how he felt about his life, the lives of those around him and the dead. It was an author's thought, a conceit that if it had come to him before he finished his book – *that book* – before he had sent it to be printed and carried to those important to him, he would have written the words down. But it had not.

It was a month since he had laid his quill down.

A month since he had sent it to his brothers and sisters and heard nothing. Had he expected them to reply? To acknowledge his demands? He had, but he had not been surprised by their silence. Their voices did not matter, anyway: those around him that spoke endlessly, constantly, they were who mattered, they were who he owed.

They asked for food and warmth. For simple desires, denied to them. They asked for the comforts of the living.

Their want was all they knew, all he knew, now.

At the end of his path, looking over the darkly lit city, he

511

had flushed his power through them, granting them their desire.

A thousand years later, standing in the haunt of a woman who had those same demands, the man who had been known as Qian did not know why he had done it. He was aware of walking down the road, but by then his mind had fractured. He had lost track of the years, lost track of the writing. He remembered nothing of the final chapters and had not recognized the end when he read one of the surviving versions at Jae'le's.

The book had begun as a private history, a map of his inner thoughts in relation to those he had claimed to be his parents. He could remember clearly the anticipation he felt and the rush of ideas, but it faded as the years he spent working on it grew and research took him around the world, to the bodies of those he could reach and to the new gods. By the end of the book he had lost hold of who he was. He had given himself into the suffering of those around him. He had given into their demands and, in turn, issued his own.

He still did not know why, beneath the stone arc that ended his decline into the city of Asila, he had given the dead life. Oh, it was not a real life, but rather a violent corporeality by which their shattered minds could grasp their desires. Afterwards, he remembered that uncomfortable quiet of having done what he believed was right.

He had walked the streets, his bare feet navigating the fallen and lost, while his mind was quiet for the first time he could remember. He could see the haunts everywhere, their usually sketched forms solid, filled with colour, with the flush of life that they had consumed and the warmth and the satisfaction they felt.

It had remained so the whole day, and then the next; and did so for three more mornings as the morning's sun rose over the quiet, empty city, until his brothers and sisters arrived.

And then—

Well, then they had fought.

Sitting on the killing field, Zaifyr knew that he should return to his body. Though the calm of Ger's death was disconcerting, it had soothed the haunts around him. Whatever the wave of force had been – energy or life or something other, a concentration he could not explain but which was linked to Ger's divine life – it had sated the cold and hunger that the haunts felt. Zaifyr was certain that if he took hold of the line back to his body now, he would be able to follow it, to return himself with none of the threat he had previously felt.

When he prepared to pull himself from the Leeran soldier, prepared himself for that, he felt a new presence. It was akin to the wave that had lifted him after Ger's death, but not directly so. It lacked the perfection the god had, the completeness. This new presence, this new being with its flaws and failures that were so apparent, reminded him—

Hello, it said.

It reminded him of himself.

3.

The Pale House was quiet when Ayae stepped into it, a contrast to the noise that characterized the city outside. Like the streets, the lobby held only soldiers – and while she doubted that the Mireean Guards inside had once been waiters and bellboys, their presence by the doors and flights of stairwells was a reminder of how militarized the city had become. There were no more citizens in Mireea. There were only soldiers.

Meina led her up the stairs to a narrow hall, two silent guards at the end. Behind them was a suite the size of the floor.

It was furnished in a light, modern touch, dominated by whites and blacks, with steel-framed furniture throughout. In the middle of the room was a large glass table filled with food and drink, the untouched excess of which sprawled obscenely before the occupants. Gazing at the table with a faint look of distaste was Lady Wagan, her clothing sombre browns and greens. She was joined by a tired, white-clad Reila, while at the edge of the table, a short, scarred and armoured man stood in mixed chain and plate. Captain Essa, she assumed. Heast stood away from the centre at the large, curtained windows; beside him was the sleeping Lord Wagan. At the side of the latter was Caeli, who stared quietly over the city, mirroring her captain's gaze.

'Take a seat,' the Lady of the Spine said. 'Both of you, help yourself to what is here. If only so I do not feel some crime has happened in my name. How has Steel fared, Captain Meina?'

'Fair.' The mercenary took an orange from the table. 'We've been able to hold our part of the Spine without any real threat, but we haven't been tested, yet. Not since the first night. We will be soon enough, however: the Leerans have been slowly making their way through the killing field.'

'Captain Essa?'

'Aye.' His reply was more a sigh than a word. 'It's fairly obvious their strategy is to make a series of paths, but with no easy way up the Spine if we go down, we can do little but watch.'

Meina began peeling the skin. 'By tomorrow, I would expect to see bigger pushes.'

'Not tonight?'

'A night attack is a risk, especially for an attacking force who aren't familiar with the Spine. The Leeran general pushed it once and it cost him. I doubt he would do it again.'

'It will be at dusk, tomorrow.' The Captain of the Spine did not turn from his window. 'As the afternoon's sun sets. It will be our first real test.'

No one disagreed, though Ayae wanted to do so: to her, all the attacks had been strong, all had been very real threats. She had watched men and women in both forces die. Yes, the Mireean losses had been easy to count, far smaller than the Leerans'; but the deaths had been real. *Real* people had died.

515

They were not numbers, not a way to measure the intent of the enemy or a source for those in charge to support their theories.

But she did not speak. It was her first battle, her first war, even if the horror felt familiar.

'What about the talk of sickness in the city?' Essa asked. 'I've had a few soldiers go to the hospital feeling ill, but I've yet to hear much.'

'That we are addressing now,' Lady Wagan said. 'Reila?'

'There is a plague in the city.' The elderly woman's white robe, so similar to Bau's, was old and stained by blood and chemicals. 'If anyone beneath you — or you yourself — begins to feel a pain in their bones, they need to come to the hospital immediately. There is a vaccine. Last night's outbreak need not happen again.'

Ayae had not heard of any outbreak. She glanced at Meina, and the mercenary captain gave a faint nod.

'Word of this cure will get out soon enough to ease the panic,' Reila continued. 'However, it is a difficult subject for two reasons. The first is the origin of the cure. When people learn where it comes from — and people will learn, as they always do — there will be resistance to it. It will especially be resisted by the Mireeans under your command. They will view it as a witch's brew. A warlock's blood pact. It is not, but—'

'Where does it come from?' Meina asked.

'Zaifyr,' Ayae said, quietly. 'From his blood.'

'Yes. You all met him once, though you perhaps did not fully understand who he was.' The Captain of Steel snorted and the healer smiled in response. 'Perhaps you understood some, then. He was once a man named Qian, one of the men and women who created the Five Kingdoms. He was also the man, historians argue, who began the destruction of those kingdoms. It is in the remains of Kakar that his capital was based. Because of him, libraries were burned, histories were lost and wars swept our world as those he called brother and sister were hunted, unsuccessfully.

'His reaction to the disease that infects him is unique, a testimony to the power within him. If you watch the blood when it is outside the body – and to do that, you will need a little magic – you can literally watch his cells divide and recombine and alter themselves, rapidly breaking down the infection within him. I do not know if it is unique to him, or if all those cursed (forgive me, Ayae) are similar. All I know is that I have never seen anything like it. However, the making of a cure from it is relatively simple. Due to the nature of his blood when it comes into contact with the infection, it is readily available. For reasons I don't understand, the cells will cure nothing else within a man or woman, and react to nothing but this disease. For a lot of the people in Mireea, the idea of being injected with a serum that was made from the blood of a cursed man is going to be very difficult to accept.'

And for others, as well, Ayae noticed. While both Lady Wagan and Meina were unmoved, Kal Essa grunted unpleasantly and frowned. At the window, Caeli turned, mirroring the mercenary's facial expression, a rare break in her discipline.

'Which brings us to the second point: the man who created the disease in our city.' Lady Wagan lifted a folded letter up from beside her, held the white paper up for all to see. 'Our two Keepers are responsible for this disease, one more than the other.'

'You have proof?' Meina asked.

'Enough to make a case in Yeflam, if – ' she tilted the paper forward ' – we do it right.'

'That is from—'

'The Traders Union. I wrote to them yesterday explaining our situation with the Keepers. Their reply came much quicker than I thought it would, almost as if they were expecting it.'

'What do they want?'

'The Keepers in chains.'

'And if not?'

'There is no "if not". They will not promise us safety if we return with their bodies. They are saying that they do not have the political strength to defend us, with an army coming down the mountain after us, if we return with bodies.'

'They . . .' Ayae hesitated. Then, 'Fo and Bau won't surrender themselves.'

'No,' Lady Wagan said, 'but that is why we are going to send you to Yeflam with the bird and all our civilians. With that, we can force the Traders Union's hand, especially if you promise them that both the Keepers will be coming shortly.'

She made no reply.

'That task falls to Captain Meina and the Mireean Guard.' The other woman paused. 'I want you all to know that I am not a fool. I know that they will not surrender. I know that blood will be spilt.'

'I should help.'

She shook her head. 'This is not for you.'

'You're wrong.' Ayae took a deep breath. 'I am not the Keepers, and I am not Zaifyr. I can do nothing that they can, but I can do more than most people can. On the Spine I know

I move faster than anyone else. I know I am as strong as the strongest person there. I wish I could do more, but I can do something. I can stand there against them, and tell them of their law, and if they break it, then I will break it with them.'

'You can lead our people to safety.'

'And when I got there, what would I do? I cannot barter with the Traders Union. If you think Illaan's father will help me, you are wrong. He will not welcome me once he hears that Illaan is dead.'

'I would not ask this of you, Ayae.'

'You need me,' she said slowly. 'You cannot send Meina to them alone. They will resist and if I am not there—'

'They may kill you all,' Lady Wagan said.

'That will let you into Yeflam.' She was aware that all eyes were on her. 'They will be forced to hold a trial if I die. You know that as well as I do.'

Lady Wagan frowned. 'This is not the way, Ayae.'

'It is.'

'Child, you do not—'

'I am not a child.' She did not like her words, did not want to say them; but they were right, they were what was needed. 'If I was a child before Orlan's shop caught on fire, then I stopped being so on that day. This is my home,' she said, 'and I will not ask others to make sacrifices for it in my place.'

4.

It was not a child that Zaifyr saw, but rather a young man – a soldier who emerged from the edge of the Spine, his haunt marked by the wounds that had killed him. He was the only one so marked. The man's face was distorted by the pitch that had been poured over him which ruined the dimensions of his face, leaving a misshapen lump. His face looked like a mask, an apt description for the being that lurked behind it.

Ger is dead. The soldier spoke with a girl's voice, a child's voice. *My father—*

Your father?

He was one of many who were reluctant.

They were all reluctant. What is your name?

I have none. I simply am.

He smiled in response.

You are one of the pretenders, she said. *It is fitting that I speak to you today, I believe. It is as fate promised.*

There is no fate.

There is a strand. A single strand. It is the faintest truth, one I can barely understand or comprehend.

Did it tell you Ger would die?

He was always dying.

They all are.

Yes. The broken head of the haunt tilted, the damaged eyes staring at him. *But in answer to the question, no, it did not tell me. I am incomplete. I cannot fully comprehend fate yet.*

Like us all.

No, you are a fragment, a fallen piece of fate and power. You are what you are. You have grown as far as you will. You will never be complete.

And you will?

Yes.

Around him, the killing ground began to smooth. The huge blocks of cement that formed the Spine morphed into the crumbling peaks of the Eakar Mountains. When it had finished, the barren, windswept soil of the valley emerged. There, from the ground, a sphere of dirt began to rise, as if the poisoned ground gave birth. Men and women – memories, not haunts – flickered into being as they emerged: white-skinned, they fell to the ground in homage before the sphere. In their faces, the young and old, Zaifyr could not see sickness or the toll that the toxic land had taken of them; instead, he saw a fatigue hidden behind a fevered belief, a need to rest that was pushed aside by magic as they began to rip open the sphere with their hands.

This is my birth, she said. *I was not born of woman, like you. I was not born flesh, like you. I was made from the very being of the divine.*

You were born in poisoned dirt.

I lay in the soil Linae made for me. She constructed me, saw the need for me as fate told her. In my birth she must have seen her death, but did she see the prison that you were confined in as well? It was derelict to the men and women who found me, of no interest to them. But—

521

A crooked tower came into view, which Zaifyr knew intimately.

On the tiled roof of it, however, sat a brown mountain eagle. The claws of the bird – of Jae'le – made faint scratching noises when it landed and when the eagle took flight.

But the man you call your brother. He was interested.

Zaifyr was unsurprised.

He followed the men and women who came for me, my Faithful. He followed them for each year that it took to bring me home.

The landscape changed: the Spine returned to its truthful structure and a large wagon passed through its gates. Pulled by a pair of heavily muscled oxen, it was heavily laden, a thick, discoloured canvas cover pulled over its cart. The driver was one of the older men from the Eakar Mountains, while those who had stood with him ringed the cart on horses. The fatigue he had seen earlier was now etched even deeper into their features. In the back of the wagon – through the opening of the canvas – sat a crumbling sphere of dirt, the poisonous casing barely visible.

In its cracked crown lay a child.

Still quite young – too young, Zaifyr thought, when compared to how those around her had aged – she was wrapped in a dirty cloth and slept soundly as the cart began its steep descent of the mount. A wild dog lurked behind, following from the edge of the Spine before it disappeared into the bush.

He never took control of the oxen, never thought to slow us. He but watched until we arrived in Leera, then returned to you.

Where, Zaifyr knew, the door to his prison was soon unlocked.

Interesting, but I never sensed you at all, he said. *For a thousand years there was only the dead—*

Who spoke of you. The images faded, revealing the broken killing ground, the flags, and the stillness of it all. *I did not have a form for a long time and so I did not sense you, either. But I knew of you. I was told about you. It was not until much later that I realized you were not a haunt like them, that you were not their dead king who would not serve me.*

A haunt serves nobody.

They do. He sensed pleasure, a smile through the soldier's still lips, and frowned. *I do not yet know all of fate but I can feel its strand, as I said. Its length is one I can grasp, if not know. And I know that it affects not just me, but you and all the living and all the dead. The haunts on the mountains knew this. They knew I would give them life, give them birth, again and again.*

You cannot.

It is my right.

No—

I can keep them dead, or I can let them live. Her voice rose. *It is my will, my power—*

Then why do your Faithful use blood to work their miracles? Why not just gift them what they ask for in prayer?

The movement was a shimmer, a slam into his chest, a burst of pain across the haunt he was in. The intent, he knew instinctively, was to drive him out of the haunt, to shock him with the power she wielded. In that, she was not entirely unsuccessful. For a while he kept the body of the haunt, kept his control over her. He also felt an echo in his being, a reverberation that left him with the sensation of being hollow. He could explain it no better and took the second slam to experience it again, but when she made to hit him a third time, the arms of haunts emerged from the ground and wrapped around the legs of the soldier.

You are different, he said to her, slowly.

I am the last God, she said. *I am Fate. I am Divine. I am the Child. You may have power here but it is a feeble thing. You do not wish to stand against me.*

Not if I have a choice.

And, suddenly, the anger and the power drained from the haunt of the soldier. *Yes, you have a choice,* she said softly. *At this instance, it is before you.*

He shook his head.

Do you not believe me?

No, you are different. I imagine that my brother knew, as well. I wonder if he felt as if a part of him were drawn in, being consumed as if tiny mouths were trying to pierce his very being?

The laughter was a girl's laughter: musical, light and sinister through its innocence.

But I have no interest in the return of gods, especially if you do as you say, and keep the dead here. His voice grew cold. *If you have done that, you are nothing but my enemy.*

To that, there was no response.

In front of him, the haunt of the soldier began to dissolve. His head crumbled first, sinking into his chest, collapsing until the rest of his haunt began to do so, and the man stopped existing in any way that Zaifyr knew.

5.

Before they entered the Spine's Keep, began walking through the long, empty corridors and stepped onto the open bridge before the silent tower, Meina returned to the Spine.

She had said only that she wanted to gather others, offering little to Ayae in terms of advice or tactics. When the meeting had finished, the mercenary captain had nodded to Lady Wagan and stepped outside, waiting for her — the Lady's final words to Ayae had been a grasp of her hands, a whisper that she stay safe — and had fallen in beside Ayae as they descended the stairwell. If she had had words to speak it would have been there, but she had none and it was not until they reached the bottom that Ayae realized that while none of the doubts she felt were voiced by Meina, her quiet and straight mouth were not the contrast she first thought that they were.

Outside, she said, 'You ever done anything like this?'

'First time,' the mercenary replied.

'It'll probably hurt the first time.'

'It always does.'

'There was less pain the second time. That was my experience.'

'For me, it was the third. Maybe the fourth.'

'We're lucky there's another twenty-five in Yeflam. I'm sure we'll be able to enjoy it by the end.'

Meina's laugh was short. 'You don't have to come for this,' she said. 'Those two will fight before they surrender. And we're—'

'Going to hurt for it,' she finished. 'If anyone should go alone, it should be me.'

'I'd never hear the end of it.' The mercenary began walking towards the Spine. 'It might be that the Mireeans would agree to it, but Steel never would. They don't abandon their own.'

Ayae did not reply. She had not been given the rotten straw as Meina had, she had drawn it. Yet, she could not lie to herself and say that she wanted to face Fo and Bau alone, and did not, in truth, want to face them at all. Oh, she knew why she had to, and she knew that even if she did not have her power and Meina and Steel had been ordered to enter the Keep, she would have followed regardless. As the captain had said: you did not abandon your own. But that she was part of the mercenary band without having joined was a strange sensation. Yet, as she drew closer to the Spine and the faces of those she had fought beside came into focus, she acknowledged that it was not entirely untrue. She had fought beside the men and women before her, watched others die, and she had saved more than once. She was bonded by friendship, blood and experience, bonded in the same way that she was to her home, here, in Mireea.

As she reflected on that, Ayae watched Queila Meina gather ten mercenaries to her. The tall woman pulled herself up onto the wall of the Spine, walking among the battlements that had already been patched and repaired. She looked at home there: a dark-haired, pale-skinned, lean figure raised on war, on its violence, its devastation and terror. She was more comfortable in its company than in the suite she had just left.

The mercenaries she chose numbered four women and six men. Each was a scarred and even-gazed veteran who nodded and rose with a sword and shield.

'Are you sure you won't take more?' Bael asked as the two returned.

'The Spine still needs to be defended. If we cleared the wall it would be a signal to the Leerans to swarm, and rightly so. Besides – and I want this to be clear – if we don't come back, I don't want you or Steel going up there. Take them out of this city.' Then she added quietly, 'There will be nothing to be gained if we fall.'

'Queila, think about this, please. The Innocent has slain—'

'The Keepers are not Aela Ren,' she interrupted. 'And we do not go alone.'

Ayae met Bael's gaze and smiled, feeling none of the confidence that she should. He began to respond – to point out, she thought, the inadequacy of Meina's statement – but stopped when twelve members of the Mireean Guard arrived. They were reporting, the large, lean man who led them said, on the orders of Captain Heast. They had the look of veterans, professional soldiers in well-kept and well-worn boiled leather and chain with heavy swords by their sides.

'What's your name, soldier?' Meina asked.

'Vasj.' He offered no rank, no introductions to those behind him.

The Captain of Steel did not expect either. 'You seen these shields we have before, Vasj?'

'We have.'

'Do you know how to fight beside them?'

'Yes, Captain.'

Shortly after, they set out for the Spine's Keep.

It was the silence of the building that struck Ayae deeply as she passed beneath the gate. The only reminder of Lady Wagan's staff — and of the Lady herself — was in the recently planted gardens, the moist and mulched soil around the new life. But there was no sign of who had carried the watering can from the well or left the deep prints in the dirt. There was only absence. Stillness. A mixture of loss that mirrored Ayae's own feelings from earlier, and grew as they entered the Keep, as they walked the long halls, the walls unlit, their quiet footsteps echoing loudly, interspersed with the clink of chain mail and the low breaths of each.

And then they were before the door.

Meina moved ahead, but Ayae's warm hand fell to her shoulder. 'I should go first,' she said, the words threatening to catch in her throat.

'It will be cramped inside,' the other woman said. 'There will be no fighting room with all of us there, but that's okay. We'll pen them in. We'll use our numbers like a weight. Let the shields stay close to you. Don't step out of them.'

She nodded and pushed against the door.

It opened easily.

Inside, the room was still, quiet. The boxes remained pushed against the empty benches, the furniture isolated comforts. Yet there was a quality about it, about the pronounced nature of it that she thought, as she stepped further into the room, spoke of the two men who had taken residence in the tower.

A quality that spoke of their emotional state, of an absence dissimilar to the one she felt; of a singular notion and a selfish need.

'Upstairs.' She heard Bau's voice. 'Don't be shy now.'

The Keepers stood by the window of the second floor. Two chairs had been moved to the window, but the remaining furniture was untouched. 'Ayae,' the Healer said, as soldiers and mercenaries followed her. 'Little flame. You are going to make us break the rule.'

6.

When he was sure that she was no longer there, when he knew that he was – for as much as he ever was – alone, Zaifyr took hold of the tether that would return him to his life. It was not physical, yet he could feel it. It was not real, yet it guided him away from the haunt he had hidden in, away from her pain and the dim sense of loss in her. He was careful, his steps that were not steps slow, fearing the calm that had followed Ger's death would break – as it must. *As it must,* he repeated to himself, drawn by a truth in the words, though he did not fully understand it. As with the steps that he took, the cord that he held, it was a realization of truth with no easy defin-ition and no physical counterpart. It was not like the tents that emerged around him, forming like huge white waves that threatened to fall over him as he drew closer to his body. For the first time he wondered just what he would do when he reached—

His eyes opened, his breath a startled draw that turned into a cough, that drew the attention of all to him.

It was the elderly healer, Reila, that reached him first.

7.

'We have come to take you into custody,' Ayae said. 'You have—'

'Ger has died.' Bau spoke, ignoring her, while Fo's scarred eyes drifted lazily over the men and women around her. 'A god is dead. Do you feel the difference? It is as if a wound was drained and you can suddenly move that limb freely, again.'

She tried again. 'You—'

'You can feel it, can't you?'

Around her, soldiers and mercenaries began to encircle the room, Queila Meina falling in beside her. 'I did not know it was that,' she said finally.

'The men and women beside you won't understand what you felt. To them, Ger is already dead; he has been dead for longer than history records. But you and I know that is not right. He has been dying. Dying for thousands and thousands of years until he is gone. Just like that. In less time than the word itself takes to speak. And we – you and I and Fo – are left with the absence. We, and only we, are the ones who can feel it. Only we can question it. We must ask ourselves what we will feel when one of us dies. Will we have that sensation of loss? Will our awareness of each other, so much smaller than our awareness of Ger, point to a similarity between us and him?'

She felt a flatness in herself, an emptiness in her stomach, and her hands – her warm hands – fell to the hilt of her swords. 'There are rules,' she said. 'You said so yourself. No immortal can attack another.'

'Little flame.' His smile was a knife's cut in his handsome face. 'No one even knows for sure if you are a god.'

'And besides,' Fo said, finally speaking, 'who said you could judge us?'

Her reply was lost in the sudden push.

Meina's command was a hand signal, a movement in the corner of Ayae's gaze, her palm flat, her spread fingers tightening. The heavy shields in the hands of the soldiers from Steel led the way, the Mireean Guard following. In seconds, the room shrank, the walls no longer defined by brick, but by metal. Ayae watched as Bau took a single step backwards, while the scarred, bald Keeper slid his gaze to those around him. His lips puckered as if he were going to speak . . . but with no apparent hesitation, he spat.

Onto the shield before him.

The shield that webbed with fractures, that began to crumble—

That the Keeper's fists broke through, plunging through the suddenly exposed guard of the mercenary behind, and into the man's face.

Meina's order was sharp – '*Face!*' – but Ayae, unable to tear her eyes from what happened before her in drawn-out seconds, saw the man's face begin to crumble, following the pattern of destruction that had afflicted the shield. It was not the force of Fo's punch that did it, no; the impact after he broke through the shield was hard, but not enough to do what she saw. He screamed, falling back with one mercenary grabbing him as others swarmed Fo, shields smashing into him, the shape of each falling apart as he curled into himself, refusing to submit.

She started to call out, to shout that they had to attack not just him, but Bau, that Bau was *important*, that they couldn't just *let* the other Keeper stand there, that *nothing* would happen if they did that, when Vasj vaulted over the shields. The words died on her lips and she shifted forward, aware that she was standing at the back now, that she was the last person in the room.

Vasj's heavy sword levelled at Bau, intent to take his head from his neck . . . and he stumbled, the sword dipping, the strength leaving his body.

The floor erupted in a sickly green light, driving back those attacking Fo.

Slowly, the Keeper picked up the fallen man's sword with his scarred hand. 'Everything can contain a disease, a rot. Steel, wood, flesh: it matters not to me.' As he spoke, a faint green glow began to emanate from the blade. 'Imagine, now that Ger has finally died, what will happen to the foundation of this mountain? As the rot sets in, even the ground you stand on will not stay safe.'

Green lines began to emerge around his feet, webbed from each step. She saw those who had fallen around him bloat, saw their flesh split and crack . . . and before any of those standing – the dozen that included the Captain of Steel – could react, Ayae found herself suddenly, surprisingly, next to Fo.

Her swords led the way, thrusting high and low, forcing him to raise the sword in his grasp, to parry both her blows. Still, quick as he was in his defence, she was quicker, and her left blade sliced through his shoulder.

As she thrust again, as she pushed that wounded arm, she saw it heal.

With a grunt, she drove Fo backwards. But with the rush of her emotions fading, she realized that she had made a mistake. She had stepped into his unhallowed ground, ignored the very advice she had given herself moments before. She could feel weakness in her feet. As she took a step back, the sole of her boot gave way, the leather splitting from sudden age, her balance lost and saw Fo's sword—

—caught by another.

Meina twisted, thrust the sword away, and mercenaries and guards barrelled into Fo, thrusting him to Bau, threatening to take both out of the window.

She could not watch. The pain in her feet was unbearable and she needed Meina to steady her. When she met the gaze of the mercenary, she saw a dark fatalism there. It was justified. The pain she felt was a fraction of what the guards and mercenaries who had led the attack felt. They lay in crumbled heaps, their skin sagging, their bones piercing their skin in angry, red protrusions.

It had taken only a handful of heartbeats for the two Keepers to accomplish that. The tiniest fraction in all their lives to kill them.

Ayae pushed away Meina, her anger fuelling her, but as soon as she placed her weight on her feet, she screamed. The bones in each foot cracked, fractured. It was as if she could feel each break, as if each foot were on fire, as if she were on fire—

And she was on fire.

The pain of it ran through all of her, so suddenly and painfully, like burning liquid in her joints. The pain in her feet evaporated, her consciousness slipping for a moment. The world went dark. She could hear nothing. She felt nothing. And then — a sudden rush of noise, of crying, shouting, of steel clashing and voices calling out orders, calling out for Meina, the woman who had been forced to step away from Ayae by the heat that had ignited the floor of the tower.

A burning floor that she stood on without pain.

'Captain—'

'—where did—'

'The injured—'

'—Captain!'

'*Ayae!*'

She heard Meina cry her name, but her steps had already been taken, her path cleared by the flames around her. Flames that did not and *would* not terrify her. Flames that she could control, that bent to her desire and intent. As she ran, the flames bent to reveal crumbled shields and twisted swords, men and women who no longer looked as if they had ever been alive, who had been robbed of their humanity and their dignity. It was especially clear to her in the body of Vasj, of the man who had appeared so strong but now lay on the ground, curled in on himself as if his skeleton had lost all that it took to keep him straight.

It was Fo who saw the danger first, how close they had come to the window, and he cried out, too late, too late—

She broke through the glass with both men.

8.

The Captain of the Spine saw the fire before it was reported to him. He saw it spill out of the tower, its flames pale fingers beneath afternoon's sun, raised on cinders and char. He did not have a smile, not even a grim one to match his dark thoughts, his hope for success; rather, he spoke to the runner beside him, conveying orders not for the fire to be put out, but to be left to burn for the moment; he added that another order be taken to the Spine, to strengthen the guard there, and these words he spoke as he shifted his eyepiece to the broken killing field.

'Sir!'

He turned to the speaker, the young soldier who had interrupted him.

'Sir.' He was breathless, catching it between words. 'Sir. The man. The man you sent me to watch in the hospital.'

'Is he awake?'

'Yes, sir. He is heading towards the Keep, sir!'

9.

The fall did not kill her.

The glass shattered and, with both Fo and Bau in her grasp, the tower fell behind her fast, impossibly fast; she panicked and lost both Keepers, aware that they were drifting away from her and that Bau was reaching for Fo. She told herself that she had to catch them, to hold them — but the thoughts came too late as the rush of air deafened her, as the heat in her body was lost to the wind around her. The wind that tore through her, stealing her strength and resolve, threatening her consciousness that was lost when she hit the ground moments later.

It was a weak touch on her shoulder that brought her back.

'Ayae.' The voice that belonged to that touch was soft, raspy. 'Ayae, please. You have to get up. They're not dead. I can't, I can't — Ayae, please.'

A body slumped to the ground beside her.

'Ayae.'

Meina.

The words were not said aloud: she could not speak them, so horrified was she at the sight of Queila Meina. The tall mercenary was on her knees, hunched over, her skin blistered with sores and open wounds that she had sustained not from a sword, but from when her sword had struck Fo's. Ayae could see the mercenary's weapon behind her, a twisted, distorted shape so similar to its owner that their entwined nature could not be denied.

Meina's hand — the hand that had held that sword so strongly — had no strength when Ayae took it.

Still, she had made her way from the tower. Meina must have left after the fall, for it burned fully now. She would not have left alone, either. Half of the ten members of Steel who had come with them had been alive when she went out of the window, a quarter of the Mireean Guard: but none were in sight of the captain, none had made it out of the Spine's Keep. Ayae had the grisly vision of their bodies lining the halls, having fallen to similar ailments, their flesh breaking down until only one was left, only one could limp, slowly, agonizingly, to her.

And she could do nothing.

'Only you left now.' Fo's voice was even, monstrous in its lack of acknowledgement of what he had done. 'But that is how it should be.'

She released Meina's limp hand.

'The gods did not fight with mortals,' he continued. 'They knew they were too frail for any battle, any true test, not that it stopped those who had faith fighting in their name. Every part of our history is filled with men and women who raised a weapon, a fist or a voice, in the name of their own god. They did it regardless of whether their god demanded it or not. They did it because they wanted to do so, because they *had* to do it, because they were the image of their god, the divine creation. But the truth of it is, they never needed to go to war: in the fullness of their power, the gods were terrifying beings, just as we are.'

Her first sword lay to her right. She picked it up as she rose. The second, not far from that, followed.

She met Fo's gaze as fire ran the length of both.

She had no words, no thoughts. Yet, when her swords lashed out, it was as if she screamed. It came from deep in her, deep from within her grief not just for Meina behind her, or for Illaan, but for her city, her home, her life. Unable to open her mouth, her weapons contained her rage, held the burning distillation of everything that she had known two months ago and been sure in. Everything she had derived her happiness from. Everything that she had lost.

She wanted nothing more than to feel her swords hack through Fo, to slam — not cut, but *slam* — through his flesh, to beat him down, to tear through him as if she were the basest, most rabid animal to reach the man behind him, the man she knew she would have to kill first.

Beneath her bare feet, she could feel broken, diseased black dirt, an emanation that Fo left with every step he took backwards, every cut he sustained. She did not let that bother her, did not allow the weakness to take hold as it had before. She burned whatever felt alien against her, whatever felt wrong inside her own body: an awareness she had never had so fully, so completely as what she did now. One that, in another time, would resulted in her immense curiosity, and perhaps a satisfaction, but which now left her feet and legs feeling as if they were made from liquid, as if they were not truly flesh, and allowed her to push her attacks quicker, harder, scoring cut after cut on Fo's shoulders and hands, edging closer to his neck, his face, knowing that she would soon overpower him.

Then, suddenly, the Keeper dropped his guard.

Her sword pierced his shoulder as he drove into her. A quick step back and she slashed her blade across his abdomen; but there was no return stroke. Instead, he smashed his head into her own. She reeled, crying out in shock not from the hit, but from the sudden blindness, the loss of her sight, the complete and utter blackness that surrounded her.

It returned in a flash of pain to show his healing wounds, but so startled, so unprepared for the move was she that she had no time to counter Fo's head a second time. No time to counter his hand as it closed around her throat.

Her sight came back again, blinkered, a series of still moments that revealed a figure at the gate of the Keep, a figure behind Bau who was deep in concentration, deep in knitting the wounds Fo had taken, keeping the strength in his body as his fingers tightened around Ayae's throat.

The knife that came around his neck cut deep and straight as it had across the throat of a dead man, weeks before.

And like that time, it saved her again.

10.

The deep wound across Bau's throat began knitting shut the moment Zaifyr's blade left his skin, but he did not bother to keep hold of the man. He had gained Fo's attention, had stopped the Keeper as his hand tightened on Ayae. It did not matter if Bau, clutching his throat, was scampering out of his reach. Oh, Zaifyr knew that if he wanted to kill Fo, he would have to kill the Healer first. That was obvious to him, just as it was to Ayae. But her tactic to drive the Keeper back to the other, to cut one down to reach the other, had been brutal and fuelled by rage, and had failed.

He would not make the same mistake.

'They have gone to take them into custody.'

Reila, earlier.

Her cold hands pressed against his throat, probed behind his ears, and stopped only when he brushed her hands away a second time. 'Fo has been releasing diseases into the city.' Her voice was soft, for him alone. 'Both he and Bau are trying to stop us from going to Yeflam. Ayae and others are going to stop them, put both in chains. But you know neither will be arrested. Neither will agree with that. They will fight. They will—'

He did not need to hear the rest of the words, to hear, *they will kill.* He had staggered to his feet, his mouth dry, an awful taste in it that he could not identify. He found water, but it didn't help. The last of Fo's poison, he decided annoyed, spitting on the cobbled stones. By then, he was out from beneath the tents, leaving the white wave of their shape behind, heading towards the Keep.

Movement felt good. Each step made him feel better, undid the sensation of not feeling right in his skin, of feeling as if he was both too big and too small for the tangible frame he felt thrust into. The charms in his grasp helped a little, reassured his panic. Each step did the same. And each step did more: it helped him adjust to the haunts he could see, the dead that milled in the street, that were moving slowly, as if they were also coming awake, that their awareness — limited as it was — returned to them.

Slowly, he came up to the Spine's Keep, the burning tower a beacon that drew only him and no soldiers. He was surprised by that — *Heast,* he thought, spitting again — but had little time to think of the intent behind it.

Ayae and Fo were fighting.

And Bau.

Bau stood behind both, his stillness revealing his focus, his burnt clothes an indication of the fight so far, the broken ground likewise.

He did not make a sound when Zaifyr grasped his head and wrenched it back.

'I have waited for this a long time, Qian.' Before him, the scarred Keeper approached in a measured stride, his heavy sword easily held in his right hand. 'I knew it would come. If

I were to create fate, if I were to truly be a god, then this moment would happen. It simply must. There was no other way for it. Others urged me not to want it so. Aelyn warned me against it, specifically. She said I was too young. She said that I had not understood what age meant, but she was wrong. She came to Asila after it had fallen, after *you* had fallen. But I was in it when it fell, an ageless, blind beggar, a man without a family.

'I heard you walking through the streets, heard your conversations with the dead, heard your urges and your tears.'

'I am sorry you experienced it, Fo.'

'I am not.' He stopped, the dirt black, the bloody stain of those who died by his hand. 'I held what you did against you for many years. For much of my youth I wanted to break open your tower. I sought it out once, and stood before the door. I could not open it, no matter how I tried. Was it luck? I do not know, but I have come to accept what happened there and in Asila. I have peace in terms of emotion and of event. In hindsight, I believe that is what stopped me from opening the door, and it is what has brought us here today. Today, I will show the hypocrisy of our lives to be true, I will return us to our natural form, to where we fought for our dominance, where our power decided the fate of the world.'

'You're a fool.'

Fo's lips curled into a snarl and he took a step forward, only to find that he could not.

The hands that emerged from the ground to grasp the Keeper's ankles came from a haunt, but it was not the haunt that drew itself out of the ground in an agonizingly slow set of movements after the first set of hands. The second haunt, an old miner, wrapped his cold hands around Fo's to stop him raising his arm.

'The War of the Gods was terrible.' To his left, Bau, his throat a heavy red line, struggled to his feet only to find that he was held down by another pair of haunts. 'It was not that the gods fought that was the horror. Those battles were barely witnessed, except for their aftermaths. That was the true tragedy. It turned the weather extreme. It made for decades of drought. Decades of flood. We lost the sun. We had famine. We had plague. We had war. Species were killed entirely. Entire civilizations were destroyed.'

'They can be remade!'

'By who?' A hint of anger entered Zaifyr's controlled voice. 'By you? You want to start a war but cannot even realize that you are a victim of one! You lack the simple self-awareness to realize that the War of the Gods never ended, that we have been living in its carnage for thousands of years.'

Behind the Keeper Ayae climbed to her feet, the flame from her swords gone.

'There is a child, Fo. A true child of the gods,' Zaifyr said. 'It was here, but you didn't feel it. You felt only Ger's death and exalted in that. You did not see what he freed himself from. But you will. You will see things power can do. You will see what the war has done to us.

'I will show you.'

Aelyn would not forgive Zaifyr for what he had done.

She would call a trial in Yeflam, to hear and judge, but in the moment his will flushed through the dead in Mireea, he knew that it would be a farce. His death would be decided for him, and he accepted that. It was necessary to show them what was at stake: to show them that a god, a true god, did exist and what it had done to generations of souls, to over ten thousand years' worth of dead. Dead that he alone had seen and heard, a horror that he had thought his own, a weight he must carry for ever.

He had been wrong. It was not his punishment. He ran his power though the cobbled streets of Mireea, flushed it through the haunts that rose from beneath the rough, wooden gates dividing the city; to the generations who had lived in brick houses and hotels; to those who stood on the Spine of Ger beside soldiers; and to those who lived in the fallen cities beneath. With his power, Zaifyr made clear the horror that he had lived with for thousands and thousands of years: that the souls of the dead did not move on, that they were trapped, their personalities dwindling into a desire for warmth and food.

For a moment, for just one, single moment as his consciousness was connected to so many, Zaifyr was tempted by the dead.

He thought of giving them warmth and sating their hunger, of doing as he had done in Asila. But, it was just for a moment, for when his eyes opened he saw Ayae. On her face was a look of horror, born from the dawning realization of the tragedy unfolding around her. He had seen it earlier, when she learned what he had done in Asila and had stepped away from him. It struck him at his very core, a recognition of what he had felt for so long, the horror he had tried to become immune to in the crooked tower. And as the needs of the dead assailed him, he retained his control. He closed his eyes to the vision of Ayae, but his sight did not leave her and he kept his will strong, directing the dead to the one crime he had known he was going to commit, the one act that was intended to change everything. With it, he would ensure that his brothers and sisters would no longer sit idle.

Fo screamed first, a cry for Bau as his scarred flesh was torn from his body, his bones revealed to be black and brittle. But his cry went unanswered as Bau, unable to stand, found his flesh stripped, cold hands and mouths plunging into him, opening his stomach even as he thought to heal the wounds. Wounds that healed over the haunts, over the forms that had a sudden tangibility, though not of a kind to be trapped in the knitting wounds. And as more of the dead came to him, more and more of his power was tested until it gave way. His body, all its flesh and blood torn apart in a frenzy, was consumed, just as Fo's disease-ridden body was.

Once they were done, Zaifyr left his power in the dead – not as haunts that only he could see, but as ghosts, for all.

Epilogue

You and I are the godless. You and I live in a world where there is no divine judgment. You and I decide what is right, what is wrong. You and I decide our rules, our yokes, our morals and our authorities. You and I celebrate. You and I punish.

—Qian, *The Godless*

1.

He entered the ruins of Ranan, the capital of Leera, as the afternoon's sun sank over the horizon.

Bueralan had ridden hard. He had pushed both horses to the limits of their endurance, just as he had done to himself. As a consequence all three entered the city exhausted. It was a mistake, he knew, for he would be unable to help Dark if they required it. But a certain fatalism had overcome him in the final days of his journey, one of which he was desperate to rid himself.

In the week since he'd left the Spine, Bueralan had not seen a single person alive. The humid, sweating towns he passed through were all the same: populated by swamp crows, stripped of material for siege engines and war and surrounded by empty fields. Outside the towns, marsh and bogs and unploughed acres of shallow, mean farmland lay like old wounds. The dotted remains of scarecrows and field hand equipment, both in equal states of decay and rust, were his companions until he discovered the cattle. The bulls had gone wild and now made their homes in gullies and ravines, watching him intently as he rode past, drawing ever closer to the city.

He had been to Ranan a decade ago and was surprised, not just by the emptiness of the roads and silence of the buildings, but by the disrepair that he found it in now. Then, the city had been defined by its use of wood for building, by the natural look that allowed a visitor to believe that it had been part of the land for thousands of years, that its vintage appeal came from generations of vines that wrapped around the structures. That sensibility had never extended to any of the towns around Ranan, but it did not change the fact that the first experience a person had when he or she stepped into the city was to gaze upon a green-tinged, sprawling city; one that felt as if it had been drawn from the swamps so prevalent in Leera, a lost artefact restored.

His return to Ranan, however, saw him return to ruins. Beyond the stone archway, none of the wooden houses remained whole: there were but the markers for blocks, the opening of cellars and the litter of furniture and clothing. He was tempted to correct himself: in the first few blocks it was not ruins that he saw, but rather emptiness; Ranan had been stripped to its base by the Faithful as they prepared for war, leaving nothing behind. But slowly, as he and his tired horses made their way along the dirt road, half-formed buildings did emerge. Broken wooden frames stood open to the sky, while shattered window frames lay between choking vines and moss and trees that had been felled. Clothing and toys and cutlery lay scattered around, a story between each.

Soon after, he discovered stone blocks in orderly lines across the road, as if they had been dragged from a quarry and set, ready to be used in building. It was impossible, of course: there was no quarry in sight, and the blocks were as tall as he was. They easily weighed such an amount that they could not be settled upon each other without teams of animals and people, all of which were clearly not in sight.

Then he saw the man.

He was a stout figure, naked from the waist up. His pale skin was deeply tanned and his hair, short and brown, was as unremarkable as the rest of his face. But the man had strapped ropes across his thick chest, ropes that connected to the huge stone block that he pulled across the ground. The effort strained him, but not unduly. He himself was clearly not unremarkable.

When he saw Bueralan, he let the ropes fall and approached him. 'Another for the cathedral?' he said.

'Yes.'

'You will find it soon enough on this road. You are expected, I believe.'

'The others that came, do you remember them?'

He shrugged. 'Men, women. I have my task, they have theirs.'

'And yours?'

'To rebuild the city.'

'Did you . . .' Bueralan hesitated. 'Did you speak with the people who came before me?'

'They did not want to be spoken with.' He returned to the huge block. 'But they were expected, just as you are.'

The earlier fatalism returned to him strongly. *They were* . . . No, he refused to say it. There was still time. He was not too late. He was not.

Following the road, Bueralan picked his way through the ruins of Ranan, to the cathedral, the only complete building in the entire city.

2.

The Floating Cities of Yeflam shimmered in the distance, an elegant construction on the edge of the Leviathan's Blood, a beacon that promised rest, security and heartbreak.

Ayae knew the last to be true, though it was entirely possible that she was the only one of the men and women on the road who did. Four days behind them, Mireea remained on the back of Ger's Spine, its cobbled streets alive with ghosts – both the dead who were known and those who were not.

It had been a horrific event for all, her included. The Mireeans did not share a single belief about the afterlife; and what belief they did share was agnostic, a fatalism bought out of the fact that they all knew and accepted that death was part of life. For some, death was the end and you no longer existed after you died; others thought that you moved on, to a better world, a new world, that your soul endured; while others still, believing in the same endurance, said that you returned. But the sight of the dead, of men and women and children who were friends and family, had shown to all that they had all been wrong, that something much, much worse happened to you when you died.

Ayae had experienced it just as everyone else had. As the

flesh of Fo and Bau was stripped beneath invisible hands, the dead began to appear around her and the first she had seen was Queila Meina.

The mercenary captain was not as she had been in death, and for that Ayae was thankful. But there was a terrible sadness in her spirit, and her mouth moved wordlessly to convey words, all of which failed to emerge. It was the same with all the ghosts that had appeared; despite their sudden density none could speak or be felt. They moved to do both, but the result was only that a sense of futility was emphasized, and the sense that they — that all the dead — were trapped, grew.

By the evening, all the living in Mireea had fled, beginning a march down the mountain, as the first of the earthquakes began.

The Mountains of Ger had begun to move.

To those around her — who gave her a wide berth — the answer for the sudden quakes was a mystery. But the result was that, in combination with the city of ghosts, a wedge was driven between them and the Leeran Army. As the morning's sun rose there was no sign of the opposing force, and according to the whispers among those on the road they were in prayer, even as the ground around them shuddered.

As for herself, Ayae had been mostly silent as they made their way down the great road to Yeflam. Oh, she had spoken: she was invited to the meetings Lady Wagan held, and said her piece there as she saw fit, but her topics were limited to Zaifyr, the Keepers and what she had witnessed.

She had spoken to Bael and Maalen as well. Meina's two uncles had taken the news of her death stoically, as if they had expected nothing less.

When she had pointed this out quietly, Bael turned to reply.

'This is a business of mortality,' he said. 'War is paid for in blood and tears, no matter what side you are on. If you do not expect that, the grief will only be harder.'

'What will you do now?'

'Finish this business, see you to Yeflam.' Behind, the line of refugees had begun to stretch out, and a pair of Mireean Guards rode past, to bring it up. 'After, we will disband. There is no Steel without Queila Meina.'

'She has a child,' Maalen said. 'We will tell her.'

She could not imagine the conversation, but both appeared to be burdened under the weight of the words they would need to speak as they left her.

Her silence was not dissimilar. As Yeflam drew closer, as the smell of blood and salt – the smell of the black ocean – reached her, Ayae felt her ability to form words dry up so much so that she attended meetings mutely, while within her mind her words tumbled effortlessly and disorganized. When she entered the city, she knew she would have to speak. First to Aelyn Meah, to the leader of the Keepers, and then to those around her; and then at the trial, for there would surely be a trial, a huge and public one where Zaifyr would stand at the front in chains, a villain, a man who deserved to die.

He had told her that, in the Spine's Keep.

'Leave!' She stood apart from him, confused, horrified, driven away by what she had just seen, drawn by the sad knowledge in his eyes. 'We can go down the other side, through the Leerans, to— to—'

'To nowhere.' His empty hands showed themselves to her, an offer she could take. 'Yeflam is the only place to go.'

'Even if it is in chains?'

'I must look harmless.'

She looked around her, looked at the ghosts that pulled themselves from the ground and drifted through walls. 'You could not ever be, Zaifyr.'

His smile was sad. 'War is coming to us, Ayae.'

'You don't have to be part of it.'

Behind her the tower cracked and began to crumble, the flames destroying its support.

'I do. We do. We all must, for it is a war between us and a god,' he said. 'Look around us. You see the dead. I have lived with this for a life longer than nearly all others. I thought it my own fault for the longest time that they suffered, a failing of my own to help them, but it is not true. They are held here by a god who needs power, by a being who has not enough to do what she wants, and so draws on the souls of the dead just as a witch and a warlock do. Imagine that. A being of such power that she can keep the dead here, trapped, but even that power is not enough. I have been witness to that for thousands of years and I will be witness no more. I will go to war, and the men and women of Yeflam will know that I do so, with or without their consent.'

She glanced behind her at the Spine of Ger in the distance. It ran like a thick, stone vertebra along the mountain, broken only where Mireea was and the tallest parts of the Spine's Keep were visible. She could no longer see smoke, the remains of the fire that had died the evening they left the city, a sudden rain quenching it. But what would it matter if it had? Her home was defined by the ghosts in it, by the dead that had slowly dissipated along the road.

556

Except that they had not, and no one in the train to Yeflam believed that to be so. The dead were with them, invisible, silent, unseen to all but the man who had asked Heast to put chains on him.

Zaifyr had said to her once that she would be sad on the day that she learned the true power of her peers. He had not been wrong. It had cost her deeply, in terms of friendship and of her home. But more than that, it terrified her, not just because of him, but also for herself and what she was capable of, what her potential was. She had already begun to dream of her fall from the tower, her subconscious mind reinforcing what she knew: that she had survived not because of fire, but because of wind and earth, an acknowledgement that only deepened her connection to the men and women who could create atrocities.

It seemed to her that there was now no longer any respite from that. Not even, she admitted, in death.

3.

A quarry lay near to the cathedral: a huge, rectangular pit twisting down in a pair of narrow ledges that a single man, the Builder, could follow. Without the huge man there, all that lay in the lonely pit was a single, dented shovel.

Further up, Bueralan saw the cathedral sitting in front of the marshland of Leera. In the afternoon's final, melting orange-red light, the building looked as if it had emerged from fire and destruction. The twisted limbs of trees behind it were like giant fallen bodies, the hands held up in supplication, in forgiveness to the god who lived inside the tall, imposing building they had fallen behind. If such a god had paid attention, the saboteur did not know: but the cathedral was big enough, sprawling enough and tall enough that it spoke of an institution of belief, of an institution of care and neglect to the people around it, and not a single individual, though he knew it was a single individual who resided inside, and no more.

No more, unless . . .

There were no horses outside, nothing to suggest the passing of Dark. He would have taken comfort in that if he could not turn and look over the ruined city behind him and know that there was simply nowhere else for them to be.

The cathedral door opened easily.

Inside, the light from thousands of half-melted candles greeted him, a faint, still air of smoke falling like a curtain, and limiting his vision.

Bueralan stepped inside, his hands dropping to the hilt of his swords, the blades the old man had given him. The candles lined the walls and the edges of the alcove, the smoke thick from the sheer number of them, but it was not until he stepped into the next room that he fully appreciated what the half-melted white stumps obscured. Through their smoke, he could barely make out the thick, new pews and the windows against the wall. Likewise, he struggled to know the full size of the impossibly huge, blank roof that the smoke swirled around – just as it obscured the length of the cathedral, the path he slowly followed. All that he could make out clearly was the shadows of flames along the ceiling and walls, dark fingers that beckoned him to come further, to walk deeper.

It was not long until he came across disturbed candles and the fatalism that he had felt earlier was realized.

Kae sat on one of the long pews, snuffed candles around him. With his eyes closed and his back straight, it looked as if the swordsman had stopped to pray, had found peace. Until Bueralan noticed the first of his broken swords at his feet. The second lay next to it, also broken. What both had broken against was unclear. What was worse, however, was the darkness around his stomach, and the realization that it was not a failure of the candles to complete him, but of flesh.

Bueralan continued down the aisle, pressing through the

smoke, the taste of the unreal in it growing, suggesting more and more unworldly a presence.

Ahead, the pews became a jumbled collection, strewn across the floor with the candles.

There, he found Ruk and Liaya close to each other. The first's legs had been stripped to bone, as if acid, or worse, had consumed the flesh, while the latter had died behind him, her hands on his back, her intent to help him clear, the contents of her pack strewn across the floor, a dark pool of blood and chemicals that reinforced the act. On her, however, the marks of death were not cannibalistic, but it was clear that what had struck her had done so from above, coming down through her face, her throat, her chest. Ruk's sword lay just beyond him, in the darkness, torn from his grasp but with no blood, nothing to suggest, as with Kae, that he had wounded anything.

Aerala he found shortly after, her bow shattered, her spine likewise.

It was when he bent to close her eyes that he heard the laughter: a young girl's laughter. A child's laughter.

He did not draw either sword. There was no point, he knew: even had he not been exhausted by the week's ride, he would not have been able to kill, or to defend himself against whatever had killed the others. What had killed them all, he corrected. He knew that he would find Zean shortly, and Orlan. He would find what had killed all of them and then he would follow. He doubted he would even, at the moment it came, resist.

The smoke parted.

It revealed the end of the cathedral, a huge, bare stone wall with a single, closed door to the left. But it was the dais that drew Bueralan's attention, the upraised platform that held hundreds of melting candles in a series of circular patterns, while in the centre of them sat a child. A pale-skinned, blonde-haired girl, who wore a simple dress of white and regarded him with clear, green eyes.

If not for what surrounded her, he would have thought nothing of her.

But at her feet lay Zean, having fallen on the short flight of steps to the dais, his body a mix of cuts and slashes, a knife and sword close to him.

While behind her—

Behind her was Samuel Orlan, a series of dark, shadowed hands having dropped from the smoke and drawn him against the bare wall, still alive.

'God touched,' the girl said. 'Another god touched man to visit me. But the last to ever be touched by one of the old gods, yes?'

Bueralan made no reply.

'It is wise not to draw your weapon on me. I am protected here. I cannot be hurt and you would not survive, just as your friends did not.' She lifted up a small, dark crystal, held it before her. 'But I have a gift for you, Bueralan. One that will show how kind I can be – to you and your blood brother, Zean.'

'You have to capture a man's soul in a bottle for it to be true,' he whispered.

'A stone or a bottle, you believed in neither.' She rose, stepping through the candles, to stand over Zean's body. 'But it matters not. Any item will hold a soul and I have done it for you. I have done it despite the fact that you killed my favourite.

She was to bring me back my father's power, but you snapped her neck, so, so easily. I do not hold it against you, though. It was not all you, I know that. My father had his own desires, so I have forgiven you for your part, and to show you that, I give you my gift.'

She placed the crystal in his hand and he knew — he *knew* — she spoke the truth.

'Don't.' Orlan's voice was a damaged rasp. 'Strike her. Strike now. Don't believe. The dead are her power — the dead are used for all her lies. She will never — she will never give up even one!'

His hand closed around the crystal.

'Return to your home,' she said softly. 'Take Samuel Orlan with you. I cannot kill him, not now, not yet. But if he stays, I will not know such restraint as you see now.'

From the huge dome of the cathedral there emerged a sound, similar to flesh moving against stone, a sense of movement that did not linger above where he stood, but which resonated through the entire length of the building.

'And remember,' said the girl, 'that you may call on me. But once, just once. But, dear Bueralan, call only when what is at stake is innocence.'